PRAISE FOR STACEY MCEWAN

"This book is immediately gripping. I was invested every step of the way, and loved the visceral world of the ledge. The cold might not be alive, but these characters definitely jump off the page, and the enemies to lovers romance hit all the right spots. Stacey's debut novel is a triumph for all fantasy lovers, and I can't wait to see where this series goes!"
Raven Kennedy, author of *The Plated Prisoner* series

"The Maas mob will devour this trilogy. *Ledge* reads like Laini Taylor's lore set in Leigh Bardugo's Fjerda, penned with Katherine Arden's prose. The narrative pacing, playfulness, and deliverance will delight fans of Ilona Andrews' *Innkeeper Chronicles* and Holly Black's *The Folk of the Air*."
Angela Armstrong, author of *The Unflinching Ash*

"I fell in love with the fierce and clever main character, Dawsyn, and I can't wait to follow her on the rest of her journey."
Vanessa Len, author of *Only a Monster*

"Stacey has followed through on the promises made in *Ledge* with a pacy, compelling sequel - no mean feat for a second book in the series. Her lovable characters grow more complex as the plot stakes rise, but continue to delight with their quirkiness and repartee. Stacey understands the tropes of the genre so well, she's not afraid to have fun in the fantasy space. The series manages to bring together thoughtful world-building and vivid character development, with joyful playfulness. Can't wait for the conclusion (no pressure, Stacey)."
Jo Riccioni, author of *The Branded Season* duology.

"McEwan, a popular figure on BookTok, has written an ambitious fantasy debut. The plot and worldbuilding are thoroughly fleshed out and make this novel a great start to the Glacian Trilogy."
Library Journal

T0285224

Stacey McEwan

VALLEY

THE GLACIAN TRILOGY, BOOK III

ANGRY ROBOT
An imprint of Watkins Media Ltd

Unit 11, Shepperton House
89 Shepperton Road
London N1 3DF
UK

angryrobotbooks.com
twitter.com/angryrobotbooks
Soaring, flying

An Angry Robot original, 2024

Cover by Sneha Alexander
Edited by Gemma Creffield and Dan Hanks
Maps by Thomas Rey
Set in Meridien

ISBN 978 1 91520 241 3
BAM ISBN 978 1 91599 888 0
Ebook ISBN 978 1 91599 849 1

Printed and bound in the United Kingdom by TJ Books Ltd.

9 8 7 6 5 4 3 2 1

MIX
Paper | Supporting
responsible forestry
FSC
www.fsc.org   FSC® C013056

To all the wild-eyed, sharp-tongued, fire-breathing girls.

CONTENT WARNINGS:
gratuitous violence
suicide
torture
sex scenes
sexual assault

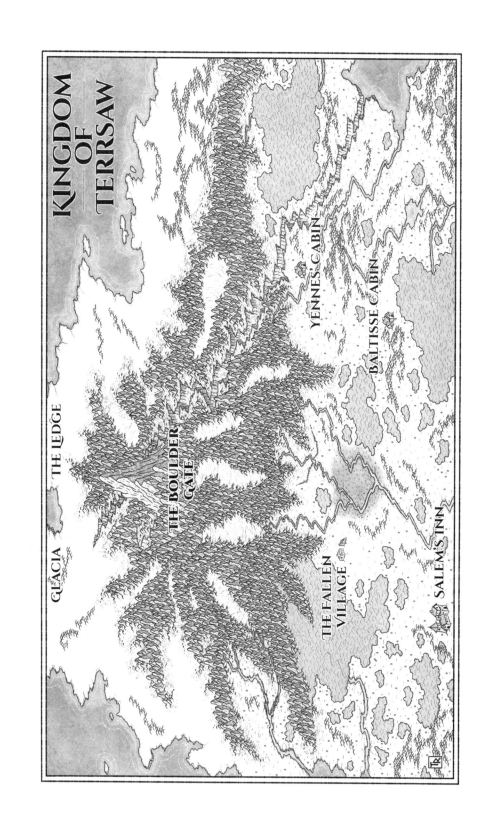

CHAPTER ONE

The Queen Consort of Terrsaw keeps pace with her wife through the corridors of the palace, her tone blithe and her smile even more so. It is the mark of any good spouse to a monarch, she thinks, to be exceedingly vapid. Perhaps even ineffectual. Or, at the very least, one in her position should *appear* that way.

Queen Cressida has learned all the ways to thrive and fail in her role. She has both held and mishandled the deference of the palace's delegates. She has won and lost the favour of her constituents with the passing of years. In fact, if she looked closely enough (which she never did – one needn't inspect the opinions of a commoner), she felt sure she would find the populace of Terrsaw held her in quite low regard. They might even hate her.

In this, she had failed her role, because as well as appearing of little consequence in the shadow of her wife, Queen Alvira, Cressida had also been charged with the task of being well-loved.

Of course, there was no ordained manual for wedding a Queen. In fact, when Alvira had been newly crowned, Cressida had envisioned the role adjacent as a robust one. One of influence. A role in which she might hold some sway.

She swiftly learned there was no sway to be had. No, her only duty was to be the gem on Alvira's finger. The living embodiment of an ideal. Stand tall, blush, smile prettily, wave. Be demure. Don't scowl.

How quickly she had miscarried that duty. Even quicker had she come to despise it.

Cressida nods to her wife, who walks, as always, just slightly ahead, skirts blocking the space directly at her side.

"…and the Fallen Woman will need clearing, of course. The townsfolk still insist on cluttering its dais with candles."

"Is that not what a shrine is for?" Cressida yawns. It is always best to dilute snide with indifference.

"Perhaps during a commemoration," Alvira scoffs. "But this is a royal jubilee."

Cressida tsks. "The candles shall matter very little if the entire affair is disrupted by Dawsyn Sabar and her... radicals." Another technique she has found handy – diverting any line of conversation to the focus of one's choice.

"I am well aware," Alvira quips.

"I only mean to hold the bigger picture in mind, dearest."

Alvira looks ahead as she says, "I worry just as much as you do. But my mind is capable of worrying about many things at once. Perhaps it is a defining trait of a leader."

Cressida presses her lips into a tight smile, as one demeaned by a Queen should. "Perhaps," Cressida allows. "And is the defining trait of a leader's wife not to stream the doubts and fears into something traversable?"

Alvira smiles in the way that she always has when looking upon her wife. With deep affection. With gratitude. "It is," she says, reaching back to grip her hand for a moment. Alvira is never happier than when Cressida defers to her lesser role.

Still, beneath the bitter tang of resentment, the boiling restlessness, Cressida's pulse quickens at the feel of Alvira's fingers in hers, not so different from the way her wife's warm touch made her heart race fifty years before.

"You know I value your insight."

"I do," says Cressida. How very easily they can both lie to each other.

They descend the winding stone staircase, deep into the bowels of the ancient castle, Her Majesty first. "If this traitorous leech should not be of any further help to us then–"

"Yes, yes." Cressida waves the thought off. "You'll string her up. The woman is well aware of the direness of her situation. I assure you; she is ready to be of use."

Alvira continues to stomp down the narrow steps, holding her skirts above her ankles, mumbling beneath her breath. "Such a future to squander, all for a mere speck of glory," she says. "I had high hopes pinned on that girl."

"A pity indeed. I suspect she has since realised the gravity of her choices."

"Be that as it may," Alvira says, reaching the floor of the dungeon. "I will put her neck in a noose should she stick it out a second time."

The guard standing sentry at the entrance to the cells straightens as his Queens come into view, staring somewhere just above Alvira's head. "Your Majesty," he greets, his tone the very essence of devotion and fear.

Alvira continues past him without any acknowledgment. "Ugh, but I *hate* the air down here. It is putrid." She stops at the end of the room, where the last cell gate stands, and looks within. "Putrid air for the vermin it hosts. What say you, Captain?"

Cressida joins Alvira at the cell gate, and together, they look in upon the form huddled on the ground, her clothes tattered and unsightly, her long hair in great disarray.

Ruby looks up from where she lies and says in a raspy voice, "Your Grace." It seems to take all the breath from her lungs. All the strength from her bones. She does not rise from the stone floor.

Alvira sniffs. "Have you had a moment to ponder your recent ventures, Ruby?"

A nod. "I... I have."

"And is it true what my wife says? Do you regret the day you left your duties to follow Dawsyn Sabar up that mountain?" Alvira's eyes narrow like a bird, eyeing its prey from a great height.

"It was a... moment of weakness," Ruby murmurs. Cressida is surprised she talks at all with her face so bruised and swollen. "One I hope to rectify."

"Well, little traitor," Alvira says. "Pray that whatever information you might have for me on the Sabar girl proves useful."

Ruby breathes slowly, her eyes screwed shut, either in pain or determination.

Cressida watches keenly. Her fingernails bite into her palm. *Get up,* she thinks. *Tell her!*

"Speak," Alvira commands, and the walls encasing them rebound her voice until it fills their ears, their minds. Until it rattles them all the way through.

Ruby's eyes open. She places the flat of her palms beside her head and lifts herself inch by torturous inch.

That's it, Cressida thinks. *Get up.*

When the beaten and broken captain is as close to sitting as she can manage, she lifts her chin to Alvira, her ropey black hair shielding much of her face. "The Sabar girl is filled with Glacian magic," she croaks, pinkish spittle bubbling from her lips. "She is imbued with it."

The fine lines on Alvira's jaw become taut, her eyes wide and dangerous, not with anger, or bloodlust, but fear.

"Guard!" Alvira calls, summoning the sentry by the dungeon entrance. "Open this gate."

CHAPTER TWO

Inside our breast
Amid our walls.
Among the bones
We dealers call.
Dealt are ends
Of pain or peace
Of withered cries
Of sweet release.
Strangled pleas
Or tender falls.
Inside our breast
Amid our walls.

Somehow, the lament had filled her as she'd slept. It seeped inside her. An insidious melody she had never heard before. She fell asleep in the dark and awoke in that same darkness, brimming with verses not her own.

Dawsyn blinks sleep away and hears the song still. It drifts off slowly, fading into something insubstantial. It disappears into the blackness, becomes nothing at all. A dream. Intangible.

She rolls her head to the side, until her cheek meets the ash and grit. Particles of it drift into her nose. It smells of fetid earth, of damp decay. Something long ago buried, never meant for the surface.

Ryon lays beside her, his back to her front. He is unmoving in sleep.

Dawsyn lifts a hand. "Igniss."

The slow-flickering flame in her palm illuminates the inky outline of blood on his torn shirt, where the blade punctured through. Dawsyn touches the fingers of her other hand to it now and feels the hybrid, her hybrid, shudder delicately. He does not wake.

The iskra magic stirs within her, already summoned by her thoughts. Her mage blood sings, alight and ready. Together, the two sides of her, dark and light, fuse willingly. No longer combative.

Ishveet to repair, Baltisse had taught her. *Bones or blades. Anything broken. They are not so different.*

"Ishveet," Dawsyn murmurs now, her voice as ashy as the earth beneath her. Her palm glows with the magic, growing steadily brighter. She feels it flowing through her blood, but before it can do much to mend Ryon's wound, the glow flickers. It recedes.

Dawsyn feels the depletion. The magic crawls back to its crevices inside her.

She sighs. Then she sits. She tries to see.

At first, the only discernible things are the pockets of glowing amber – torches left alight, ends buried in the ground. But soon, Dawsyn can make out other things. The darkness isn't so absolute. It strangles one's sight at first, but soon envelopes you, welcomes you into its folds, and shapes begin to emerge. The blindness lifts.

The bottom of the Chasm stretches out before her. Its width is less immense than she'd imagined. Littered between walls are the slumped and sleeping forms of maybe a hundred people, layered in furs. They lie with their heads on sacks and bags, bundling their children into the curve of their hunched bodies. Others sit alert, watchful, unable to sleep for any amount of time in a place so strange, so odious.

The walls of the Chasm glisten where the torch light reaches its sharp edges. The rock cuts inward and juts outward, slicing jagged patterns up and up. There is only a narrow strip above them that reveals the day. A thin belt of white she can only see if she squints. There is, oddly, no teeth in the cold. The air is close and still, not biting. It does not reach the bones.

Every sound in the Chasm echoes on and on, following those cutting paths of the rock face to its escape. Moving bodies, hushed conversation, the languid tumble of water that meanders down the middle. The living vein of the Chasm.

Soon Dawsyn, Ryon and the others – Tasheem, Rivdan, Hector, Salem, Esra and Yennes – will need to wake the rest. They will need to begin the journey to the Chasm's end.

Dawsyn prays another end exists at all.

She stands and dusts the strange dirt from her body. It seems to cling to her. She hates to think what particles might reside in it. Every so often, she sees the remnants of what might be white bone half-buried in the ground. How many have fallen off the Ledge in fifty years? How many have been thrown in from Glacia?

Dawsyn paces carefully over sleeping forms. First, she passes Esra, rolled up on his side, huddled inside a thick fur-lined cloak, then Salem, who frets in his sleep.

She passes Yennes, who does not appear to have slept at all. The older woman sits with her back against the rockface, hands trembling, mouth pinched and eyes alert.

Two paths, both are filled.

Dawsyn nods to the woman. She knows Yennes defies all sense in being here, helping them. She prays that Yennes, so timid and meek, does not need to suffer the Chasm long.

Finally, she comes to another familiar body. One that's perfectly still. Covered head to toe in a cloak, and unflinching at the permeating cold of this place.

Baltisse.

Dawsyn lowers herself to the ground beside the mage and reaches for the cloak. She pulls until it reveals a vacant face.

Dawsyn Sabar has seen many unsettling things in her life, but none are so unnerving as the sight of a once powerful sorceress reduced to nothing but a shell in the dust. Baltisse's fair hair has already lost its lustre, the sheen from her skin is marred in dirt. Her eyes, always so molten, so visceral, are now a pale innocuous blue. She is here, and not. Dawsyn hopes she has already found her way to that other realm, into the arms of a Holy Mother who showed her little mercy while she lived.

Dawsyn swallows and traces a vein at the mage's neck with her fingernail. "I am sorry," she whispers to her. And she is. She is made only of her remorse. Her regret. She feels it in every single cell. Every trace of her. Her being shakes with it.

"Dawsyn?" comes a voice. She turns to find Esra, his eyes swollen and red. The man, his face ruined and then put back together by the dead mage before them, blinks in rapid succession. Usually so tall, his spine seems curved with the strength of his sorrow. "Is she..." He hesitates, swallows thickly. "Can she be moved? Must we leave her?"

Dawsyn's fingers clench around the mage's cloak. *No. We can't.* But what she says is, "She must stay, Es."

Esra kneels beside Dawsyn, the tears shining on his cheeks. "She would loathe it here," he says. "Though I think it an appropriate grave for a witch."

Dawsyn smiles wanly at him, placing a hand on his trembling shoulder. "She isn't here, Esra."

"No." He clenches Dawsyn's fingers. "Already, it feels different. Do you feel it?"

She does. There is a… hum missing from the air around them. A vibration they had once taken for granted leaves an eerie, hollow silence in its absence. She nods to Esra, the action painful.

Silence consumes them, heavy and slow. But when Baltisse does not rise from the earth with ethereal redemption, Dawsyn asks, "Why did she do this?" The words have been stuck in her throat for hours. She has been unable to swallow them.

Esra seems uncertain when he responds, as though it is the easiest of answers, the most obvious of the lot. "To *save* you," he says, eyebrows lifting. "To save Ryon."

But Dawsyn shakes her head. She rejects the thought. It is an intolerable one. She grips her thighs until it hurts.

"I don't want it to be for me."

Esra sighs shakily and wipes his wet eyes. In a hollow way, he says, "She was a desperately unhappy woman, Dawsyn." He gently holds Baltisse's fingers. "She spent much of her life blaming herself for the misfortune of many. She lived with blood on her hands. There was not a single word to be said that could save her from her own persecution. Salem and I had long ago accepted that." Esra sniffs, peering down at the woman he had claimed as family. "I think she would be happy now, knowing that she helped these people. She freed herself from that guilt that had festered so long inside her. For that," Esra muses, his voice weak and without conviction, "we must forgive her."

Dawsyn takes her last look at the mage. She wonders how it feels to be released from responsibility. Released from self-persecution.

Ryon is suddenly there beside her. He kneels gingerly on Dawsyn's other side, his pain evident. He presses a kiss to his fingers and rests them on the mage's cheek for a moment. "Sleep well, my friend," he says, his deep timbre reverberating. He lifts the cloak back over her, shielding Baltisse from the ugliness of this place in the world's middle.

Esra muffles a sob. "Couldn't we just–"

"She cannot come with us, Esra," Dawsyn says once more. She tries not to let the steel find her voice. Not this time. "She isn't here at all."

Salem comes to pull Esra to his feet. His own face, illuminated by torch light, tells a story no better than theirs. "C'mon, lad," he says gently, wrapping an arm around Esra's hunched waist. "Leave Baltisse be. Yeh've harassed 'er enough fer one lifetime."

Esra leans into Salem's substantial frame, and the older man guides him away. Dawsyn cannot yet bring herself to follow.

She still hopes for a shiver of presence. She lingers in the vain hope to absolve herself. *I'm sorry,* she thinks. And even deeper. *I won't let another die.*

An impossible promise.

"You always reminded me of her," Ryon utters. He stares at the cloaked body, his jaw tight, dark eyes clouded. "She carved a place into a world that refused to make room for her, just as you have."

"As *we* have," she corrects him. But if there is a place within any kingdom they can claim as theirs, she is yet to know it. "I am unsure the world will ever make room for people like us."

"Then we must insist it does," Ryon says, standing to his full height, despite the pain it causes. He holds his hand out to her.

The people of the Ledge begin to wake. They stir in groups. Dawsyn passes intermittent fearful faces, thrown into haphazard relief by orange glow. They stare up at the thin line of daylight above, then around at the expansive nothingness.

Slowly, some make their way to the water that runs through the Chasm's middle. They cup their hands into its shallow depths and feel it slip over their fingers, moving of its own accord. Their eyes widen, seeing for the first time water that flows, water that sings. They marvel at its strange dance.

"Will you speak to them?" Ryon asks her as they carefully traipse around the groupings.

Dawsyn supposes she has little choice. "They will need to be made aware of the provisions we have. There will need to be... agreements."

"No fighting?" Ryon asks, though his expression tells her there is little hope for the endeavour.

"Yes," Dawsyn says. "They've lived fifty years fighting for rations from the Drop. Now, they will need to... *share.*" Dawsyn sighs at the word and looks around once more. Already, the group shows how insistent old habits can be. She can see a woman named Helenia shoving the chest of an older man until he falls over backwards. Another group are tussling on the ground, likely over something as meagre as a torch.

She feels the enormity of the task ahead swallow her once more.

Then, Ryon's fingers slowly slip between hers. She feels the pulse at his wrist jump alongside her own. When she looks up, his face is turned down to hers, reverent and gentle. She isn't alone.

It will be like the slopes of the mountain, the untraversable plane they walked together to reach the ground. This newest undoable task will not be a solitary endeavour.

Dawsyn presses her lips to the back of his hand, holds it there for a moment, then lets it fall away. "Pass me a torch," she says.

It does not take long to acquire the silence she needs to speak. Her voice, when raised, catapults from wall to wall, amplified by the Chasm as it climbs. The people within stop almost immediately when she calls out. They turn to her, their faces expectant.

Dawsyn stands beside the stream. In every direction she turns, she is met by the face of someone she recognises. All of them are here because of her.

She takes a deep breath. "Before we leave this place," she calls, loud and gravelled. "We must make certain that we are of the same mind. We have provisions." Dawsyn points to the sacks at her feet. "A small amount of food, and water from the Chasm. But the food will not last for any long period of time. Even less, should our desperation overcome us, as it did on the Ledge."

There is a slow rumble among the crowd. Old neighbours eye one another. Grow defensive.

"The food will be dispersed fairly among us when we stop for rest. There will be no stealing. No fighting. If we are going to find safety, we must do so together, in a way we have never sought to unite before. Let our past quarrels be put to rest here. If we are to survive, it will not be the few. It must be the many, or we might as well have remained on that Ledge and let the Glacians continue to pick away at our numbers."

Some faces look determined. Of what, Dawsyn can't be sure. Some seem suspicious or resigned.

"The length of the journey..." Here, Dawsyn stumbles. "The length of the journey will be long. Prepare yourselves accordingly. Mind your sick, your young." She pauses again, hesitant. She looks up to see Ryon; Rivdan and Tasheem are at his side. Yennes waits behind them. Her hands tumble over one another, her lips moving as though chanting a prayer.

Dawsyn squeezes her eyes shut, then opens them once more. "We... we are not alone in this Chasm," she calls, and hears her voice echo back. It is soon joined by a resounding shudder of shock, a rumbling dissent. Dawsyn speaks again before it can grow any louder. "There may be creatures, here at the bottom. Should we meet them, we will defend ourselves, just as we were never permitted to do upon Selection. Here, you will fight your way through any obstacle. Any–"

"What creatures?" someone calls.

"We were not made aware!" Another shouts, and the sound of fear rings through the rest, stirring them. Bridling their own uncertainty. The tremors multiply. Breed.

Dawsyn grits her teeth. The magic within her bristles. "Quiet!" she calls, but the crowd takes no heed. The fear swells.

Dawsyn fills her lungs. "QUIET!" She bellows, and her voice rings down the Chasm, further and further, replaying in a continuum as it follows the water downstream.

She huffs, surprised once more by the immediate effect it has on the people. They stare, waiting, mouths still.

"We have met enemies before," Dawsyn calls, ensuring her words reach all the way to the brink. "And when we meet them again, they will be unprepared for our ferocity. We can no longer allow fear to rule us."

Some nod. Chins jut in the air.

"How many times did we stand before our homes, obedient lambs waiting for slaughter?"

Another rumbling, of assent this time.

"We are freed of that now! And if we are threatened on this path, it will not be met with compliance." Dawsyn turns to Ryon, to Rivdan and Tasheem, to Hector, Salem and Esra. She finds them watching her, waiting. Grinning. "Hand out the weapons," she calls. "And we will be on our way."

The people raise their fists, cheer. They converge forward toward the Glacians, not away from them.

"Watch the Chasm!" one shouts.

"Watch the Chasm," others chorus in reply. The chant slowly grows, turns to a war cry. It chases the songs that mumble to Dawsyn of blood and bones and ends.

"Watch the Chasm! Watch the Chasm!"

"WATCH THE CHASM!"

CHAPTER THREE

The people of the Ledge ready themselves to journey. They don their hoods and pull sacks over their shoulders, sling bags across their backs. The children are fed meagre amounts and led to the stream to drink. All energies seem renewed, with the exception of a few.

Ryon, Tasheem and Rivdan wear the remnants of their battle. There is a gash along Tasheem's cheek that looks days old, though it isn't. She limps badly, her left leg barely able to bear weight. Rivdan is little better. He holds his arm close to his chest. Dawsyn remembers the sight of a blade sinking into his shoulder up on the Ledge. When they escaped the battle and fled into the Chasm, both seemed near death. It was Yennes who saved them, though her already depleted power made healing them to completion an impossibility.

Ryon is still wounded. Dawsyn watches him wince as he bends, his shoulders shaking, brought back from the brink of demise but not nearly whole. Dawsyn is bruised and sore but otherwise unharmed. It is the weakening of her own magic that bothers her most.

As for Yennes, the woman seems… unstable. She is exhausted. That much is clear. She had folded many times into this Chasm, healed and helped as many as she could, pushing her capabilities to their limits. But Dawsyn suspects it is not her expended labours that ail her now.

Yennes' tightly curled hair begins to free itself from the head scarf she uses to encase it. She gives Dawsyn the impression of a cornered animal – fearful and frenetic, twitching at each sound and movement. As is her tendency, the extent of her discomfit is channelled through her hands. They fret and worry incessantly.

Dawsyn approaches the woman, grabbing her hands through the darkness. Yennes startles.

"Easy," Dawsyn tells her, her voice low. "I didn't mean to frighten you."

Yennes gulps, eyes wide. "Dawsyn." Her head whips back and forth. "We must go. We've remained still too long already."

Dawsyn nods. "Are you well?"

Despite the chill, a bead of sweat falls from the woman's hair line and slides down her cheek. "We must go!"

"Walk with Ryon and the others," Dawsyn says. "Nearer to the front. It may ease your nerves to have them close."

The woman gives a dry huff of mirth behind pursed lips, a shudder rippling through her. "I fear they'll be no match for what lurks here."

Dawsyn takes Yennes' hand and begins to lead her away. "Whatever comes," she says, "will not have met a group quite like this."

Yennes looks around at the glint of knives and swords reflecting firelight. At the hardened stares of people tried and tested on the Ledge. She seems to quell a little. Her hands slow, if only slightly. "I hope you are right, Dawsyn Sabar," she says. "Or may the Mother have mercy on us all."

"We've come this far," Dawsyn reminds her. "Perhaps the Mother favours us already."

Yennes grimaces. "If She truly favours us, She will make this journey upstream a short one."

"Upstream?"

The familiar voice is close – to Dawsyn's immediate left. This darkness is disorientating. How easy it is for shadows to lurk.

Nevrak stands there, his brows pinched in confusion. The Splitter, they call him, after his propensity for splitting skulls as easily as timber. The man's grey beard reaches his chest. He stands easily a head taller than Dawsyn and he uses his height to his advantage now. "Did the woman say 'upstream'?"

Dawsyn glimpses his tensed hands. She answers carefully, aware that others nearby have halted to listen. They turn to hear her answer. "Yes," she says, and means to move on.

She takes not two paces before Nevrak calls to her back, attracting even more on-lookers. "But... Surely we should follow the water?" he asks. Dawsyn turns to see him looking at bystanders for their assent. Some of the men and women nod. "Does the water not lead to the valley, girl? You said you'd lead us off this mountain."

Yes, Dawsyn thinks. But leading them to the valley means leading them into the arms of a queen who would entrap them once more. A queen who, learning of their presence in her kingdom, would see them as an invasion. A threat to the peace she'd traded them for in the first place.

Dawsyn has no intention of leading them out of the hands of one tyrant and into another. But, how to explain to them?

The people of the Ledge do not know of how Queen Alvira sold them to the Glacians all those years ago. Most were born on the Ledge, like her. They only know as much as she did before she left it.

How to tell them all now that she will lead them away from the promise of a green valley? How to tell them that, instead, she intends to lead them to a place unknown, toward mere possibility? How to tell them now without having them turn their backs, without them fleeing in the other direction? How can she be sure they will listen, that they will follow her to uncertain ends?

Dawsyn realises she cannot.

If they know, they will not follow.

They'll run to Terrsaw.

To their recapture. To their end.

Dawsyn's breaths come faster. Her fists ball. The faces around her wait impatiently. Confused. They grow ever more persistent with every wasted second.

Dawsyn spies the rest of their party across the way and they too stare. She silently begs them not to contradict her. Silently, she apologises to them.

"The water leads to an ocean," Dawsyn says, loud enough that her voice carries. "We cannot reach safety that way." This, at least, is not wholly untrue. "We will travel upstream."

"In the opposite direction?" Nevrak asks. His voice hits her from several angles, refracting from the rock. "Where does it lead?"

Dawsyn does not hesitate. She turns on her heel to look back at Nevrak and meets his eye. "It will take us to Terrsaw," she says.

She feels the emitted tension from Yennes. She notes the uncomfortable shift in the posture of her friends, now complicit in a plan made of lies. Remorse floods her.

But the Ledge people around her are unsuspecting. Their ignorance is what Dawsyn depends on. "The path will take us back," Dawsyn says now.

"And have you seen it yourself?" Nevrak calls once more. His is the only stare that appears dubious, though there is uncertainty too. The deeply etched lines around his eyes flinch with it. His son stands at his side, and Wes imitates his father's stance, though he is not half Nevrak's height. He pushes his chest out, looks down his nose at her.

Dawsyn smiles coldly. She takes a step toward them and Wes's feet shuffle back an inch.

She tilts her head to the side and laces each word with arrogance – the only language men like Nevrak are likely to understand. "I've seen a great many things," Dawsyn says. "But I've no time to paint you a picture. By all means, walk yourself into that ocean," she nods her head down the Chasm. "You don't need to take me at my word."

She can see Nevrak biting down on his tongue. His jaw rolls beneath his beard.

Dawsyn can suddenly feel Ryon standing close behind her. She feels the threat exuding from him, all the way to her bones.

Nevrak and his weasel son must feel it too. They back away several paces, conceding.

Dawsyn nods to them one last time and then shows them her back.

"Dawsyn," Ryon says immediately, his face one of grim reproach. His eyes beseech her.

Dawsyn barely meets them. There are too many people watching. Listening. "Time to move," she says simply, and walks by him.

She meanders through the horde, looking for its end, but Ryon follows close behind. She can feel him at her back once more.

"Malishka," he rumbles darkly.

"Not here," she bids, tunnelling through the people at greater speed. Space lies ahead, away from the crowd. Space and more bleak darkness.

The second they are free, Ryon has her wrist in his grasp. It is a testament to her affection for him that she does not immediately wrench it free. Instinctively her body tenses, combative.

Ryon pulls her to the wall of the Chasm, pulling her in front of him, so that his body blocks her from view of the others.

"You lied to them?" he says at once, his voice so low, there would be no hope of anyone else overhearing. His eyes flick back and forth, searching her face. Always searching.

Dawsyn is momentarily distracted by him. The closeness of him always drives her mind far away from the set course.

"*Dawsyn.*"

"Yes," she says, finally. She looks away. "I lied."

"Why?"

"*Why*?" she repeats. "What do you believe they will do now if I tell them that the kingdom below is just as wretched as the one above? Just as dangerous?" Dawsyn awaits an answer that does not come. Ryon's expression only darkens. "Do you truly believe they will follow me deeper into this Chasm with no knowledge of what lies before us? With no reassurance that it won't all be for nothing?"

"They followed you *here*, Dawsyn. And you did not need to deceive them to do it!"

"And it was a miracle," she replies icily. "The quantum of which will likely never be matched."

Ryon shakes his head at her, his temper rising. "You must tell them the truth, Dawsyn. *Now*. Before it makes folly of this plan."

Dawsyn grits her teeth to keep her voice from rising. And yet, shame climbs the walls of her throat. "I'm sorry," she tells him. "I'm sorry for not speaking with you first. But *I* know these people. I understand how they think, how they behave. They will not follow me down that path, Ryon. Not unless they believe it has a known end."

Ryon gives a frustrated huff. "Then you have very little faith in them," he says.

"Just as they do in me," Dawsyn rebuts, quietly seething. "I have persuaded them into this hole. I will not test the extent of their leniency once more."

Ryon's jaw ticks. He stands tall, looking over her head, and down into the interminable nothingness of the path ahead. "You test their leniency already, malishka," he says grimly. "We have no idea what may lie in wait here."

"No," Dawsyn cedes. "But I know what lies in the opposite direction. And if I must use their ignorance against them to give them freedom, then so be it."

With that, Dawsyn leaves his side. She steps closer to the middle and holds her torch high above her.

Soon she sees the glow of a dozen torches rise in response, signalling their willingness to be led through the dark.

Dawsyn turns, facing the road ahead.

When you lie within the mouth,

The cost will be no fewer.

* * *

They go against the flow of water, lumbering with aching slowness. Trepidation coupled with the lack of light means they must trek slowly and yet still people fall. The ground hosts sharp rock that seems to appear from nowhere. Dawsyn remembers the feel of differing terrain beneath her feet the first time she stood on ground that was not covered in snow and ice. It makes their steps overly cautious, their gait unsure.

The glint of flame that reflects the black rockface plays tricks on the eyes. Dawsyn finds herself walking with her ax in hand, if only to quell the rising fear in her belly. The magic within her is disturbed by its surroundings as well. It roils at each foreign echo, each speck of light.

Dawsyn looks behind her often, letting the light of her own torch shine over the hoods of the horde behind her. All squint and bend their heads to the ground, trying to make out the hazards there.

Tasheem and Rivdan have remained at the back of the horde to ensure none fall behind. Dawsyn suspects it also allows them to hide their ailments from her and Ryon. They seem to struggle to keep pace. Salem and Esra stay close. Every so often, Dawsyn can make out Esra's despair – the quiet sniffs and rattling breaths. Salem murmurs to him in an attempt to mollify, but the sniffing continues.

"Dawsyn?" says a voice. Hector's. His face is suddenly thrown into relief, hanging there in the dark as though detached from his body. "Mind if I walk by you?"

Dawsyn grins wanly, but doesn't break pace, "You've never asked permission before."

"You weren't the almighty leader of our people before."

"I am hardly that now," she scoffs. "The word 'leader' implies compliant underlings."

"That's rather tyrannical of you," Hector comments. "Alvira and Vasteel probably thought the same." This gives Dawsyn pause. "I think the word 'leader' implies the action of leading. Which you seem to be doing as we speak."

"It isn't democratic. These people would rather have me out front as their sacrifice."

He shakes his head. "There's never any point arguing with you. If I point to the sky and call it 'up', you'll call it 'down'."

"And yet," Dawsyn drawls. "You can't seem to help yourself."

Hector shoves her lightly and she smiles. How different the setting for such familiar habits. He has always managed to claw even the most reluctant grin from her. It is possible that Hector, despite the similarities in their upbringing, has retained a nature that is whole and good.

She prays she has not forsaken it. Guilt swells once more. "Do you think I made a mistake?" she asks. "Deceiving them?"

Hector's footfalls, dulled by the ash, are all she hears for a moment. He seems deep in contemplation, though she can't make out the nuances of his face. "I understand why you felt you had to. But... I do not think deception a good tool for a leader."

"I'm not a–"

"You *are*, Dawsyn." Hector's interjection slices the thinness of her refusal in two. "Whether you choose it or not, whether you believe yourself capable, the charge of these people has fallen to you. Denying it will do you little good." Hector raises his head to the thread of sky above. In a whisper, he says. "Should they find out you have led them astray, you will have made an enemy out of every one of them."

Despite herself, defensiveness encumbers her. "And if I lead them to their salvation, they will be none the wiser."

"Quite the gamble," Hector remarks casually, though there is a shake to his voice, a barely contained dread. "But as you know, I've placed my bets with you."

She feels the weight of it, of all of them.

Hector continues on beside her, staggering every so often over stray rocks. He leaves Dawsyn to dissect the enormity of this journey and all the lives she has put on its course. Entrapping them. Enslaving them to it. She thinks of Ryon and Hector and their small band of rebels. Should the Ledge people learn that she is walking them away from Terrsaw, and not to it, their wrath will not befall only her.

CHAPTER FOUR

If Dawsyn believed the slopes above were a test of great endurance, they now appear child's play in the wake of the Chasm's path.

It seems to her that this middle world was made torturous by design. The graphite walls narrow and widen without warning, giving Dawsyn the impending dread of constriction. At times, the path becomes so thin the water spans from wall to wall. If she walks with her arms outstretched, she can touch either side. Here her heart stutters, her throat closes. She becomes sure the next bend will reveal the meeting of those two walls, pulverising any hope for freedom – a dead end.

She walks with her hands pressed to either side as though she might hold those walls apart, praying they do not collapse their efforts. Then, miraculously, they begin to widen once more.

Those walking between them fall constantly. The Chasm echoes their grunts and groans as ankles buckle against the hazardous rocks protruding from the path. Dawsyn's palms are torn from catching herself on the ground. The children often need to be carried, and it only serves to slow them all.

Slow… agonizingly slow. They travel at such an aching pace. It is perhaps the most painful torment of the Chasm. This black abyss thwarts any attempts of haste. The only sign of time passing is the strip of light miles above them and its incremental changes. The growing amber, the slow waning to grey. Without it, the illusion of night would be uninterrupted. It is the only measure of their progress. The only tether they have to the surface.

When it seems they have pushed onward as far as they can, Dawsyn calls for rest. They will eat and drink, sleep a while. After, there will be nothing else to do but forge onward.

The people of the Ledge let their bags and burdens fall with resounding groans. Many converge at the stream and lap up handfuls of water. There is very little conversation among the groupings – evidence of lives lived in wary solitude. They seem to struggle with the proximity of their neighbours now. Dawsyn watches them clamour for safer positions along the Chasm's wall, where their backs are protected. They huddle their possessions behind them, lest they be stolen. There is not a single ounce of trust among their number and Dawsyn cannot blame them. It would be so easy to rob one's fellow here in the dark.

She sighs as she lets her own pack fall from her shoulder. It is full of the most valuable resource they have – food. Dawsyn trusts only her inner circle of outcasts to carry it. Somewhere in this crowd, Ryon, Salem, Esra and Hector carry more. Combined, it still amounts to very little. Enough to quell the appetite of a hundred for a couple of days. Beyond that, they will be walking against the pangs of growing hunger, against time itself. If the end of this Chasm does not reveal itself to them soon, then more dangerous measures will need to be taken. Ryon, Tasheem and Rivdan will be sent atop the mountain in search of sustenance, but only if they are recovered enough to fly – and even in this, Dawsyn has her doubts.

She wipes her tired eyes with the back of her hand, and shuffles with her torch through the bodies to an open space.

"Stifle your torches," she calls. They must preserve their torch light for travelling less they burn down to cinders. Gradually the halos of light among their party diminish, except for her own. Without the orange glow illuminating patches of dark, the blackness is practically absolute.

It does not take long for Ryon to find her. The torch is a beacon in the dark, and for all Dawsyn knows, perhaps the charmed necklace she still wears around her neck beckons to him as well. Perhaps it mimics this constant searching she feels within her at his absence.

He says Dawsyn's name and it is close enough that she hears it alongside a hundred other reverberated beckonings. A swarm of murmured human voices weaving through the dark to find their kin.

"Ryon," she responds.

A hand touches hers, then moves to her waist. No visible arm attached. The outline of a face with no discerning features as it speaks, but unmistakably him. "There you are."

It is said on an exhale – a quiet blessing. Then his forehead is pressed to hers. And though she cannot make out the finer details of him, she feels their breaths combine, she feels the flicker of his eyelashes on her skin. She can imagine his shoulders falling and rising with each exhalation. He takes her torch and extinguishes it.

She winds her fingers in his and they willingly grip hers in return. "Are you well?" he whispers quietly, grimly. His voice travels over her lips, vibrates against the shells of her ears.

She contemplates her answer, wonders if there is any benefit to lying. "No," she murmurs back. "Are you?"

His hands tighten around hers. She feels his head shake.

Dawsyn wants more than anything to sink to the ground with him at that moment. She wants to allow her knees to buckle and give in to the crippling exhaustion in her muscles and rest in the reprieve of him, give him the reprieve of her.

"We cannot sleep yet," she says quietly, wary of the listening ears.

He sighs. "I know."

"How many are injured?"

"I stayed to the middle most of the way. I counted six, perhaps seven who fell. There were likely more toward the back, though I'm yet to find Tasheem or Rivdan to ask."

Dawsyn nods woodenly. "Let us see if any of this magic is restored enough that I might be useful. I'll try to heal who I can."

"You've walked all day, Dawsyn. You're exhausted. Today hardly granted conditions for you to replenish."

"And still," Dawsyn presses, "I'll heal who I can."

"The injuries I've found so far are superficial," comes another whisper. Yennes. "I've done what little I can for the more concerning injuries, but I'm afraid I am still weakened."

Dawsyn turns to the sound of the woman's voice. "We all are," she says. "But we cannot remain idle and wait to heal."

"No," Yennes replies, her outline shuffling uncomfortably. "Ryon? Is... is your back–?"

"I'll survive." There is something oddly sharp in his tone. "Do not spare me your healing if you have any left to give."

"I disagree," Dawsyn argues. "If you are healed, you can fly ahead to mark the path, warn us of anything that might lay ahead."

Ryon sighs. "Then you might heal Tasheem first, or Rivdan. Either can do the very same."

"I fear their injuries are more severe than your own," Yennes says gravely. "We may not be able to do much for them yet."

"All the more reason to focus your attentions on them." Ryon slides his thumb over Dawsyn's fingers. "Please. I'll begin rationing."

Dawsyn wishes she could see his face.

She feels the tendrils of dark iskra lurking in her core and brings them forward. She summons that light in her mind and lets the two collide in her palm.

"Igniss," she says, and watches as a spluttering flame ignites in her hand. It threatens to flicker out but remains long enough that she can glimpse Ryon's face, the glow reflected in his eyes.

For a second, their eyes meet, then the flame extinguishes. She sees his lips descend to hers before the light dims, and he kisses her hard. She relishes the feeling while she can, before he pulls away, disappearing once more into the blackness.

Yennes and Dawsyn take a torch each and light them, making their way around the resting bodies. At the other end of their camp, they find Tasheem and Rivdan in states of collapse. They pant, chests heaving. Tasheem's face glistens with exertion when Dawsyn holds her torch closer. Her eyes remain shut as she speaks. "A good few already seem too weary to continue," she says, the sound of her usually loud voice lost now. It seems an effort for Tasheem to speak at all. "I suspect they were already made weak by hunger before we took them off the Ledge."

Dawsyn kneels before Tasheem, peering into her sallow face. A magnificent shade of purple blossoms from her jaw. Her leg is propped up atop a hessian sack and she winces at the slightest movement. How she managed a day of walking across ground so treacherous, Dawsyn can only guess at, and her bets lie with Rivdan. She suspects the male half-carried his friend this far.

Rivdan lies on his back, cradling his arm to his chest. He stares with deep concentration at something above and breathes through his nose, his body quivering. Yennes attends to him.

Dawsyn summons every ounce of her magic, though she feels how thin the threads are, how frayed.

"Brace yourself," Dawsyn murmurs to Tasheem, and then places her palms to the female's battered leg.

Tasheem gasps at the contact.

"Ishveet," Dawsyn intones, directing the cold and the warmth in her palms, showing it the path to Tasheem. She feels it radiate outward, searingly bright, seeking a destination. Something broken to mend.

Tasheem bites out a curse, but it soon turns to a groan of relief. The back of her head hits the earth, her body slackening.

Still, it isn't enough. Dawsyn feels the magic retreating before it can complete its work.

"Thank you," Tasheem says, smiling tiredly at her. She seems to breathe a little easier.

"I fear it did not do much at all," Dawsyn says.

"Well, I no longer wish to tear the fucking thing off, so you've at least spared me the dismemberment."

"Can you fly?"

But Tasheem shakes her head. "Not well," she says. "Not while I'm weakened."

"Riv?" Dawsyn asks. "What of you?"

Yennes' hands leave the male's shoulder, and he rotates it experimentally, his eyes scrunched in determination. "I might try to, if you wish, prishmyr."

But Rivdan's voice still hitches with the force of his pain as he moves his arm, and Dawsyn cannot ask it of him. Not yet. She shakes her head. "Find your rest," she says to them. "And heal. Lame Glacians are no help to me at all."

Tasheem smirks as she closes her eyes. "I was going to say the same of lame mages."

Rivdan chuckles, lying back.

Yennes and Dawsyn make their way through the rest, calling for those injured to make themselves known. A surprising amount have already fallen to sleep without eating. Ryon, Salem and Esra can be heard passing out rations of food in the dark. Perhaps Tasheem was right, and they were already conflicted with hunger before arriving in the Chasm. It worries Dawsyn that they should be spent so quickly, so early into the journey. What will become of them if this trek were to last another week? Or will they all be thwarted before fatigue sets in?

Dawsyn tries to heal twisted ankles and shallow gashes among them, but many are still left only mildly relieved from their pains. "How did you run through the Chasm, that first time?" Dawsyn asks Yennes, baffled. "How could you see?"

She feels Yennes shudder delicately beside her. "I could not see," she says. "But I could hear them."

Dawsyn frowns. "Hear who?"

"Have you not been listening? Do you not hear it?"

She means to say "no." She means to say, "I hear nothing"' But curling into her ears are the unrecognisable whispers, the taunts, singing to her once more.

We dealers call… 'til you heed the fall… Strangled pleas and sweet release… Lie where sorrow dares not be… Cease your breath…

Cease your breath.

Amid our walls.

Inside our breast.

"One must run," Yennes says now, her voice breaking the illusion of others. "When being chased."

With that, Yennes leaves Dawsyn in the darkness, taking her torch with her. Moments later, the light is snuffed.

Dawsyn makes her way toward the sound of the stream, stopping when the toe of her boot splashes into the shallow water. Everything creeps up on her here, never quite as close, or far, as she judges. She cups her hands to the brook, letting them slowly fill, then brings them to her lips. The water is gritty with sediment, and as she swallows, Dawsyn thinks she detects something metallic, but it is better than nothing.

She finds her way back to a wall she can slide down, finally. She sighs as her backside finds the ground and lifts her chin to an approximation of the sky, but now sees nothing at all. Night has fallen on the surface.

Dawsyn finds the charmed necklace beneath the layers of her clothing. She runs her fingertips along its chain. She wonders where Ryon is.

Like a call answered, she hears a body moving toward her, coming ever closer. And then his voice is saying her name again.

She says, "I'm here," and "take my hand," and his fingers are back in hers. They rest upon the cold ground, side by side, her forehead pressed into the curve of his neck, where she can feel the pulse of him and nothing else. Not the rising panic in her gut or the weight of obligation. Just that who she loves and oblivion.

It doesn't seem such a bad fate.

"We could stay here." Ryon whispers, his mind aligned with hers, and she smiles.

"The very opposite of our objective, if you'll recall."

"Indeed," he groans, for a moment not sounding noble at all, but more as though the presence of anyone else in their vicinity is a gross invasion. "Do you think these people will notice if I fly you to the surface for an hour or so?"

"An hour?" Dawsyn grins. "Would you need an hour?"

Ryon squeezes her waist in his hand, and she buckles beneath it, smothering her outcry in his chest. "You wound me," he murmurs.

Dawsyn reaches up to trace his face, the skin beneath his eyes gritty. "Wounding you has become a favourite pastime of mine," she tells him, her breath catching when his teeth graze the pad of her thumb.

Ryon chuckles, the same way he did when Dawsyn once held a knife to his throat. It brings to mind how his body felt beneath hers, coiled and tense, rigid with consuming anticipation, with brilliant desire. Just as hers had been.

The spark in Dawsyn's mind – that shining zeal that encompasses her mage ancestry – suddenly doubles, pulsing heat throughout her. She feels it rekindle with Ryon beneath her touch, stroking the hair back from her face, as though he were its life source. *Her* life source.

Think of a time you were happy... content, Baltisse had once bade her, coaxing Dawsyn's mage magic to the surface. There had been only one memory powerful enough to conjure it.

Dawsyn lifts herself higher onto Ryon's chest and his hands assist her, gripping her beneath her clothes. Hands that somehow find their way through to her skin. She leans over him, her face hovering above his, and waits for the dark to creep back, waits for her eyes to adjust, and find the finer features of him she has come to rely on. She needs to drink them in again. Needs to retrace them. Needs them to anchor her here, where nothing seems real at all.

Dawsyn presses her mouth to his and lets her tongue trace the curve of his lips. She drinks in the deep rumble that rises from his chest and cannot help but press in closer. It is all she can do not to push further. It is a torture not to let that resonating light in her mind expand, let it move her hands beneath his clothes.

She can feel the urgency in his grip on her ribcage. He holds on fiercely, his fingers twitching each time her tongue flicks into his mouth. She knows how badly he wants to move them. Wants to let them ignite that light in her mind. Wants to make it detonate.

Instead, she sighs. She lets her lips slow, lets them mould around his with something less desperate.

Ryon sighs too. "What I wouldn't give," he whispers, moving his mouth to her ear, "to fly you away."

They wake again with no knowledge of how long they have slept. The thread of light above them appears grey. Dawn, perhaps. There is no way for them to tell. The mass of people rouses with reluctance, sluggish and haggard. They look at Dawsyn and Ryon with petulance, even bitterness, as though they were captives and Dawsyn their captor.

As Dawsyn passes with her lit torch, she hears whispers.

Should have remained.

Worse than above.

She can't be sure if the voices are real or imagined.

Her fingers itch for her ax.

If possible, they forge ahead at a pace even slower than the day before, and the path keeps winding interminably onward.

"Sabar," calls a voice at the back, accompanied by a hacking cough and the harsh clearing of someone's throat.

Dawsyn looks over her shoulder, holding her torch higher, and illuminates Nevrak's face. *The Splitter.* He wipes his mouth with the too-long sleeve of his cloak.

"Nevrak."

"Slow down, girl. Ain't all of us have kept our youthful gait."

Dawsyn groans internally. Until now, she has kept any conversation to the likes of Hector, Esra or Salem, who keep close behind her, but now she sees that they lag behind. She has indeed made headway. Hector keeps hold of Salem's upper arm. The older man has had no small number of tumbles on the trek.

Clenching her fists, Dawsyn paces her steps. "What do you want, Splitter?"

"Come now. Ain't a need for cruel nicknames."

"There wasn't a need to split Old Percy's skull in half either, but the rumour goes you did it on principle."

Nevrak clicks his tongue. "I was a younger lad then. And Old Percy had made a few unsavoury passes toward my lady. Not to mention a rather crude groping in the middle of a Drop. Who would I be if I'd let it slide?"

Dawsyn considers for a moment, remembering the disturbing stare of Old Percy and how it had clung to one's skin. Her guardian, Briar, had always forbade her from walking by the man's cabin.

She shrugs, ceding the point. "Fair enough, Nevrak, we'll call it a term of endearment. What do you want?" He coughs again, and the wet sound of the hacks sound woefully familiar. Dawsyn is at once transported to her cabin on the Ledge, where her grandmother would wake them nightly with uncontrolled gasps and spluttering. "You have lung sickness," she says plainly to the man, watching his beard tremble with the force of his breaths. Even in the weak light she can see his eyes watering, the purple veins stark on his forehead.

He nods. "So it seems. Neither here nor there, if you want the truth. I've already lost my wife, my daughters. Only Wes remains now, and he's full grown. I only need to see him reach safety. I have strength enough for that."

Dawsyn recalls the shapes of two little girls wrapped in furs, lying in the snow, their father and brother protecting their bodies through the night. Here is a man who, like Dawsyn, committed atrocities on the Ledge in the name of protection. And who, like Dawsyn, only means to fulfil obligation. A man of the Ledge, cornered into a character he was forced to adopt, if only to survive long enough to see his son freed.

It is why she could not simply disappear into the folds of the valley and be content with her own freedom. It is why she is here in this godforsaken place, leading the unwilling to somewhere that might balance their bad fortune of being born on the Ledge.

"What we all want to know, Sabar, is how long this journey will take?" Nevrak asks now. "You surely have some inkling."

Dawsyn swallows. She cannot simply refrain from answering. "A few days."

"Not very precise."

"Precision is difficult to achieve with a hundred or more people in tow, Splitter," Dawsyn intones. "Our pace is not as steady as I'd hoped."

"There are many that are weary already," he continues. "What do you mean to do if some fall behind?"

"No one will fall behind. There are enough strong backs among us that we can carry who we must, should it come to that."

Nevrak scoffs. "A fool's errand."

Dawsyn turns toward him. "And what do you suggest we do?"

"Leave them," he says simply, his stare piercing. "Leave the weak to their unfortunate fate and let those strong enough forge ahead."

It is the answer Dawsyn suspected he'd give. She tsks at him. "And you speak to me of being cruel?"

"What *is* cruel is burdening those who stand a chance of surviving this grave you've thrown us into."

"Thrown you into?" Dawsyn repeats, ice creeping onto her tongue, seeping into her voice. "Do you wish to return to the Ledge already, Nevrak?" She says it like a promise. A threat. "Would you prefer that you had not followed me into this Chasm? Are there others that would like safe passage back onto that fucking shelf?"

Nevrak's eyes narrow. "I want reassurance that you're prepared to do what is necessary. It will come to pass either way, princess."

The moniker makes her jaw clench, and she tastes blood on her tongue. He means to use it to demean her, to lessen her, but it brings other questions to Dawsyn's mind. They are long overdue for the asking.

"While we're being painfully honest, Nevrak. I have a few questions of my own."

"Make your ask then, girl. Ain't nothing else for us to do down here."

Dawsyn steps carefully over a sharp boulder, then continues. "How old were you when you were brought to the Ledge?"

Nevrak pauses before answering. "Who's to say I was not born there?"

"You seem the right age for it," she says. "It does not take a genius."

Again, Nevrak hesitates to answer. "A boy," he says, "seven... or eight, perhaps. I've long since stopped counting years as they pass. I was old enough to be afraid. Old enough that I've retained the memory of the cold when it first grabbed me."

The cold is not alive, Dawsyn hears in her mind. The voice of her grandmother. And yet the people of the Ledge only ever speak of the cold as though it were a sentient thing.

"Old enough to remember more," Dawsyn accuses. "You knew that Valma Sabar was Terrsaw royalty."

Nevrak levels her with a derisive stare. His lip curls. "Course we knew," he says, and the plurality catches Dawsyn off guard. "She came screaming into that village while it burned, got snatched up just like the rest of us. Knocked the crown right off her head."

Dawsyn bristles at the resentment in his voice. "She came to warn you all," she says. "To tell you to run."

"And it was too fucking late." Nevrak's tongue flicks over his lip, jaw rolling. "Likely it was her frumped-up skirts that slowed her down, and she got herded up that mountain just like the rest of us, weeping and pleading with the Glacians the entire way. Woman had never known a day of discomfit in her life."

Bile crawls up Dawsyn's throat. Nevrak's description is much like the one Dawsyn would give Alvira or Cressida. But never Valma. Her grandmother was the opposite of pomp and privilege. The image of bravery. Even Dawsyn's imagination cannot conjure a realm that would have seen Valma Sabar stooping to beg for mercy.

Dawsyn wants to argue, to reject the insult to her grandmother's name, but Nevrak is speaking freely now, his eyes glazed with memory, and she resists the urge to stop him.

"We were thrown on that Ledge with nothing but a few scraps of food, and the fighting started straight away, as you can imagine. The princess stopped it. Started decreeing laws and ordering folk about. They all listened to her at first," Nevrak comments. "She was royalty, after all. Bossy. Put her nose in everything. Wanted everything divided fairly," Nevrak chuckles, as though it was unthinkable. "Thing is, up there on the Ledge, people soon figured royalty didn't mean a fucking thing. Weeks went by and there was no sign of King Sabar's calvary. No one came to find us, to save us. And here was another Sabar, still dangling her rank and dishing orders. They got sick of her mighty fast, I'll tell you. At some point, a fellow challenged her," Nevrak's tone turns darker, dangerous. "She'd hoarded some food for herself, or so he'd said. He demanded that she give it up," Nevrak shakes his head. "When she refused, the man fisted her hair, and dragged her to her feet. He pulled her all the way to the Chasm, kicking and screaming."

Dawsyn's palms grow icy at the thought.

"Some folks tried to stop him, but even more held 'em back. They were angry at the entire monarchy, see? The palace had failed them, failed to rescue them from the Ledge. People were dying in the snow each day, and still no one came. I think it were pure frustration. We were all maddening more 'n more each day. That man pulled your grandmother all the way to the ice, and just as he was about to let her slip over, she pulled a knife out of nowhere and shunted it into the base of his mouth. Pushed it all the way to the hilt. We watched him sag onto the ice, and it carried him all the way down and into this fucking hole." Nevrak shakes his head, the memory still confounding him. "He weren't the only one to try and take their vexation out on her, either," he continues. "It became clear that the Ledge had no leader. Your grandmother slunk away just as the rest of us did. We armed ourselves and stayed vigilant. Trusted only a small few. I don't remember a single person deferring to her after that day. She weren't royalty, just a prisoner, as we all were. And we all knew that only the lucky few would survive that place. Only the hardiest. The most pragmatic. Your grandmother knew it, same as the rest of us."

Dawsyn shakes her head, swallowing that unnameable emotion that threatens to weaken her voice. "And not one person thought to mention to me, or to my sister, that we were the granddaughters of a crown princess?"

Nevrak chuckles darkly then, ending on another forceful cough that bends his back. "And why would they bother themselves to? The last time I heard someone refer to your grandmother's rank, I had not a single hair on my chest, and she tacked their hand to a tree with an ax," Nevrak shrugs. "She gave up the title long before you lived, girl, and we heeded her warning. The Ledge has no royalty."

Nevrak nods to Dawsyn and falls back, allowing her to walk on ahead with her torch, with her eyes squinting into the dark, with her mind on the Ledge and her grandmother, where she'd denounced her own title with a blade.

A princess made a monster.

And now a monster made a princess.

CHAPTER FIVE

Thirty years before Yennes re-entered the Chasm, she was pulled from its mouth.

The sea had clawed for her ankles, the tide ravenous. It strained to take her into its grasp, beneath its surface. An hour she had stood there at the tips of the tide's fingers, warring with fear. And all the while, the voices that filled her sung of different paths.

They had taunted her since she'd found herself in the Chasm's basin. They had followed her here, to the very end.

Slice the limb, rid the ache.

She had run from its call. Run until her feet bled, until her chest felt torn to shreds.

Cease your breath.

"How?" Yennes had said aloud. Days, she'd spent in the Chasm. Days of torturous sameness. Of darkness. Of whispers for company. But there at its edge, facing not a safe harbour, but an ocean, she felt the first tremors quake within her. She was so tired.

Whatever valour she'd been made of before had been leeched from her. Now she cracked.

She could not cross the ocean.

Cease your breath, the Chasm whispered to her, from a refuge deep within.

"*How?*" she asked again, eager to be shown any end to her suffering.

Go into the water, it bid her.

And suddenly her mind was filled not with the thrashing of water on rock, nor the hammering of her own blood, but the burnt horizon, where the orange bled to tender pink. The world turned silent but for the whispers that bid her forward.

The water is warm, it waits.

Where before the water seemed frenzied and vicious, it now slowed. She could see the careful undulation of each wave, each ripple that grew and peaked. It was suddenly beautiful. Gentle.

The water that now cradled her ankles was indeed warm, where before it had chilled her to the bone.

It waits to embrace you, the voice said, and Yennes felt her body move of its own accord.

The ocean guided her forward, tugging on her clothes like an insistent child. She laughed and succumbed to its nudges. She let it envelope her thighs, then her hips. And if she shivered, it was only for the beautiful mercy of this end. If her breath caught, it was only for the sky's performance, painted in colours she had never seen it wield. Her hands shook, but only with the last vestiges of some forgotten dread, now rendered meaningless. Soon, there would be nothing left to fear. There would be nothing but this warm bed beneath brilliant heavens, and she would never feel the cold's touch again.

Yennes looked her last at the bruised sunset, then went under.

The water pulled her in slow circles, danced over her skin, and she chuckled. She felt the water drench her throat and heat her chest, but no pain found her.

Close your eyes, said the voice. *Sleep.*

How simple it is, Yennes thought, *to yield.*

It was some time before she felt the first upheaval. The ocean that had playfully tugged her this way and that suddenly wrenched and tore, but it did very little to rouse her.

All right, steady on, she thought. In her mind, a young girl pulled ruthlessly on Yennes' coat, coaxing her into the grove.

Hurry, Yen! she brayed. She ran full pelt through the drifts, snow spraying either side of her, arms raised as though they'd lift her into the sky.

I'm coming! Yennes called back, watching the girl's black hair disappear into the mist of the grove.

But Yennes was lurched in another direction, then another, several hands pulling her, tearing at her clothes. As though she were among the fray of the Drop, scrapping for bundles. She fought the hold they had on her but there was something burning her throat, her chest.

She was so cold. It engulfed her then with stunning ferocity. It stabbed at her skin. A different cold than that of the Ledge – that was a cold one could see. It was the mist of breath, the virgin snow, blackening skin. Slow moving frost that crept closer if you didn't stop it.

This cold was unstoppable.

Sleep, the voice crooned to her, giddy in its triumph. *Sleep now.*

But what rest was there to be found in pain this terrible? Amongst hands that threw her in circles until she was dazed. And that icy burn in her belly – it blossomed within her, climbing into her chest, down her arms. It sliced pathways through her body and up into her mind.

Away, Moroz, the voice said, already shrinking, diminished. *Away!*

But her mind was flooded with the chill of this new creature, and its anger was insatiable.

Yennes felt her body collide with something unyielding. Then again. She was struck on all sides as she tumbled, battered across the head, her shoulder, her hip. Her eyes and mouth filled with salty grit. Her back collided with something solid, and she felt the water pushed from her lungs. It stung her nostrils.

It took a long time for Yennes to realise that she was no longer moving. A while longer to become aware of the orange glow leaking through her eyelids, the warmth on her face, the stinging breaths she took.

Yennes could hear the ocean, but it was no longer within her, around her. When she opened her eyes, it was to find that same sky, those same shades of pink above her.

From somewhere deep in her core, a very different voice whispered – not of painless ends or ceasing breath – but of something entirely other.

Release me, it said. *Release me.*

And then it sunk into some unreachable place within and left her entirely alone.

"Not *entirely* alone," came a voice, melodious and precise.

Yennes turned her head in slow degrees, pain lancing down her neck. On the shore beside her sat a woman, dripping wet and wearing an expression of deep petulance.

A woman so beautiful, Yennes hardly believed she was real at all. Yennes squinted at her as she rose from the sand with ethereal grace, shaking out her dress.

"Who–" Yennes coughed, her voice desiccated. "Who... are you?"

"Baltisse," said the woman brusquely. "Mother above. Close your eyes a moment, would you?"

And then there was a burst of white light.

CHAPTER SIX

Serpent spine and temptress tongue
Silent wails and bargains sung
Bowl the heart and drink it dry
Run...run...run...

Dawsyn jolts upright, gripping her chest. It is collapsing inward, suffocating her. Something with claws digs its nails into her flesh. She drags in a rasping, wild breath, and the feeling disappears.

She blinks but sees nothing. Her chest rises and falls with ease, unhindered. Sweat beads on her forehead, collecting in her palms, but she is unharmed. Her chest is intact, her heartbeats decelerate. Just a dream. It was just a dream.

Yet still, those ungodly voices and their slippery verses echo within her. She can no longer say if they did not originate inside her to begin with.

"Dawsyn?" Ryon rouses. She feels the warmth of his body at her side. "What is it?"

She lets her eyes sweep back and forth but it is a useless endeavour. The Ledge people sleep through the night, their torches stifled, the blackness all consuming. "Do you hear that song?"

Ryon is silent a moment before answering. "A song?"

Dawsyn nods – another useless endeavour. "Voices? They woke me."

Ryon pauses again, presumedly to listen.

Serpent spine, skip down each rung.

Back to where the end begun.

But he only chuckles. "I am surprised you hear anything above Salem's snoring. He could rival a hog."

Fear slides its way down Dawsyn's throat, into her stomach, joined immediately by iskra, rising to the call of turbulence. Still, she hears it, the last whispering tendrils leaking away as though the wind carries it.

Slice their bellies,

Carve the skin.

"What do you hear?" Ryon asks now, all traces of humour gone. He must feel her rigidness, the threat emanating from every pore.

It is strange. Dawsyn has met a great many terrible things in her life. Things that troubled her, scared her. Living, breathing foes that stood taller and numbered greater, all with the desire to kill her. And yet here where she is not touched, where she can see no foe – in this darkness is where she is most afraid. She is gripped by terror. Choked with it. "I hear…" Dawsyn begins, only she can hardly describe it. "I hear…"

Before she can respond, another noise makes itself known. It springs out of the quiet, black nothingness without warning, and stills Dawsyn and Ryon both.

A high-pitched cry – muffled. As though a hand were pressed tightly over a pair of lips. It is immediately followed by rustling and a whispered refrain. The refraction of the Chasm's walls makes it difficult to discern whether it is a distant sound or not, or what direction it comes from.

Dawsyn rises to her feet and twists her head. She takes the ax from its sheath on her back, turning it over with her hand.

This is a sound she knows. It is not the murmur of something bodiless. This is horribly recognisable.

She does not light a torch. Instead, she calls fire to her palm and lets the small light serve as her guide. Dawsyn hears Ryon make haste at her back, just as alert. She hears the singing of metal as he removes a short sword from its scabbard. She has little doubt that the sounds are recognisable to him as well.

She follows the sounds of the smothered whining. Softened terror is the most heinous kind. It heats Dawsyn's blood. The flame in her palm brightens, yet the people she passes seem unperturbed in their sleep. Deadened. It disquiets Dawsyn. How has the noise not woken them?

In a crevice along the rockface, a woman's legs kick out against the earth, one after the other, as though attempting to gain traction. She lies with her upper body hidden within that fissure. Atop her, a dark mass shifts. A man's form holds her down, and the quiet refrains continue, the muffled sounds of torment.

"Shut up!" the man hisses.

Ryon reaches them before Dawsyn – a stroke of fate, for the magic within her has gathered at her palm, ready to explode, and she sees very little reason not to let it.

The assailant turns at the sound of Ryon's approach. Though she cannot yet make out his face, she hears the crunch of bone as the butt of Ryon's blade collides with his nose.

The man is hurled sideways, his head hitting the side of the jutting crevice. He collapses in a heap on the ground, a pitiful moan escaping him before he is quiet and still. The woman in the shadows struggles to stand. Dawsyn hears her panting, then spitting something onto the ground, and when Dawsyn holds the mage fire closer, she sees that the woman is hardly a woman at all.

"Abertha," Dawsyn breathes on an exhale.

She couldn't be more than eighteen. She tries to straighten her cloak and don her hood, concealing the auburn curls that tumble wildly about her face.

"Fucking mongrel," she rasps, wiping her mouth aggressively with the back of her hand. "Sat on my chest as I slept and tried to pin me there, as though I haven't won every fucking match against him since we could walk. Coward has to wait until I'm asleep to claim a victory."

But Dawsyn spies the discolouration around Abertha's lips, the angry red patches on her throat "He tried for much more than that," Dawsyn says darkly. It is not a question.

Abertha spits once more. "I was handling it."

"Are you hurt?" Ryon asks, his voice quiet, his face still turned toward the assailant, likely considering further injury.

"Course I'm not," Abertha mutters.

Dawsyn grimaces. It seems a common defect amongst Ledge women to want to bear the burden of their aggressors alone. Dawsyn can see it in Abertha's face now. The determined set of her eyebrows. The rage that masks the insult, though there is a slight shake to her voice. The girl turns her face away in a show of disinterest, but Dawsyn makes out the glistening of her eyes in the firelight. "If you don't mind," Abertha says dismissively, and begins to stand, brushing herself off.

Dawsyn knows better than to expect a person of the Ledge to show gratitude. She doesn't dare embarrass the girl with coddling; Dawsyn does not possess the flair for it, and it would only compound the insult. Instead, she does the only other thing that ought to be done. She turns to the man on the ground and kicks his side until his body flips over.

Wes, son of Nevrak, lies unconscious at her feet. A trickle of blood flows freely from a cut on his scalp, but he is alive. His eyes move behind their lids.

"The fucking weasel," Dawsyn murmurs, lip curling in disgust.

The boy's pants are halfway undone, as if there were any doubt to his intentions with Abertha. Dawsyn's eyes run over his gap-toothed mouth, his plain, round face and bent nose. She raises her ax.

"What is this?" comes a voice, much louder than necessary. It bounces off the rock face, stirs the bodies that lie nearby.

Nevrak disentangles from the gloom. Behind him are two other men of the Ledge, standing behind him like pillars. Nevrak looks down at his son, lying lame and bleeding on the ground, with his trousers askew. Then, he looks to Dawsyn and Ryon, who hover over Wes with their weapons drawn.

Nevrak's eyes narrow, and he pulls a dagger from his sleeve, spinning it in a menacing circle. His chums do the same.

"Nevrak," Dawsyn says, trembling with fury. Others have begun to rouse. They gather beyond Nevrak, some of them lighting their torches. "You ask an excellent question. Why don't we confer with your kin?" Then, without waiting for an answer, and with unceremonious violence, she launches the toe of her boot into Wes's side once more.

The boy jolts upright as Nevrak hastens forward, raising his dagger. But Ryon meets him with his sword. "Watch your step," Ryon says in a voice that promises death, and Nevrak is forced to halt.

Wes coughs and splutters into his own lap, gasping painfully as he grips his side.

"Pa?"

Dawsyn lowers to her haunches next to him, placing the blade of her ax beneath his jaw. "I'm afraid not," she says flatly. "Now stand."

Wes gulps against the edge of the ax blade but does not dare reply. His eyes do not leave hers, even as she applies pressure against his throat. He rises unsteadily, keeping his chin lifted as the ax follows.

And with the absolute imbecility of a man cornered, he reaches for the sheath at his hip.

Dawsyn's hand arrives first, and she grips the hilt of the blade in his belt. She could happily slice his throat open now, let him spill out into the Chasm.

"I wouldn't," she warns, her voice a void.

"What the *fuck* is the meaning of this, Sabar?" Nevrak demands. Rage was seeping into his reddened cheeks, spittle dampening his beard. Here was a man she had only yesterday begun to sympathise with. A man she thought no different to herself. She laughs through her nose, and it seems to rattle him. His eyes flit between the ax at his son's throat and Ryon's sword tip. "You dare threaten my son?"

Dawsyn turns her gaze back to the weasel boy. His lips quiver. One of his eyes is swelling shut. She waits until his stare meets hers. She waits for the pupils to dilate with fear, for the swallow at his throat to reverberate against the ax blade. Then she says, "Go ahead and tell Pa all the bad things you were doing in the dark."

Wes's eyes flick to Nevrak's, silently pleading. "I…"

"Louder," Dawsyn orders.

Sweat beads at Wes's lips. "I… I…"

But Abertha shuffles forward into Dawsyn's periphery. "It was a fight," she says loudly, her voice far stronger than the boy who tried to pin her down not minutes before. Abertha looks with contempt at the people closing in around them to better watch the proceedings. People who would gawk and spectate but would never once raise their hand to protect her. To shield her. On the Ledge, every eye is turned away from their neighbour. Turned inward solely to mind one's own welfare.

"We were fighting," she says loudly, for all to hear. "And Sabar stopped us."

Dawsyn's eyes shut. *No,* she thinks.

"It's done," Abertha continues, and in the silence that follows Dawsyn opens her eyes to find the girl piercing her with a stare like the tip of a knife. It beseeches her. Begs her. "It's done," she says again.

Beyond Abertha, those watching seem to lose interest. They back away, falling into the darkness. Just another tussle, nothing more. They were ripe for picking on the Ledge.

Dawsyn seethes quietly, but her eyes don't leave Abertha. They stay glued to the girl's throat, to the graze on her jaw, to her bruised lips.

"Wes lost," Abertha snaps at Nevrak. "Again. Shame you lost your dear girls. They were twice as strong as your bastard-born son."

The veins in Nevrak's furrow bulge slightly. "Gloating is unbecoming on you, Bertie. Born with a bitch's tongue, like your mother."

"Such is my burden," Abertha says dryly, then she shoves past Nevrak, disappearing quickly.

Dawsyn is left with Wes in her grasp, the ax blade still biting at his throat. His breath seems steadier, as though knowing he has not been bested, as if he believes himself out of the thicket. He even grins up at her. "If you don't mind, Sabar," he says thinly. "Lower the ax."

"Unhand him, Dawsyn," Nevrak adds. "And tell your *pet* to step back."

Dawsyn looks over her shoulder at Ryon, still blocking Nevrak's path with his raised sword. Nevrak eyes Ryon with something intended as contempt, but instead only appears scared, dwarfed.

Dawsyn grabs the blade from Wes' hip and throws it before any can react. With precision it embeds into the toe edge of Nevrak's boot, likely just nicking the skin inside. Nevrak curses and stumbles backward, saved from falling by the arms of his fellows.

"Bold of you to insult a Glacian," Dawsyn says. "I wouldn't make a habit of it."

Ryon chuckles good naturedly and sheathes his sword.

"You almost got my foot!" Nevrak shouts.

"I'll admit, I was a little short," Dawsyn allows. "I was aiming for a toe."

Nevrak rights himself, pushing away his two cronies and pulling out the blade. "Get off me," he mumbles to them. And then to Dawsyn, "Ain't a single person here that needs you to show us the way, Sabar. Only two directions and you've already pointed the way."

"An interesting threat," Dawsyn intones. "Why don't you make good on it?"

Nevrak hesitates. "What?"

She nods in the direction of the Chasm's path. "By all means, be on your way. And take your pitiful excuse of a son with you."

Nevrak says nothing. His eyes sweep between Ryon and Dawsyn, now quelled by hesitancy, by fear.

Dawsyn huffs a breath of mirth and turns her eyes on Wes. "If this... *stain*... touches one more person indecently..." Here, Dawsyn pauses, raking her eyes with revulsion over Wes's face. "If your hands find their way beneath one more skirt, I *will* cut off your cock, Wes. Do you understand?"

He swallows. "I didn't–"

The denial is choked off by Dawsyn's ax. Beads of blood spout along the skin. "Do you understand, Wes?"

The boy's eyes water, but he nods this time, refraining from speaking at all.

"Good," Dawsyn says. With that, she finally withdraws the ax. After one last warning glance, she turns her back on him.

"Morning is breaking," she says, and indeed, a sliver of grey light has appeared high above. "If you wish to blaze the trail, Nevrak, you ought to make haste."

"We will allow you to lead the way," Nevrak mutters darkly. "If I have your word my son and I will not be threatened again."

Ryon laughs and the sound is laced with violence. He steps toward the Splitter, and it serves to illustrate how much taller he is, how much more imposing. Nevrak swallows and holds his blade up again.

"I'd be more concerned by her *pets*," Ryon says.

With the magic in Dawsyn's palms pulsing, she leads Ryon back toward the creek, where many are huddled to drink or douse their faces. Dawsyn breathes through her nose, reimagining the sounds of Abertha's cries.

"I'm surprised you didn't kill him."

Ryon's voice slides over her shoulder. He is looking down at her, brow furrowed.

It isn't an accusation, nor a reproach. She frowns. "Perhaps I should have."

"No. The last thing we need is a revolt."

Dawsyn supposes he is right. The miracle of rescuing the people from the Ledge will be for naught if they cannot herd them to the Chasm's end peaceably.

"I only mean that I expected to have to stop you," Ryon elaborates.

"You mean that you expected to tear me off him, kicking and screaming."

Ryon grins. "Yes."

But Dawsyn cannot find the humour in it. Men like Wes walk amongst them still, when they should have been left to starve on the Ledge. Instead, she will personally escort them to their freedom, should the Mother bless them all.

"You did what was necessary," Ryon tells her.

But Dawsyn can't help feeling that necessary acts so often contradict with what is right. Wordlessly, she reaches to take Ryon's fingers in hers. They are warm to the touch, and she shivers.

Without needing any further prompt, he wraps both arms around her, forearms resting against her chest, and pulls her into the enclave of his body. "We'll make it, malishka" he says, lips glancing her neck.

Dawsyn shivers again. "Whatever comes?"

She feels him grimace. "Whatever comes."

CHAPTER SEVEN

A strange ache seizes Dawsyn as the hours trickle by. It begins in her stomach, a small, muted pulse, easily ignored. She barely notices its presence among the other small pangs of foot travel – the sting of her heels sliding within her boots, the pull of the sacks she straps to her shoulders, the strain of her eyes as she tries uselessly to peer through the unending dimness.

But, insidiously, the ache spreads. It reaches her muscles and makes each step laborious. It shortens her breath. She finds herself coughing with the exertion.

And she is not alone. The Chasm is full of the sounds of ragged breath and dry coughs. Dawsyn wonders if it is something in the air that parches their throats and turns their breath to sand.

Esra walks close by her side, and he eyes her suspiciously as she coughs again. "You sound like a goat," he says. "If a goat were to choke on its own testicles."

Dawsyn snorts. "I wonder if you work to be indelicate or if it comes by you naturally."

"Pariahs are renowned for their shocking indelicacy. *Princesses* however–"

"How many times must I denounce that! My grandmother was a princess, not I."

"No," Esra agrees. "You are, in fact, a goat."

"I've been accused of worse," she says with a grin, then coughs again, her eyes watering.

Esra frowns, but he does not raise further concern. "You would make quite a monarch, you know," he remarks, stumbling over a half-concealed boulder. "A great one."

Dawsyn sighs. "Of what kingdom?"

He doesn't answer immediately. The silence stretches a few moments longer than he would usually allow. "Any kingdom," he says eventually. "All kingdoms need fair leaders. *Moral* leaders."

She grimaces at the mention of morality. After all, should she wish to, a flood of barely vindicated brutalities could be conjured from her memory wherein she was left with a bloody ax and a hollow chest. If morality is a requirement of royalty, then a crown will likely burst into flame should it ever meet her head.

"I've rarely seen fairness and morality meet at the same table and not come to blows," Dawsyn says. "Balancing the scales of fairness often requires... immoral acts."

"You are right, Dawsyn dear, as you so often are." Esra nods morosely. "Morality might well be a faraway dream. But fairness, Dawsyn... *'the balancing of scales'*, as you say. That dream, I believe, is far closer to you than anyone else. And a pariah like me," he says, taking Dawsyn's hand and squeezing her fingers, "can only hope to be led by a queen, even if she were a goat." He smiles at her, but another boulder catches his toe, and he lurches forward, breaking the moment. "Fuck me!" he shrieks.

"I've rarely seen one person stumble so often," Dawsyn remarks dryly.

"Princess, I walk cobblestones in a gown with a three-foot train while villages throw rotten lettuces at me, and I don't miss a step. I'm fucking blind in here."

Dawsyn laughs again, thinking it must be a person of truer magic than hers to make light of a place so grim.

They stop earlier than Dawsyn intended. She raises her hand to call for a halt, too tired to raise her voice, and hears the resounding relief from the mob behind her.

They follow the same routines as the previous nights. Hector, Salem, Esra and Ryon ration out the last of what little food they had managed to bring. Dawsyn and Yennes comb through everyone in search of any that might need aid, and the people of the Ledge drink from the slow-moving creek. They try to find quiet corners and crevices to sleep in along the rockface.

Dawsyn drags her feet. With each expenditure of magic, no matter how small, the fatigue worsens. She finds herself longing to find Ryon, to seek in him that strange sense of renewal.

"Miss Sabar?" comes a voice from the ground. Dawsyn peers down, letting her torch reveal a woman huddled, a child in her lap. The small boy appears waxen in the low light. His lips horribly dried. His eyes are closed with something that resembles sleep and even though he gives a small cough it does not rouse him.

"My son," the woman says. "He grew ill throughout the day."

Dawsyn frowns. "Does he have a fever?"

"No," the woman says. "Only this cough. And he complained of tiredness, though we are all tired. I carried him most of the way."

Dawsyn grimaces. The boy looks to be about seven years old. It can't have been easy to carry him. She crouches next to the woman. "Diedre, isn't it?"

She nods. "And Leon," she looks down at the boy.

"I can try to… fix it," Dawsyn tells her, grimacing at her choice of words. "But I am a novice with this magic. It may not be completely effective."

"Please," Dierdre begs, the lines in her forehead deepening. "We'll fall behind if I must carry him another day."

Dawsyn readies herself. Slowly she places her hand to the boy's throat. "Close your eyes," she warns Deirdre.

Palm to the site of disrepair, Baltisse had told her.

"Ishveet." Dawsyn encourages the waning magic to rid the child of whatever ails him. She feels it flow through her to him, feels it move through his blood.

The small boy startles as the magic touches him, clutching tightly to his mother in fear. Too soon, the magic pulls back, thinning into something insubstantial. It flees back into her palm.

The child, wrapped in furs, stares wide-eyed at Dawsyn, but his cheeks hold their colour, he appears alert. When he coughs, it is faint and innocuous.

"There we are," Deirdre sighs, gripping her son tighter. "It's all right, you are well."

But Dawsyn fears he won't remain well for long. She nods to Leon, then to Dierdre, and forces herself to stand.

The limitations to her magic are endlessly frustrating. She coughs into the crook of her elbow and wipes the wetness from her eyes, wincing against the pang in her throat and chest.

Still your lips… cease your breath… amid our walls… we dealers call…
Dawsyn stills.

Lie where sorrow dares not be… amid our walls… inside our breast.

A tangle of verse, over-lapping and intertwining as it breathes into her ear. She whirls in a circle, bringing her ax forth. But as with each time before, there is nothing that embodies the hissing. A trio of women seated a foot away stare at Dawsyn warily, disquieted only by her, and not by the bodiless voices only she seems to hear.

"Dawsyn?" Yennes calls to her, the glow of her torch bobbing steadily closer.

Dawsyn gives her head a shake, clearing the noise as Yennes comes into view. The woman peers up at Dawsyn for a moment before looking away. "I've seen to as many as I can tonight. I'm afraid I can do no more." Her voice quavers as she speaks.

Dawsyn watches Yennes' fingers grip and regrip her cloak with restless urgency, her hands always revealing her discomfort, and Dawsyn is suddenly struck by a thought, a niggling suspicion. "Do you hear them?" she asks abruptly.

Yennes seems to shrivel. She shakes her head, not in refute, but rather as a warning. *Do not speak of it,* she seems to say. *Please.*

Dawsyn recalls again Yennes' mutterings in a voice not quite her own. *Two paths, both are filled. Two paths, both are filled.*

Filled with what? Dawsyn had asked her in the cove. *Tell me.*

I cannot begin to describe, Yennes had hedged.

Try. Please.

A… presence, she had said. *The presence of something… most sinister.*

Dawsyn had breathed a sigh of relief. *A presence is easily ignored.*

Not these, Yennes had said, her eyes closing against something imaginary. *These won't be ignored.*

Dawsyn feels the tightening in her chest again, something weighing her down, and she coughs. She splutters without drawing breath, until all the air is expelled from her lungs and Yennes has to grip her arms to keep her upright.

"How many did you come across with the same infection?" Yennes asks her now, patting her back ineffectually.

Dawsyn is doubled over, panting raggedly with her hands pressed to her knees. Her ax lies before her, discarded. "In…fection?"

"Yes. The coughing. The fever."

"Ten, though I hear many more." And indeed, the Chasm's silence is splintered over and over again by splutters from every direction.

"I saw to six of them," Yennes says with a sigh. "Though I couldn't clear their chests completely. It is difficult to cure an unknown sickness."

"Where has it come from?"

"I suspect it is the water. Though it could be the air, or a virus carried here from the Ledge. Or... something more insidious altogether."

"You mean a presence within the Chasm?"

Yennes doesn't answer. For whatever reason, the woman does not give voice to what they both so obviously hear, what they both feel.

"If there were something here that wished for our demise, there are far quicker ways than the spread of a cough," Dawsyn says quietly. She is well aware of the women nearby who might be listening.

"Then, we must consider some kind of contaminant."

Dawsyn curses. "How are we to continue if the water cannot be drunk?"

"I do not know, but we have exhausted our food stores this night, Dawsyn."

"Yes, I know."

"A day faster than we had planned for."

"I *know,*" Dawsyn repeats.

"You cannot take away water as well,"

"I am well aware."

"And yet, it seems we've come no closer to–"

"–to the end. *Yes,* Yennes. There is no one in this fucking Chasm with a better grasp on the depths of our dilemma than I."

Dawsyn's voice rises with each word. She runs her free hand over her face and ignores its trembling. Three days they have been in the Chasm. Just three.

"There is nothing to be done," she murmurs, struggling to reign in her temper, her fear. She cannot ask that these people fast from water without knowing if it is indeed contaminated. Dehydration will weaken them faster than any infection can. "We will help who we can, and hope that the end of this journey draws near."

Yennes hesitates, biting her lip. "And if it does not?"

Dawsyn closes her eyes. She breathes deeply, fortifying herself. "Then we will get everyone out."

Yennes does not say the obvious thing, that the Glacians are still weak, that Dawsyn has not yet folded successfully, that Yennes' own magic is dwindling, that getting these people *into* the Chasm was a feat all on its own, a challenge of which will not likely be matched.

Instead, Yennes says, "We fight against time now," and then she looks about her. "We ought not waste too much of it remaining idle."

Dawsyn raises her torch to illuminate as much as she can and sees her people sleeping in their disturbingly deadened way. People who she will allow to drink from this Chasm, despite the sickness it may or may not spread. "Idleness is our enemy," Dawsyn mutters, only it is not her own voice she hears. It is her grandmother's. It is Briar's.

Yennes sighs. "Indeed."

"Please, say nothing of the infection. It will not serve to spread panic."

Yennes nods once, then turns away.

But it is sheer, undiluted panic that Dawsyn feels herself, watching Yennes leave. She coughs again and feels a stab of corresponding pain in her chest, in her throat. It is all she can do not to sink to the ground where she stands and submit to sleep.

Seal your eyes and sleep... lie here with us...

There is only one resurfacing thought that stops her, that forces her to turn back. *Ryon,* it tells her. It promises to fill her, ease her. *Find him. Then sleep.*

So concentrated is she on this promise, that she doesn't see the person waiting there in the dark until it is too late. A man blocking the path mere feet from where she stands, well within hearing range.

Dawsyn falters as he steps into view. Her heart plummets into her stomach.

The man leers at her.

"Nevrak," Dawsyn says.

CHAPTER EIGHT

In a meeting room of the Terrsaw palace, a likeness hangs of the former King Kladerstaff. It seems an apt placement to Alvira, to have him preside over every decision of strategy that pertains to Terrsaw. After all, he has long been hailed the greatest tactician in the kingdom's history. Alvira stares at the painting now and recalls the story her father – a nobleman – once told her, of the ancient Terrsaw King who sought to rid his kingdom of the Dyvolsh infection.

The tale of the terrible Dyvolsh was her least favourite. She would have preferred to hear of the tailor's daughter who sailed out to sea and returned with exotic fabrics, or the tale of the Mirror Queen, who was swallowed by her own reflection when she looked too closely. However, six decades of retrospect lends Alvira the surety that the Great Purger Kladerstaff was more educational for a future Queen.

The tale goes that Kladerstaff's subjects were falling into the grip of some unseeable disease. It would tire them first, weighing their muscles until they ached before it invaded their chests. Within a week it would take their sense of time and place, then descend them into an incurable state of delusion. Mere days, and the disease or the madness would claim them completely.

Dyvolsh, the kingdom whispered in the old language – *the devil.* They bolted their doors and shuttered their windows and refused even the most desperate of their neighbours, terrified that Dyvolsh would seep into their homes, under their skin, and drive them to insanity.

A woman tied her ankles to a horse's saddle and let it pull her through the Mecca. A man sat in his cabin while it burned around him. People of all ages hurled themselves from rooftops, plunged knives into their bellies or tied ropes around their necks. Scenes of unimaginable violence were escalating, and the unaffected seemed powerless to stop it.

All the while, Kladerstaff watched from the palace windows, unable to find the source of the infection, unable to locate the crucible that plagued his kingdom. It seemed they were completely helpless to the blight. Kladerstaff was a benevolent king, a kind and merciful ruler of Terrsaw, and yet his people were being ravaged under his watch, and he could not avail himself to stop it.

That the delusion was contagious became apparent quickly. Families would fall to the illness one after the other, and then their neighbours. The disease spread like ink spots on a map, slowly blackening each doorway in an ever-expanding radius.

First, Kladerstaff ordered his people to stay indoors, but such an order could only keep for so long before the water pails ran dry and the food was gone. Despite it, Dyvolsh found his way through the kingdom with relentless pursuit. The deaths continued, each more gruesome than the last.

Kladerstaff's own wife soon fell ill. Born on the mountain, she had taught the populace of its beauty, its resource, and of the protection it offered, barricading them from the fiercest of winds. Queen Yerdos was her name, and she was widely adored. The people believed the Holy Mother had sent the woman to Terrsaw herself, for with her came favourable weather.

Queen Yerdos stopped eating. Kladerstaff thought it was stress that stole her appetite, for she loved the kingdom and was as helpless as he. But then, she awoke in the night, coughing and retching, and it was clear that the infection had staked its claim on her. Kladerstaff was removed from the bedchamber, separated from his wife. He was forced to leave her with Dyvolsh.

A week later, as Queen Yerdos died, a patron saint was born. The Queen broke a vase and ran a shard of glass across her throat. Her blood pooled on the bed she had shared with her husband, and she was known thereafter as Saint Yerdos – beholder of the mountain.

Kladerstaff quickly became near delusional himself. His queen was dead, his kingdom would soon be annihilated by an enemy he could not fight – he was desperate. He had to purge the province of this contagion. And if all were to perish, it didn't seem such a mighty cost to rid the kingdom of a few.

He concocted a magical fire in the Square. His wife had been known for her spiritual nature after all, and if anyone were to devise an antidote to Dyvolsh, it would be Queen Yerdos. Kladerstaff beckoned all to leave their houses and join him. He pointed to the raging pyre and said, "This magic was left to us by our beloved queen, and it will purify the sickness that blights us. Bring forward all those afflicted and watch as it cures Terrsaw."

One by one, those deluded by the plague stepped into the fire willingly, drawn to its flame like a moth. With each sacrifice, the flames grew higher, until they could be seen by all, and soon, each and every person infected heeded its call.

The kingdom of Terrsaw was rid of its infection by dawn. The loved ones of those who sent their kin to the pyre waited for their return, only to find that the fire was only fire, and the magic Kladerstaff had promised was a farce. When the flames finally died, only ash and bone remained.

Kladerstaff was prepared for anger and outrage. He awaited the storming of his castle and was ready to allow his subjects their retribution. But instead of a great uprising, the nation rejoiced. The devil had been slain by their king along with hundreds of his own subjects, and yet the surviving populace hailed him a saviour, not a murderer.

One might argue (and Queen Alvira often did), that Terrsaw's current monarch had achieved feats rather similar to Kladerstaff's on the day she'd made a deal with the Glacian King and sacrificed the people of a fringe village to the Ledge. A long-lasting blight to the kingdom was gone in a matter of hours, and yet not a soul had ever hailed her efforts. Alvira had traded a forgotten shire and was met with distaste, yet Kladerstaff had ushered double the humans into his purification fire, and his statue was erected in the Mecca – a patron saint of wellness, right alongside that of his wife.

It was the tale of Kladerstaff that had driven her to make the bargain with King Vasteel fifty years ago. Kladerstaff's act of decisive leadership had saved Terrsaw from extinction, and so too had Alvira. A true leader, she knows, makes the decision all others are afraid to, and then withstands the shudder of its recoil alone.

Every man, woman and child in Terrsaw reaps the benefits of her quick action, her continued action, and yet it is not her name they chant in the streets. It is not in her name that they rally.

It is for Dawsyn Sabar.

Alvira has taken to grinding her teeth to dispel the chorus of voices mocking her. Taunting her. It seeps through the castle walls. It finds her through the corridors.

Long live Sabar! Long live Sabar! LONG LIVE SABAR!

By the week's end, her molars will be ground to dust.

Impertinent imbeciles. Ungrateful leeches. She should throw them all beyond the Boulder Gate, feed them all to the–

"Your Majesty?"

Alvira jumps. She is loath to be seen jumping, yet she seems to startle easily of late. "Yes?" she says gruffly to her chief advisor. The nobleman appears to be awaiting her answer. In fact, the entire table waits, all faces turned to hers. To what question, the Queen could not venture a guess.

"I was inquiring as to Your Majesty's wishes for the continued search of Miss Sabar?"

Alvira exhales, not bothering to hide the air of irritation. "Sixty days since she swung from that noose," she mutters, mostly to herself.

"I'm sorry?"

"I was pondering the ineptitude of my guard," she says loudly now, enough that it rouses looks of contrition from the faces of her noblemen. "A thousand strong, last I counted, and yet still not enough to find a singular girl."

Silence follows the statement, and Alvira lets it fester. None dare speak. She hopes it chafes, to have failed so brilliantly.

To her immediate left, her wife peers down her nose at the advisors and strategists, just as disillusioned, Alvira imagines, as she is herself. Cressida may not have many ideas of her own, but she certainly heeds the sense of a good one. The chief advisor, Chen, keeps his eyes downcast, fiddling with the edges of the maps splayed out before him. His underlings follow, two indiscernible men whose names she cannot recall and does not care to.

And to Queen Alvira's left, is Ruby. Once captain of the Terrsaw guardianship, and now the repentant servant, tethered to the palace until she proves herself useful once more. Which thus far, she has yet to do.

"Perhaps," comes the quaver of Chen's voice, eyes looking anywhere but to his Queen. "It no longer benefits the kingdom to continue our pursuit of the Sabar girl and her... followers."

Acid soaks Alvira's tongue. "*Followers*," she repeats, testing the word aloud. She relishes the sight of seeing Chen flinch. "As though she were a messiah. A deity."

Cressida scoffs beside her, and Alvira can imagine how her eyes must roll in that derisive way. That keen ability to cut and slice by way of expression and gesture.

"N-no, of course not, Your Majesty," Chen says.

"Tell me, sir. Do you harbour a fondness for Dawsyn Sabar?"

Chen's eyes flicker once to the side. "No."

A lie. Alvira's fists clench. "And yet your advice is that I let her roam free on Terrsaw territory, despite her attempts to murder myself and my wife."

Chen turns a worrying shade of red and sweat beads his upper lip. "I only mean to glean your majesty's wishes. Our battalions have had no success in locating the girl's whereabouts across Terrsaw, and your people... well, I fear they..."

Alvira raises an eyebrow. "Spit it out."

"I fear they have grown... weary."

Accompanying Chen's comment, the distant chanting of the Mecca grows louder. It swells quite inconveniently.

Long live Sabar... Long live Sabar...

"Their houses have been ransacked. Their businesses disturbed. I fear that further efforts in this endeavour may create an unwelcome stir," Chen continues delicately, as if the stirring hadn't already given way to a rising mutiny.

Alvira's molars clack together.

Ruby clears her throat at Alvira's side. "The continued search for Sabar need not include the disruption of peace in the Mecca," she says now. It is most annoying to hear how strong her voice is, how wilful, when Alvira's specific instructions had been to clobber the will *out* of her. "The search of the Mecca is fruitless. Sabar is unlikely to be found there. It is the Ledge she seeks," Ruby says assuredly. "If we wish to find Dawsyn Sabar, then we would do well to look there."

Alvira turns her shoulders until she is facing Ruby. The girl has always been tenacious – it was obvious from her initiation into the guard. But she was never petulant. Never stupid. People hear conviction in a woman's voice and call it conceit or more often bitterness, but Alvira hears it for what it is – power.

She no longer sees power when she looks at Ruby. Instead, she sees a snake. A viper that sheds its skin when it likes, slithering back into the cracks and crevices when it meets a more forceful strike.

Ruby is not a woman of power; she is a pest.

Alvira laughs at the suggestion. *Go to the Ledge indeed!* "If she has gone to the Ledge," she says, tapping the chains that still clad Ruby's wrists – a firm reminder of her tenuous seat at this table. "Then she is *exactly* where I want her."

"Your Majesty!" The doors to the meeting room ricochet off the walls as they collide, having been thrown open by a footman. He appears out of breath, as though he ran the corridors.

"Mother above," Cressida gasps, clutching her chest. "Treecher! How dare–"

"It is urgent," Treecher gasps, eyes wide and haunted.

Alvira stands. Ice trickles down her spine.

"The King of Glacia is here," the footman continues, ignoring the gasps around the table. "Adrik."

Fear floods Queen Alvira's stomach. "Here? Now?"

"Yes, Your Majesty."

Alvira turns to her wife. She wears an expression that likely mirrors her own. One of sickening dread. "Get out," she says abruptly to the room. "Now."

Chen and his advisories snatch their maps from the table and practically fall through the doorway without bothering to bow their heads to her as they leave. Ruby makes to follow.

"Not *you*," Alvira barks. "*You* will remain. Should this beast come for blood, it will be you I offer first."

Ruby's eyes darken in response, but she does not argue. She bows her head politely, then returns to her place at the table, without the decency of even appearing afraid.

"Well, well," comes a voice ahead of the creature. It steals down the hall and into the meeting room, as unnatural as its owner. "What a fine home you keep."

The creature turns the corner, his frame filling the entire doorway. Flanked on his sides are two others, just as tall and menacing.

Immediately, Alvira is transported back to that fateful night five decades ago, when a king named Vasteel broke through the glass ceiling of the throne room and snapped the Sabar King's neck. Vasteel's skin had been just as translucent, his hair just as startlingly white. Though his wings, admittedly, had been a sight bigger, and clear of troublesome abrasions.

In fact, this Glacian before her appeared… battered. It was hardly several months ago that Adrik had visited the palace and pronounced himself the new Glacian King. His skin hadn't been so colourless then, nor his hair.

He has transformed, Alvira thinks. One look to her right tells her that Cressida has deduced the same.

Alvira hears an intake of breath, and from her periphery, sees Ruby's chest rising and falling. But not with fear, with anger.

Mother above, but the snake is moronic. Adrik will snap her like a twig if he spies her boldness.

"King Adrik," Alvira intones carefully, and is relieved to hear that her voice does not shake. "What a surprise."

"Is it?" he snarls. He appears to wilt slightly where he stands. The day grows oppressively hot, and Alvira imagines this new pure-Glacian has not grown used to its toll. "I rather thought your guards might be expecting me, Your Majesty." And indeed, Adrik seems somewhat put out. As though insulted by the lack of due precaution.

Alvira treads carefully. "With our current understanding in place, I had come to think the extra fortification… unnecessary."

"And I thought you would have known I would come, what with the sudden growth in your populace."

Alvira's mouth closes with a snap. Whatever she had expected the beast to say, it hadn't been that.

Adrik's pale eyes swivel between Alvira, Cressida, and – annoyingly – Ruby, as though she were a noteworthy thing. "Where are they?" he asks slowly, dangerously.

Alvira swallows but lifts her chin. "I assure you; we are putting every effort into recapturing the Sabar girl, and–"

Adrik growls, effectively cutting her off. Within a moment he has approached the round table and swiped a hard-backed chair out of his way. It splinters as it hits the wall. "Not *her.* Where the fuck are my *humans*?"

The silence that follows is broken only by Adrik's harsh breathing. He sucks air through his bared teeth with growing intensity. "The only thing saving your skin is the existence of more convenient stock, Queen. Have you forgotten? *Where are the Ledge-dwellers?*"

Alvira's throat closes. A dark, insidious cold seeps through her. It makes her next words brittle. "Are they…" she hesitates. How she *hates* to hesitate. "They've escaped?"

"Mother above," Ruby mutters, and the awe in her voice grates on Alvira's skin.

Adrik is riddled with it – this calamity. Ropes of veins stand prominently along his neck and down his collarbone. His eyes exude the urgency of a man strung out. He is desperate.

No danger more grave than a desperate man, Alvira's father once told her. Now she knows how wrong he was, for surely no other danger could equate a desperate Glacian.

Where are the Ledge-dwellers? Alvira thinks, and then: *She succeeded.*

"WHERE ARE THEY?" Adrik roars, and the table beneath his hands gives an alarming crack as its legs begin to buckle.

"In case our dumbstruck expressions weren't answer enough," Cressida says, in a voice far more superior than it ought to be, "we are no wiser to their whereabouts than you. Though I assume we can thank Dawsyn Sabar and her band of miscreants for their absence?"

Adrik seethes for a moment, his jowls positively trembling with rage.

"You look rather worse for wear," Cressida remarks now. "Thoroughly trounced. Am I to take it *that* victory is hers too?"

Adrik rounds the table in the space between heartbeats. He has Cressida's throat in one hand and his eyes on Alvira's in a moment. Something unhinged pulses behind his eyes. Something deranged.

"Where. Are. They?"

"Not here!" Alvira exclaims, her hands raised uselessly, as though they might protect her wife. Should this Glacian decide to flick his wrist, she will be no more. "I swear it! If they walk on Terrsaw soil, we have not been wise to it!"

"We've searched the entire mountain," Adrik continues, the manic glint in his eyes remaining. "Turned over every boulder and searched every cave. There is nowhere else they could seek refuge."

Alvira bids herself to think, to speak, and all the while, Cressida's face colours from pink to red to purple.

This is what Alvira does best. She acts. She does not stutter in the presence of adversity. She stomachs what she must. She, alone, untangles the messes of this kingdom while the rest scurry away and quail. She thinks of Kladerstaff, who was decisive when no one else dared to be. She thinks of King Sabar, who neglected to protect his own people from the Glacians, and then she watches Cressida's eyes implore her. Beg her. Alvira opens her mouth and says, "I know where they have gone."

Adrik's eyes narrow. His lip curls back over his teeth.

"I know where to *look*," Alvira amends. "I did not know they had been freed from the Ledge, but if what you say is true, then I know where to find them."

"Where?"

"I will have them returned to you. But…" and here, Alvira ignores the bile in her throat, the rapidity of her pulse. "If you kill my wife this night, your livestock will run free."

Adrik laughs wickedly, though his hand loosens around Cressida's throat. "You make threats?" he says. "I could rid this palace of its souls this night. I could pluck the strays from the streets if I wished. I have no use for *you* at all."

"Except, you are weakened," Alvira retorts, the words coming faster now. A plan forming. Her eyes sweep to the Glacian's torn wing. "You are battle-weary. Just being here, so close to sea, taxes you further, does it not?" Alvira awaits an answer that does not come, so she continues. "You cannot endure our climate for long. If you could, you'd search for them yourself. You do not fool me, Adrik. You are not here to reign terror on Terrsaw. You are here to have me do your bidding, of which I have just pledged my willingness to do. Do not insult me with empty threats. Besides," Alvira does not allow herself a smirk; she should only push the beast so far, "knowing they are out there – Dawsyn, Ryon – it would be intolerable for a… *being* in your position. You would live out your reign awaiting their return to Glacia, awaiting the day they come to seek your throne." *Just as I wait*, Alvira thinks.

Adrik's eyes tighten, as does the fist at Cressida's neck. Cressida make a strangled whimpering sound.

"But you've already surmised as much, haven't you?" Ruby interjects, and Alvira's skin prickles with irritation. "You haven't come here to raid the Mecca. You've come because you fear Ryon. You betrayed him, after all."

Adrik drops Cressida, and she topples to the ground gracelessly. Alvira goes to her side immediately, sickened by the bruises already blooming along her throat.

"Ryon betrays his very nature," Adrik growls, though the droop in his shoulders diminishes the menace. "He betrays *me,* and I will savour the day I wring the life from him. As for the girl…" And here, Adrik's eyes turn impossibly paler. White and ghostly. A creature most unnatural. "I will drink the life from her. She is but a human. She will taste the same as all the others. I will pitch her slackened body into the Chasm after I've reaped all essence from her core, and never think of her insignificant name again."

Adrik pounds his fist to the table, and it gives way, caving in the middle. All three women startle.

"Find them," he says, his chest heaving. "Send word when it is done. You have until the change of season. By then," Adrik pauses, sneering, "it will be growing cooler here in your kingdom. I might find the land beyond the Boulder Gate more to my liking."

"The hostile season comes in a week," Alvira states. "It may take longer to track down the–"

"Send word," Adrik repeats. "Or we will cross the Boulder Gate." He nods to the henchmen who flank him, smiling most cruelly. "And we will help ourselves to as many as we can carry."

The silence that descends the room upon the Glacian's departure is deafening. It drowns out the rebels in the Mecca. It rings in the Queen's ears, pulses violently in her brain.

"She did it," Cressida exhales, her voice no more than a whisper. "She freed the Ledge."

Alvira does not reply. Her mind is a loop, echoing the same question back to her. *How? HOW?*

She squeezes her eyes shut. The day she has always feared, coming to pass. Worse still, that it passes at the hands of a Sabar. She can envision her now, toting her barbaric ax, wreaking havoc upon whatever she touches.

"You have no idea where they are," Ruby says levelly. Her tone is neutral, a simple statement of fact. "And we have a mere week to find them."

Alvira has never reduced herself to physical violence, but the snake tempts her. "*We?*" she says acidly, cocking her head to the side. "No. *You.*"

Ruby swallows, finally humbled.

"*You* have a week to find them. A week to prove yourself worthy of continued existence. And should you fail," Alvira's voice finally gives way, quivering in the wake of each word, "then you will climb over that Boulder Gate and deliver the message yourself."

CHAPTER NINE

"An interesting conversation you were having," Nevrak says, his nose not two inches from Dawsyn's. "What was it the witch said? The part about the water?"

Dawsyn does not take her eyes from his, though her mind races. Her hand goes to her back reflexively, and it is only then that she remembers she discarded her ax on the ground, somewhere behind her. Never in her life has she been so complacent. The thought rattles her. "I'm not likely to impart the private conversations I have with my friends, Splitter," she mutters with a confidence she does not feel. "Eavesdropping is for children."

Nevrak does not speak for several moments, does not move. He simply appraises her, his eyes travelling the planes of her face. It is intrusive, and damning.

Then his lips part, having calculated the exact thing Dawsyn hoped he wouldn't. "You'll tell me," he says lowly, carefully, "or I will sound a warning to this entire Chasm. What was it you said to the witch? *'It will not serve to spread panic.'*"

Defeated, Dawsyn exhales, closing her eyes briefly. When she opens them again, Nevrak is nodding to his side, gesturing her to follow him somewhere more secluded, though the people around them seem too weary to wake and overhear.

They clamber around people, their hands to the Chasm wall, letting it guide them. They leave everyone else behind, too far away to listen.

"Despite what you may think of me," Nevrak begins, "I have the very same desires as you. We all do. We wish to find our way to safety. If you cannot do that, then you've deceived us all."

If you knew the truth, Dawsyn thinks, *you would split me where I stand.*

"What is wrong with the water, Sabar?" he asks forcefully.

She sighs. How she longs to sleep. "I do not know that there *is* anything wrong with it."

"I heard–"

"You heard conjecture," Dawsyn interrupts. "We suspect the spread of infection among us. There are many who seem to be falling ill. It is there for anyone to see."

Nevrak looks over Dawsyn's shoulder, likely listening to the echoing coughs with new understanding.

"Yennes and I are aiding as many as we can, but we must know what the illness is if we are to fight it. We were simply deliberating the infection's origin."

"Lung sickness," Nevrak says at once. "The cold has always slowly choked us."

"It is not the cold. The illness spreads some kind of... contagion."

"And you believe the water to be the origin?" Nevrak asks, his eyes widening.

"It is one theory," Dawsyn allows. "Among many."

"Tell the others. Warn them."

"To what end? If they do not drink, dehydration will kill them faster than any infection. They are already weakened!"

Nevrak chews his tongue for a moment, deliberating. "How long until we reach the Chasm's end?"

"A few days more," Dawsyn lies, ensuring her eyes do not blink. She holds her chin strong and sure.

There is a sheer moment when she thinks he isn't fooled by her bravado. His stare is penetrating, unforgiving. The lines around his eyes deepen and Dawsyn's stomach falls away. But then, Nevrak is stepping back, shaking his head. "A few days more ain't gonna kill the lot. The water will matter little." He looks back into the Chasm. "I will not stir fear where I ought not to. But should the end of this fucking path not come soon, I will shout your secrets for all to hear and I very much doubt our neighbours are the understanding kind." Nevrak's shoulder knocks hers as he passes, and weak as Dawsyn is, she teeters off-balance. "You best find us that green valley," Nevrak calls to her. "Soon."

* * *

When Dawsyn wakes, she finds her hands bundled in Ryon's. He remains asleep, his neck bent awkwardly atop a burlap sack. She knows it will be empty of any food. There is nothing left for them to carry but weapons.

His eyelids open to reveal slits of pupils. He blinks at her wearily. "Sleep well?"

With her head still against the black earth, she nods. Then she coughs.

"Liar," Ryon mutters, pulling her closer. She rests her head against his forearm, and closes her eyes once more, wishing away the hours ahead. The days. The weeks.

No, there will not be weeks of this.

"There is sickness spreading," she whispers to him. "Yennes thinks it could be the water."

Ryon gives a world-weary sigh, then presses his lips to her forehead. "So what now?"

Dawsyn lifts herself onto her elbows and looks as far as there is to look in this pit. "Now, we pray."

They rouse all that can be roused, but there are some too weary to do more than murmur and cough, their eyelids fluttering.

"I can carry this one," Tasheem tells Dawsyn, pointing to a boy no younger than sixteen. His eyes roll in his head, detached from reality.

"You're still injured," Dawsyn says. "Better that you heal properly before we count on your heroics."

But Tasheem only flashes her a tired smile and hefts the boy into her arms. His head lolls over Tash's forearm. "I'm healed enough for this," she says.

Dawsyn touches her arm, tensed muscles working beneath her fingers. "Thank you."

"When we reach this utopia," Tash tells her, "I want a statue erected in my honour."

They stumble onward, Dawsyn at the spearhead. The hours pass with nothing but sameness before them. The path meanders on and on, narrowing and widening. The utter darkness does not lift, giving Dawsyn no cause to believe that the end is any nearer than it was the day before. Behind her, the coughing grows louder.

She wrestles with the idea of sending Ryon or one of the other mixed above, or ahead. None are healed enough to fly with humans in tow. This journey certainly hasn't allowed for rest. It seems dangerous to stretch their limitations, not to mention there are Glacians they may encounter up there.

Mother above, her chest hurts. Her feet hurt. She feels every jostle, every ounce of weight from the weapons she carries. She coughs and it makes her eyes water.

The hurt, the ache... tear it out.

Dawsyn startles. The voice in her ear, in her head. She cannot be sure if it is hers.

Why suffer when you can belie your fate?

Not hers. That other entity of the Chasm comes to whisper torments once more. Only this time... this time the voice sounds less threatening. It... comforts. Calms.

Take up the reigns and belie your fate.

Climb the walls of Mother's gate.

Like a balm, the words come. Smothering out any other noise, tampering the sights and smells around her. *Mother's gate,* Dawsyn thinks, or perhaps it slips past her lips. Her grandmother told her of Mother's gate. The realm of spirits in the afterlife. A place of eternal peace.

Rid the ache. Tear it out.

How her throat burns. She wishes she could rip the sickness from it.

Tear it out.

"How?" Dawsyn asks, the word slurred. She can barely see. Her torchlight is a haze of orange in her periphery, not real at all.

Cut it from the skin, that silky voice says, and though something deep within quails at the thought, this voice makes violence sound gentle, welcoming. She imagines how simple it would be, to part ways with all that makes her hurt and ache and suffer. She could surrender to Mother's gate. She could...

All at once, the iskra within her awakens. It meets in her chest with the mage magic and combines – light and dark.

She hears a keen screaming. It fills every crevice of her mind, so loud that it pains her, and then it is stifled all together. The magic suffocates it, flooding her mind with light and darkness both.

"Dawsyn?"

A hand comes down on her wrist. Squeezes it so tightly that her fingers are forced to open, forced to drop the knife she holds. She hears the sound of its clatter as it hits the rock beneath her feet.

Her vision swims. She coughs in a great hacking stream. Something dark comes loose from her throat and she spits it onto the ground.

"Prishmyr?" comes Rivdan's voice. His hands are on her sides, preventing her from falling forward.

Dawsyn retches. Loose hair falls from her hood into her face.

"Breathe," Rivdan says calmly. "Just breathe."

She gasps at the air, taking in great lungfuls of it, and with each breath, the urge to heave lessens. She feels a stinging at her arm and sees that her sleeve has been rolled to her elbow. There is a shallow cut on her wrist.

"That's it," Rivdan is telling her, pulling her upright. "Steady."

She blinks up to where his face should be, struggling to make it out.

"Shall I help you walk?" Rivdan asks quietly, urgently. His head turns to peer over his shoulder. Dawsyn realises that others must be close behind, waiting for them.

But Dawsyn's wits are scattered. She cannot completely rid herself of the fog that clouds her mind. Instead of answering, she simply stares stupidly up at Rivdan. "I –" she stammers.

"Do you need to rest?" he presses, eyes skirting over her face.

Dawsyn shakes her head, and just this small movement dizzies her. Iskra retreats deep into her core. The glow of her mind is dulling. She looks once more to the small slice along her arm, then to the knife on the ground. Her knife. "The voices," she says. "There are voices here."

Rivdan's eyes, full of alarm, widen. "Voices?"

Dawsyn closes her eyes. Nausea brews in her stomach and the Chasm tips on its side. She tries to shake it back into place. They cannot stop. There is no time for rest. There is only the end of this unending path, or the surrender to it.

That is all it wants, Dawsyn thinks to herself, hearing again the echo of that slippery voice. *It only wishes to see us all fail.*

"I – I forgot myself," she tells Rivdan, finally meeting his eye. He has never looked more disturbed. "Lost my senses for a moment, I think."

"You haven't eaten," Rivdan allows, though his expression tells her that he is not the least bit mollified. "And barely rested. All this healing, it has addled you."

Dawsyn nods, hardly vindicated.

"The others are waiting. Can you continue?" Rivdan asks.

Dawsyn nods, allowing Rivdan to gently pull down her rolled-up sleeve. He takes the pack from her back and slings it across his own shoulder.

"You walk with me now, prishmyr," he says gently, taking the back of her forearm in his hold.

Dawsyn merely nods her assent.

In truth, she does not wish to walk alone.

CHAPTER TEN

Yennes stood on the beach and watched the sun sink into the Terrsaw sea. "It's beautiful," she said quietly. All her life, this sun had alluded her. Now she knew its hiding place.

Yennes stretched her arms experimentally, but they did not ache as they should. "You healed me?"

"Mm hm," said the woman named Baltisse. "Though I suppose you'd rather I hadn't," she tsked and moved her wet, ropey hair over her shoulder. "If you wish to do away with yourself, there are far better methods, sweet."

Yennes frowned. Her body might have been renewed, but her head remained sluggish. "Do away with myself?"

"I could hear your thoughts from the beach. Awfully loud, they were. Sounded like you were crooning yourself to death. Tell me, are you mad? Is that it?"

"What?" Yennes frowned. "N-no."

"Only a simpleton would take joy in drowning themself."

"I wasn't trying to drown myself."

"No?" Baltisse raised a slender eyebrow. "Your mind spoke otherwise."

Yennes blinked stupidly, her thoughts too frayed to form quick retorts. "You... you heal *and* hear thoughts?" she asked, looking the woman up and down. Had she not sensed something unnaturally elegant about this woman on first sight? Something entirely other? "Are you magical?"

"How kind of you." Baltisse smiled and it was the first softening of her expression that Yennes had seen. While the woman's body was supple and languid, her face was held rigidly, with a sort of practised dispassion. "I've been called much worse."

Yennes returned a blank expression.

"I am a mage," Baltisse said carefully. "Though I'd rather keep that information away from the palace, if you don't mind. Unless you'd like me to toss you back into the wash." Baltisse nodded to the sea, then gathered her sopping skirts into her hands. "Tell me, girl. What led you into the ocean, if not the promise of dying?"

Yennes' mouth hung open for a moment, then she shook her head, putting aside the casual mentioning of palaces and mages. "I... I didn't... I came from the Chasm."

Upon the utterance, Baltisse froze, rendered still and silent by the word. She stared at Yennes anew. Shrewdly, intrusively.

It was only then that Yennes noticed the way the mage's irises churned like liquid gold. "Say it again," she said eventually, glancing over Yennes' shoulder to the Chasm's end, where the cliffs divided to allow the ocean passage.

"The Ch–"

"Mother above," Baltisse interrupted, eyes widening. "And what, pray tell, were you doing in there?"

An answer fumbled around Yennes' mind. It was mixed with the sounds of her own harsh breathing as she'd run through the Chasm, the voices that had chased her. She remembers the light that had shone from her hands in her desperation, some strange power creeping into her palms and lighting the way before sputtering out. She sees once more the vein of sky above her, impossibly far away. And in her belly, she feels a resurgence of the urgency that had driven her down the path, the desperate plea she had uttered over and over, that she had chosen the right one.

"What were you doing in the Chasm, girl?" Baltisse repeated. Her face had lost all lustre.

"I was escaping," Yennes mumbled, voice trembling.

"Escaping what?"

But Baltisse didn't seem to need an answer. Her eyes skittered across Yennes' face as she remembered the Chasm, then before it Glacia, and before that...

"The Ledge." Baltisse exhaled the name, as though it were some ancient myth. "You have come from the Ledge."

* * *

Baltisse walked her up the shoreline, over the long stems of lazy grass stalks that bent away from the ocean. Yennes trailed her fingers along the tips, marvelling at their number.

Here, the cliffs tapered back and made way for a cove. In the cliffs' shadow, a timber cabin stood. Its many windows were filled with glass, revealing the inside. It struck Yennes as odd. Cabins on the Ledge did not have windows.

"Where are we?" Yennes asked Baltisse then. The breeze that tracked over her clothes chilled her but did not sting. It whispered, rather than howled. And the sky was enormous, stretching endlessly over the ocean, unshrouded. Everywhere she looked, the land was covered in trees, shrubs the likes of which she'd never before seen. Surely, this was paradise.

"Terrsaw," Baltisse said instead. "The very corner of it."

Baltisse opened the door to the cabin and stepped within. "Come," she said to Yennes. "You must eat."

Eat. It had been an age since Yennes had eaten. Her stomach flipped at the mention of it. The mage set to work in her cabin, lighting a fire with a mere wave of her hand. She set a pot atop it and fetched limp game from her rafters – the plumage of the bird was unrecognisable to Yennes.

"Pheasant," Baltisse told her. "Meat is what you need."

Yennes hovered uncertainly in Baltisse's doorway, staring wide-eyed at the cabin's interior. Yennes thought it smelt peculiar – a mix of burnt foliage amongst other things. It left a strange taste in the back of her throat.

Through the windows, Yennes could see the scope of the ocean clearly. It stretched endlessly. It surrounded them. After her recent tussle with it, it made Yennes blanch. "Will… will…" she stumbled. She cleared her throat and tried again. "Will… the ocean–"

"It cannot reach you here," Baltisse answered, not waiting for her to finish. "The tide is on its way out. Had you waited in the Chasm but a few more hours, you could have waded through the shallows to reach the shore."

Yennes had no clue of what the tide was, but she knew she could not have waited for it to aid her. "The Chasm would not have allowed me to stay," she said firmly. Her hands began to tumble over one another, revealing her frayed nerves.

"What could you mean?" Baltisse asked, her lips pressing together firmly.

"I... I ran from its voices."

Baltisse's gaze drifted over Yennes once more, and it only unsettled her further.

Without warning, Baltisse brought a large, square-edged blade down on the pheasant's neck with a loud thwack, and Yennes jumped.

"We eat first," the mage said. "Then we shall see about this Chasm and its voices."

After the pheasant meat and vegetables were boiled and spiced, Baltisse ladled a generous helping into a bowl and passed it to Yennes. The smell emanating from the pot was almost too much for Yennes to bear. It was a task to take the bowl from Baltisse without snatching it from her grasp.

Though it burned, she devoured the stew in moments. When she held out the bowl to return it to Baltisse, it was inexplicably full once more.

"Have some more," the mage ordered. "Slower, this time."

Her belly was distended by the time she was done. It was the most food she had ever consumed in one helping. Her body did know how to hold so much, and she vomited soundly into a basin by one of the windows.

"I did tell you to eat slowly." Baltisse grimaced, her nose wrinkling.

Yennes did not bother to apologise. It did not seem the woman cared much for the wasted meal. "Thank you," she said instead. "For saving me. For the food."

Baltisse stared at her. "But what are we to do with you now?"

Her posture was casual – cross legged in a chair by the hearth, her form slouched, and yet still. Yennes could not help but feel malice in those words. Danger.

"You can unclench those hands, sweet. I do not mean you harm."

Yennes had no weapons to wield regardless, not since she left the Ledge and was stripped naked by Glacian brutes. Even if she possessed a blade, her hands could not cease their trembling. She doubted her ability to use it against a mage.

"Hm. I cannot imagine the life you have lived," Baltisse said then, turning her gaze to the fire. "Imprisoned in such a place."

Yennes offered nothing. Once, she would have said something cutting, quick-witted. But too much had befallen her. Too much had been stripped away. She could not summon the fierceness she once depended on.

"Tell me," Baltisse said. "How many still survive on the Ledge?"

Yennes looked curiously at the mage. "Several hundred. Maybe less. I do not know."

"Poor souls." The flames danced in the mage's eyes. She remained still for several moments more, seemingly lost in whatever thoughts plagued her.

"How many remain here?" Yennes asked, forehead creasing. "In Terrsaw." She had heard stories of the valley as a girl. Stories that seemed more like fairy tales. It was the place her parents had been taken from. She had never given thought to those who might have survived the Glacian's raid.

Baltisse chuffed derisively. "A fair few more."

Yennes nodded. "The people on the Ledge… the ones that lived in this valley before they were taken, they do not like to speak of it."

Baltisse's head tilted to the side. "Oh?"

"My mother and father… they did not like to reminisce on what was lost."

"What *did* they tell you?"

Yennes fell quiet again. In truth, she could only remember half-stories. Mentions of forests and streams and music and festivals that fell from her mother's tongue when the yearning softened her, but the sentences were always cut short, always followed by abrupt reproach.

No point in longing for what is lost, pet, her mother would say, shaking her head. *We keep our eye on what we have now, lest someone snatch it.*

Her father was worse, falling into fits of rage at the first murmurings of the valley. *They ain't coming to fetch us,* he'd thunder, throwing what little crockery they had at the walls. Trinkets they had fought so hard to scrounge from the Drop. *They ain't deigning to cross the Boulder Gate. And we ain't deigning to remember them.*

Who *they* were had remained a source of mystery to Yennes. Though she'd gleaned some knowledge, she'd dared not question either parent further.

Baltisse seemed to have heard Yennes' answer, despite her silence. She nodded now, and Yennes garnered that this woman did not often make a show of compassion or sympathy. Yet Yennes felt it in that cabin. The woman's eyes grew glassy as she stoked the hearth.

"Well," Baltisse said slowly, quietly. "Best you know it all, then.

Chapter Eleven

The fourth night comes without seeing the end of the Chasm and the people slump to the ground, forfeiting the pretence of conversation. Dawsyn sees their faces and feels their defeat, and the guilt in her gut screws deeper. *They're dying,* she worries. *And they don't yet know it's by my hand.*

Yennes and Dawsyn walk amongst them for a time, as they've done each night before, but they find very few they can help. More than half are now plagued by whatever cruel affliction the Chasm has meted out. They splutter in their sleep as she passes, the force of their coughing still not enough to rouse them. They have not paused to catch their breath all day.

"Miss Sabar?" says a voice in the dark.

Dawsyn turns to her left, holding her torch out to reveal a woman sitting cross-legged on the black earth, an infant in her lap. The woman has bundled the baby in layer after layer, and even so, the child's cheeks are reddened by the chill.

The mother's own cheeks are leaked of colour. Her eyes are haunted, forehead marred by the dust that has collected in her frown lines. Her cracked lips part, and she coughs soundly.

"My son," she finally says when the coughing abates. "I have no more milk for him." She touches her chest as she says it, her eyes glistening. "There is nothing left."

Nothing left.

Nothing left.

"There is always something," Dawsyn says to herself, to the woman, to the voices that hound her.

The baby stirs in the woman's arms but doesn't open his eyes. The small whining he utters sounds listless to Dawsyn. It chills her. "Has he taken ill?" she asks, praying as she says it.

"Not yet, but he needs milk." The woman's voice shakes as she says it, her eyes too dry to release tears. "He needs me." And then she coughs again, and something wet and dark loosens from her chest, spat out onto the rock-strewn earth.

Dawsyn feels how stretched and thin her magic is, how huge the resistance, but it matters very little. What is her magic for, if not this?

She looks down at the sweet face of the baby in his mother's arms, disturbingly still in sleep, breaths rapid and uneven, and she turns to the mother.

Dawsyn places both hands to the woman's chest, above her heart, and with every ounce of her might, she coaxes whatever vestiges of her power remain, intending to ring it dry if she must.

"Relencia," she says clearly, bidding that the woman be replenished. "Ishveet," she says next, repairing something unknown and unseen, knowing full well that it will not do. It won't be enough.

But the woman's cheeks have pinkened when Dawsyn opens her eyes and looks up. She breathes a deep sigh of relief, her shoulders slumping.

"Drink as much water as you can," Dawsyn tells her, knowing the risk it may hold. "Feed your son."

Dawsyn passes the woman a waterskin, then lingers while the mother latches her baby, her own weeping now replacing the sound of her son's. "Thank you," she tells Dawsyn, shaking her head in disbelief. "A walking saint."

"If only I was," she says ruefully, but offers the woman no more.

Saints martyr themselves, lead their people to safety. What will this woman call her, should Dawsyn lead them to their demise instead?

Spent, she can no longer expend her magic to relieve the sick or heal even the smallest wounds. She is a stranger to this craft. An amateur. These people do not need a saint, they need a true healer, someone of far more power than what Dawsyn is capable of. Someone like Baltisse.

How it would comfort her, to be beside the mage once more. Her teacher. Her friend.

There was too much to learn and she is not half the mage that Baltisse was. It suddenly seems unbearably cruel of fate to have taken someone so strong and leave Dawsyn as consolation. A sorry substitution.

Dawsyn finds Ryon in the dark. They always sleep ahead of the group, finding spaces tucked away against the wall. He waits for her there, his eyelids falling as soon as she descends into his arms.

Dawsyn watches his chest rise and fall for a long time before she submits to the drag of her heavy eyes. He coughs every so often, just small expulsions that do not rouse him, and yet it spills a pool of dread into Dawsyn's belly. She puts her palm to his chest.

"Ishveet," she whispers, and feels the magic intertwine in her palm, escaping through her fingertips and into Ryon's chest.

His breathing eases, becoming quiet and even, though Dawsyn knows it will not hold. It never does.

She drifts into unconsciousness, her mind full of a great unravelling. She can no longer picture the Chasm's end and all it may behold. It occurs to her, not for the first time, that it might be more painless to simply lie here and let the Chasm claim…

Jarring sounds rouse her. Voices grow louder and more fervent. Then suddenly, the air explodes with a chorus of screaming, shouting.

Ryon is torn from his sleep at the same time as Dawsyn, though her own reactions seem slower, more sluggish. As he hurls himself into the middle of the Chasm, she hurries to follow behind, trying to pull her ax in front of her. She is not even aware of the direction of the noise, only that it tears through them all, glancing off the walls.

She thinks – *no more. Please, no more.*

They run back through the rousing mass of humans, stumbling over rocks, retracing their steps from the day before. They splash through the shallow stream to better avoid colliding with bodies and keep running down its length. Ahead of them is a brilliant glowing, though Dawsyn cannot think of its source.

They run until they are clear of the Ledge people, following the cracks and bursts of light and the screams accompany it.

Ryon stops, and Dawsyn follows suit. Before them is a raging fire.

There have been no campfires along their venture; the torches and oil have been saved for travel. There is nothing to burn here at the bottom, so it bewilders Dawsyn at first, to see tall, licking flames, and the stricken faces of a dozen people basked in its glow, staring into its centre in horror.

"Mother help him," Ryon mutters, aghast, hastening forward.

Him? Dawsyn thinks, peering at the scene, blinking wildly until it comes into clearer focus.

A man lies ablaze on the ground. A blanket, thrown over him in an apparent attempt to smother the flames, is quickly disintegrating. Some are trying to beat the flames with their coats, scooping armfuls of dirt onto the blaze to no avail. Two men run toward the fire to throw buckets of water onto the poor soul within, but it only sizzles when it meets the flames.

"WES!" Nevrak is screaming, his hands reaching into the flames only to be hauled back by the others. He beats his hands into the earth by his sides, his breaths ragged, full of anguish. "MY SON!" he bellows. "Help him!"

But Dawsyn knows no spells to extinguish flame. She only knows of the way fire consumes. The way it destroys. It is too late to save Wes. He is nothing but blackening flesh. The smell of meat fills the Chasm, assaulting them all.

Dawsyn goes to Nevrak, who wails incessantly, staring into the pyre as though he might lay himself atop this last child. She finds nothing to say. What words could mend this?

"Gone," Nevrak whimpers. A stream of tears running into his dirtied beard. "They're all *gone!*"

And Dawsyn sees again his girls, their bodies wrapped and waiting in the snow. She knows what he feels now is the terrible, yawning understanding of utter aloneness. She lays a hand upon Nevrak's quaking shoulder.

The fire crackles and spits as it devours, an insatiable beast.

"Who did this?" Ryon demands, the timbre of his voice not to be ignored.

At first there is no answer. Just the appalled silence of the bystanders, watching the flames lash at Wes's flesh.

And then comes the young voice of someone to Dawsyn's left. Someone Dawsyn hadn't noticed. "He... he did it to himself," the girl says. "I saw him. He – he *doused* himself in oil."

"Abertha?" Dawsyn asks.

The girl's auburn curls quiver as their eyes meet – hers wide, fearful, and full of the firelight that consumes Wes. The boy who, not so many hours before, had been her assailant.

"Abertha?" Nevrak pants, peering up at the girl suddenly, his voice quieter. "Abertha." His jaw tightens. His eyes vacillate between his son and the girl.

Dawsyn can practically see the conclusion being drawn in the man's mind. She can hear the cogs of his thoughts turning in one direction.

"Nevrak," Dawsyn warns, pulling her ax handle against the man's throat. "Wait–"

Nevrak goes to lunge for Abertha, slowed only by the pull of the ax handle against his windpipe. Dawsyn wraps her arms around the man, wrestling him back onto the ground.

The breath is pushed from her lungs as he scrambles back on top of her.

"BITCH!" Nevrak shouts, despite the pressure against his throat. "SHE KILLED MY SON! SHE KILLED MY–" the sentence is swallowed by the strangled sounds of his cries.

"Calm yourself, man!" Ryon is shouting somewhere above. Dawsyn can barely see around Nevrak's body atop hers. "The girl did not do this."

"My son!" Nevrak wails. "He... he..."

"He is gone," Ryon finishes for him. "He's gone."

"We were going to get out of here," Nevrak rasps, the fight finally beginning to leave his body. Dawsyn knows he will be unconscious in moments.

"The girl didn't do this," Ryon tells him again, but Dawsyn's grip against Nevrak's throat has stayed too long, and the man's body slumps.

Dawsyn groans as she releases her hold, the weight of the man nearing unbearable. Ryon takes Nevrak's shoulders and lifts him off her at once and deposits him on the ground, then he looks down at her anxiously, turning her chin in either direction with his large hand to check her over. He mutters something fierce in the old language.

"He'll come to in a few moments," Dawsyn pants, looking for Abertha and finding her. "Go. Now."

Abertha scrambles to her feet, stumbling away into the dark, face stricken.

Ryon holds out his hand, then heaves Dawsyn to her feet. His eyes run over the length of her. "Do you believe what she said?"

Dawsyn doesn't know. She is assailed by the smell of burning flesh.

Nevrak's son slowly disintegrates in the unnaturally vehement flames, and she cannot imagine anyone choosing this as their end.

But then she hears again that silken voice that wheedles and worms its way into her mind.

Take up the reigns and belie your fate.
Climb the walls of Mother's gate.
Rid the ache.
Rid the ache.

CHAPTER TWELVE

Ruby paces the servant's corridor, biting her fingernails as she waits – only two remain. The rest were pulled by the shaking hands of a guard so green he might have passed as her son.

The curtain that separates the servants from the dining hall suddenly stirs, and Ruby holds her breath, but no one emerges. It settles once more, and Ruby resumes her pacing.

One week, the Queen had given her. One week to yield the impossible. Ruby cannot begin to venture where Dawsyn Sabar might be hoarding a hundred or so humans. When last she saw her, Dawsyn had been merely grappling with the quandary of it.

Ruby had given her what she saw as the only possible solution: to parade the survivors through the Mecca, to force the Queen to publicly accept their arrival.

Dawsyn had, at the time, seemed to have considered the idea. Yet not a single new arrival had been sighted across Terrsaw, much less a hundred of them. The forests and villages were teeming with guards, and if Dawsyn meant to stash them somewhere in Terrsaw, she imagines they would have been found by now.

No, Ruby thinks. *They're not here.*

But if not Terrsaw, then where?

The curtain stirs once more, but this time it is drawn back. Silk skirts appear, heavily embellished in Terrsaw wildflower embroidery. Garish crystals line the hem, the waist, the bust, matched by diamonds hanging from the neck of Cressida, the Queen Consort. The entire garb loses its splendour as soon as the curtain shuts out the light. Here, in a servant's hallway, Cressida seems smaller. Just a woman in costume.

But her glare is still disintegrating.

"Ruby," she greets, her voice hushed.

"Your Majesty," Ruby returns. Mother forgive her but she cannot do away with the formalities so easily. Years of training forbids it.

Cressida looks furtively to the curtain and back again. "This is foolish," she hisses. "I told you whatever need be said must wait until nightfall."

"In case you were too deprived of oxygen to hear it," Ruby hisses back. "Time is running out."

Cressida looks torn between slapping her and gouging out her eyes.

"I have summoned the iskra witch to the palace," Ruby continues. "She is due to arrive this night."

Cressida narrows her eyes. "The iskra witch? And what exactly do you plan to do with her?"

"She might be of use. Perhaps she has a way–"

"The iskra witch is good for very little," Cressida interrupts. "And completely at the mercy of my wife, as you well know."

"Which may make her a motivated ally. A powerful woman, forced to remain an outcast, threatened with the full might of the palace–"

"And as unstable as a three-wheeled wagon," Cressida finishes. "Truly, the woman is of limited substance. You cannot expect to bribe a hermit with societal freedom."

"I do not expect to bribe her at all," Ruby says. "I expect *you* to."

Cressida barely contains a huff of mirth. She shakes her head. "The iskra witch cannot help us."

"And yet, she comes. We may as well glean all we can from her. She will not answer to me, but to you," Ruby nods her head to Cressida, "she may reveal something useful. Perhaps she has some method to find those who want to remain hidden."

A small clamour comes from somewhere beyond the dining room.

Cressida's eyes go cold. *"Glacians?"* she mouths.

"No," Ruby says, ushering Cressida backward. "Just the guards returning through the Eastern tunnel... with the iskra witch."

Cressida delivers her most lethal of glares. "So I see you've forced my hand."

Ruby stares right back. "As you've forced mine."

* * *

Despite being freed from the dungeons, Ruby is not free to wander the palace at will. She is confined to a servant's sleeping quarters and only allowed out when summoned by Alvira.

Thankfully, years of servitude to this castle has lent her the knowledge of every hidden hallway, every servant's stairwell, and the benefits of courting friendships with most of the palace staff. Darius, the kitchen hand, has been most instrumental, given his tendency to leave lock picks in her food.

Ruby makes her way to the throne room through a private corridor. It is the same one the guards would use to evacuate Queen Alvira and Cressida should they need a quick escape. One only needs to access the library to find it, hidden behind the colossal map of Terrsaw that adorns the wall.

She has never walked these ancient tunnels without feeling slightly panicked. She curses those ancient kings and queens for constructing tunnels so impedingly narrow. Ruby must turn her shoulders sideways as she hobbles down the passageway, biting her lip against the throbbing in her hip and ribs. Cobwebs catch her eyes and mouth, and she resists the urge to splutter and spit. These walls aren't so thick as to muffle her presence.

When the passage curves to the opening of steep steps, she breathes a sigh of relief. At the bottom, she turns to the wall and runs her fingers between the stones until she finds the seam. She follows it down to a handle – a hidden door to the side of the throne room, concealed only by the Terrsaw flag hanging on the other side. She will have to hope it is enough to conceal her now.

Carefully, Ruby pulls on the handle. In small increments, she widens the gap, until she can place one side of her face to it. She doesn't dare allow anything more than the width of one eye – just enough to see.

Beyond the edge of the green flag, Ruby spies Alvira and Cressida, adorning their respective thrones. Alvira's expression is regimented, alert, while Cressida (and for this, Ruby must credit her) looks bored. Her eyes drift slightly to Ruby's and then away.

"I gave no orders to summon the iskra witch," Alvira is saying, her brow furrowed.

"I did," Cressida answers seamlessly. She waves her hand in front of her as if the matter is of little import. "It seemed a good time to pull out all our tricks."

Alvira scoffs. "The iskra witch is hardly that."

"In any case, Your Majesty, we were unable to locate her," comes the voice of someone unseen. A guard.

Alvira pauses. "You went over the river?" she asks.

"Yes, ma'am. When she did not respond to our signals, we crossed the river to find her."

Alvira swallows discreetly, her eyes remaining trained. "Without orders to do so," she quips. An aching silence follows, broken only by the clearing of someone's throat, the slight jostling of the guards' armour. "So the iskra witch is missing?"

"Yes, ma'am," comes the answer. "We found her cabin, but that was not all, Your Majesty. It seems that she knew to expect us. We found a letter. Addressed to you."

Ruby's heart pounds. She watches as a guard comes into view, approaching the throne with his head bowed and his hand outstretched. In it is a folded piece of parchment, blotted with a wax seal.

Alvira takes the letter, suspicion clear on her face. She holds it up to the light, turning it over in her spindly fingers. "Very well," she says without looking back to her audience. "Go."

The sound of clanking steel announces the departure of the guards and in their absence the throne room becomes eerily silent. Even the sound of Alvira's breaths echo.

Ruby watches as the Queen slits the wax seal with her fingernail, and as she does so, something falls into her lap. Something too small for Ruby to make out.

Alvira retrieves it and holds the small object at eye level, her expression clearly bemused. If only Ruby could make it out. She presses closer, squinting, trying to see–

"You might as well come out, Ruby," Queen Alvira says dispassionately. She does not bother to look in the direction of the concealed door. "You did orchestrate the witch hunt after all, I presume?"

Bile descends into Ruby's stomach; her spine turns rigid.

"Come out, little rat," Alvira beckons. "No use scurrying away into the walls now. Let us see what you make of this."

Ruby draws in a deep breath; her pulse hammers, her hands sweat. Despite it, she is determined to walk out of this hole with her chin held high.

Cressida's eyes flash with something like fury as Ruby steps into the light of the throne room. *Stupid girl,* they seem to say.

In contrast, Alvira does not deign to spare Ruby a glance. "Whatever your intentions were in fetching yourself a witch," she says, "it seems they have been lain to waste."

Ruby speaks quickly, before she loses all nerve. "I only sought her assistance," she says, "in locating Dawsyn Sabar and her... band."

"Her band?" Alvira repeats, the inflections lashing the air. "Is it a rebellion she leads, or a merry crew of misfits?"

Ruby says nothing. Her years at Alvira's knees have taught her when to stay silent.

"Well, it seems the jolly *band* has gained itself an iskra witch," the Queen continues. "Yennes is with Dawsyn Sabar as we speak."

Ruby's eyes widen. She stares at the parchment in Alvira's hand, wishing it were transparent. How did Dawsyn come to find the iskra witch? How did she convince a woman so timid to follow her to the Ledge?

Whatever questions arise, they are suddenly thwarted by something more alarming; Alvira does not scowl at the parchment before her. She does not crush it between her hands at having lost another asset in this battle. No. Instead, the Queen's eyes glint. She grips the page with something akin to mania. She smiles, and it reminds Ruby of animals. Wolves.

"You shall have to thank whatever saints you pray to, Ruby," Alvira states. "They have indeed provided you with a way to redeem yourself."

Cressida's eyes spark with warning, flicking between Alvira and Ruby. *Careful,* she seems to say.

With energy that belies her age, the Queen alights her throne. She walks briskly past Ruby, shoving the letter and the object it encased in her hands as she sweeps by. "You have a journey ahead of you, Ruby. Alert me when your scouting party is ready." And just before she leaves through the heavy double doors, she adds, "Oh, and if I find you meandering in the tunnels again, I'll throw you back to the dungeons."

The doors close behind her.

Ruby lets out a breath, her chest aching at having held it in for so long.

"What does she mean?" Cressida says lowly, her voice icy. "What is it?"

But Ruby cannot answer. She can only stare down into her palms, at the abused parchment, inked in words meant for the Queen.

Your Majesty,

I've left the means with which to find me…

Whatever else is written remains obscured by the object that rests upon the cursive.

A slightly bent, silver ring. A gaudy bauble of little value, except perhaps for the small onyx stone it encases. Ruby recognises it instantly.

Ryon Mesrich's ring.

Chapter Thirteen

"How much farther are we to walk?" a boy asks Ryon. He blinks up at him from the ground, his irritation clear at having been roused.

They all ask it. Every face that wakes and spots Ryon's through this fucking darkness bids him to relay the very same. *How much longer? Are we nearing the end? Surely, we are close?*

Ryon turns his face in the vague direction of the voices and says, "Not far," though it is a lie. Each time it is said, the lie grows heavier, more difficult to carry.

The fifth day within the Chasm looms ahead.

He raises his arms to stretch out his shoulder blades and winces. The wound in his back has closed but not healed. He feels it ache as though the knife still remains. Around Ryon, the Ledge people rise from their makeshift resting places and gather their belongings. They are not the same people who entered the Chasm days before. They are lesser. Diminished. Each wears the same weary expression of fatigue.

Humans weren't meant for the dark, Ryon has decided.

The echo of hacking and coughing is inescapable. It grates on him. Fingernails on the inside of his skull, scratching at the same spot, over and over. He should be thankful that he has not succumbed to the same illness. But enduring the sounds of it around him feels draining enough.

Ryon bends to shake the shoulder of a late riser – an older male, covered by a threadbare blanket. "Wake up," he says, shaking the man's shoulder harder. "We must go," but the man's body simply slumps over, his face pressing against the ground. Ryon raises his torch higher, and only then does he make out the ring of darkened soil around the man, as though something had seeped from him.

"What happened?" comes a voice – one he can distinguish even in complete obscurity, if only for the thrum in his veins when he hears it. Dawsyn.

He turns to see her in the light he casts and watches her approach. He notes how grey her pallor looks, how far the dark circles beneath her eyes stretch.

"Dead," Ryon tells her. "His throat has been sliced."

"By his own hand, it seems." She nods to that which Ryon had overlooked. The blood-crusted blade clutched within a stiffened fist. His torchlight glances off the rusty metal.

Dawsyn's looks down to her own feet. "Fool," she mutters, though her voice quavers. "Escaping the Ledge, only to lay down and die in the Chasm." She presses the heels of her palms to her eyes, pushing against whatever thoughts plague her. It seems she is always plagued. Always pushing.

"We will find the end, malishka," Ryon says. "Not all were equipped to see the journey through."

The words are meant to reassure her, though Ryon himself is far from reassured. He looks at the man, sees the ring of his blood and feels disturbed.

These Ledge-dwellers, ones of hardy breeding, who forge an impossible existence against such callous land, they are not the kind prone to quitting. This man makes the second human who took a violent end by their own hand and saw it as the lesser of two evils.

Ryon squeezes his eyes closed against the image of Wes, burning amidst flames.

Dawsyn groans, swaying where she stands.

"Steady, girl," Ryon says, placing his hand on her hip. "Are you all right?" For a moment, Ryon thinks she'll scoff, or perhaps make some flippant remark and carry onward. Onward with the quest. Headfirst through the next obstacle, and then the next.

Instead, she teeters sideways. Her head falls heavy against his chest.

There is a remarkable sensation that fills him in these small moments – these fragments of time where she devests some invisible outer shell and entrusts herself to him. If only she were aware of his deepest desires, his most selfish wishes. That he covets her. That he would become happily entrusted to shield her for the remainder of his days and forever wonder at his good fortune. He only ever wants to be *this*. Forever. He wants to be the place where she lays.

But she is a creature easily startled by hasty advances. And so, he settles for brushing the hair away from her neck and placing his hand against her skin. He draws her subtly closer, though he cannot quite stop the protective curve of his frame creating walls around her.

"What can be done?" she asks, A small surrender. One he cannot yield to – there is little to be done.

"We continue down the path," he says in lieu of anything serviceable.

"And when we grow too tired? Half are sick. More will become sick still."

A tendril of panic unspools in his stomach to hear her resolution waver.

"We carry on," he says firmly. "Whatever ails them, it does not seem so sinister. As long as they remain on their feet, there is hope."

"I feel it," she whispers to him. It is a secret breathed into the fabric of his shirt. "This infection. It has hold of me. It speaks."

The panic blooms. A *voice* speaking to her? Cajoling her? "What does it say?" he demands. For a moment, she is silent, and Ryon thinks she won't relay it, that she'll crawl back within the armour she has forged and withdraw.

But then the words come.

"It wants me to surrender," she confesses, the way a starved man speaks of supper. The words curl with deep yearning. It is a voice Ryon does not recognise in her. Not in this human, so impervious. So strong.

"Yennes said the Chasm was not empty," Ryon growls, his pulse jumping, muscles tensing. "Perhaps she spoke of more than one threat."

Dawsyn nods, pulling her body away from Ryon's, likely feeling how cool his blood has become.

"Do not heed it, malishka," Ryon says suddenly, taking her jaw in his hands, angling her face to his. "Do you hear me?"

She turns her cheek into his palm, then nods.

Too easy, the submission comes.

"All right," she says, though her voice is a faint imitation. "Time to march on."

Ryon stays to the middle of their convoy as they journey, as he has done each day. He cannot see Dawsyn who leads, or Tasheem who herds the stragglers. Indeed, he can only see the faint outline of those closest to him.

But he hears them all. The straggled breaths, bodies hitting earth as they stumble, the pained cries as they glance their shins and knees along the hazardous path, littered by invisible traps.

And the coughing. The coughing is all around.

"I can hold that awhile, Ryon." Yennes appears at his shoulder. He can just make out the familiar profile of her face. She taps the torch in his hand.

His arm has been growing weary from holding it aloft. Ryon passes it to her. "Thank you."

"No trouble." Her words always seem so muted, so hesitant around him. And he cannot help but feel uneasy around her in return. Perhaps it is her innate furtiveness, her skittishness rubbing off on him.

"Tell me," she says in a voice that could be aloof if it weren't so timid. "You grew up in the Colony, or the palace?"

Ryon is taken aback by the question. "You know of the Colony?"

"Tasheem and I have spoken some."

Ryon hesitates a moment. "The Colony," he relents. "I made my way into the palace when I was full-grown."

A pause, and then, "How did you manage it?"

He sighs. It isn't a tale he enjoys telling – one full of deception, fouled remembrances, old ties. Even more unpleasant, that he should tell it to a near stranger.

But Yennes was a friend of Baltisse. Someone she had trusted enough with Dawsyn's life. Yennes has aided them greatly, helped Dawsyn, closed his wounds. His distrust in her is irrational at best. She deserves his leniency.

"I had a… friend," he begins. "A Glacian noble. He trained me to fight, looked over me as I grew. He eventually persuaded the King to permit my entrance into the palace. As a servant."

Yennes is quiet, but he can feel her practically vibrating, absorbing each word. "And that was what you wanted?" she asked. "To leave the Colony?"

"It was what needed to be done, to learn the ways to tear down the palace."

More silence. "Your benefactor," she says. "He must have been a very generous being."

Ryon grits his teeth. "I assure you, he is not worthy of any praise," he says darkly. "He was merely loyal to the memory of my father. Not to me."

"Even so," she says. "A generous Glacian indeed. I knew them to be the opposite. Brutes."

Quite, Ryon thinks. He has a hundred memories of a hundred bodies snapped and shoved and hauled from the pool. "They regarded themselves so highly they could no longer see the difference between themselves and gods," Ryon intones. "You were very lucky to escape their cruelty."

Yennes doesn't respond. Ryon can hear her walking alongside him, see the golden reflection of fire in her eyes, but he cannot discern her expression, her thoughts.

"Who flew you to the bottom of the Chasm?" he asks abruptly, tired of having this one thing unanswered. "You said you did not know the Glacians to be a generous breed, yet it must have been a pure-blooded brute who offered you an escape into this pit. I watched a hundred or more soulless humans fall into it. No amount of iskra could bring one back," Ryon waits until she gathers the courage to look at him squarely. Her face a mere shadow. "Who was it?" he asks.

Yennes takes a deep breath. "I did not know their names, Ryon," she says. "Only that their pool could not have me and that there was at least one Glacian among them still human enough to see me to the bottom of this hole." She utters this last with a mixture of venom and trepidation. "And even imbued with iskra, I barely survived it."

Ryon considers her words for a moment. "What did you encounter, here in the Chasm?" He is sure his efforts will be wasted. Dawsyn and he had both questioned Yennes on what they might find here in the world's middle before they'd left Terrsaw, but the woman barely uttered an intelligible word. She had clammed up, her lips pursed and trembling. Her hands had clenched and unclenched, giving way to whatever anxiety lied within her.

Horrible things, she'd said. *Bodiless beasts*. That was all Ryon had interpreted amongst the quiet muttering. Yennes had a tendency of retreating inward, speaking to herself in hushed murmurs. She did so now, mouthing what could have been answers or spells for all Ryon knew.

"Yennes?" he says to redraw her attention. "*Yennes.*"

"Death," she says. "Death and Dyvolsh." Then she says no more, for she has doubled over, her body spasming with racking coughs that erupt from something dark and insidious within.

Hesitantly, Ryon stops alongside her. He allows others near him to pass by. He places a wary hand on her shoulder to support her, lest she teeter face-first to the craggy ground.

Her muscles jump beneath his hand, spurred into action by that which consumes her. Consumes many of them. Even now, Ryon hears Yennes' expulsions echoed by ten others, twenty. An unending melody that only seems to grow more frenetic as time passes. An insidious crescendo. Somewhere down the path, Dawsyn likely joins the chorus.

Ryon had lain awake the night before as Dawsyn coughed in her sleep, her breaths choked and disjointed. And yet still she had not woken, touched by that unnatural slumber of the other humans. Trapped in sleep, not roused even by their own gasps for air.

"Dawsyn is hearing voices," Ryon says, though he remains reluctant to offer this confidence to Yennes. "Is that what you mean, when you say Dyvolsh is here?"

Yennes straightens. Wipes her mouth. Whatever her expression, Ryon cannot see it. She does not answer him.

"Do you hear them, Yennes? The voices? Answer this much, please."

"Mother help me," she mumbles, the words hardly discernible. "I hear *every* whisper." Then, she stoops once more, the resounding hacks erupting from her chest.

"Damn it," Ryon growls, grabbing her shoulders as she begins to fall. "It is this sickness. It must be. It addles the mind."

"N-no," Yennes splutters, more vehement than Ryon has ever heard her. "The voices belong to the Chasm."

"How could you possibly know?"

"Because they are no different to those I outran when I was last here. And they have haunted me since."

He can feel it vibrating from her, that marrow-deep knowledge. He feels her muscles coiled beneath his touch, as though she resists some deep-seated instinct to flee.

And yet she has not.

"Why did you come?" he asks her, and this time his voice is softer. Whatever misgivings he may have, he cannot ignore her sacrifice, her courage.

She turns toward him, and though her features are shrouded in shadow, Ryon is sure he is being searched, measured.

"There are things here that I could not simply turn my back on," she says.

With a fortifying breath, Yennes passes the torch back to Ryon. "I'm afraid I may topple should I try to journey with it."

Ryon nods to her as she walks onward, disappearing into the folds of darkness.

And Ryon is left with a faint glimmer of hope.

…They are no different to the ones I outran when I was last here. And they have haunted me since.

These voices, Ryon thinks, looking ahead to where he imagines Dawsyn might be, dragging her feet along this cursed path. *These voices can be beaten.*

Chapter Fourteen

Yennes found herself on the beach once more, hurling shells into the whitewash. "Where does this ocean end?" she asked the mage beside her – a woman who seemed content to stand immobile, staring at the horizon for hours at a time.

"It is not known," Baltisse answered. Her face was turned up to the sun, her eyelids turned pink from its heat.

"Have you never wondered what lies beyond it?"

"Of course," Baltisse said, her lips flattening with annoyance at the interruption. "But I am not stupid enough to seek ends I am not ready to meet."

Yennes frowns at the tumbling waves but quietens. In the last few weeks, she has swallowed more words than she has spoken.

"Try again," Baltisse ordered, not bothering to open her eyes. "If you've finished taking your anger out on the waves."

Yennes huffed. They had been working for hours. The sun was near setting. Yet she lacked whatever audacity she once possessed that bade her to argue. She lifted her palm instead and concentrated on it. "Igniss."

"Find the source first," Baltisse reminded wearily.

Yennes groaned but closed her eyes. She found that strange, dark mass in her belly. The one that seemed content to slumber within. "Igniss."

"Coax it out," Baltisse said, her voice bored now.

"I am trying."

"Barely."

Yennes gritted her teeth and bit back a retort. She addressed the iskra instead, angling her thoughts toward it. *Will you come?* The iskra rolled but did not rise. *Please... come.*

"You sound like my first lover," Baltisse said conversationally. "He had the very same whine in his voice."

Yennes rolled her neck. The mage was beginning to grate on her nerves.

"A little assertion goes a long way, sweet," Baltisse instructed. "Convince it. Do not *beg.*"

Yennes steeled herself. *Come out.*

Leave me, the iskra replied, vapid and listless.

Come!

A lance of pain sliced a path up her spine, and Yennes fell to the sand, gasping. As quickly as it had struck her, the sizzling pain was gone.

"Too much assertion," Baltisse tsked, not bothering to offer Yennes a hand.

Yennes let loose a frustrated growl, pounding the sand with her fists. "I can't reach it."

"Odd," Baltisse remarked. She was busy intertwining her hands with the wind, as though it existed to dance between her fingers. "I'd have thought that one such as yourself would have more dominance, more grit."

"One such as myself?" Yennes queried. She could feel the iskra stirring to the call of her rising temper.

"Mm," Baltisse assented. "A Ledge-born. I can't imagine someone so faint-hearted would have survived as long as you."

"You've little idea what was survived and what wasn't."

"I've some idea," Baltisse rebuked, tapping Yennes' forehead once.

Yennes' fingers dug into the ground. She could feel that strange biting cold coating them.

"If it was not fortitude that kept you alive, then it must have been something other. Your *wiles* perhaps."

Yennes stood. She faced Baltisse with glistening hands, laced in frost. The iskra pounded through her blood.

"No shame in it," Baltisse continued, her fingers gracefully curling before her. A whorl of sea mist followed the movements, obediently led in the dance. "I'm sure there was many a man or woman who'd have lent you a side to their bed. One must find warmth somewhere in a place like that."

"I bartered many things," Yennes bit out, her voice shaking with vexation this time, rather than fear. "But never my *body.*"

"Never?"

Yennes froze. In her mind, however, were not images recalled of home and any bedmate she may have taken. She did not remember a lost lover of the Ledge. But other memories assaulted her, and they melted the iskra from her palms in a matter of moments.

Baltisse could see those memories. Hear them. It was clear on the mage's face. Her eyes widened, her lips parted ruefully, and she was immediately sobered. "Oh," she said. Gone was the goading lilt. "Yennes... I–"

"I've done a great many things to stay alive," Yennes begins, her voice louder than she had dared to raise it in a long time. "I've killed. I've taken food out of the hands of the hungry. I've cut dead flesh from my own body. I've lied and pretended and tricked my way to safety many times over." Yennes lets the memories assault her once more, sure that the mage sees it too. She makes Baltisse relive what she had to endure.

The mage's skin turns sallow as she watches and listens. When it is over, Yennes' hands are trembling again. They seek each other, clasping and unclasping in a frenetic tumble. "If the opportunity arose for me to fuck my way to safety," she says with more bravado than she feels. "Then I would have done so. I'd say there is a fair amount of grit to be found in that."

Baltisse stares at her for a long while, and Yennes is loath to look away, but she does. Gone was the girl who would slash and cut the foe on her path. Gone were the ways she could shape her words into barbs that pierced skin. In the back of her mind, she could still hear the words sung to her inside the Chasm. Words that picked her apart and burrowed deep. They no longer rang with that fresh echo. The voices were just memories now, ghosts that she could not rid herself of. But they rattled her, unsettled her, just as they did inside the Chasm.

"You made it out," Baltisse reminded her, laying a slender hand on Yennes' anxious ones. "You are safe here."

Yennes closed her eyes. She felt the tears trickling down her cheeks. "I should not be."

"Yet you are."

"My father," Yennes muttered, tears dripping down her lips. "And... and my–"

"You needn't cling to what you left behind," Baltisse said fiercely, gripping Yennes' wrist. "Those thoughts will consume you."

Yennes shook her head. "I do not know how to forget it all."

"There's no forgetting I'm afraid," Baltisse said, wiping the moisture from Yennes' cheek. "But you can unburden yourself. You do not need to borrow blame. Your fate was not your doing, after all."

Yennes thought she would very much like to know whose doing it *was*. What cruel being had designed a path so impossible to travel?

"Not impossible," the mage said, smiling sadly. Her eyes flitted over Yennes' shoulder to where the Chasm's opening swallowed the tide. "An unlikely survival is not the same as an undeserving one."

Yennes and Baltisse stood on the beach a while longer, until the former's eyes dried. The mage did not wrap an arm around the other woman's shoulder to comfort her. Instead, she lifted her hand to the wind and manipulated the sea spray into beautiful spiralling patterns with her fingertips, and Yennes watched on.

She watched the sun sink into the sea. She watched the night bleed the sky of its spectrum. And only when it was dark did she lift her hand and close her eyes.

"Igniss," Yennes said, and a small blue flame danced in her palm. Cold and strange.

"Well done." Baltisse smiled. "As good as any mage-born."

"Baltisse?" Yennes queried, letting the flame sputter out. "Will you teach me to fold?"

Chapter Fifteen

The fifth day passes with a fading sense of awareness. There are times when Dawsyn is wise to the path underfoot, the walls around her, the noises behind her, the ache in her feet and legs and chest and throat. Other times, she is only aware of the noise of her mind, sounds of a more soothing nature. Words and melodies that rid her of even the memory of pain.

But each time, that magic within her rises to the threat of invasion. It strikes, serpent-like, forcing that other inhabitant into silence.

And then the Chasm returns, and she finds herself stumbling down its spine again. All of the aches reawaken with a vengeance.

She thinks of the mothers carrying their children. She thinks of the husbands carrying their wives. She feels the burn of each cough that rings up the rockface and prays for this to end.

If the valley is heaven, and the mountain is hell, then surely this is the purgatory between, an infinite torment. A path with just one true end. The other is a winding maze, entrapping those stupid enough to follow it.

No, Dawsyn thinks, shaking the thought away. *This will end too*. It has become her mantra, her war cry. *Stay alive*, she commands herself. *It is all you have to do.*

Twice, they stop, so that someone can kneel and leave their kin on the ground, their body having succumbed to this wretched journey.

"A mistake," Dawsyn hears, over and over. Words that find their way to her down these obsidian walls. "Leaving the Ledge was a mistake."

She cannot bring herself to look them in the eye. She suspects they might be right.

The third time they stop, it is a different energy that passes down the convoy, raising the hairs of Dawsyn's neck.

"Stop!" she hears Ryon command. And they do.

But there are whimpers, shouts, the sound of bones and flesh meeting that accompanies the call. The dismay of bystanders bellowing and pushing one another.

Dawsyn doubles back, knocking into the chests and backs of those who bear the misfortune of blocking her sightless path. She follows the glow of the torch held high above her head, for surely Ryon is its carrier.

The sounds of fighting grow louder, more vicious. It is the very same accompaniment one would often hear when these sorry fools graced the Ledge. It is the chorus of her childhood as the Drop came. The canticle of every feud, every transaction, every settlement of grievance.

But there is no time for public exhibitions here. No energy to be expended on frivolous quarrelling. Dawsyn barrels toward the noise, toward Ryon's beacon, and draws her ax forth, however heavy it may feel in her hand.

"Move," she calls, nearing the commotion. "*Move!*"

"Ah, here she is!" comes a voice. The last spectator moves, and Dawsyn takes several moments to blink the scene into view.

Nevrak stands before her, straddling the stream. Beneath his hand is someone on all fours. Their fingers claw into the earth on either side of the water's edge. By the sounds of their laboured breathing and the way Nevrak's fingers are twisted into their hair, it seems their grip on the ground is necessary, lest Nevrak decide to bury their face in the brook again.

"I won't ask it again," Ryon is saying, his sword tip levelled with Nevrak's bared teeth. "Drop her."

The girl in Nevrak's hand, spits, whimpers, water cascading from her clothes and hair. Hair that glints auburn in the flicker of torch flame.

Abertha.

"She. *Killed.* My son," Nevrak shouts, his jaw trembling with the force of his rage. "Burned him. *Alive.*"

"He –he set it –himself!" Abertha pants, her face screwed up tightly in pain as Nevrak yanks.

"SHUT UP!" he bellows, incensed. "Enough lies!"

Abertha cries out, then thrusts her hand upward in an attempt to grab Nevrak's beard. In turn he pushes her back down, her face breaking the surface of the water.

"Stop!" Dawsyn calls, stepping forward, holding her ax aloft. She waits until Nevrak finds her in the gloom, his expression only darkening. Slowly, he lifts Abertha's face.

The woman gasps violently, spitting grit and icy spatters back to the ground.

"Killing the girl will not bring him back," she calls, but the volume of her voice ignites that waiting flame in her chest and throat, and her abrupt coughing dulls the sharpness of the words.

"Thought she'd pay back my son for deigning to notice her," Nevrak bleats, ignoring her. His face bears the fiery, veined conflict of man far surpassed of his rational nature. "Too fucking high and holy to bear his attention!"

"He forced himself on me!" Abertha spits, her cheeks billowing with the strength of her gasps.

"And you *set him alight.*" Nevrak growls. His teeth are bared. The fist that holds Abertha captive pulls her head from side to side.

"No!" she cries.

"NEVRAK!" Dawsyn bellows, but Ryon now touches his sword tip to Nevrak's throat.

"Do it," Nevrak hisses. "Cut us all down. Put an end to this *nightmare.*"

"Listen to me," Dawsyn asks abruptly. "Was your son hearing voices? Whispers?"

Nevrak hesitates. "What did you say?"

"Did your son talk of voices in his mind?"

"How could...?" Nevrak frowns. "He spoke to you of the same?"

"It was those *voices,* Nevrak," she says exasperatedly. "They drove him to madness. It was not Abertha."

"LIAR!"

"Did you hear him scream in that fire?" Dawsyn pushes. "Did *anyone* hear Wes scream?"

"Ask *her,*" Nevrak barks, nodding to the woman in his grasp. "She was the only one with him. Fucking convenient, I'd say! That a man she had grievances with had the misfortune of combusting before her fucking eyes." Nevrak's voice breaks. Sobs make the spittle fly from his mouth. His throat pushes against Ryon's sword. "He was just a *boy!*"

"He was sick," Ryon says calmly, though his sword does not lower. "No one is at fault."

"My – boy," he says, the shudder of pain breaking his words. His chest rises and falls with rage turned to sorrow. In painstaking increments, Nevrak loosens his hold on Abertha, his fingers detangling from the tendrils, and she falls away from him, scrambling on her hands and knees. "No one's fault?" he asks, tears dripping from the end of his nose, disappearing into the first bristles of beard. "There's always fault to find. Anyone that dies here in this hole, dies by your hand."

He points at Dawsyn.

Ryon lowers his sword but does not take his eyes from the man. There's a muscle feathering along his jaw and Dawsyn knows he wrestles with the desire to crush Nevrak. His eyes flicker to hers, awaiting her say so.

Perhaps she should give it. Perhaps she should rid their journey of the threat standing before her, of a voice far louder than she would prefer. If Nevrak wanted to attack her, there would be a million opportunities to do so down here.

But the man's belly and shoulders still shake with the force of his loss, and Dawsyn knows well the feeling. She brought this man into the Chasm so that he might escape the early clutch of death, and she does not want to be the one to bring it about. Maybe there was a time when she would have split this Splitter for daring to challenge her, but Dawsyn finds that while she has enough reason, she does not have the energy, nor enough hatred left. Perhaps this sickness has sapped even that: the rage that keeps her upright, keeps her moving.

With a small shake of her head at Ryon, Dawsyn lifts her chin. "Nevrak," she says, "And every other here!" This time she bellows it, finds the face of any close enough to be illuminated beneath Ryon's torch. They stand by, watching her with waned expressions, hollowed eyes.

Dawsyn takes a breath. "On the Ledge, we settled our grievances in the way animals do. "We slashed and clawed for what we needed, and anything else besides. We could not turn to each other for charity and compassion when there was not enough to go around. We were given imbalance, and it forced our hand, tilted the odds," Dawsyn finds Ryon watching her keenly, and for a moment their eyes lock – his dark and awed, as though she were a spectre. "We can no longer afford to settle debts in blood. We cannot continue to tear each other to shreds as if our neighbours were our enemies. Our enemy lives above, and we needn't aid them." At that, Dawsyn coughs violently into the crook of her elbow.

Close your eyes... sleep.

"No!" The word rips from her lungs, though she feels the pull to unconsciousness. Whatever magic she still possesses floods her mind, her palms, rushing to heed her call. Her palms glow brightly, leaking light, and the voice becomes nothing at all.

Around her, people stare at her hands. Shocked. Afraid.

"The end to this Chasm nears!" she says it like a prophecy, a divine proclamation. She wills it to be true. "And we will not litter what remains of this path with our bones. We have enough adversaries without turning on each other." Dawsyn sways, weakened by her own rising voice. She nods to Nevrak. "Mourn your son." Then she nods to Abertha, who has made it to Dawsyn's side. "But if you lay a hand on this girl again, I will take it from you, neighbour or not."

Nevrak spits to the ground before Dawsyn, his expression remaining red-splotched and pained. "You do what you must," he tells her, finger pointed as though it were a weapon. A stake to run her through with. "And so will I."

"Be on your way," Ryon tells him, and the timbre of his voice brooks no protest. The short sword in his hand quivers with eagerness.

With one final sneer in Ryon's direction, Nevrak lumbers away.

The others follow quickly, disappearing back into the shadows until Ryon and Dawsyn are the only ones standing in the torchlight's reach. Dawsyn lets loose a breath, and feels the world turn sideways.

Ryon's arm comes around her in moments, winding around her back and grasping her side. "Easy," he tells her softly, though the old malice still simmers there, an undercurrent, hastily dampened. He gives a huff of frustration. "You need rest."

Dawsyn says nothing. They all need rest.

"I should kill him now, malishka," he mutters, leading her away from the stream, guiding her around the obstacles, both natural and human. "Before his control wanes again."

But Dawsyn shakes her head.

He emits a gravelled sound, a low growl. "You've killed men for much less," he says, the anger winning out. "As have I."

"He would deserve it," Dawsyn murmurs, leaning heavily on Ryon's embrace. "Abertha is not safe sleeping so near to him."

"Then why–"

"Because it would divide the others," Dawsyn says. "Those who believe Abertha killed Wes, those whose ears Nevrak has already filled.

He suspects I cannot bring them to the end of the Chasm. Each day, these people grow wearier, less certain, less hopeful. Killing Nevrak will only spread distrust. I will not allow factions to be created before we've even reached a place to settle."

"And if Abertha's throat should be cut in the night?"

"I will send Hector to watch her. Guard her, if he must. He is well equipped to handle Nevrak."

"That human is dangerous, Dawsyn. Leaving him alive is a mistake."

"I will not have those I lead watch me cut him down."

"When will you accept yourself as worthy of following? These people will see it for what it is – a threat to be eliminated."

"That is a Glacian's ploy. Human's do not always carve inroads by killing that which blocks the path."

Ryon huffs mirthlessly and Dawsyn sees too late the line she has redrawn between them. "Humans kill plenty," he says acidly. "You are no exception."

She stops. Ryon has walked them away from the others, where no one will hear. She unwraps herself from his hold. Staggering as she regains her footing. Her neck heats. Her hands clench.

"I do not deny it," she says, aware of the way her chest smarts with a new ache. "It is not *goodness* stopping me from killing a man like Nevrak. These people will turn their backs to me the instant they believe I cannot be trusted."

"Then you have already lost," Ryon rebukes, his expression steely. There's something desperate beneath the surface, something entrenched in fear. "You sabotaged yourself the second you lied to them and led them away from Terrsaw."

Again, that ache. It strikes her chest anew, doubling the pain. Ryon lifts his eyes from hers and looks to the heavens, where not a single star shows itself. He curses lowly. "If you had but told them everything, allowed them to make the choice to follow, you would only risk dooming yourself in this venture," he says, shaking his head. "But you chose coercion. And now, you may doom them all." And still, he looks skyward, refusing to meet her eyes. Keeping from her that light she can always find in him, the confidence and awe and reverence he reserves for her.

He withholds it now. His jaw ticks with agitation. His hands rise to scrub his face. "I've followed you without question," he says. "And it was my choice to do so. But you have tricked these people into doing the same."

"Yes," Dawsyn says, the hurt quickly solidifying to contempt. "And I did not do it lightly. I know what it is to be coerced. *Lied* to."

There they are - those old pains, the old treasons. She hurls them into the space between them now, as though they are shields. She barricades herself against whatever cuts he might inflict. Inside, she boils.

Ryon gives a long-suffering breath. In it, she hears his exhaustion. And still, he holds his stare up and away from her.

Dawsyn follows his gaze. Somewhere above, the Chasm opens to the heavens. How it must beckon him, she now realises. How easy it would be for him to escape this fate she leads him to.

"Go," Dawsyn says now.

Ryon looks down at her, confused. "What?"

"Go," she says again, nodding to the sky. "If that is what you wish."

Ryon scoffs again, his lips curling into a sneer, into something that masks hurt. "You know absolutely nothing of what I wish."

"You stare at the sky as though you would bid it closer."

"Name a person here who doesn't," Ryon growls, he steps closer, lowers his face until it is an inch from hers. "Do you think I would leave you here? Leave our friends here?"

"You say I have doomed them all." Her voice quavers, her heart racing with something unspent, something she desperately tries to strangle into silence. "If that is what you believe, then I will not scorn you for making your escape."

Ryon turns away from her, mutters the old language in a hot stream. He exudes frustration, disappointment. Lines cord down the back of his neck. Yet, his wings do not appear. He does not summon them.

He turns until he can meet her eyes and says, "Mother above, girl. I've been run through by talons and swords and blades, but *you* are still the biggest pain in my arse." And then he leaves, cursing loudly as he goes.

Dawsyn stands there in the darkness alone and finally lets the shame wash over her.

Chapter Sixteen

Ryon wakes long before he should, disconcerted. Beside him is the form of a person he does not recognise. A woman not his own, and then he remembers... Abertha.

The night before, he had returned to the camp and found Hector. Ryon had always thought the human scrawny, but no doubt stronger than he appears. Life on the Ledge would not have forged a man of meek temperament.

Still seething, Ryon had woken Hector who laid on his side, his front to Esra's back.

"I need a favour," Ryon had said in a low voice and waited for the man to find his feet.

"It is Dawsyn?" Hector had asked, rubbing the grit from his eyes with his equally gritty knuckles.

It should have set his teeth on edge, he thinks, to hear Hector enquire after her in that intimate tone. But Ryon has watched Dawsyn and Hector interact since they delivered him from the Ledge, and he knows their relationship is not, and has never been, romantic. It is something else entirely.

And by the way Hector gravitates toward Esra, Ryon needn't hold further concern.

"Stay close to Dawsyn for me," Ryon had said, nodding to the gloom due North, where Dawsyn surely still stood, seething as he did. "She is coughing more and more. Watch over her?"

Hector's eyes had widened with worry. "I will."

Ryon had given a stiff nod, then left in search of Abertha.

Now, sick dread pools in his belly to not have Dawsyn lying by him, and he regrets stalking off as he did, leaving her in the dark. If the blight worsened her in the night, he'll curse himself.

Abertha breathes easily beside him, still asleep. The Chasm is still, quiet, despite the yellow river of light above them, signalling daybreak. It seems the longer they remain in this canyon, the more life it leeches from these people. *Soon,* Ryon thinks, *they won't rise at all.*

Donning his sword sheaths across his shoulders, Ryon retrieves his unlit torch and stands. Each morning, he steals away. It is an easy thing to do in a black hole like this. He finds the wall, feeling along its sharp edges, putting distance between him and the others. Then he closes his eyes.

He rolls his shoulders, searching inward. He feels the place between bones where his wings nestle and stretches them carefully. It should feel as easy as stretching one's legs; the muscles and tendons giving a dull but satisfying ache. Instead, Ryon's eyes screw tightly shut. His wings spread reluctantly, sending a shock of pain down his spine from where the blade pierced his back. Had that knife been an inch closer to the centre, Ryon is sure he would not be able to walk, much less fly.

His wings shudder as they extend fully, but they do not vanish this time. It brings him a measure of relief. He is healing, if slowly. And it is far more than he could have hoped for.

Yet still, he thinks of Baltisse, who would have had him flying again within moments, had she not given her life to this ploy.

He sags. His friend, Baltisse. How desperately he wishes to confer with her now. No doubt the mage would bolster him, tell him to buck up and walk on. She would bring reason to whatever ailment plagues Dawsyn and the rest, curing them all. She would call Dawsyn a fool and rattle her until she saw sense.

But Baltisse is gone. Dead. Before he even had the chance to repay her for all the ways she fixed him, right from their very first meeting.

Gritting his teeth, Ryon raises his wings, as though he might lift his body from the ground. The pressure in his back is extraordinary, but he manages to hold the weight. His wings remain aloft until he cannot bear the strain, and he finally relents. They vanish, and he falls forward toward the Chasm wall, catching himself with his hands.

"Fuck," he pants, feeling sweat drip down his chest. Dawsyn had accused him of wanting to fly away. If only she knew how impossible a feat it would be, even if he wanted to.

He recalls the look on her face. The shame and hurt, quickly veneered by her usual indifference, her slow-simmering ire. He wonders if he'll ever truly see her with those layers stripped away, if she'll ever fully reveal herself to him.

Or will he always trail after her, scratching the surface, hoping for a chance to see inside.

Last night, he had stared at the sky, and wished he could fly Dawsyn away. That desire still burns hotter than any other now. It is brighter than his irritation with her. Bigger than his fear. And yet, she still doubts his loyalty to her. His attachment.

Perhaps, he thinks, a bitter taste cloying in his mouth, *the attachment is one-sided.*

Sometimes, it is an easy thing to believe – that she doesn't need him, even if she wants him. But there are those other times, like when she seeks him out. He can feel it then – the tether between them. Those moments when she buries herself in his embrace and recedes within him. In those small seconds of surrender, he believes that they were meant to find one another. "This girl has the power to destroy you, Ry," Baltisse had once told him. "Best weigh your choices carefully."

"I think it might be too late for that," Ryon had grunted, watching Dawsyn sleep on a narrow cot inside Salem's inn. Baltisse closed Dawsyn's wounds and brushed her hair back, still damp with river water. "Then Mother help you."

Ryon had stared at the mage, asking her silent questions, letting her read his mind.

"I don't tell fortunes," she had said. "I do not know if it will work. I only know that the connection is... strong. Strangely so. Sometimes these things are better off left alone."

"I can't," he had whispered, staring at Dawsyn's blood red lips, darkened by the cold.

"Then stay with her," Baltisse had said. "And brace yourself. She will not make it easy."

Ryon shakes his head at the memory. "Pain in the arse," he says again, looking upward.

One day, Dawsyn will finally lay down every tangible and intangible weapon before him, and he will say, *See? Do you see now, how exactly right we are?*

And until then, he will scratch. He will pull the hair from his scalp and curse the Holy Mother until there is no more resistance.

* * *

"Riv," Ryon calls, finally finding the male. He has been searching each crevice of the Chasm for him.

Around them, people are gathering their meagre belongings, preparing for another endless trek. More than once, he hears the discontented murmurs – some angry, but mostly tired.

"What use is there walking onward?"

"She told us it would only take several days."

The sixth day inside the Chasm dawns, and Ryon cannot shake the feeling that it may be their last, whether the end comes or not.

"Brother," Rivdan says as Ryon approaches, nodding solemnly.

"How many?"

"I counted two," he says in answer. "Tash found one other."

Ryon sighs. Three more dead. "How?" he mutters quietly, carefully, aware of lingering ears.

"One tied a leather swath around his face. He was blue when I found him. Not certain about the others. Seems as though they died in their sleep. Many of them were already weak when we brought them here."

Ryon nods. "I'll tell Dawsyn."

"Today, it is three. Tomorrow it may be ten." Rivdan is quiet a moment. "It is odd," he says, "these deaths."

"Suicides," Ryon corrects. "Though I do not think we could call it deliberate."

Rivdan raises his eyebrow.

"What do you mean?" comes Tasheem's voice. She joins their halo of light, brow furrowed.

"It's this sickness spreading among them," Ryon tells them. "I think it may be driving some to insanity. I've heard mentions of voices."

"Voices?" Rivdan says, and then he falls quiet again.

Rivdan has always offered few words by nature, but his silence now alerts Ryon. He has known the male long enough to be able to discern the subtle differences in his quiet. The set of his lips, the distant stare; he can see the contemplation, some spark that has been ignited at the mention of hearing voices.

If there is one among them who knows tales of a contagion such as this, it is surely Rivdan, the storyteller.

Ryon grasps his shoulder. "Riv? Do you know any stories like this? Of people plagued by delusions? Possibly madness?"

Rivdan seems to chew on his tongue for a moment. "There is *one*."

Dawsyn eyes Ryon warily when he finds her, but he doesn't allow her time to speak before he grasps her upper arm and lifts her from the ground. "Come with me," he says simply, ardently. "And for once, just do as I ask without arguing."

Her eyes dilate, startled. He hauls her away without waiting for a response.

They wind their way back through the clusters of bodies, sitting and standing, until Ryon finds Tasheem and Rivdan again, waiting solemnly.

"What is it?" Dawsyn asks them all, her eyes flicking to each of them, but inevitably settling on Rivdan's.

His are furtive. Unsettled.

"Rivdan may have some knowledge of... of a contagion. Just like the one spreading among us."

Dawsyn raises her eyebrows. "Does he now?"

Rivdan locks eyes with Dawsyn for a moment, and then looks quickly away. "There is a story. Though I do not know how accurate."

"All stories are born from seeds of truth," Ryon says. "Is this not your belief?"

"It is," Rivdan allows. "Though the story often travels a long way from its origin."

"Tell it anyway," Ryon bids. "It may help us."

Rivdan exhales, once more trading that curious glance with Dawsyn. And then he speaks, the timbre of his voice easing into that of someone far older, worldly. It is why he was monikered the storyteller in the Colony – the way his voice drew in his listeners and subtly ensnared them.

"Glacia was not yet a true nation when they were first tested by the Mother's greatest weapon. The Glacian numbers were small and vulnerable when an affliction threatened to annihilate them. Yerdos had risen from the Chasm."

"Yerdos," Dawsyn mumbles. "The *hawk*?"

Rivdan frowns. "No. The creature of the Chasm," he corrects.

"You mean the *saint*," says a new voice.

Ryon turns at the sound. Salem stands just beyond his shoulder, his face only partially illuminated by the glow of firelight. "Yerdos," Salem reiterates. "The patron saint o' the mountain. The first Terrsaw saint."

As one, they stare at Salem, bewildered.

Salem's expression, however, is stricken with growing alarm, as though some new understanding has formed within his mind.

Rivdan continues, though his frown remains. "I know nothing of Terrsaw saints. The Yerdos of *our* stories was a spirit who rose from her prison in the Chasm, maddened and vengeful. Her touch wound its way first into the lungs of the Glacians, and then into their ears. They grew sick. Weak. But these symptoms were the very least of Yerdos' torments. Her madness, they say, was catching. Soon, Glacians were surrendering to the call of Yerdos – she beckoned them into the Chasm's depths. They walked to the edge and dived, fell on their swords, or cut their throats. The Glacians believed they would soon all be overcome by Yerdos' voice. Her sickness.

"It was Vasteel who saved the remaining Glacians," Rivdan tells them. "Or so he says. He called to Yerdos and tried to make a deal with her. 'Let us live,' he told her, 'and we will help you seek revenge on that which banished you to this Chasm in the first place.'" Rivdan pauses, and as he looks to each of them, Ryon realises they have all leaned closer by increments. "But Yerdos refused. 'It was the cold that banished me,' she said. 'I will not seek deals from the cold's creatures.'"

"This was an admission not missed by Vasteel, and in it, he found Yerdos' weakness. He filled his body with iskra, and when next he called Yerdos from the Chasm, it was to display the full force of his Glacian power. Vasteel's blood turned icy, his breaths were the winds of the hostile season, and in him, Yerdos saw that she had met her match.

"The other Glacians feasted from the pool, and soon they were filled enough to fend off the affliction that ailed them. Their bloodstreams burned with the cold of iskra, and Yerdos' affliction retreated. Unable to call them into the Chasm, she returned to its depths, forgoing her revenge on the cold."

Rivdan's voice dissipates as he reaches the story's end, dispelling to nothing. The others stare with blank expressions, mouths slightly agape.

Two paths, Ryon thinks, his chest constricting. *Both are filled.* He looks to Dawsyn with renewed understanding. "Stories are born from seeds of truth."

But Salem is shaking his head vehemently. "No," he says, his tone belligerent. "Yerdos were a *Queen*. Blessed by the Holy Mother!"

The others share looks of astonishment at the conviction in his voice.

"She died by the devil's infection, not by the hand's o' that ruddy *bat*," he continues, spitting to the ground. "Can never remember the old language word fer it. Deevilsh? Denvish?"

"Dyvolsh," Tasheem, Rivdan and Ryon say together. *Devil.*

"That's the one," Salem nods. "The Dyvolsh infection."

Death and Dyvolsh, Yennes had said to Ryon, just days ago.

"I've not heard of it," Dawsyn says, shaking her head.

"It was, oh, a thousand years ago. *More*, probably. Folks thought they were sickened by the devil. Convinced 'em to do mad things. Wiped out a good half o' the population – Queen Yerdos included. She became a saint after that. Legend has it, she were a woman of some strange magic. Connected to the land. Folks still pray to her fer good weather, rain, fertile soil an' the like. I never believe in tha' brand o' nonsense though. Complete horse shit if yeh were to ask me my opin–"

"What was the Dyvolsh infection?" Dawsyn interrupts, her tone blunt.

"Same as what Riv described," Salem answers. "Or so they say. Somethin' that drove 'em all to their deaths."

"The two stories don't make sense," Dawsyn shakes her head. "Yerdos cannot be a martyr and a vengeful spirit both."

"You said she was a hawk?" Ryon adds, his mind whirring through the tangle of story. "What did you mean?"

Dawsyn sighs, then says, "It was a legend my grandmother would tell my sister and I on the Ledge. There is no knowing if it was anything more than a child's tale."

"Tell it anyway," Ryon presses, and awaits the third fable of Yerdos to begin.

"Ach, some folks get carried away with their tales," Salem barks. "Said tha' Queen Yerdos became a hawk after she died, flappin' all o'er the mountain. Protectin' it. That's where she came from, see? King Kladerstaff found her up on the mountain by herself an'–"

"*Salem!* Let Dawsyn speak, man," Ryon growls.

"Oh. Pardon me, lass."

Dawsyn only frowns, her head cocked to the side at Salem's rambling, but she gives it a shake and begins. "My grandmother told us of Yerdos, who took the shape of a great hawk, as big as a man. She was the keeper of the mountain before Moroz came."

"Moroz?" Ryon questions.

"The cold," Dawsyn explains. "The cold is not alive, but at one time, people believed it was."

"Moroz," Salem mutters, turning the word over, as though it were familiar. "Now, where've I heard tha'?"

"Continue," Ryon ushers Dawsyn, his eyes glued to her.

"Moroz came to the mountain and froze the ground. It shrouded everything in snow, chased the animals from the slopes, and Yerdos could do nothing to stop it. So, she flew to the peak of the mountain, where no mortal can reach, and consulted the Mother.

"The Mother only laughed at Yerdos. She would not lift her mighty hand to stay the frost that had smothered the mountain. Enraged, Yerdos sought to destroy the mountain all together. She soared from the mountain's peak, diving until her indestructible beak collided with rock. When it finally did, the mountain split in two. A great chasm was formed, and Yerdos descended into its depths, where she became its keeper instead."

All are silent as they listen to the final ringing notes of Dawsyn's story, reverberating back to them, courtesy of the very Chasm she spoke of.

"Terrsaw legends," Salem mutters, his head shaking. "Fuckin' drivel."

"If you're talking of me *again*, old man," comes the raised voice of Esra as he joins the circle, "I shall have to tell everyone about the bouquet of roses you have tattooed betwixt your nipples. And I seem to recall you threatening my life should I reveal a secret so intimate, so–"

"ESRA!"

"Tit for tat, old man. Or two tits for tat, in this case."

"We was talkin' about Saint Yerdos, yeh fuckin' knuckle-brained, arse-mouthed–"

"Oh! I do love the exchange of ancient legend."

Ryon pinches the bridge of his nose. "How unfortunate you missed it then."

"Did you tell the tale right, Salem? Of Queen Yerdos? And her revenge plague?"

A beat of silences passes. "What?" Ryon utters.

Esra smacks Salem heartily in the belly, making the other man double over. "Should have known you wouldn't have told it right!"

"I told it like yer 'sposed to, yeh lech. Stop hittin' me!"

"Shut up, both of you," Dawsyn snaps, and miraculously, the might of her stare seems to quell them. "What did you mean, Es, when you spoke of a revenge plague?"

"Well," Esra says, his expression animated. He squares his shoulders as though he were a stage man addressing an audience. "Terrsaw is rather divided on the history of Queen Yerdos, you see. Most believe she was a benevolent saint. Our dear Baltisse used to say she was stark raving mad. If you ask me, I think she was simply misunderstood. And then there is a certain subclass of people who rather think she was a nasty bitch with a chip on her shoulder."

"She was touched by the *Holy Mother*, yeh imbecile!"

"She was touched in the *head*, Salem. You can kiss the feet of every statue erected in her name, but it won't change the facts."

"Do you think he'll actually relay the facts anytime soon?" Tasheem asks of Ryon, her brow furrowed. "Or should I choke it out of him?"

"Unfortunately for you, queen of the bat people, I only invite that brand of bed play in fellow gentlemen."

"Esra!"

"Right." Esra clears his throat. "There are plenty of ancient journals that recount a rather different course of events during the Dyvolsh infection. Journals of noblemen, servants, even Yerdos herself. The real tale begins with King Kladerstaff, who ruled Terrsaw a fucking long time ago. He took long explorations over the sacred mountain, back when it wasn't a frozen bloody wasteland, obviously. It was during one of these treks that he came across a tribe of mages living peaceably on the slopes. Amongst their small number was Yerdos. It seemed that Kladerstaff had grown bored of all the flesh afforded to him by the women of Terrsaw, because he had the tribe slaughtered, and took Yerdos for himself."

"Rubbish!" Salem barks. But he is silenced by the resounding glares of the others.

Esra smiles sweetly at Salem, then continues. "Yerdos was taken captive and made to marry Kladerstaff, a man far older than she. He stripped her from her home on the mountain and forced her to use her powers to his benefit. I'd imagine his subjects were rather thrilled with him, procuring a magical wife who could manipulate the weather and ensure plentiful crops.

"But Yerdos did what all women ought to when tied down and forced to yield. She set a plague on the whole sorry lot of them. Turned them all into raving lunatics. And when Kladerstaff finally realised what she had done, he killed Yerdos himself, slicing her throat. Now, that's where the old journals fall short. Of course, no one knows what happens to one's soul once they perish, but I'd rather think a woman like that would return to the place she was taken from." At this, Esra looks pointedly to Dawsyn. "And let hell reign down upon those who try to take her away again."

Ryon hears his own breath fall heavily in the silence that follows. Dawsyn's eyes are scrunched closed. In confusion, perhaps. "A mage," he thinks she is saying.

"This version of the story makes better sense," Rivdan says. "A vengeful mage, turned malevolent spirit."

"What Yerdos was, and whether she cast the infection matters little," Ryon says, his heartbeat beginning to race again. "We need only know that the same infection spreads among us now." He looks to Dawsyn as he says it, and even in the dim, he can see the impending panic in her eyes.

"Moroz," Salem is muttering. "Swear I've heard tha' somewhere."

"Moroz?" parrots Esra, his voice obtrusively loud for this glib discussion. "Baltisse's spell?"

Ryon's breath stutters. Dawsyn's eyes have darted to Esra. "Baltisse?"

"She used it to cool my burns after the fire," Esra tells them, looking down at his arm unconsciously. Beneath the layers he wears, Ryon knows the new skin remains mottled and scarred, despite Baltisse's best efforts to heal him entirely.

"A cooling spell," Dawsyn utters, her breath coming faster.

"Made my veins feel like they might freeze over," Esra nods. "Didn't Baltisse aid you with it once before, Salem? Something about burning urine?"

"I will kill yeh as yeh sleep, Es."

"Riv," Dawsyn interrupts. "You said that the Glacians drank iskra to cure themselves of Yerdos' madness?"

"Yes," Rivdan nods.

"Moroz," Dawsyn says under her breath. She flips her hands and looks upon her palms. They glow dully, pulsing softly. Even Ryon can feel the sudden eagerness of her magic.

When she looks up, it is his gaze she finds. "The cold is alive after all," she says.

Chapter Seventeen

"Come with me," Yennes said again, awaiting a familiar response.

Baltisse only shook her head. The mage stood at the basin before one of the wide windows, her gaze on the ocean.

Those windows still made Yennes uncomfortable, despite the lack of any other being in the bay. She could not rid herself of the sense of vulnerability. The cabins in Terrsaw were not built the same.

She stood with feet planted in the doorframe, though apprehension clawed at her throat. "I'll go without you."

"Then do so," Baltisse said. "I'm sure you'll find your way."

That was just it. Yennes had no idea where to go, or indeed, where she was going. She just knew she could not remain in the bay forever, never seeing another scrap of Terrsaw. Baltisse had shown her maps. It was an unfathomable mass of land, stretching many sides. She didn't need to remain here, so close to the Chasm, where the voices still found her in the night. Sometimes she was unable to discern if they were real, or the simple torture of memory.

It would aide her to leave this bay. Find another speck on the map, where she did not have to watch the waves roll and think about the way it felt to be drowned by them.

But more than that, she sought help. Favours. Favours that Baltisse would not grant her.

The mage still would not teach her to fold.

Despite knowing that she could not stay, turning away from the bay and outward made her falter. She knew nothing of this land. Knew nothing of its people. She erred on the stoop. Equally determined and frightened.

Baltisse sighed dramatically and leant her weight on the countertop.

"Very well," she relented. "I will accompany you. But when we go out there and find nothing worth finding, I'll expect you to heed my advice in future."

Yennes grinned, but said nothing to provoke the mage as she readied herself to journey.

"I hope you neglected to eat breakfast," Baltisse said, gathering a small hand-woven swag.

Yennes frowned. "Why?" She had not turned down a single piece of food since arriving a little over a month ago.

"I know how you hate to waste a meal."

Moments later, Yennes' hands were splayed against new territory and her stomach turned up every morsel it held. Her limbs, newly decompressed, popped at the joints. "*Fuck,*" she gasped, overcome by another wave of nausea. "You didn't think to mention how very unpleasant that would be?" She closed her eyes as they swam.

"If I had, you wouldn't have done it, would you?"

Yennes groaned. "I've changed my mind. I do not wish to learn how to fold."

"That's a relief," Baltisse muttered. "Perhaps you'll cease pestering me. Though if you wish to see that bay again, you will need to find a way across the river, and you swim like a helpless infant."

"I've no desire to return to that bay," Yennes said, more firmly than was her habit of recent days.

Baltisse did not refute it. Instead, she pressed her lips into a thin line, and averted her eyes. "We shall see."

Once Yennes had reclaimed enough composure, Baltisse guided her wordlessly through woodland. They walked a weaving, trailless path for a time, and the mage did not bother to check if Yennes followed. Though the sound of her mind was likely telling enough.

The land overwhelmed her. Its ground dipped and rose with the interweaving of tree roots, thickening into trunks with bent backs and hollow stomachs. Trees that leaned over one another, their foliage draping over her as she walked beneath. And the colour... the colour was everywhere. Newly formed buds sprouted all around, some opening as Baltisse passed by, drinking whatever energy she passed to them through the proximity of her fingertips. The mage hummed as she walked and the forest hummed back – a quiet symphony Yennes could only gawk at. Despite the questions that brewed, Yennes could not bring herself to break the spell.

Eventually, the forest parted to reveal a well-worn path. The dirt compacted here, strange trails marring the dust.

"What travels here?" Yennes asked. The marks were unbroken, thin, accompanied by round, almost fully circular tracks. They did not resemble an animal or person she recognised.

"Wagons, mostly," Baltisse answered. "Horse-drawn."

"Oh," Yennes answered. She did not bother to tell Baltisse that she could not picture a horse, though she'd heard it mentioned before.

The mage sighed. "There is much you will not recognise." The words were somehow foreboding.

When the sun had reached the middle of the sky and Yennes' borrowed chemise and cotton blouse were moist with sweat, she began to wish for rest.

"We've almost arrived," Baltisse answered, reading the direction of her thoughts. "No point in stopping now."

"I had not realised there was a destination in mind." Yennes frowned. Mother above, it was hot. She had not known the sun could grow quite so biting.

"The temperature will peak in several weeks," Baltisse answered. "The season has only just turned. You will be glad for the proximity of the ocean then."

"I don't plan to see any ocean again in my lifetime," Yennes quipped, but she did not continue to badger the mage with questions of their travel. The forest had begun to thin, heating the air she breathed. The wagon path widened. Soon, Yennes could see an end to the trees' border. Beyond it, wide open fields awaited. They stepped to the forest's edge and looked out, catching their breath.

It was an ocean of long, golden grass stalk, bending to the will of the breeze. Rolling hills of it, stretching in every direction.

"Wheat," Baltisse answered before she could ask.

Yennes could only stare. How could such an impossibly vast place exist? And yet no one guarded it. No one kept watch.

"It belongs to the Queen," Baltisse answered, starting forward again. "And no one would dare take it from her, lest they wish to go without their share… or their hands."

Yennes followed Baltisse out into the wheat fields. "This Queen," she began, pressing stalks to the side with hesitant movements. "Have you ever met her?"

Baltisse chuckled darkly. "Those like me know better than to find ourselves before a royal."

Yennes pressed her lips together. Baltisse had told her as much before. "You said the Queen was intolerant of your kind?"

"Of *our* kind," Baltisse answered. "Magic courses through your veins as it does mine."

"But I am human," Yennes argued. "The magic I have was taken from the Glacian's pool. I was not born with it."

"And yet, you can wield it. The Queen will not care how it was gained, only that you carry it. You're a threat to her, whether you acknowledge it or not."

"I am from the Ledge," Yennes pressed. "Will the Queen not be gratified by the return of one of her people?"

Silence follows, and then, "I have told you this part already. The Queen sacrificed your people to that Ledge... to the Glacians. She will not be pleased to see you back." Baltisse turned and looked at her, halting their progress. "I bid you not to go looking for her, Yennes. Do not put yourself in her path. Explore Terrsaw if you must. Settle wherever you might settle and pay that fucking castle no mind."

Yennes tempered the response that rose to her lips. It did not seem to matter much to Baltisse that there were people on the Ledge who still lived, trapped like animals. She did not seem to care for the gruelling conditions of their survival, the harshness of the frost, the proximity of the Chasm. She did not know the feel of talons through skin, biting into the tissue and sinew that held one's shoulders together. None of it seemed a compelling argument to someone like Baltisse, living safely in her glass-window cabin in her quiet bay.

Nothing can save them, she had told Yennes over and over. *Best you find a way to reconcile with it.*

But if the Queen knew what it was to live on the Ledge, if the people of Terrsaw knew the truth – perhaps they'd feel compelled, as she did, to aide them. To bring them home.

Many years had passed since this Queen of Terrsaw had made her deal, and time, Yennes knew, brought regret.

"Dangerous thoughts," Baltisse called from ahead, "find dangerous ends."

Yennes bit her tongue.

Chapter Eighteen

Dawsyn has been lying to herself for days. Lulling her doubts with the thought that the end to their struggles is just around the corner, or perhaps the next. She has told herself that every inch travelled brings them closer. She gave herself to the delusion that the end of the Chasm would bring the end of this affliction and all would be well.

Every time she has lain her hands on the sick, they have come away prickling. Whatever mediocre ministrations she had offered were not enough. They barely scratched the surface.

But now…

She can feel the eyes of her friends on her, and she pays them no mind. Instead, she turns her hands over and inspects her palms, admiring the rippling frost that comes and goes along the lines. The iskra courses just beneath the surface.

And then suddenly, as though it realises this might be its last chance, the whispers become shouts, bellows.

Seal your lips, cease your breath,
Rid the ache. TEAR IT OUT.
TEAR IT OUT!

But the words no longer have strings to pull her this way or that. It is only a hollow echo; it does not lull her.

She feels the burning cold of the iskra, the warm light of the mage magic, collecting to oust this thing that has made a home in her chest and heart and mind. A cursed plague, created by a seeker of light and warmth, can only be subdued with cold. With suffocating darkness. Even now, Dawsyn can feel how this entity shrinks away from the iskra.

Yerdos was defeated by Moroz. Dawsyn had always seen the latter as the enemy. How strange to see it as salvation.

Dawsyn closes her eyes. She finds the light in her mind, the one that burns resolutely with all the warmth she possesses, and she bids it to make way for the iskra. She fills her body with the strength of the cold, lets the burn flood through her. It travels the length of her limbs, makes claws of her blood. It burns away the grip on her chest and mind as furiously as fire.

"Moroz," Dawsyn says aloud, and the magic within her rejoices.

Beyond her eyelids, the world turns into a brilliant spectrum of colour, and she is immediately reminded of Baltisse and the way her touch illuminated the world.

"Mother's tits, give a man some warning next time, Dawsyn. My fucking eyes!"

"Yeh big baby!"

"Shut up!" comes Ryon's voice, and then his hands are on her neck, her face. "Dawsyn?"

She opens her eyes.

It is the same damnable darkness. The same gaunt faces in this hopeless hole, and yet she smiles.

"It worked," she pants, silently thanking the Mother.

Ryon mutters something beneath his breath, but then lowers his forehead to hers for a moment. She feels his trembling lips glance off the bridge of her nose.

Dawsyn breathes in and out, marvelling at how easily it comes. She hadn't noticed the weight that had burdened her lungs, the grip on her throat, the fog clouding her mind. In its absence, she feels free. Hopeful.

"I can help the others," she says to herself, her chest heaving with newfound levity. Then, she says it louder. "I can cure them. I know how."

Rivdan smiles, his eyes glowing as though they'd caught the brilliance of Dawsyn's light. Tasheem claps once, then bends to brace herself on her knees, laughing quietly. Salem has his hands pressed together, and he seems to be consulting some higher power, tears glistening in the corners of his eyes, and Ryon paces in a circle, gripping his hair with shaky hands. He hides his face from them all.

"Apologies," Esra says. "But could someone explain to me what the fuck is happening?"

"Shh," Salem says, patting Esra's shoulder.

"Well then," Tasheem calls, slapping Rivdan heartily on the back. "This changes things."

And Dawsyn isn't sure how or why, but she feels it too. The shiver of new hope. After days of compounding despair, this one victory feels like enough. Enough to see them through.

"I'll find Yennes," Dawsyn says hurriedly. "There are many we must see to."

"I think I saw her by the stream, up ahead," Esra says. "Poor woman looks exhausted herself. Spluttering and mumbling to herself. You ought to start with her, I say," he tells Dawsyn pointedly. "I'm fairly certain her mind was somewhat addled *before* Yerdos decided to fuck her up."

"Esra! Yeh cad. *Mind yer manners.* If anyone's a marble short, its surely *yeh.*"

Dawsyn almost laughs. Almost.

"I'm strong enough to fly a while," Rivdan says now, rolling his shoulders tenderly. "I'd like to fly ahead, see what I can find."

Dawsyn eyes him dubiously. "Are you able?"

"I won't get far, but yes. I can try, prishmyr."

"Not alone," Ryon says. "We do not know what lies in wait."

"I'll go with him," Tash says, limping forward. "Mother knows, it will be better than dragging this fucking leg behind me all day."

"Go easy," Ryon warns, clearly agitated that he cannot accompany them. "And mark the time passing. We need to know the distance that remains."

"And if we can't find the end?" Tash asks. "What then?"

"There's an end," Dawsyn says, pulse thrumming. In her mind she sees the Chasm winding to its last corner, the path tinged in light. Each step eases with the promise of open land. Uninhabited territory, waiting for their claim.

Her body burns with that certainty. Her skin turns feverish. Even the forgotten necklace beneath her furs grows warm.

Yennes is indeed by the stream when Dawsyn finds her. She stoops to its edge, cupping her hands in the flowing water. She startles when Dawsyn touches her shoulder, despite her having called to the woman several times already.

"Sorry," Dawsyn offers, frowning. She waits for the woman's nerves to settle. "I called to you."

"It's hard to hear beyond the Chasm's screams," Yennes says.

She holds her hands in the icy water, apparently oblivious to the cold. A lit torch stands waiting, its end buried in the silt by the woman's side.

"Come," Dawsyn says, wariness marring her voice now. She places her hands on the woman's upper arms. "Your feet are slipping into the water."

She helps the older woman stand, pulls her back an inch from the stream's edge. "You'll catch your death."

Yennes stumbles, limbs shaking, and when her hand reaches to grasp Dawsyn's wrist, she notices how weak her grip is. Yennes' trembling fingers are slick with something far warmer than the stream. "Alas," she whispers. "Death caught me first."

She slumps, falling to the ground, limbs splayed.

"Yennes!" Dawsyn calls, squinting in the dark. In the faint glow of the torch light, Dawsyn can see her closed eyes, her parted lips.

"Igniss!" Dawsyn gasps desperately, using the conjured flame in her hand to better see. She bends over the woman, pressing her hand to Yennes' chest, and then to her neck, feeling along her jawline for the fading pulse beneath. "*Shit.*"

Dawsyn's light passes over one of Yennes' hands, and it reflects back to her coated in brilliant, dripping blood. It flows freely from beneath the cuff of her cloak and collects in her palm.

Dawsyn rips back the sleeve. There. Two long gashes, cut precisely down the arm. Even in this dim light, Dawsyn knows they are deep. Deliberate.

"Baltisse!" Dawsyn shouts in a moment of sheer panic. *Help,* her mind screams. *Get help.* But Baltisse is long gone from here. The only mage power left in this Chasm resides in herself.

She presses her palms to the wounds and feels the blood seeping over the webbing of her fingers. She finds the spark in her mind and urges its expansion. "Lussia," she tries, remembering the way Baltisse had used the spell to bind things back together. She imagines the skin stitching itself into clean lines, but looks to find the skin is barely rejoining, fighting against the tide of the blood. "Ishveet!" Dawsyn says, begging the wounds repair, to heal. "Ishveet... Lussia!" She says the words over and over, but it seems, for long moments, that they do nothing, that the wounds are too deep, the blood too fast. "*Lussia!*"

Dawsyn cries, and finally, slowly the bleeding subsides. The gashes start to close, giving in to the will of mage light shining from Dawsyn's palms.

She refuses to close her eyes as she works, despite the way the light stings them. She lets the tears course down her cheeks and her eyelids tremble, battling to remain open. Even as her magic wanes, she keeps her hands pressed to the wounds, until two, angry pink scars are all that remain of them, trapping life source beneath.

But the ground is wet with blood. So much of it. Dawsyn moves her stained fingers to Yennes' neck to find the weakest of pulses still thudding intermittently, a slow prelude to its final beat.

"Shit," Dawsyn heaves again. She looks at the woman's face, scared, even in sleep.

Anyone that dies here in this hole, dies by your hand, Sabar, comes Nevrak's voice once more, warning her from the darkest recesses of herself. It seems particularly true of Yennes.

If death has found her here, then Dawsyn will push it back. Yerdos has collected enough of their number, blanketed her burrow with enough of their remains.

Yennes will not be hers as well.

Dawsyn shouts into the air, something inhuman and unintelligible but most certainly a call to battle. She presses both hands to Yennes' chest, feels the remnants of light coil tightly inside her, and shouts, "ISHVEET!"

She hears her name called, feels hands on her shoulders. But her focus remains on Yennes, whose chest rises from its middle, lifted by some invisible force.

The stretched magic reaches its limit and snaps.

The recoil throws Dawsyn back and she feels the impact push the breath from her lungs as she slams into something solid.

And everything around her disappears, but for Baltisse, who smirks at her quietly over the rim of a full glass, perfectly at home in the shadows.

CHAPTER NINETEEN

"Dawsyn!"

Hands pull aside her coat. They press firmly against her chest.

"Dawsyn. *Wake up!*"

"What happened to her?"

"Dawsyn!"

She blinks, the outline of a familiar face hovers above her. Rough hands hold her waist.

"Yennes?" Dawsyn asks Ryon. But it is not Ryon who answers.

"She's fine," Hector says from somewhere over Ryon's shoulder.

Ryon's answering growl, however, contradicts the word *fine*. "What the fuck were you doing, Dawsyn?" he says, shaking her slightly.

Dawsyn sits. Pushes his hands away. She feels unsteady. Bleary. "Saving her."

"Bleeding yourself dry," Ryon corrects. "As surely as Yennes was."

"She was dying," Dawsyn utters. She is unsure if he hears.

Ryon growls again, standing and then lifting Dawsyn onto her feet easily. "And many more might yet die," he states. "Should I expect that you will sacrifice yourself to save them all?"

Dawsyn does not answer. In truth, her mind is still blanketed by that numbing haze, but she hears his question and thinks: *Of course. Of course I will.*

Perhaps her silence says enough. Ryon grips her face in his hand, and though his tone is rough, his fingers are controlled. They lock her jaw in place. "We've a lot to talk about, you and me," he says, so low and dangerous, it makes her shiver. "But if you care for me at all, you will consider what it might do to me, should you burn yourself out."

126

Rattled, she nods. She wonders if she has ever submitted so quickly to another.

"Mother help me," he mumbles to himself, eyes leaving her face. He drops his hold and stalks away from her, leaving her to stare at Hector's outline.

And behind him, the form of another rising.

"Yennes?"

The woman's lips move, but the words she mouths are soundless.

Dawsyn sags, her lips stretching into a grin.

"She is well," Hector says, his hand around Yennes' elbow, ensuring she remains steady. "What happened?"

"Yerdos," Dawsyn answers coarsely. "Yerdos had her."

Hector frowns. "The hawk?"

It makes Dawsyn laugh, however wearily.

Yennes weeps quietly and when Hector holds a torch a little closer Dawsyn sees the woman's clothes are drenched in red.

She goes to her, wrapping her own shaky arms around the woman's frame. "All is well," Dawsyn breaths, relief washing through her. "The Chasm should know it can't have you that easily."

Yennes' splutters a weak laugh and for a moment she buries her face into Dawsyn's shoulder.

An unfamiliar sense of pride fills Dawsyn, to have succeeded, to have accomplished this much.

Yennes' pulls away and her lips fight to form words. "I'm sorry," she manages.

"Your mind wasn't your own," Dawsyn says, more gently than she knew herself capable.

"The voices... they have lived with me. All this time." When Yennes opens her eyes again, Dawsyn can almost see the ghosts in them, lurking beneath the surface, tormenting Yennes long after she left the Chasm, and reclaiming her when she appeared within it once more.

Dawsyn thinks of the slithering whispers that plagued her own mind for just a few days and cannot imagine the torture of it making a home there, year after year. Dawsyn thinks of the iskra within Yennes' blood, keeping Yerdos and her madness at bay.

"They won't speak to you anymore," Dawsyn tells her, brushing her cheek with the pad of her thumb. "You'll banish them."

She tells Yennes about Moroz and how they will use it to rid them all of infection.

Yennes smiles at her as Dawsyn speaks. It is despondent, and does not hold for long, but Dawsyn is calmed by it. Once more, she feels the awakening of true hope. Despite her waned magic, she feels, for the first time, powerful enough to defeat this Chasm and deliver each one of them to its end.

Surely it exists. Some innate knowledge tells her so, and if these obstacles were made to keep them from finding it then they will lay them to waste.

"Yennes, you and I can cure the rest, we must–"

But her words are swallowed by the sudden uproar of voices, shouting from the south. Dawsyn stands abruptly, reaching for her ax.

Hector pulls forth a dagger and stares in the same direction – into the interminable darkness that roars back to them. A collection of angry shouts and the contact of flesh.

"For fuck's sake," Hector growls. "How can they possibly muster the energy to fight now?"

"Dawsyn!" someone calls. Salem's voice, searching for her in the gloom.

Dawsyn takes the torch from Hector and hastens forward. Toward the clamour. "*Salem?*"

"Dawsyn!" And then he appears, grabbing her arm and tugging her forward. "It's tha' son o' a bitch," he yells. "The Splitter."

Her stomach plummets. The sounds of fighting continue. "Nevrak."

"He's gathered a mob," Salem huffs, stumbling over debris. "Ryon's holdin' 'em off!"

Dawsyn lets the ax handle slide into her trembling hand until her fingers find the worn grooves at its end. She leaves Salem behind her and follows the light shining from several torches ahead, barely illuminating the scuffle before them.

"I SAY WE WASTE THE GLACIANS!"

The bellow is met by a hearty roar of assent. Fists rise in the air.

Dawsyn pushes through to see Nevrak standing in the middle of the mob, his forearm locked around Tasheem's throat. She winces, holding her injured leg aloft. Her calf dangles sickeningly, no doubt re-broken.

Nevrak holds a knife beneath her eye, the tip caressing the side of her nose. The small crowd of men clear a circle for him, and each have weapons drawn. Their faces are ruddy with hatred. They stare at Tasheem hungrily.

Ryon and Rivdan are the only ones standing between the mob and Nevrak. Dawsyn can see the few who have tried to pass and failed. They stagger stupidly with cut lips and swelling eyes.

Dawsyn counts twenty or so men, all heeding to Nevrak's call.

"We've lived beneath the press of their talons long enough, haven't we?" Nevrak calls to them, and they respond with resounding assent.

"Call your men off, Nevrak," Ryon says quietly, though his wrist turns his sword over and its glint is as menacing as his stare. "I do not wish to make them walk without their limbs."

Nevrak spits onto the ground. "We ain't sheep to be herded! We've let ourselves be led down this merry path, when you Glacians could've flown us out at any time!"

"Mesrich, kill this idiot," Tasheem spits. Her hands pull on the constricting arm around her neck. "Before I do."

"Oh, ho! You see, lads! I say, this path ain't leading us to Terrsaw. No kingdom of the free. There ain't no field of whores waiting to ravish us all on the other side!"

The men laugh, riled and vengeful.

"No. I'd wager that the only thing we'll find at the end of this fucking path, is another corner to confine us to! ANOTHER FUCKING PRISON TO TRAP US IN!"

"Enough," Dawsyn says. She steps into the circle. Turns her back on the watching crowd.

Ryon moves slightly to guard her. "Easy," he murmurs. She can feel his adrenaline as she passes.

She faces Nevrak. "Don't be a fool, Splitter."

Nevrak pins her with a glare so hateful, she almost feels its touch digging into her skin. "A fool?" he says, that maddened veneer sheathing him once more. "I turned a fool the day I let your mongrels drop me into this *fucking hell hole!*"

"And I'll not let you leave it, if you don't put down your blade," Dawsyn says. They are so close to the end. So close. She can feel it. She won't allow Nevrak to impede it.

"Ha!" Nevrak barks. "You Sabars always did have more arrogance than was good for you. We've let it guide us far enough, girl. You ain't in charge anymore."

"No? And I suppose you'll be taking my place?"

"You're damn right," Nevrak growls, steam rising from his lips. He pulls Tasheem tighter. "And unless these bats fly us over that edge up there," he juts his chin to the sky above, "I'll be leaving their useless carcasses here, among the other fools unfortunate enough to have listened to your lies."

"I'll ask it nicely once more, Ryon," Tasheem huffs. "Kill this imbecile."

Ryon eyes Tasheem in silent warning. "All of us were injured, Nevrak. We will be lucky to rescue ourselves from this Chasm."

"Another fucking lie, no doubt!"

His supporters shout their agreeance.

"Think it through, Splitter," Dawsyn says, stepping carefully to the side. She can spy one of the armed men stalking closer to her in her periphery, where he thinks she will not see. "What you claim makes no sense. You are delirious. Hungry. Heart sore."

"YOU'RE FUCKING RIGHT I'M HEART SORE!" he bellows, spittle showering over Tasheem's shoulder. "My whole fucking family is gone!" Nevrak scrunches his eyes shut a moment, as though he can squeeze the pain out. "And I ain't dying on a ledge, or in a hole, or corralled into some trap like an animal! I'm getting out of here. We all are. NOW!"

"You'll either journey down the path, or you'll die here. Those are your choices."

"Nay," Nevrak pants, then nods subtly to someone over Dawsyn's shoulder. "I'll choose neither."

The man with the ice-pick lunges toward her, his footing so unsure, Dawsyn hardly has to move to fell him. In one swift action, she slides her inside foot back and throws her elbow around in an arc. It connects with the side of the man's head, and he wails as he falls to Dawsyn's feet, his ear already bleeding. It will likely ring for a week.

"Don't," Dawsyn says, holding her ax aloft on her other side, where another has stepped forward with his blade raised. The man halts in his spot. He eyes her ax warily.

"*Fuck*," Nevrak mutters, his breaths coming faster. "Tell your friend to take me above, Sabar!" He moves the blade to Tasheem's throat, nicking her skin with the tip. "TELL HER!"

"Tasheem is injured. She could not take you even if she were inclined."

"You forsake her then! You'd rather I kill your Glacian pet, then let me leave?"

"It's not her death I worry for," Dawsyn says. "It's yours."

"I've got a knife to her neck, Sabar. I'd say she's closer to meeting the Mother than I."

"I assure you," Ryon sighs. "That's not the case. Last chance, Nevrak."

"YOU AIN'T IN CHARGE NO MORE!" Nevrak bellows and the others shout in raucous assent. "We're taking our own way out now and if this spawn of the devil won't fly us out, she is of no use to us!"

More cheers. Nevrak throws his head back in apparent rapturous victory, howling maniacally.

Tasheem, however, only looks sullen. "Now?"

Ryon shakes his head in dismay. But then squares his shoulders. "Now."

It is over within moments. Tasheem thrusts her head back hard enough that the resounding crack of Nevrak's nose reverberates. She twists his wrist and the man's blade clatters to the ground. His lips and neck are slick with blood by the time he topples, eyes dazed, jaw slack.

Tasheem hisses a stream of old language, none of it recognisable to Dawsyn and surely none of it refined. She holds her wasted leg aloft, her face scrunched in pain. "He broke my fucking leg, Dawsyn," Tash mutters. Shaking her head. "Attacked me from behind with an ice-pick."

"So I see," Dawsyn says. But her attention returns to the mob before them. Twenty or so men, now holding their weapons with less conviction. Some are backing away.

"You're a murderous fucking devil," one says to Tasheem, hocking a gob of spit onto her boot. But he too retreats.

"He isn't dead," Tash says viciously. "Yet."

As though in answer, Nevrak groans.

"Enough of this," Dawsyn calls loudly, so that all can hear. "We will reach the end this day! I am sure of it."

"And how many will we lose in the hours before?" another calls, a woman this time.

Dawsyn will not let that old weight fall heavy on her shoulders again. She won't let it wane the light she feels. "Yennes and I will see to the sick," she says. "We can help them."

"You can't!" someone says from the gloom. "Your remedies only go so far!"

"We've found the cure," Dawsyn calls, refusing to be talked over. "We will attend to those–"

But her words are strangled, for the necklace at her chest suddenly grows shockingly hot. It pulses against her skin, in time with her racing heartbeat.

She grabs at it through her clothing, then looks over at Ryon.

"What–?" she mutters, confused. But Ryon is not gripping his knuckles in the way Dawsyn expects him to.

He looks back at her, concern clouding his face. "Malishka?"

Dawsyn does not answer. While the necklace heats her skin, her focus resides on Ryon's hand and the bare fingers that host no ring – magicked or otherwise.

Chapter Twenty

The Chasm sings.

But this time its voice is a deep drone. A subsonic drum that slowly crescendos. It makes Dawsyn look to the ground, where pebbles and debris quiver. She expects to see cracks forming between her feet – opening to finally swallow them all.

But then comes the sound of echoing voices. Of armour. Of horses.

The Chasm walls collect the noises and surround them with it, so that the cacophony comes from everywhere, all around.

"No," Ryon breathes, eyes wide. He is as struck as she, frozen in stupor, in disbelief. "No!"

Hector steps toward her, gripping her elbow. His touch is cold.

A glow appears, growing warmer, brighter. It is the same light Dawsyn has seen in her imagination, the same building illumination that would precede their freedom. Paradise.

Only it does not arrive from the north, but from the south.

They come.

On their horses and on foot. With their pulled wagons and glinting armour. They come toward them aglow with lanterns and torches – a travelling nimbus.

It reaches Dawsyn's face in increments, making her squint. She raises her ax. "No," she utters. That burgeoning hope, the last vestiges of confidence within her, already it is ebbing, slipping away. "No." Her voice is louder this time, and she pushes her way forward, through the faceless bodies of her people, toward that brilliant light and the sounds of nickering and clashing armour.

Not now, her mind screams. *Not now!*

"Halt!" She hears from ahead, inside the nimbus, and the voice is familiar. Dawsyn does not pause to reason its owner, she retrieves a blade from her side and launches it through the air, to the place where the first horse comes to a standstill, still twenty paces away.

But the rider raises a shield, and the blade clatters off it before it can find its mark. The knife falls to the ground, and the mount jumps, startled.

"Stop!" says that same voice from behind her shield.

This time, the voice catches. It sticks to the sides of Dawsyn's mind. Then quickly it rots, turning viscid and foul.

"Ruby," Dawsyn exhales, and it is not a sigh of relief, or of welcome. Because Ruby mounts a horse blanketed in Terrsaw green, and she is flanked by Terrsaw armour, and the shield she holds before her bears the emblem of her homeland. Of her Queen.

"Dawsyn," Ruby answers, and only then does she lower her shield. Just enough so that Dawsyn can see her face.

The same brown eyes and rich skin. The same lips pressed firmly together, the same cleft in her chin. And not a mark on her to be found. Not a single one.

On her finger is a ring, one not present when last Dawsyn saw her. Dawsyn cannot see the silver band clearly, but the necklace against her collarbone beats its heated pulse, and she feels sure the ring does the same.

Ryon's ring.

"Easy!" Ruby calls, but she looks beyond Dawsyn, raising a placating hand to those behind her. "Peace!"

But the people of the Ledge are backing away. Most have never laid eyes on a horse, never seen weapons hewn of such fine silver. The light is blinding after days holed up in darkness. It burns their retinas. Dawsyn feels them raising their weapons and retreating.

Already, they know what Dawsyn knows. This is a fight they cannot win.

Ryon is pulling on her arm. "Fall back," he yells, holding his sword defensively, his eyes pinned on Ruby's.

"PEACE!" Ruby yells again, and the word seems to be for Dawsyn, for the captain looks to her imploringly. "Dawsyn! Go easy. We do not come to fight!"

Nevrak crawls to his discarded blade and staggers to his feet. "Who are you?" He calls, his front bathed in blood. "What business have you here?"

Ruby looks to him, one hand on her reigns, the other holding her shield. "We are the royal guard of Terrsaw," she tells him.

Dawsyn feels the turning before the first word of dismay is spoken. The realisation slithers through the crowd, weaving through their number. A shiver of comprehension, of confusion.

"You have come from Terrsaw?" Nevrak asks. Dawsyn watches the terrible knowledge dawn, watches it break over him.

"Nevrak–"

"We have," Ruby calls. "And we've been looking for you."

Dawsyn braces. They've been looking for them. Looking to capture them, imprison them. She raises her ax.

"We will ensure your safe journey to the valley," Ruby says now, looking over them all, her eyes growing wider as she takes in their dwindled number, their sunken faces, their ragged attire. "We've brought horses, carts. Your wounded needn't be made to walk further."

"We've been *journeying* to Terrsaw," says a confused voice. "To the valley."

Ruby frowns. She looks once more to Dawsyn, and it takes her moments to see it – Dawsyn's deceit.

And only a moment longer to take advantage of it.

"You're headed the wrong way. Our valley lies South," Ruby calls for every hearing entity in the Chasm to bear witness. "I'm afraid," she says, and here she swallows. The grim set of her lips turns apologetic. "You've been led astray."

Nevrak's jaw quivers. He turns to pierce Dawsyn with his glare, and with him, Dawsyn feels every single one of her people turn on her in kind. She feels their accusations, the heat of their rising fury.

"You swindled us," Nevrak says simply, almost serenely, like the strength of his voice has been swallowed by rage.

Dawsyn's breaths come shorter, faster, her heart sprinting. Her hands rise in a desperate attempt to subdue. "No–"

Ryon is moving to block her, to shield her. But it was not he who lied to them. Tricked them.

"You told us the water led to an *ocean!*" Nevrak says, his words gaining impetus.

"*Listen to me,*" Dawsyn shouts loudly. "Please–"

"Just where were you taking us?" Nevrak juts his finger at her, his chest hitting Ryon's hand. Ryon shoves him backward. "To your Glacian's den? Some fresh circle of hell?"

"Terrsaw isn't *safe,*" Dawsyn shouts, turning in a wild circle, her back to the guard, so desperate is she to stop this thing from slipping between her fingers. "The Terrsaw Queen is the very *reason* we were condemned to the Ledge in the first place—"

"On the contrary," someone calls.

It slides over her skin like oil, this voice. Cloys in her ears. Spikes her blood. Dawsyn's head snaps back to the guard.

"I am most eager to welcome our long-lost kin back to their rightful home." And like a shadow collecting substance and forming some tangible nightmare, a black horse comes forward, and its rider pushes back their hood to reveal the silvery braid, the map-lined skin, the thinly pressed lips, the ever-calculating stare.

Queen Alvira's gaze roams over the crowd, catching on the faces of the Ledge people. Her lips turn downward in something akin to compassion.

And then her eyes meet Dawsyn's. The corner of her mouth quirks – a miniscule crack in the façade.

Dawsyn turns cold.

"Miss Sabar," the Queen of Terrsaw says. "I've been looking for you."

Chapter Twenty-One

Ruby's horse knickers nervously and retreats several paces, spooked by the sudden shout that rents the air.

Dawsyn lunges forward, slipping the grasp of Ryon's outstretched hands as he makes to stop her. Her ax flashes as she spins it in her palm and heaves it over her shoulder.

Dawsyn is a woman burning. Ruby cannot find another way to describe it. She is made of rage. It exudes from her every cell. It is trapped in her eyes and building. Soon she will combust, obliterate them all.

But while her hands glow hotly with whatever sorcery she commandeered from that Glacian pool, Dawsyn does not explode in the way Ruby expects – in the way she once saw her do on the Ledge.

The guards raise their shields regardless, forewarned and ready. Ruby pulls the reigns of her skittish horse until it collides with the Queen's and raises her own shield to conceal them both. Ruby only just hefts it upward in time for Dawsyn's ax to clang against its steel, the force of the reverberations felt all the way to Ruby's marrow. It makes her teeth shake.

Her head ducked, Alvira emits a shriek.

But no white light follows. No blast of divine power.

Ruby looks over the ridge of her shield to see Dawsyn's hands dulling, the fine ice lace receding back into her palms. Dawsyn stumbles over jutting rock and barely catches herself. *She is weak,* Ruby realises, then looks around at those she knows – Ryon, Tasheem, Rivdan are closest. *They all are.*

She reads it in the stoop of their shoulders, the drawn lines of their cheeks, their dark-circled eyes slowly blinking. She would say they were all near death itself.

Dawsyn, always so intrepidly fierce, so war-weary and unflinching, now so cruelly thwarted. It physically pains Ruby to see how far she has crumbled. "Dawsyn, *halt*, please! You cannot win."

"Get away!" Dawsyn says in a voice not her own. It is deranged. Nonsensical. "Get away from them!" Tears course down her filthy cheeks.

Ryon comes to hold her, tries to whisper to her but she seems beyond reach.

Ruby hears Alvira's muffled laughter. It is a close-lipped murmur, but still Ruby hears it. It fills her with fresh disgust. How callous a person can be, to look upon this shattered woman and find humour.

"People of the Ledge!" Alvira cries now, her voice unmarred by sufferance or starvation. It rings higher than Dawsyn's had. It drowns out her rabid outbursts. "You are weary. You've travelled down this path for many days, following the word of this girl." She does not look at Dawsyn, who tries to escape Ryon's clutches with increasing desperation. "And her Glacian comrades. But I'm afraid each step has only led you even further into the mouth of this mountain, further from your home. Your *rightful* home."

Ruby can see the Ledge people beginning to converge, as she has so often seen the men and women do in Terrsaw – drawn by the surety they hear in Alvira's voice, magnetised to the majesty of it.

"A kingdom of your own people, waiting for you. Ready to rejoice when they hear of your return. Long have they prayed to be reunited with the ones we lost all those decades ago, when the Glacians shattered our kingdom and took you away–"

"Because of YOU!" Dawsyn bellows, though her cracked voice dissipates, the force of her anger not enough to sustain it. "Because of–"

"*Archer,*" Alvira calls, her voice flat with careful propriety, and before any can react, an arrow is shunted from a dark corner, and lodges into Dawsyn's shoulder.

She is thrown backwards, hits the ash.

Ryon's face twists in horror at the sight of blood spilling down her sleeve. He roars. The Chasm is suddenly filled with its sound.

"Dawsyn!" Ruby urges her mount forward.

But like a call to battle, Tasheem and Rivdan's wings emerge. They advance with weapons in hand, Tasheem's teeth bared and ready. One leg held aloft. "Back!" Rivdan calls. His eyes affixed to Ruby's. She has never seen them look quite so deadly.

But it is incomparable to the ungodly wrath that consumes Ryon, who turns his sights on the Queen. His wings unfurl with horrific suddenness. Their magnitude unnerving.

He is inhuman. Made of blackest anger.

And Ruby can see the end before it comes – Alvira's plan aligning perfectly. The Glacians will attack, the guards will overwhelm them in numbers alone, if not with their swords, then with their archers and arrows set ablaze.

The arrow in Dawsyn's shoulder was only the catalyst, the first flame to ignite the inferno. When the smoke clears the Ledge people will be at the mercy of the Queen, in territory they do not know.

"RYON! STOP!" Ruby thunders, thrusting her voice into the air the way she would to command an army, to lead a battalion to war. She hopes it is enough now. "HEAR ME, RYON!" she roars, bringing her horse between Ryon and the Queen, directly in the line of his ire. "YOU CANNOT WIN!" She looks to Rivdan, to Tasheem. "Not in *here*," she pants. Imploring them. Pleading for them to see. "Not in this place."

Ryon shakes from head to toe, his bloodlust a tangible thing, pulling at its leash. But his eyes oscillate from Ruby to the guards, their number reaching both sides of the Chasm and disappearing back into the gloom. Surely, he knows he cannot fell them all.

And that Dawsyn would die among the fray.

See it, Ryon. Ruby begs him silently. Refusing to let her eyes lift from his. *Do not give this bitch what she wants.*

"That was a warning to you, Miss Sabar," Alvira prods, her gaze not on Dawsyn who lays on her side on the Chasm floor, desperately trying to get her feet beneath her. Hector hunches over her, trying to stay her movements. Instead, Alvira pins her glare on Ryon, baiting him. "You have led these people astray for the last time."

Ryon bares his teeth, the swords in his hands shake. But he does not advance. He stays his ground. "Stop," he growls to Tasheem and Rivdan, who have crept forward, closing strategic gaps like the practised fighters they are. "Not here," he repeats, glaring at Ruby.

It is difficult to tell whether the Glacian wishes to trust her or slice her to pieces.

"Do not let this girl deceive you any longer!" Alvira continues. "We have food, wagons and carts for your sick and injured, horses for those too tired to walk."

Ruby can see the horde rouse at the mention of food. They look in desperate need of it.

"We will reach Terrsaw in mere days," Alvira promises. "With enough lanterns to light the path, and sustenance to strengthen you. You will be seen to safety on the other side."

"What of the ocean?" a Ledge man calls – bearded and bedraggled. "Does this stream lead to an ocean that will trap us?"

"You needn't fear it," Alvira answers, her tone placating, gentle. "The Chasm empties of its tide long enough for us to reach Terrsaw soil. And there you will claim your dues. You will have freedom in all its forms – fertile land, forests, rivers, community. There is plenty for the taking, and you have suffered long enough. Please," Queen Alvira implores sweetly, almost sickeningly. "Allow us to provide you with the comfort you have so long been without. Let us lead you home."

There is a pause. But it is short.

The bearded man moves first. With one last withering look to Dawsyn, he takes a fortifying breath and squares his shoulders. "The blood is on your hands," he says simply. Clearly. Then he deliberately walks past Ruby, and into the frontline of guards before the Queen, passing between the gaps of their shoulders. They let him through.

The rest take no more time to deliberate. They funnel between Dawsyn and the Glacians like sand through an hourglass, some spitting on her as they pass.

"Stop," Dawsyn says weakly, stringy hair half covering her face. "*Stop,*" she says, and her voice quavers. It comes undone.

Ruby looks down at her, at the arrow protruding from her shoulder, the blood blossoming along her chest. She looks at the pathways made by her tears cutting through the grit on her face. She looks at the way Dawsyn's eyes plead, a crippling mix of fury and defeat.

I am sorry, Ruby thinks.

"I will kill you," Dawsyn splutters at her. Each heaving breath seems to cause injury.

"Stay down," Ruby says to her. "It is done."

"Archers!" Alvira calls again.

And more arrows come. This time, they cut through the wings of the Glacians.

All three howl in agony, the leathery membrane of their wings torn. They stagger, holding their weapons upright once more.

"Stay down!" Ruby calls once more. Pulling on the reigns.

"Arrest them!" Alvira shouts.

"No," Ruby calls. "Halt!"

The guards dither on either side of Ruby, hesitating.

"They will die here," Ruby calls. "In the Chasm, where they cannot attack our number or fill our wagons," Ruby's heart sprints. She prays silently to the Mother. "We agreed they would not take from the provisions we have brought. There are many who are weak, Your Majesty. We should not burden ourselves further by carrying the enemy."

"They will be brought to Terrsaw," Queen Alvira commands. "They will answer for their crimes."

"It is not what we agreed," Ruby says. "They are injured. They should be left–"

"These guards will not answer to the likes of you, child," Alvira says plainly. "Take them all."

CHAPTER TWENTY-TWO

"Take them!" the Queen repeats, her voice reverberating up the Chasm walls until it fills the sky.

Oblivion is preferable, Dawsyn thinks. Her innards feel splintered, fragmented into a million parts. The glow in her mind sputters pathetically, the iskra in her belly is heavy and listless. It does not rouse even to the thought of demise, of utter obliteration.

The magic is as willing as she to have death's hand take her instead.

Dawsyn's sight is blurry, but still she sees Ryon before her, blocking the path between them and the guards, even as they advance.

Behind her, she can hear the whimpers of Esra. The low consoling mumble of Salem. She feels Hector's hands in her hair, a companion till the very end. She thinks that death in the cradle of their presence might make it less terrible.

Dawsyn peers up at Ruby, a hazy mirage atop her Terrsaw horse and she means to ask the captain for this one last mercy. Let death come and take her from this place. Let it take them all from this world that refused to accept them.

Dawsyn closes her eyes. She waits.

A blast of ice knocks her down. Her forehead cracks off the ground. She rolls and feels the arrow imbed further into her muscle and flesh, and it takes her breath away.

The sound is immense. A roaring blast that leaves a ringing in her ears. The light it emits burns the skin of her face.

It seems a long time passes before the ringing begins to fade. The neighs of fretful horses and the clatter of retreating guards rent the air alongside it. Alvira's voice is loudest – panicked and indignant. It is enough to make Dawsyn peel back her eyelids, despite the glare.

A blinding barrier spreads out before them. A glowing, white wall made of threads of ice. It stretches the width of the Chasm and climbs its walls, cold mist swirling in menacing patterns, separating the Queen and her guards, and the people of the Ledge. All of them back away with haste. Some have been knocked from their steeds, or off their feet. They scramble away.

"Hold!" Alvira shouts. "Hold!"

Then the Queen's eyes find something through the haze of the magical barrier. They enlarge at that sight of it.

Dawsyn feels someone step over her crumpled form. They walk toward the translucent blockade.

Yennes.

The woman's hands are outstretched, the mist flowing freely from them to secure the barrier. She teeters under the weight of it, and then the power seems to rebound, finally expended. She stumbles back, clutching her hands to her middle as though they burn.

The barricade remains, luminescent and tall.

"Iskra witch," Alvira snarls.

Yennes pants, but levels her gaze, meeting the Queen's more fiercely than Dawsyn has ever seen.

Without warning, a guard fires an arrow from the other side, but it merely clatters against the barrier and falls. It cannot penetrate the iskra.

"You've no need to take them," Yennes says, her voice quavering but still reaching, still clear. "Leave them here. You already have those you seek."

Alvira's eyes spark. "Are your alliances confused, witch? I had thought you'd be more welcoming. The letter you left me, and the means with which to find you, was most inviting."

There is a pause and then, "My ring?" Ryon says. His voice is hollow. Pitch black.

Dawsyn's chest tightens with fresh betrayal. Yennes turns side on to look at Ryon, then Dawsyn, and her expression is full of the depths of her sedition. "I am sorry," she says. Her hands begin their chaotic dance. Whatever valour she had harnessed is now sapped.

"Let us through, Yennes," Alvira commands. "Now!"

"I will not," she says. "Cannot. These people need not be taken or killed."

"People?" Alvira roars, and the guards join her in their noises of outrage. "Half-breeds and a collection of bandits. I'd say they hardly count."

"Then they should remain," Yennes answers. "Left in the Chasm."

Alvira's frustration is palpable. Her eyes return to Dawsyn's over and over. Ravenous. "Am I to believe you have chosen your side, Yennes?" the Queen asks. "Are you to remain here after all?"

Yennes lifts her eyes to the Queen's and though they flinch she does not avert them. "I wish to return to Terrsaw," Yennes says clearly. "I have done my duty to you. My debt is paid."

Alvira says nothing. She narrows her eyes.

"But you've now seen the extent of my power," Yennes continues. "And if I cannot travel alongside you peaceably, I will use it to protect myself."

The women trade knowing looks, seemingly communicating beyond the scope of words.

"You know my wishes," Yennes says. "They have not changed."

Alvira says nothing. Only seethes at having been thwarted.

"I brought you here," Yennes continues. "And I only bade you to leave the others, to let them go their separate ways. But if you will not abide that condition, then I will make it so."

Alvira's lips curl into a cruel, mirthless smirk. "Such a backbone you've acquired since we last spoke."

Yennes falls quiet, awaiting the Queen's answer.

I saved you, Dawsyn thinks at the woman. *I trusted you.*

"So be it," Alvira says. "Let her pass."

Carefully, Yennes passes through the barrier, the iskra parting upon her presence and then sealing behind her. The Terrsaw guards do not advance upon her as she approaches. They allow her to disappear within their folds.

Yennes gives one last parting glance to Ryon and Dawsyn before she vanishes from sight.

"Let us make way," Alvira says now. She gives Dawsyn one last appraisal, her lips turning upward. "These vermin are near enough to death that we should not mind."

Alvira pulls on her reigns and turns. The frontline of guards retreat with their eyes glued to the barrier, lest it fall. The Ledge-dwellers meander away, not bothering to glance back at Dawsyn. They leave her on the basin floor.

But the captain of the guard hesitates. Her horse paces nervously on the spot as she stalls. Her expression pained.

"When next we meet," Dawsyn says, and she does not know if the words reach Ruby's ears. "Run."

As Dawsyn's vision blackens there on the ground, so too does the Chasm, the light of the Terrsaw guards receding, taking away their captives. They herd them back to Terrsaw in much the same way they were first herded to the Ledge and Dawsyn's last thought is to wonder which fate will prove worse.

The world blackens once more.

Chapter Twenty-Three

Beaten, broken and bloody, the liberators of the Ledge lie strewn.

The glow of the barrier that saved them is dulling, beginning to curl in on itself. Dawsyn watches it recede from her place on the ground. She follows the filigree of frost with her eyes as it diminishes, the glow eventually fading. She remains staring long after the Chasm is returned to its lightless void.

If the others are conscious, they do not make it known. She assumes they lie dormant as she does, paralysed by disbelief, the slow ruining of this failure quietly splintering them.

She is amidst collapse. She can feel every torturous degree of it. The slow-moving avalanche that builds momentum with every gained inch. Soon, she will be nothing but rubble.

So close to the end, she thinks to the sky, over and over. It is a loop she cannot break. *How could we come so close, only to fail?*

She still feels it – that other side is within her grasp, and yet it might as well be a thousand miles more. Her people are gone.

Dawsyn rolls onto her side and stays there a while. She listens to the gentle tap of her tears sliding off the bridge of her nose onto stone. She is struck anew with the thought of staying there on the ground, and never getting up.

Only there is no whisper this time to tempt her. No bodiless voice coaxing her to lay down and die, but for the one in her mind.

She hears a groan. It is, perhaps, the only thing more unbearable than her own pain.

"Ryon," she mouths silently, and her lip trembles.

Then, as though she'd summoned him aloud, sounds of scuffling come from beside her. More sounds of pain. An arm encircles her. It wraps around her stomach and pulls her back into the hard, warm planes of a familiar embrace. She feels his breaths on the delicate skin behind her ear, his weight pressing into her, and despite the jolt of pain it sends through her shoulder, she is grateful. She is relieved.

It is far less painful to break here, in the safety of his arms.

Her chest gives way. Her sobs are noiseless, but she shakes with the might of them, and Ryon only holds on tightly. He pulls her in even closer when it seems all restraint is lost. He keeps her there and does not allow her to lurch herself over the precipice of oblivion.

"They're gone," she whispers hoarsely, pushing the words beyond the shuddering of her body.

"Shhh," Ryon says, his lips in her hair.

"They left," she mumbles. "Ruby... Yennes–"

"Will pay," Ryon interjects, though his voice is a croon, said to appease her. "I'll make them pay."

"Alvira... she'll... she'll kill them."

"We do not know that."

"I did this," Dawsyn says now and here lies the crux of her failure, the core of her torment. For no one else slung half-truths and false promises. She sees Nevrak in her mind and hears his accusations and he was right. He was right.

"It is done, malishka," Ryon tells her. "It's done now."

"You told me it was a mistake," Dawsyn continues, squeezing her eyes shut as new pain washes through her. Shame. Regret. "And now they are at the mercy of the Queen, and they have no idea what she'll do."

"Stop, Dawsyn."

"I – I should have told them," she cries quietly, her chest heaving. "I have killed them all."

"Enough."

"I tried," Dawsyn says, louder now. Her hands grip Ryon's arms. They claw at them. "I tried to *save* them!" These last words are unleashed. They ricochet. The echoes build in her mind, in her belly, until every part of her begs for release and she screams. She beats her head to the ground and roars her devastation into the dirt.

All of it was for nothing.

All of it.

Ryon waits until the scream tapers and turns to pants, to sniffling. He waits until her nails retract from the skin on his arms, and when she is finally quiet and still once more, save for the tremors that come unbidden, he rolls her over.

She cannot see him. He is merely a series of shadow. But she can picture him. She imagines his brown eyes, pulling her apart and fracturing her senses. She can see the short, tightly curled black hair that one can lose their fingers in. She sees the scruff that lines his jaw, his chin, the slope of his nose and indents of his cheekbones. She could draw the curve of his eyebrows from memory.

That is how often she has looked and memorised and marvelled. She knows him by heart.

"Ruby betrayed us," he says. "Yennes, too. Alvira. Cressida, Vasteel, Adrik. These are the ones responsible for the fate of those people. It is not you who should shoulder their blame."

"I promised them safety."

"And you were the only one in fifty years brave enough to attempt it."

Dawsyn swallows the fresh wave of emotion that threatens to pull her back under. She lifts her shaky fingers in the dark and finds Ryon's lips. She traces them.

Then she presses her mouth to his, and for a moment, she is transported out of the Chasm. She feels his breath mingle with hers, the soft, safe warmth of him surrounding her.

"Your wings," Dawsyn says when they part, though she cannot bear to move further than an inch. "Will they heal?"

"Ah," Ryon answers, his voice a low rumble. "You needn't worry. I have the benefit of travelling with a mage who loves me."

Dawsyn smiles weakly, though he cannot see it. "I do," she says. "Love you."

"I know you do."

Around them, Dawsyn can hear the others beginning to rise and move. She hears the stones scatter with their footsteps, the pained grunts as they fight their fresh injuries.

She expended her magic when she healed Yennes, moments before the woman betrayed them all. How cruel fate is, to twist the knife ever deeper.

"Ugh. My fucking ears are bleeding, Salem," comes a voice, louder than the sombre occasion could ever warrant.

"A taste o' yeh own medicine," a harsher voice grunts. "Me ears've been bleedin' from the sorry second we met."

"The old man lives," Esra replies dryly. "Hurrah."

"Ow! Fuckin' trousers are full o' stones."

"The only rock-solid thing they've ever rubbed up against, no doubt."

"Mother almighty."

Suddenly, a flame illuminates the dim. A halo of light erupts from a torch. Hector's face stands in its glow. He replaces the flint to his pocket, and squints at the faces surrounding him.

Tasheem and Rivdan are awake. They sit alongside each other, stooped over bent knees. Salem and Esra continue to bicker as they lumber to their feet, seemingly unhurt.

And there, just behind them, is the form of another. A face obscured by shadow.

"Who's there?" Hector says suddenly, seeing the figure in the same moment Dawsyn does. He thrusts the torch threateningly in their direction, a blade sliding into his palm from his sleeve.

The figure rises slowly, unsteadily, then steps forward. Her untamed, auburn hair gives her away immediately.

"Abertha?" Dawsyn asks, her voice cracked, but loud enough that it travels.

The girl nods, her eyes remaining on Hector's blade.

He is already lowering the weapon. "Bertie," he says. "You remained?"

The girl looks around at their group – at Esra and Salem shaking pebbles from the legs of their trousers, to the wounded Glacians barely able to sit upright. And then she looks to Dawsyn. "Yes," the girl says, her voice purposely firm.

"Why?" It seems unfathomable to Dawsyn, that she should still be here.

Abertha takes a fortifying breath. "I do not know where that path leads," she says, nodding upstream into the gloom. "But I can't imagine why you would lead us away from Terrsaw, unless there was something there to be avoided." She chews on the inside of her cheek for a moment, glancing at each of them in turn. It is the first time her nerves show. Eventually, her eyes find Dawsyn's again. "You saved me twice. I'd bet you could manage a third."

Dawsyn wonders if the girl can see the fresh moisture in her eyes, or if the Chasm has at least given her the mercy of discretion.

She remembers seeing Abertha play in the snow drifts as a child, closely guarded by her mother. She would watch from the grove for longer than was wise, haunted by visions of Maya playing those same silly games. She quickly learned to avoid crossing the girl's cabin. She learned to avert her eyes, lest Maya fill her mind once more and suck the will from her body. Those first years alone offered no reprieve, no solace. Her only chance was to keep her mind on the work, her eyes on the Chasm, and pray the hole inside her closed.

Even now, Abertha stirs the ghost of Dawsyn's sister, who would have been of similar age, had she been born to a different corner of the world.

"I do not know if there is another end to find," Dawsyn says. She will tell it all to this girl. She will do what she should have done all along. "We have not seen it."

Abertha's eyes do not leave Dawsyn's. The girl waits, shrewd and patient.

"But I know what there is to find in the opposite direction," Dawsyn continues. "I know that the Queen of Terrsaw… she does not seek to offer you sanctuary in her kingdom."

"Why not?" Abertha asks forcefully. "Tell me."

And Dawsyn does. She tells the girl the tale of Princess Valmanere Austrina Sabar, who fled to a village on the outskirts to warn them and was swept up in the raid of the Glacians. She tells Abertha of the bargain Alvira struck with the Glacian King and of the fear that guides her plans. She tells Abertha of the plan she concocted to find another place – any other place – big enough for their people to occupy, without the threat of Glacians or Queens or the cold.

When she is finished, Abertha's mouth hangs open. And strangely, after all she has heard, the first thing she utters is, "You're royal?"

The others chuckle meekly and it serves to warm Dawsyn, if only slightly. "So I'm told,"

"Right." Abertha squares her shoulders. "Then I should like to follow you."

Dawsyn shakes her head. "It may be to your own detriment."

"So be it. If I'm to follow one royal or another, it will be one from the Ledge. We should make haste."

Dawsyn sighs. She does not know how they can simply stand and walk on. They are battered, wilted versions of themselves. Each time they rise, something comes to cut them down. She cannot even begin to reach the mage power, nor the iskra. Both hide like whipped animals – abused and indignant.

"I'm not dying in this hole," Tasheem says from her spot, though her face is pinched with pain. "If those fuckers want to launch themselves into enemy territory, so be it. But I'm seeing the sky again," she says, turning her face upward.

Above them, the thread of light weaves an uncertain line into the distance, then disappears.

Dawsyn sighs. "To the end," she says, though she is not filled with conviction, nor determination. No. It is the last vestiges of survival that cling to her now, propelling her forward. Idleness is her enemy, as it has always been.

It is close, she thinks to herself. *Around the next bend.* And yet, her legs do not allow her to stand.

"Come, malishka," Ryon says, wincing as he stands beside her. "This is no place to give up." He proffers a hand.

Dawsyn shakes her head at the ground, pulling rattling breaths through her teeth. How utterly stubborn they must all be, to return to the path. "First," Dawsyn says, "someone pull this fucking arrow from my shoulder."

Chapter Twenty-Four

"If you've cured them, why do they drop like stones round each bend?" Alvira snarls.

The iskra witch stands before her, nervously eyeing the mare that Alvira holds by the reigns. The horses don't seem to be taking well to the dark. Either that or they've sensed something most sinister in this god-forsaken pit. It spooks them. If left a moment unleashed, they sprint down the Chasm. They have already lost two of them.

As for the Ledge runaways, they've lost plenty more. Fifteen, by her count. "I thought you'd found a way to drive out that madness," Alvira snaps when Yennes doesn't respond. She wouldn't be surprised to learn the witch was mad herself. It was likely what made her so pliable.

"I have. But magic is finite," her eyes turn distant as she says it. "I cannot not spare enough to cure them all *and* fold you back to Terrsaw."

Alvira groans. Already this trip grows tiresome, and they've barely travelled a day. "How many still have the... *infection?*"

"I do not know," Yennes admits. "But it is not only the sickness that fells them. They are weak. They have gone without food–"

"Daft fucking lunatic," Alvira mutters. "What use would it have been, walking these people to death?"

Yennes merely remains silent. Smart of her.

"The food stores will see them to Terrsaw," Alvira says firmly. "They will live if they don't kill themselves along the way."

"They will die if the voices are not driven out," Yennes says. "And if I must fold with you, then I cannot expend it on curing them. Already, my power is depleted."

Alvira makes a sound of frustration and turns her head to those who litter the Chasm floor. Dirty little creatures. All of them. Covered head to toe in badly stitched hide and fur, faces blackened with filth. And the *smell…*

Alvira sighs. She would rather cut off her nose than stay in this corner of hell a moment longer. But should this party return to Terrsaw without the numbers she needs, Alvira feels certain the new Glacian King will cut off far more.

"Cure them," she commands, ever the leader, the first to sacrifice. "We need them alive."

Yennes nods and Alvira detects relief in the way the witch's chest sags.

"But if you warn them," Alvira says, "if you utter a singular treasonous word against me, I'll consider our arrangement voided. Do you understand?"

Again, the witch nods but says nothing. She disappears quickly into the mess of humans.

Alvira, however, turns back to her mare. She mounts it after several moments of gritting her teeth and willing her strength not to fail. Her backside falls into the saddle and a lancing pain shoots up her back. She is too old to be riding. Too old to be forging through Chasms. Alvira pushes herself upright. "Ruby," she calls in no particular direction. "Someone bring her to me. *Now.*"

She hears the voices of the guards volleying the message and moments later, Ruby arrives on foot.

Alvira suppresses a sneer. She is loath to see the woman back in Terrsaw armour. But the stripes of her authority as captain are at the very least missing.

"Your Majesty," Ruby greets.

The captain stripes may have vanished, but noticeably still present is the bold glint in her eye. A shame the dungeons had not snuffed it.

"I am to travel on ahead with an assemblage of guards," Alvira says. "The iskra witch will not fold me away after all."

Ruby frowns, then nods obediently.

"You will ensure the rest of these… *people* are brought to Terrsaw alive. Force the iskra witch to heal and cure at knife point if you must. They are no good to us dead."

"How many guards will leave with you?" Ruby asks.

"Six." Alvira stares intently at the former captain, daring her to argue, wanting to see if that streak of rebellion still resides. *Call me selfish for taking so many,* she thinks. But Ruby only nods once more. Alvira continues, "I will take the provisions we need, though without the encumbrance of the slow walkers, I suspect we will end our journey in another day."

"Yes, Your Majesty."

"Do not tarry," the Queen warns her. "Our friends in Glacia will be waiting for word."

"We will put the slowest of them on horses or in carts," Ruby says, ever-pragmatic. "We will rotate them out and walk through the nights."

"Good," Alvira says. "Do not fail."

Ruby bows her head a moment, then turns on her heel, approaching the first guard in sight to relay the Queen's orders.

"Fenrick," Alvira calls now, ushering another guard to her side, though this one has not left the saddle of his horse. A fair boy, no older than sixteen by her estimation, though the armour always tricks the eye to see a grown man. Fenrick lowers his head briefly.

"I trust that you'll watch the former captain with a steely eye," she says quietly. She does not allow the boy's gaze to drop from hers. "The witch as well."

Lifting his chin, the boy nods. Young men's egos are so easily stroked.

"Should she appear to divert from the course, you will kill her."

Again, the boy nods. He puts his fist to his chest. "I will, Your Majesty."

Queen Alvira leans to pat the boy on the shoulder and then trots on, trusting that the bodies filling her path will scatter as her horse nears.

Soon, she will be rid of this fucking Chasm and back in the arms of her wife. Back in the safety of her palace.

Chapter Twenty-Five

In his youth, Ryon had been beaten often enough to warrant days of bed rest. He recalls the sensation of minced insides – so battered and sore that he was surely nothing more than pulp beneath the skin.

He feels as such now, ambling along the path. So pitifully tender that he cannot separate the aches.

Tasheem and Rivdan walk ahead of him somewhere. He can hear their low grunts, their tormented breaths. He wonders how much they regret the decision to join him all those months before. Ryon imagines most fates now look more attractive than this.

Esra and Salem stay close by him. They drag their feet as unwillingly as he does, and they fall often. Abertha and Hector help to prop them up when needed. Their bodies are more intimate with the pains of exertion and starvation, and they seem to bear the journey with more grit. But when Ryon catches sight of their faces in the torchlight, he is struck by how gaunt they have become.

Another day and their bodies will begin to fail them completely.

Another day and no amount of determination will help them stand. They will simply wither away in this basin with their useless wings, along with Dawsyn and her expended magic, all of them unable to climb out of the hole they have sunk themselves in.

"Ahead," Dawsyn's voice calls, croaky and frail. "Just ahead."

She says it often, though Ryon is not sure to whom she speaks. Perhaps to herself. She seems convinced that this unknowable end is near. It is likely a shield she holds between herself and the possibility of no end at all. The possibility of failure. After all, rage can only propel a person so far, Ryon knows.

He worries. He worries for what will become of her, what she will have left, if this end should not appear.

Then again, the torment will be short-lived. This Chasm has hovered and bided its time. It will soon swallow them whole.

He hears Dawsyn, but he cannot see her. Her pained breaths are closer than they were before. Perhaps she has slowed, or he has lengthened his strides. It is difficult to tell in the haze of hunger and weakness. The trails of thought run together.

"Ryon?" she says. He has never successfully snuck up on her.

"I'm here."

He reaches out until his fingers glance off her shoulder, to keep from colliding with her.

"Walk with me," Ryon says. And he takes her hand in his, feeling the sharp edges of her broken fingernails and the grit caked onto her palm. His hands are no different. "Have you had water?"

"Yes," she says. Her fingers intertwining with his. "Though the stream runs thin here. Did you notice?"

Ryon nods, forgetting she cannot see him.

"We're almost at the end and those fools turned their backs the moment they were about to stumble upon it." That same bitterness colours her words, turns them vicious. Her hand tightens in Ryon's.

"I think it's time to prepare for the possibility of no end, malishka," Ryon says now, too tired to pretend for her, though he wants to. He does not want her to feel the weight of this failure as well, not when she has fought so hard.

"No. It is ahead."

"We grow weaker each hour," Ryon says. "If there is an end, I fear we will not live long enough to reach it."

She pauses in her speech but not her stride. She pulls him onward. "If I must be the one to haul us all to its end, then I will. I am not surrendering."

And this is where they differ, for if Ryon must die in this Chasm, he is prepared to do so, solaced by the consolation that Dawsyn might be by his side. That he will see her in that other realm, both whole and repaired, and they will be together.

But Dawsyn will walk in her anger until death thwarts her. She will not grant herself the small mercy of taking those last breaths against his chest. She would rather face death wrapped in her rage.

"Malishka–"

But Dawsyn has suddenly halted in place. Ryon's shoulder glances off hers as he passes. "Dawsyn?"

"Do you feel that?"

He stills. Each hair on his neck rises to the disquiet in her voice. His senses awaken, reaching to detect whatever foul thing Dawsyn has already grown wise to. But he hears only the harsh breathing of their comrades, sees only the faint outline of Dawsyn's figure. Feels the pounding of his blood and little else. "I–"

"It is warmer here," she says firmly. It is not a question. "Do you feel it?"

Ryon tries to feel what she does and fails. His body, over-exerted, has run hot since they entered the Chasm and seldom has he rested long enough to cool. Even so, his blood is allied with the cold. He does not feel the cruelty in its touch. The air feels no warmer to him here.

He wonders if Dawsyn has become addled in fatigue. She walks on, her stride determined, leaving Ryon no room to question her. "Come on," she says, her voice inexplicably stronger, though she should be sapped of any strength.

"Dawsyn, go slow!" Ryon calls. "You'll fall."

"Watch the others," she says over her shoulder. "Be sure they don't fall behind."

"Dawsyn!" But she has disappeared from his sight. His eyes reach desperately to find that faded outline again, but he can't see. "Fuck," he grunts. He hears the others behind him, remaining close to Hector's torchlight. They will be safe enough together, walking their achingly slow trail.

"Fuck," he says again. He can no longer hear the clatter of her footsteps ahead. They have disappeared as quickly as she. *Damn it, girl.* Ryon moves ahead, cursing the boulders that his shins bounce off, the slanted rock his feet slide over. He plunges on, his eyes squinting out of sheer habit. *"Dawsyn!"* he calls, and his voice is fed back to him like a taunt. "Dawsyn?"

He hits a wall and feels along its jagged edge. It curves toward him – a corner. He follows it, feeling his swords clatter against the stone. The walls taper in dramatically, leaving little room to pass through. He turns sideways to keep his shoulders from glancing against the sharp edge of rock. This corner is severe. Ryon has the strange sensation of being turned in a circle. It collapses further inward until Ryon's breaths shorten, panic beginning to seize him. And then his hands find open space. The walls disappear on either side.

And then he sees her.

Not just her outline, nor the shadows that dart as she moves. He sees Dawsyn in full.

Ryon sees her as he would before first light, when the night loses its lustre and turns an anaemic grey – hazy and diluted. But even dimly lit, it is a clearer picture than he has seen in days.

She stands in the middle of the basin, looking down at her feet. The walls of the Chasm have opened to create a wider path here, and she looks around at the lifting gloom, as he does.

He steps out toward her, his eyes rising up the Chasm walls, finding that the light does not extend to its heights. The sky is no closer to them. They do not owe the lift of darkness to the sun.

Ryon wanders slowly to Dawsyn's side, his mouth agape.

Dawsyn's, however, is not. She studies, of all things, the ground. Her toe disturbs the fragmented rock there. "It is dry," she says, her eyes rising to his.

Ryon peers down. When had the stream run dry?

Dawsyn crouches, a strike of pain flashing across her expression, and places her hand to the ground. "And warm."

Ryon frowns, but when he kneels and places his fingers beside hers, they absorb the heat quickly, as though he'd laid a hand on a sun-soaked boulder.

He lifts his eyes to hers, and for the first time in an eternity, he can see the colour of her irises – an impossibly deep brown. They are not marred by the reflection of flames. He can see the dip in her cheek as her lips lift, he can see the fan of her eyelashes, the slope of her nose.

"We're almost at the end," she says, and a single tear catches in those eyelashes.

Ryon exhales in a gust, his chest releasing its dread and relenting to hope. He holds Dawsyn's face in his hands and lays his forehead to hers.

The warmth, the light. Surely, that is what it all leads to. An end.

"Almost there," he says, his smile matching hers.

Salem, Esra and Hector come first, squeezing themselves through the gap between walls and falling out into this opening. Like Ryon, it takes a moment for them to comprehend the changes in the Chasm, but soon their eyes grow wide. They look around for the source of light and fail to find it.

"Ry," Esra says. "Have we died?"

Tasheem and Rivdan break through the curve next, then Abertha behind them, clattering clumsily in outward.

"Fuck," Tash utters, her sword loosening in her palm.

They all look wretched. Ryon has never seen Salem look so gaunt. Even his rotund belly seems less inflated, his face ashen.

Esra, Hector and Abertha are no better. Hector casts a worried look at Esra, who leans heavily against his shoulder. Hector grasps the man's waist firmly to keep him from falling.

Tasheem and Rivdan are waning. He fears they are closer to death than they allude. Even if their wings were whole and unharmed, he doubts they could now garner the strength to summon them.

Even so, each of their faces change upon sight of this new Chasm – illuminated dimly by something unknown.

"Come," Dawsyn says. She grins over her shoulder at them through cracked lips and sunken cheeks. "Let us set eyes on the other side."

Tasheem laughs, eyes glistening. "This is it," she mutters. "It must be."

"Thank the Chasm," Hector exhales, wobbling under Esra's weight.

"Fuck the Chasm," Esra hisses. "Let's get out of here."

Dawsyn laughs hoarsely, her head turning up to the sky, eyes closed. Even smeared in black dust and leeched of any vibrancy, she still appears to Ryon a perfect creature. Surely the Mother never conspired to rid the world of her, when she took such precise care to sculpt her in the first place. Of course she would find her way out. Of course.

"Make haste," Ryon says. "I could use a solid meal."

Rivdan crows his assent, and they continue forward. Following Dawsyn's footsteps down the dry trail, and as they go the Chasm brightens and brightens. The dark finally chased back by the promise of escape.

Chapter Twenty-Six

Dawsyn keeps her eyes ahead, looking for the changes in direction, where the Chasm might open at any moment to reveal its end. The light turns to softer greys at first and then yellow. The air warms further and she laughs in quiet hysteria to feel sweat slip down her spine.

Upon the next corner, the light has taken on a bright orange hue, but still it does not reach the tops of the Chasm's walls. Specks of black float on the air. They fall slowly down before her face and settle on her shoulders. She lifts a palm and catches one – a small flake that disintegrates in her palm.

Dawsyn turns to face the rest. They too are covered in it. Their heads and shoulders are speckled. Hector raises a hand to inspect the flakes in his palm and he lifts knowing eyes to Dawsyn's.

Ash, he mouths to her.

"Where'd yeh s'pose this is comin' from?" Salem asks. "Up top?" The man lifts his gaze skyward.

But Dawsyn does not answer. She has locked eyes with Ryon and sees the fear she feels.

She turns and barrels on ahead, down the Chasm. If she stops a moment longer, she may not find the strength to move onward.

The air grows hot, then hotter still. The Chasm walls begin to reflect the sinister shifting of light she feared. Red and orange lick up its glistening obsidian surface. The ash swirls in whorls overhead.

The Chasm no longer sings or whispers to her. It does not muddle her senses with its ratcheting echoes. Now, it roars. It starts as an exhale, then builds into the moan of some deep earth-dwelling beast. The farther she creeps, the louder it becomes. There is a corner ahead. It glows red and hot in the distance. She can see the reflections dancing up the walls.

"Dawsyn!"

She hears, but does not heed. She is too lost in the growing noise, the intensifying heat, the drum of her heartbeat.

No, she thinks, her feet gathering momentum toward this last turn. *No*. For she knows the gate to paradise does not glow red. It does not lick her skin with a burning tongue.

She coughs and squints her eyes against the sting of smoke, her pulse hammering, her mind still gripping false promises.

She hurls herself around the narrow corner and there she finds it, almost topples into it.

The end.

Around the corner, there is no path. It falls away, and Dawsyn's feet catch on the precipice of its cliff. Here, her eyes squint, but this time it is not darkness that impedes her. It is the near-unbearable heat. The burning brightness of light.

"Mother above," Dawsyn mutters shakily.

A clamour comes from behind, and she turns just in time to ward off the crush of the others, lest they push her over the edge. "Stop!" she shouts to them, holding up her hands.

But she needn't bother. They have all frozen in their spots, having rounded that last corner. They stand stock still, gasping in awe at the sight beyond Dawsyn – at the end of the Chasm.

A lake resides fathoms below. It stretches in a perfect circle, the length of which Dawsyn would not hasten to guess. She can just barely see the walls on the opposing side, far in the distance.

But it is not a lake of water, or ice. It is a lake of fire. The molten rock churns and bubbles. Waves of red and golden fire collide and emit a terrible roar. Fragments of stone fall from the rock face and it sends a cloud of smoke and ash into the air. It cloys in the back of Dawsyn's throat.

This is the end of the Chasm.

Not a green valley, untouched and unclaimed.

Not the collision of the Chasm walls, cruelly blockading their freedom.

No. The end of the Chasm is hell. It is the fires of the underworld.

"Mother," Dawsyn hears and it is Tasheem who utters it, her hands hitting the earth before her, finally succumbing. "Mother… *please!*"

"It can't be…" Esra says, and his voice is a whisper of what it was, the Chasm having stolen his verbosity, his very spirit. "No."

"For nothing," Hector says, sinking to his knees. "Was all of it... for nothing?" It seems he asks the sky. "WAS ALL OF IT FOR NOTHING?" Then he is howling.

Every one of them sinks to the ground. They let their legs give way, having carried them far enough. They surrender there, at the path's end, having travelled the length of it only to find a slower death.

To follow Dawsyn.

Her fault. Her fault.

Ryon lowers to his haunches, his thighs shaking. And then his fist beats against the ground. He roars and turns to launch his fist into the rockface, every muscle in his arm wired in tension. "FUCK!" he shouts, loud enough to crack Dawsyn's bones.

She covers her ears. Mutes sound. She sees and hears her friends fall apart, but it doesn't compare to her own insular destruction.

And there is a justice in that – that she should suffer most.

She hears her breaths. They are impossibly heavy, uneven. She feels the blood pulsing in her eardrums. She feels the weak tendrils of iskra singing its own requiem. She sees plainly that she has led every single one of these good people to their death.

This cannot be it. They did not survive all they have only to arrive here.

She did not leave the Ledge and escape the slopes.

Salem did not lose his home and Esra his flesh.

Tasheem and Rivdan did not abandon their kind.

Ryon did not put his faith in her, again and again.

Baltisse did not die.

She did not fall in love with a Glacian, just for it all to end here.

And then she hears it once more, the silky voice tempting her into this pit of fire.

Dealt are ends
Of pain or peace
Of withered cries
Of sweet release.
Strangled pleas
Or tender falls.
Inside our breast
Amid our walls.

The voices are louder here. They do not seem to exist within her this time, but all around. It fills the bottomless cavern, and when Dawsyn turns her head, it is to find the others silent and alert. Their eyes dart warily. They all hear it too.

Make your soul unto itself;
break the bone and cure,
For when you lie within the mouth,
The cost will be no fewer.

The roar of the voice grows until it is unbearable. Dawsyn claps her palms over her ears and closes her eyes.

Seal your eyes and sleep,
Still your lips, cease your breath;
Lie where sorrow dares not be,
Free from hands of death.

Dawsyn groans, sinking to the ground at the edge of the path. And before her erupts a sight to cower a titan. It ignites a fear so deep she cannot breathe. She cannot blink.

A hawk rises from the molten lake. Its colossal wings aflame.

Ash chokes Dawsyn, chokes them all. The hawk flaps its mighty wings, rising before them. It fills the enormous cavern, sending waves of heat to burn their skin with each downward swoop.

Yerdos, Dawsyn thinks.

Her limbs do not cooperate. She tries and fails to get her feet beneath her. She hastens away from the edge, pushing her heels frantically against the earth. An arm locks over her chest and hauls her backward.

Don't go, says the voice. And once more, Dawsyn recoils from the volume, clutching her ears. But it is more discernible now. It is not the whisper of the Dyvolsh infection. This voice is pitched. Female. The words curl lasciviously. Goadingly.

You have only just arrived.

The hawk's beak does not move and yet it seems to Dawsyn that it is the creature that speaks to them, toys with them. Its great beady eyes glint menacingly, alight with predatory lust and something other... something far more human.

"Yerdos," she utters aloud.

In the flesh. Her wings swoop forward once more and heat thrusts them all backward. Dawsyn brings her forearm up to shield her face.

And you are Moroz, Yerdos says now, her voice rebounding. *Come to find me.*

"Moroz?" Dawsyn murmurs, confused.

I feel the cold within you. She continues, the words growing louder, more vicious. *You bring its creatures to do your bidding.*

Dawsyn's eyes dart to Ryon, then to Tasheem and Rivdan, who stare on in horror. She suddenly recalls Rivdan's story.

"No," Dawsyn says once more, shaking her head frantically, emphatically. Though even as she says it, the iskra within her wearily rallies in the presence of a familiar foe.

I smell it, Yerdos says. *You carry its foul breath.*

"I am not Moroz!" Dawsyn calls, though her voice is far from sturdy. She cannot seem to give it volume.

It takes many forms, Yerdos continues. *The cold is alive and well. It takes and withers everywhere it goes and the Mother lets it. She lets it roam freely. And I have been cast into these depths.*

With each word, the temperature rises. It scolds Dawsyn's cheeks and burns her eyes. She can hardly keep them open.

The Mother lets Moroz choke the life from this mountain. She punishes me!

Yerdos' voice remains otherworldly, but there is a snarl of human anguish tangled in it. A deep, dark bitterness.

Dawsyn hears frantic scuffling behind her and turns to see Abertha retreating hastily on her hands and knees.

The hawk shrieks, the sound reaching Dawsyn's marrow, a seismic wave crashing through her. A terrible quake sounds above them – the slow splintering of stone – and rock rains down. Boulder-sized pieces crash onto the path, blocking them in.

There is no leaving now you are here, Yerdos says.

Abertha pants wildly. A rock the size of her torso lies before her, an inch from her nose. She scurries backward into Rivdan.

You've come so far to find me. To vanquish me. There is nowhere to run.

"We do not come to vanquish you!" Ryon shouts.

But the hawk releases a gust of smoke from its beak, and they all bury their faces from it, coughing into the dirt.

I will take what chance our Mother offers me, Yerdos says now, her intensity growing. *I've long prayed to meet you in the battlefield again. Come, Moroz.*

The enormous hawk rises. It extends its wing. From the tips of its feathers, fiery ropes unravel, whipping toward Dawsyn and the others.

"Watch out!" Dawsyn shouts as the ropes strike. She rolls to the side, crashing into Ryon. But no pain comes. The ropes do not scorch her. When she looks up, she sees they no longer burn red. They attach themselves to the precipice.

A great wooden bridge has appeared. It stretches across the enormous pit and the fire it is made of slowly extinguishes. It creeps inward, summoned backward toward the creature that wielded it.

A creature once a hawk, who now takes the form of a human.

A woman stands in the middle of the bridge, and she glows every bit as brightly as the hawk did. Her hands are alight with the fire she collects. It courses across the wooden struts of the bridge and back into her palms, until it is gone altogether.

I can wage this war in the form of the humans, if that is your preference, Moroz, Yerdos says. Her voice still shakes the very walls. *Come.*

She speaks to you, Dawsyn thinks. "I am not Moroz!" Desperation leaks into her voice. "I want no fight with you!"

But Yerdos only laughs, and it sizzles against Dawsyn's skin.

"What do we do?" Hector mutters, again and again. "What do we do?"

"Don't move!" Ryon orders. Abertha has scrambled to her feet again, tears streaming down her face. "Stay down."

"We cannot fight it, brother," Rivdan says, and he does not try to keep the fear from his voice.

"Saint Yerdos," Salem whispers. Dawsyn can hear his gruff voice, whispering to himself. "It is her."

But the woman on the bridge no longer resembles a saint. She appears, from this distance, just a woman. She paces back and forth, her hands clenching. And though her hair glows fiery red and she moves with undue grace, she brings to mind an image Dawsyn has long since forgotten.

An image of Briar Sabar, stalking before their cabin on the Ledge, impatient for Dawsyn and Maya to return.

Dawsyn sees her guardian, her *mother* once more: red-faced, hands clenching, pacing with predatory deliberation. Dawsyn and Maya had been due back in the cabin by nightfall and the sun had retreated over the Face.

"Get inside," she had said without further preamble. *"And do not bother with excuses. One can only tease the thread of a woman so thin. You do not want to see me frayed."*

Yerdos looks like a woman frayed.

A vengeful mage, Esra had called her. Taken from her home by a king who slayed her clan and dragged her back to his castle. *One can only tease the thread of a woman so thin.*

Dawsyn rises unsteadily.

"Dawsyn! Stay down," Ryon grunts, pulling on her wrist.

But, unbearably, Dawsyn slips his grasp.

"What are you *doing?*"

Dawsyn does not quite know. She does not take her eyes from Yerdos' form. "I... I must go to her."

"Are you mad?" Tasheem splutters, choking on smoke. "Dawsyn, no!"

Dawsyn's eyes water with the intensity of the heat. Her throat stings with each inhalation, but she draws breath to say what she must. "We've reached the end," she tells them all, her eyes locking with Ryon's. They implore her to stop. Beg her. "And there is no way out," her eyes turn to the sky, so impossibly high above them. "And I've led you all here," she takes in another rattling breath, and it is filled with the weight of regret. "And if we are all to die, better I make our souls right with this Saint before we meet the Mother."

Before they can stop her or drag her back, Dawsyn hauls her ax over her shoulder, twists the handle in her palm, then closes her eyes and steps onto the bridge. A barricade tangles up the rock behind her the second her feet are free of the precipice. It is made of the same fiery rope Yerdos used to make the bridge.

Beyond the roar of flame and spitting magma, she hears Ryon bellow into the void. "Don't you dare fucking die, Dawsyn! *Do you hear me?*"

But this time, she cannot bring herself to promise safe return.

"I'll leave you my heart," she says. But the words are whispers swallowed in smoke, and they are left behind her, unheard.

Chapter Twenty-Seven

Yerdos awaits her, and the closer Dawsyn comes, the less afraid she feels.

Perhaps it is that she knows she will die, whether it be by the hands of this saint, or the Chasm she created. Her mind parts from the fear that bids her to run and she relents to whatever conclusion comes now.

She has walked all she can. Fought all she could.

And though vicious swirls of hatred and anger deep inside still leak into her mind like poison, she will not fight anymore.

She was wrong.

She has failed.

She will succumb now.

Dawsyn's hand around the ax handle is limp. She only holds it to feel something familiar. She keeps her eyes on the woman of fire. The mage. The saint. The hawk.

She is beautiful. And terrible.

Her auburn hair matches the flecks of her cheeks, her elegant neck slopes gently to her collarbone, her wild eyes are framed in pale lashes. Her black teeth are bared and her palms smoulder with the heat of her wrath. But, beneath the anger, she appears a young woman not long after reaching maturity.

"Moroz," she says to Dawsyn and this time her voice does not echo around the chamber. It simply falls from her lips.

"I am not Moroz," Dawsyn says again, lifting her chin just slightly. "I am Dawsyn Sabar. And I have not come to kill you."

Yerdos smiles, but it is not the smile of the wicked toying with its plaything. It is a veneer that conceals uncertainty. "There is no hiding from me, Moroz. I can feel you."

Dawsyn feels the iskra roil inside her, weak and afraid.

"It is the cold you can feel," Dawsyn says. "Not Moroz."

"The very same." The words hiss into the air, sizzle into specks of ash. "One and the same." She holds her palm up toward Dawsyn, fire dancing over the skin. "Ready yourself, Moroz. Let us see how the frost fares here."

She waits for Dawsyn to lift her own palm. She wants to defeat Moroz as an equal.

But Moroz is not here.

Moroz is no one.

The cold is not alive.

Dawsyn takes her last look at the woman named Yerdos. A woman turned slave turned saint. She closes her eyes. She does not look into the depths of herself to find the iskra. She does not try to call it to her palms. Instead, she reaches into the corners of her mind. She tries to find the faint speck of glowing light, as Baltisse taught her to.

She thinks of Ryon's hands, guiding her over the terrain. She thinks of his lips against hers, the sweet eclipse of her thoughts when she feels his breath against her neck. She thinks of his lips parting to reveal a smile. A smile the dark tried to deny her.

And there she finds it – that flickering spark. It strengthens with each thought, reignited by every stroke of remembrance. She feeds it more images, things she has memorised and safely guarded: the lines of his palms, the shape of his brow, the feel of his fingers laced with hers. The beat of his heart beneath her ear. She brings it all to mind. And knows that if Yerdos fells her where she stands, at least she will leave this world filled with thoughts of its greatest creation.

Dawsyn opens her eyes to the sensation of mage light, trickling down her arm. It is thin, weedy, but tangible. It collects in her palm.

She grips it tightly, lest it retreat, and then locks her gaze with Yerdos.

"Igniss," Dawsyn says, and a small flame appears.

It flickers calmly atop her palm, as small and wonderful as the first time she conjured it. Useless in battle, pitiful beside Yerdos' molten lake, but still beautiful.

Yerdos' eyes widen. They lose the edge of madness. She stares at the flame in Dawsyn's hand and her lips fall back over her exposed teeth. "Mage light?" she asks, almost whispers.

Dawsyn exhales, feeling the pull of her lungs as it strives for oxygen amongst the sulfuric air. Still, she manages to nod. "Yes."

Yerdos' own palm falls slowly, finally lowering to her side, where the fire recedes. "You are mage-born," she murmurs. Her expression turns suddenly wistful. She watches the flame dance on Dawsyn's hand as though it were something precious.

"I am," Dawsyn breathes, and she allows the mage fire to sputter out in her palm. She cannot hold it anymore. She is so very tired.

"As was I," Yerdos says. Her eyes turn distant. She does not seem to notice the heat that scolds Dawsyn. "I was born of a clan on the mountain."

Dawsyn nods. She feels grief exude from Yerdos in waves. "I know."

"My sisters. My family," she continues. "We protected the mountain. And it guarded us. Provided for us."

Dawsyn watches her carefully. "Kladerstaff," she says. "He captured you?"

Yerdos closes her eyes. Tears fall down her cheeks and suddenly she is nothing but another soul who suffered and fought and lost. She is neither mage, nor saint, nor hawk. She is a woman, trapped in the throes of her own rage and sorrow, unable to break free of it. "His guards slit their throats as they slept," she says. "I was a child. Too weak to stop them."

"A... child?" Dawsyn hesitates to ask. Even now, she looks young. Too young.

"Ten and five," she says. "Ten and five."

Fifteen, Dawsyn thinks. *A girl.*

"I vowed to my dead that I would kill every last soul in the valley. I swore I would rid this earth of those that take and take and leave nothing. And the Mother..."

Yerdos pauses. Her eyes open. "The Mother tried to take me. I refused."

"You went back to your mountain," Dawsyn says for her. "You protected it."

"And the Mother sent Moroz," Yerdos answers, anger returning to her tenor. "And she smothered everything, suffocated it all – all but the mage-born."

Dawsyn hesitates. "The mage-born?"

"Kladerstaff could not bleed them all," Yerdos says, her gaze far away, hundreds of years removed from this place. "He could not find them all."

"There was still a clan on the mountain," Dawsyn says, realisation dawning. "The mages, they originated on the mountain."

"And Moroz chased them into the valley. Moroz took them from our mountain. Just as I had been taken."

Dawsyn breathes. She remembers Baltisse telling her of the mages that still lived.

"Are you the last mage in Terrsaw?"

Baltisse rolled her eyes. "No. But you will not find the others."

"Why?"

"They do not want to be found."

"We knew the mountain's secrets and it flourished as we flourished," Yerdos continues. "We bled into its streams and absorbed the energy from its soil. We travelled the ridges and caves and it cradled us. We took and it took. We gave and it gave."

Dawsyn watches Yerdos' face vacillate between hatred and yearning, all at once young and ancient. "Kladerstaff took you from your home," she says carefully, gently. "And then Moroz took your home from you."

Yerdos' eyes turn molten, as Baltisse's once had, as lethal and scorched as the pit below. And in them, Dawsyn can no longer see a great creature of brimstone, nor an ancient saint of legend. She sees a woman burning.

She sees her grandmother, bitterness etched in her brow, smothering anything soft.

She sees Briar, lost in grief and pitching herself into its depths.

She sees Baltisse. *Baltisse.* Incinerated by guilt, slowly boiling from within.

And finally, Dawsyn sees herself, cloistering into a pit of rage that she made her own, unable to claw her way out.

Dawsyn sees a woman forged in anger, in a wrath vehement enough to split a mountain in two.

"Moroz endures still," Yerdos says. "And the Mother does *nothing.*" This last word turns vicious. It reverberates around the cavern and pounds in Dawsyn's blood.

But Dawsyn hears again that old mantra, the one that kept her among the living in a place meant for the dead. The words her grandmother passed to Briar, who then passed them on to her, and it saw her through the very worst Moroz could brandish.

"The cold is not alive."

Yerdos' churning eyes land squarely on hers and Dawsyn can feel the heat of their touch. Her lip curls back. "Moroz endures."

"Moroz endures," Dawsyn agrees, nodding her head slowly, carefully. Her heart breaks for this woman, trapped for an eternity in a hell of her own making. "But the cold does not live. It does not breathe, or move, or hold a sword," she urges. "It… it does not *love*." The words come hoarsely, with the last vestiges of her breath. "And so it cannot die."

Yerdos' chin quivers, her eyes closing again. "No."

"The earth… she gives and takes in equal measure," Dawsyn continues, speaking words of a friend she would die to see again. "Every season comes to a close."

Yerdos cries then, but it is not a terrible shriek this time. The sound is horribly human, a thousand times more painful. It is broken, and cracked, and utterly pitiful. Her lips part around the whimper and her shoulders sag. She bends under every ounce of sorrow she holds.

And as though she stood before Dawsyn herself, Baltisse's voice rings through her mind once more. It cuts through the boil of lava and the hiss of smoke. It takes her back to a forest where an edelweiss flower settles into Baltisse's touch. *"Sometimes you need to reteach a thing its loveliness."*

Dawsyn wonders if a creature such as Yerdos can be taught. "No one seeks to harm you anymore," she whispers, though her body trembles with fear. "Not even Moroz."

Yerdos shakes her head, and her long wisps of red hair catch alight, whipping smoke through the air, but it is a half-hearted movement. She holds her hands to her chest as though she seeks to rip out her own heart.

"You do not need to stay here," Dawsyn tells her.

But Yerdos shakes her head again. She breathes heavily, her shoulders rising and falling. There is a long silence, and then she says, "As long as Moroz remains, I burn."

Dawsyn knows there is nothing more than can be said to Yerdos the Saint, so embroiled in her own animus.

"You are not Moroz," Yerdos says now, her eyes searching Dawsyn's body.

"No." Dawsyn shakes her head. Her legs are moments from giving way.

"Yet you seek me," she says, then waits, a question in her eyes.

Dawsyn tries to swallow. Fails. "No. We only sought an end to the Chasm," Dawsyn says. "Another side."

Yerdos' eyebrows lift. "No end lies this way."

Dawsyn's chest deflates and her legs do give way then, sinking to the scalded wood of the bridge. Yerdos only watches her, a deep curiosity changing her face. "You seek an end." She looks suggestively to the fiery pit below, then back to Dawsyn.

"No," Dawsyn murmurs, the heat colliding with her, overwhelming her. There is little air to breathe. "No, not yet."

"Then return to our mountain," Yerdos says. "And reclaim it. You are mage-born."

Dawsyn catches herself on her palms as she falls forward. "I am Ledge-born," she corrects. Her eyes closing against the sting.

"What is your name?" Dawsyn hears. Someone bends over her; she can feel the heat of their breath.

"Dawsyn Sabar," she utters, though she cannot feel her lips move.

"Return to the mountain, Dawsyn Sabar. Seek a different path."

And then Dawsyn feels the impossible collapse of her being as she is reduced to a slither, to nothing at all.

She looks her last at the Chasm, and then she disappears.

Chapter Twenty-Eight

An animal pulled a cart toward her, its driver waving erratically, gesturing for Yennes to move from its path. She jumped aside and collided with Baltisse, who grabbed her shoulders and guided her onto the cobblestones.

"Stay off the road, sweet," Baltisse ordered. It was one of many orders she had uttered since their arrival in this bizarre settlement. Pitched roofs surrounded them, some thatched and some made of tile or timber. The narrow lanes were filled with dust as the wagons and carts trundled by, their drivers spitting and cursing, or else tipping their caps as they passed. There were children everywhere. Mothers with babies riding in slings. Stalls filled with food and goods set up on every corner.

Everywhere, people shouted. Sometimes they called to her. "Pickled cabbage!" or "Stewed goat!" followed by "Make haste, miss, they'll be gone within the hour!"

It muddled her, had her spinning in all directions. Every noise made her jump, made her quail.

Baltisse took her arm, sighing in a long-suffering way, and led her around a puddle of what Yennes figured was human muck. "...like leading a fawn, jumping out of her skin." Baltisse then pulled her to a halt as murky water dropped from above, splattering on the stones before them. Yennes looked up to see a paunchy woman hanging out of her window holding a bucket. "Watch it!" the woman shouted, as though Yennes was intersecting the water's path.

"Mother above," Yennes muttered, keeping her eyes skyward as they continued. "What is this place?"

"This is the Mecca," Baltisse answered. "It is as close to the palace as you ought to come."

Yennes almost walked headlong into a crate of birds who squawked indignantly as she skirted them. "Why did you bring me here?"

"Because it seems you need your fill of all Terrsaw has to offer, despite my better judgement," she said, then nodded to where a statue loomed high over the rooftops on the right. "We're here as tourists."

Baltisse led her down one alley and the next. The paths became cleaner here, less haphazard and mired road dust. The people were swathed in a wider variety of colour too. They met in quick conversation with one another and parted smiling. Their arms were laden with more food than seemed possible, baskets of breads and produce. There were musicians that played strange instruments and doors adorned with signs she could not read. Yennes marvelled at it all.

Ahead, a large stone structure stood. It was remarkably carved into the shape of two people. The first seemed to be the image of a man, though his face was worn and cracked. There was a crown atop his head and a staff in his mighty hand. Beside him was the kneeling form of a woman. Her hands rested benignly on her thighs, her posture deferential, and she stared at the King with almost religious zeal. Even in stone, the woman's eyes showed a depth of feeling. Yennes tilted her head and looked at the structure in wonder. She thought that whoever this woman was, she must have been in love.

"Who were they?" Yennes asked as they approached. She had never seen something so big carved into something so beautiful.

"King Kladerstaff," Baltisse said, in a voice at odds with Yennes' regard, "and his wife... Queen Yerdos."

Yennes frowned slightly, looking at the woman named Yerdos. "But she is not crowned?"

"No," Baltisse mumbled. "History is often forgetful."

"She was beautiful." There was no denying the fact. The woman's hair was wild yet fell in hypnotising waves down her back. "She must have loved him."

"It depends on your perspective. Some say she kneels before her King, marvelling at him..."

Yennes turned to look at the mage, frowned, then turned back to the monument. "She *does* kneel before him. What could others possibly say?"

Baltisse smiled sadly. Then she pulled Yennes around the monument, until they were looking over Yerdos' stone shoulder, seeing what she saw.

"Some say it is not a marvelling we see in her eyes but a longing for something lost."

From this angle, Yerdos' eyes seemed to look not *at* King Kladerstaff, but past him. They appeared aligned with the mountain in the distance, its height disappearing into deep cloud cover. Suddenly the young queen's lips did not seem parted in awe, but in sorrow. Her eyes did not glimmer in reverence, but in heartbreak.

"She was a mage, before she was a queen," Baltisse said, so quietly that Yennes looked about them, as though she might find onlookers lurking by their shoulders. "And she did not fare well as a royal. Power is alluring, Yennes. Those leading a kingdom will covet it, try to use it. Magic like ours ought to stay hidden so that it might remain our own."

Yennes couldn't help but glance back at the monument as they walked away, and once more she saw a woman desperately in love with a man.

It made her blanch.

In a tavern tucked away by the town square, Baltisse led Yennes to a table. She bought her food and water and grinned at the way Yennes' face lit up. "You are a strange sight to behold," she told the Ledge woman. "It's only lamb."

Yennes shoved the food between her teeth and paid the mage no mind. No food had ever tasted so good, arriving on platters as though she had summoned it from the air.

She drained her cup, then looked around for more. "What is it they drink?" she asked abruptly, pointing to the tall tankards of men milling about the tables.

Baltisse's eyes narrowed. "Nothing you ought to try."

Yennes sat back in her chair, compliant. Then something sloshed into her lap and forearms settled on her shoulders as someone heavy leant over her from behind. "Never mind yer matron," the rough voice growled, the heat of his breath cloying in her ear. "Open wide, lass. Have a sip." He held a tankard to her lips.

Her muscles coiled, ready to grasp the back of the man's neck and pull his forehead down to crack against the table. Her body screamed at her to act. But her mind froze. Her lips trembled. She stiffened beneath his weight rather than fight it off.

The tankard came to her lips and a bitter, warm liquid filled her mouth.

"No," Baltisse said icily. And suddenly, the weight was gone. Yennes fumbled for the tankard as the man seized on the floor, flailing wildly, then went limp.

The mage's eyes churned.

"What 'appened to 'im?" another patron asked, having been knocked to the side as the great lout fell.

"Drunk," Baltisse said, blinking innocently.

But the patron clearly saw in her eyes what Yennes could see – that ethereal glow, the blossoming gold. He turned back to his party quickly without enquiring further. Smart man.

Yennes considered the unconscious man a moment longer, and then the tankard he'd left her. It was amber, filmy and pungent. She brought the cup hesitantly to her lips and drank. It wasn't unpleasant. In fact, it coated her tongue and throat in a satisfying way. "What *is* this?"

Baltisse looked foreboding. "As I said," she answered dryly. "Nothing you ought to try."

"You brought me here to experience all that Terrsaw has to offer, did you not?"

"There is nothing at the bottom of these mugs that will help you see clearly." Baltisse stood abruptly. "Come. We'll take our leave whilst your legs are still beneath you."

But Yennes had begun to feel a pleasant buzzing in her mind. It ousted the echo of the voices. She looked about the tavern, at the lazy smiles and the free-flowing liquid that exchanged hands with a strange ease. "I wish to stay," she told the mage.

Baltisse muttered something beneath her breath, and it sounded like a curse.

Within the hour, Yennes had consumed several servings of the ale – lager, the patrons called it. One man in particular seemed intent on delivering fresh mugs to her table whenever she ran low.

With the arrival of Yennes' fourth drink, Baltisse stood. "I'm leaving. You should join me." She was a beacon for attention with her obvious beauty. It seemed she could no longer suffer the advances of every male in the dank room. "Last chance," she told Yennes, donning her shawl.

"Why not stay?" Yennes slurred. Words seemed harder to string together.

"Because this is not a place for women to linger beyond nightfall," she said. "Come with me, Yennes. Heed the warning. No good awaits you in these dark corners."

But Yennes had never felt more welcomed. "I won't go back to that bay."

"Then I'll await you outside," Baltisse said. "Until you've had your fill."

Yennes laughed. How could she ever hope to have her fill? How could the bay ever bring her the lightness she felt now? She never wanted to see or hear the ocean again. And the Ledge... Soon it would feel like a nightmare, easy to disregard. "Do not await me," she said, lifting her lager to salute Baltisse. "This is where we part ways."

"Yen—"

"I do not wish to return with you, Baltisse," Yennes said, her voice reminiscent of her former self – fierce and unyielding, albeit slurred. "I thank you for your help."

Baltisse shook her head to the ceiling, but seemed to decide against arguing. "You will find yourself in need of me," she warned, placing a silver ring on the table. It was thick-banded and marred by divots, holding a simple, unimpressive onyx stone. "This will help you trace your way back."

Yennes felt a lick of resentment unfurl up her spine. It made her sit taller. "I survived a lifetime on the Ledge and a shorter one in Glacia," she said icily, her knuckles straining against her hold on the mug. "I do not need your help to survive a kingdom that sits on its hands."

Baltisse nodded. "Then good luck to you, Yennes. I truly hope it's everything you wish it to be." Then, she left.

Soon after, Yennes was accompanied by a group of three men who seemed intent on competing for her attention. The drink had replenished her confidence, removed the incessant anxieties that plagued her so. She felt renewed. The lager was becoming easier to swallow.

One of the men at her table was hollering his tales, though Yennes hadn't kept track.

"And then I said to 'em, 'Yeh've lost yer bleedin' mind! I didn't steal no horse! Tha' one there's mine!' And – I swear to the Mother this be the truth – the guard looked me in the eye an' said, 'That's a donkey yeh rode in on, and it belongs to Mrs Habberdish!'"

The men all roared with laughter and Yennes grinned like a fool.

"Did they lock you up in the keep?" one of the lads asked – a handsome one. His eyes kept skirting back to Yennes, slipping to the opened buttons of her blouse.

"Aye, just the night." The storyteller slapped the table dramatically. "That's when I heard all tha' chatter, yeh know? 'Bout the Queen Consort. The guards kept blitherin' on 'bout how she's taken ill."

"Queen Cressida?" another asked, joining the group. "I heard the very same just this morn'. The smithy's wife says she's got some kind of fever that won't break. Infection maybe. Says the word is Queen Alvira sent for every healer in the kingdom!"

"Aye," the donkey-thief nodded. "She'll be dead by week's end, I'd wager, the way them guards were talkin'."

"Good riddance to her," the handsome one said, his eyes locked with Yennes. "Perhaps we'd all be saved from having to bow our heads to that sneering face. I'd much rather kneel to a pretty one." He took a sip of drink, watching Yennes over the tankard's rim.

Yennes smiled back.

"I don't disagree. That woman's been lookin' down 'er nose at the likes o' workin' folk fer too long."

Yennes tilted her head to the side, her eyes seeing four hands instead of two. She chuffed, slightly hysterically. "Your hands don't look like those of a working man's." She tapped the storyteller's knuckles with her fingers. Indeed, his hands were unmarked by any measure of labour Yennes had ever seen. There was a ring around his second finger on his left hand. "Is it your wife who carries out the chores whilst you steal donkeys and tell your tales?"

The other men guffawed, surprise lifting their eyebrows.

But the lout with the smooth hands looked at her with an ugly smile. "Why?" he said. "Yeh lookin' fer a husband?

Yennes rolled her eyes and sighed dramatically. "Only a man could turn an insult into an invitation."

"An invitation, ay?" said the man darkly, but the rising colour of his cheeks detracted from the malice, and in her uninhibited state, Yennes was unafraid. He was just another man, incensed by the gall of truthful women. "I ain't got a lick o' interest in a virgin. Yer cunt's likely as uptight as yer countenance. Yeh couldn't take me." He turned from her, a sneer covering his indignity.

Yennes let loose a bark of laughter. It wasn't true mirth, but drunken, unfettered incredulity. How cruel fate was to have her survive the unimaginable and be accused of frigidity. Yennes met the man's ruddy complexion with a glare of her own. His face swam before her. "Even if you'd summoned a god to bless you with something to impress me, I promise you, that cock of yours would never make measure."

As the men laughed raucously and the lout turned puce, Yennes drained the rest of her cup, then she swung her legs from the bar stool and stood. She said nothing more to the men, but she stopped to look over her shoulder at the handsome one. She had the pleasure of watching a blush creep up his neck before she turned away.

It only took moments for Yennes to find herself pressed against a badly papered wall in a badly lit hallway. The back of the tavern was quieter, but she was still surrounded by the cacophony of clinking and laughing and singing. She found that she liked the volume of it – so much louder than any sound within her mind.

Lips ran over her neck, then down to her collarbone. Hands gripped her waist tightly, then ventured to her bodice. Practiced fingers pulled at the strings that held it taut, then tugged it downward until her bosom was free of it, encased only by the borrowed blouse of thin, flimsy make. A hand took the weight of her breast, kneading it pleasantly. She moaned.

She could not see the man, could no longer remember what his face looked like. It was difficult to remember how she'd found herself here, in this corner. But the lips pressing to her flesh were warm, the touches were pleasing. Yennes didn't much care to stop. She found she could easily replace the smells and touches with the memory of another.

"*God,*" the man groaned, pressing his hips into hers and grinding them. She could feel the extent of his arousal pressing against her and she arched her back slightly.

"Touch me."

He obeyed enthusiastically, slipping his hands between their stomachs and downward until he could find the split in her skirts. He pushed them aside and brought his fingers to her thighs. "You gonna repay me?" he asked, caressing closer to her sex, where all her nerve endings seemed focussed, waiting.

Yennes' vision was uneven, her hearing dulled. She did not know if she'd answered him, only that his fingers were suddenly on her, making gentle circles, and her breaths were coming heavier. Without a mind to, she brought her leg up to rest on his hip, and felt his fingers sink inside her. "More," she told him, letting her fingernails bite into his shoulders.

His lips were everywhere. She could not keep track of them, could barely feel them. She let him take of her what he wanted, so long as he kept touching her, kept making her feel. When he wrenched the seam of her blouse over the peak of her breast she welcomed his mouth, not caring that someone might interrupt them.

The volts of pleasure coursing through her were quickening, consuming her. She bit her lip to keep from groaning. She chased its inevitable combustion, moving her hips against his hand. "Fuck," he growled against her flesh, hastening the precise strokes with which he coaxed her nerve endings, bringing them to the edge of bliss. "That's it," he panted in her ear, pressing his lips to her neck. "You taste divine."

Yennes' eyes snapped open. *Divine,* she heard in her mind. It echoed back to her again and again, in the voice of another.

She halted in her movements, her hips stilling against the wall. Her lips trembled.

She felt suddenly too hot. There was not enough air to breathe. Her body was trapped between a man she did not recognise and the wall behind her and it made her bones scream, made her lungs ache. "Get off me," she expelled on a breath. The words came broken, shaky.

The man kept moving, unperturbed by the change in atmosphere. Could he not feel how the air had been sucked from the room? "Get off me!" she said again, louder now, panicked.

His hand stilled. His face came before hers. It was difficult to make out. His features distorted. "*What?*"

"Let me go," she panted. She sucked at air that did not find her lungs. "Please. Stop."

His hands left her completely. She felt herself fall to the floor, her knees bouncing off the hardwood on impact, but if there was pain, she was spared of its bloom. There was already pain within. It had her lungs in a vice.

Yennes heard the enraged cursing of the man above her and she held up a hand to ward him off. But the man only muttered some more, then meandered away, swaying as he went.

Later, she would count herself lucky he hadn't stayed.

The liquor was finally overcoming her. A wave of sudden nausea impeded every other sense, and she stumbled for the back door behind her, opening it in time to heave onto the threshold.

Cool air hit her face. It lifted the coils of hair away from her cheeks and she gulped it in.

"Mother above," she panted, tears coursing down her cheeks. "Mercy."

CHAPTER TWENTY-NINE

Dawsyn's head snaps back against the ground. The abrupt unfolding of her body is not enough warning to catch her fall. The breath that had been squeezed from her lungs suddenly returns, and it hurts to have them filled again.

She should feel splintered. Pain ought to blossom at every imaginable site. Her shoulder, punctured and untendered, should be pulsing an incessant beat. Her head should be swimming, her throat scorched, her feet battered and bruised by relentless travel.

She should be dead.

The lack of appropriate pain certainly suggests she is. But for the small ache at the back of her skull and the burn of new breath, she feels whole.

She feels... cold. Dawsyn opens her eyes.

Familiar trees tower above her, their branches dappling what little light the sky offers. Pine trees. Their smell strikes her and for a moment she thinks she is on the Ledge.

Dawsyn sits abruptly.

Her breath mists between her parted lips. She sits upon ground that gives and looks down to find herself seated in a snow drift. It slopes away before her, disappearing downward among the dispersed trunks. Not the Ledge, then. But the mountain.

Return to the mountain, Yerdos had said and then laid a burning hand to her cheek. Dawsyn still feels it now, the heat from Yerdos' touch. She lays her own palm against her jaw and is surprised to feel a keen sting.

At the acknowledgment of pain comes the unfurling of mage light in her mind, the burgeoning of iskra in her core. It stretches like a creature departing its cave.

She frowns, then turns her steady palm to her face and stares at it. The iskra coats it in its intricate filigree of frost.

She is out of the Chasm.

"Ryon?" she calls. She needs to get her feet beneath her. Already she can feel the cold seeping through her clothes to her backside. "*Ryon!*" she shouts the name, and it does not echo. The word is swallowed by the sky, as it should be.

Yerdos saved them. She healed them. She replenished Dawsyn's magic.

"Ryon!"

She turns and uses her bare hands to climb out of the drift. Her palms burn with the sting of ice, but it does little to slow her. She finds her feet at the crest and rises, looking in all directions.

A body lies in the snow, several feet away. It is crumpled and unmoving, disguised by cloaks and furs. But the shape is familiar.

"Hector!" Dawsyn runs to him. She stands astride him and grabs handfuls of his cloak to roll him over. His skin is colourless, but for the black grit of the Chasm smeared along his cheeks. Small puffs of mist appear beneath his nostrils. Alive. He is alive.

But he is not healed. Whatever Yerdos gifted Dawsyn she did not lend to Hector. He is fading. His eyes are glassy and distant, looking straight through her.

"Fuck," Dawsyn mutters. He was too weak to fold. They all were.

Dawsyn does not know where to place her hands, where to heal. She opts for his chest, wrenching his cloak open at the ties. She slides his tunic up his stomach until his prominent ribcage comes into view, then lays her icy hands to his skin. He does not flinch.

"Ish-ishveet!" Dawsyn stutters. The iskra and mage light rush to collide and intertwine. "*Ishveet!*"

The power courses through her and into Hector. Dawsyn can feel the thrust of it, rushing through him. She shuts her eyes against the blinding light and wills the power onward. She orders it to find what is broken and mend it.

When the magic is satisfied, it returns to her, leaving her sluggish.

Hector's eyelids blink rapidly. His nose scrunches as that same smell of ice and pine assaults him, then his gaze finds Dawsyn's. "Woah," he says evenly. "You look awful."

Dawsyn lies her forehead to his chest for a moment, her breaths ragged with relief. "Fuck you," she manages to spit out. "You scared me."

Hector pats the back of her head, his body shivering. "Nothing scares you, Sabar," he reminds her. "Where the fuck are we?"

"The mountain."

"How?"

"Yerdos," Dawsyn answers, standing. She grabs Hector's arm and hauls him upward out of the snow. "She saved us."

"*Saved* us?" Hector repeats, shock widening his eyes. "But... why?"

"I can tell the tale later," Dawsyn mutters. "We need to find the others. Now."

In the distance she can hear a keen whining. It sounds like a trapped animal.

"Esra," Hector mutters, and begins barrelling through deep snow in the direction of the noise.

Dawsyn keeps pace behind him, letting Hector lead through the trees. The sound increases as they travel.

Around the next trunk, there is a disturbance in the virgin snow. A drift crumbles inward, and something within its depths disturbs it further, eroding the sides inward. A dreadful cry comes from within.

"Esra!" Hector and Dawsyn shout as one. "Stop!"

There is a short pause in the onslaught of pained grunting, and then, "Hector?" Esra's voice calls.

"Stop moving, Es," Hector orders, side-stepping his way down the embankment of snow to the hole Esra has made for himself. "You'll only be buried."

"Already... fucking... buried!" comes Esra's panicked reply. Dawsyn can hear the stress is his voice, the breathless quality to it.

"Fucking Mother above," Dawsyn grunts, coming to a stand-still beside the hole. She can just make out Esra's face below, half covered in snow. The rest of him is already buried beneath a foot of it. "Aren't you dead yet?"

"Unfortunately... it seems the Mother will not bless me... with death's sweet release," Esra says. He sucks in each breath with great effort. "Though you may as well leave me here in this grave, Dawsyn... I am not far from it."

"You're not dying, Es," Hector admonishes. He digs fervently, pulling the snow away from the small hole like a madman.

Dawsyn does the same, carefully avoiding placing her feet anywhere near the edges.

"I am dying," Esra argues weakly. "Dawsyn... darling... move your face out of the way. You look awful. If I am to look my last... then I want to look at Hector."

"You're not *dying!*" Hector says. His face mottles with exertion.

Esra's eyes close as they dig low enough to reach him, to hook their arms beneath his shoulders. Sinking their feet into the snow to leverage themselves, they haul Esra out of the hole, inch by inch.

"Leave him there," Dawsyn orders when Esra is part-way out. His legs are still buried in the drift, but she can reach his chest, and that is all she needs.

As she did to Hector, Dawsyn finds his skin and lays her hands upon it. "Ishveet," she says, and feels that same outpouring of power. It flows into Esra and quickens his blood, it warms his heart, mends what was broken.

As the bright light fades, Dawsyn opens her eyes to find Esra's warm complexion as it once was. The cracks in his lips have sealed, and the cuts on his cheeks are no more. The places where his cheekbones had begun to cut into the flesh are now round, and though the scars along the right side of his face remain, the rest of him is as it should be.

"Heavens," he says, gripping his chest. He breathes deeply, seemingly relieved to be breathing at all. Then he shivers. "Fuck my arse its cold."

Hector grabs him. He hauls the man out of the hole until his boots are free, and then lifts him to standing.

"Easy, boy! Let me—" but Esra's indignant protests are cut off when Hector presses his mouth firmly to his.

"Well, that's one way to shut him up," Dawsyn pants.

Hector holds Esra's face gently in his hands and when their lips part again he keeps his forehead pressed to Esra's. They share breath and Dawsyn grins to herself.

"Do not speak of dying again," Hector commands, but his voice is anything but gruff.

Esra smiles, then wraps Hector in his embrace. "Of course not, my love. It was all jest."

"You were crying like a baby," Dawsyn reminds him.

"I love you, dear Dawsyn," Esra says. "But sometimes I think you ought to have remained on the Ledge."

Dawsyn grins again. "Come," she says. "We do not have time for Hector to realise his feelings now. We need to find the others."

"I swear to the Mother, if that hawk-woman spat Salem into a gorge, I shall never forgive her."

Dawsyn begins traipsing her way down the slope. "Oddly sentimental of you."

"Sentimental? Ha! The half-wit wagered that Hector would kiss a *pig's arse* before he'd kiss me. I told him that if I won, I would drop my trousers, and Salem could kiss *my–*"

"Kiss him again, Hector," Dawsyn interrupts, quickening her pace. "Now. For the love of the Mother."

Dawsyn, Esra and Hector fan out and search the surrounding wood, looking for disturbances in the snow and listening keenly to any sound. The wind is, at least, oddly still. It does not try to hurl them down the slope, taking any tell-tale sounds with it.

After an hour of searching, Dawsyn becomes frantic. There are no signs of the others – not Salem or Abertha, nor Rivdan or Tasheem. Not Ryon.

If they have been thrown onto this mountain by Yerdos, Dawsyn fears they do not have the fortitude to survive it for long.

The cold will not hinder him, Dawsyn reminds herself, though it does not ease the fear. There is little sand left in the hourglass. Should she fail to find them and heal them, they will not live through the night. She feels sure of it.

Daylight is waning. The temperature is dropping. Dawsyn's magic, though recently replenished, has been depleted to heal Hector and Esra already. She does not know if it can be extended to help the rest.

She trudges carefully onward. To either side of her, she can make out the distant shapes of Esra and Hector searching as she does. She listens intently to her surrounds but hears only the squeak of boots in snow. It is a surprisingly welcome sound after the crunch and clatter of rock in the Chasm. The feel of sinking snow beneath her soles is not something she ever imagined missing.

She lifts her boot and pauses. Beneath the vast pine before her, the snow is disturbed, as though someone had sat beneath it, resting their back to the bark.

Dawsyn rounds the trunk, finding the drag marks that lead down the slope. It could be an animal, dragging its kill to its den.

But Dawsyn doesn't think so.

"Esra! Hector!" Dawsyn runs downhill, following the marks. It leads her to a pine tipped on its side, uplifted by the weight of gravity. It leaves a hole in the ground big enough for a mountain cat to seek shelter, or…

"Smoke!" Esra yells, ploughing awkwardly through the drifts toward her. Between the thick tangle of roots that resolutely tether the tree to the ground, smoke rises.

Dawsyn's heart lurches into her throat and she barrels toward the warren, allowing the snow to slip down the sides of her boots in her haste.

The glint of metal is Dawsyn's only warning before the airborne blade flies at her chest. She gasps and spins mid-stride, letting the knife fly by her. "Shit."

"Dawsyn?" a voice asks.

A face has appeared between the roots. One framed by wild auburn hair and a soot-smeared face. Abertha.

Dawsyn pants, almost laughs.

"You Ledge-folk ever thought of saying 'hello'?" Esra quips, approaching with a mixture of grunts and curses. "It's wasteful, the way you throw knives around."

"Hurry!" Abertha says. "The old man… I did what I could…"

Salem.

Dawsyn slides the rest of the way down the slope, letting her arse hit the drifts despite her better judgement. When she reaches the tree, she grabs the roots in either hand and lowers herself into the hole beneath. The warren is low, and she must squat. It smells strongly of earth and damp wood. The air is made dank by the slow burning of kindling. And at the fire's side lies the unconscious form of Salem, covered in what appears to be Abertha's fur and hide cloak. His usually flushed cheeks are sapped of colour, just as Hector's and Esra's were. Just as Abertha's are now.

Dawsyn wastes no time. She crawls to Salem's side and pushes the layers of his clothing aside to reach his chest. She feels him exhale at the chill of her touch. *A good sign*, she thinks.

This time, the magic takes longer to find the bridge to Salem. It moves sluggishly. Dawsyn finds herself pushing it onward. She comes dangerously close to commanding its will, though she knows better than to force magic's hand.

When the light dims, Salem's eyes flutter open. He looks around with a dumbfounded expression. "Dawsyn," he says, finding her in the gloom. "Yeh look bloody awful, lass."

Dawsyn grits her teeth. The insults are wearing.

He frowns. "We're alive?"

She clutches his hand for a moment. "You've Abertha to thank for that."

"Abertha?" Salem asks, like he's never heard the name in his life.

"You dragged him here, I assume," Dawsyn asks the girl without turning to look at her. She can feel her hovering close by.

"He was fucking heavy," is her response. Dawsyn grins.

Salem frowns peevishly, but says, "S'pose I ought to thank yeh."

Abertha shrugs and looks away, uncomfortable. She is dishevelled, and clearly weak, though not as dire as the others had been when Dawsyn had healed them. She is thin, haggard, certainly. But not moments away from her death.

"I can help you, too," Dawsyn tells her, gesturing down to her palms. "Return some strength."

Abertha looks sidelong at Dawsyn's hands, but then nods hesitantly. Dawsyn lays her palms on Abertha's cheeks. But the magic groans internally within her, turning reluctant.

Once more, Dawsyn coaxes. *Please. She will need it.*

The magic collides and finds its way to her hands, now moving like a petulant child, just as it had in the Chasm when there were too many people to mend and heal.

The light fades all too soon. "Damn it."

"It is all right," Abertha says softly, moving away again. "Food will strengthen me. Rest, too."

The magic has barely brought colour back to the girl's cheeks, but she is young and hardy. A girl of the Ledge. She will survive.

"Salem?" comes Esra's voice, his face appearing between roots. "Did you die?"

Salem grumbles. "Surely not. No way it'd be *yeh* sorry face greetin' me at Mother's Gate."

Esra grins. There is a spark of genuine relief in his eyes. "Wet those chops, old man."

Salem frowns. *"What?"*

"Dawsyn, move aside a moment. I need to lower my arse into this warren."

Salem looks incredulously up at Esra's toothy smile. "What're yeh blitherin' about?"

"Why, I've successfully gained the affections of the handsome Ledge boy, Salem. Our lips were united not moments ago."

Salem pauses for a moment, a small smile slipping through. "Bullshit," he pronounces.

Esra's returning grin speaks of something much more than victory. "I told you he'd fall in love with me. They always do."

"Well, I'll be damned," Salem murmurs. "Bolly to yeh, son."

Dawsyn shakes her head. "Come," she says to them all. "There are more of us to find."

"Who?" Salem asks. He notices when Dawsyn swallows. His eyes turn pained. "Ryon," he answers for her.

"Tash and Riv, too." Her heart rate spikes at the mentioning of their names. They could be anywhere on this mountain.

"We'll find them, lass."

"We will," she says, and nods to Abertha to climb out of the warren first. She does not allow herself to think of any other possibility. Already, the separation aches.

He is not dead.

He will not die.

CHAPTER THIRTY

Ryon remains on the fringe of consciousness. Even during the occasions his eyelids flutter open and his gaze fixes, he is never fully aware of his surroundings.

He can feel the weight of a sinister sleep dragging him under again and again. It dulls sound. Blinds him. The only sensation he can distinguish beneath the surface is a muted sort of pain, or rather the knowledge of pain, as though his mind cannot quite part ways with it even down here.

It is difficult to ignore, this mild ache. Incrementally it grows, a relentless nuisance to an otherwise peaceful stupor. Eventually Ryon grows irritable enough that he reaches for the surface. He claws his way to consciousness. And this time, when he opens his eyes, he makes sense of shape and sound.

"He resists death, this night wing," a voice says. Feminine, but strange. Unsettling.

Ryon blinks rapidly. The pounding in his head begs him to shut his eyes again.

"Best you follow that call to sleep, night wing," the person says. Perhaps a hairsbreadth from his cheek. "There's nothing good this side of waking."

Ryon squints, groaning through the splitting *thump, thump, thump*. He finds a woman tilting her head to the side, observing him shrewdly. Ryon rears.

"Easy," the woman says, "lest you call death too soon. I smell it on you already."

Ryon feels it. His stomach feels bowled. His limbs shake. Every remaining sensibility bids he return to that deep, dark well. But the woman's palm is held aloft and in it dances the flickers of a seemingly source-less flame.

He exhales harshly. "Mage," he utters, his voice weak, hoarse.

The woman does not nod her assent nor deny it. Instead, she acts as though he had not spoken, her eyes scoping the length of him unabashedly. Long, chestnut hair is braided away from her forehead before falling to her waist. Its ethereal beauty reminds Ryon of Baltisse and his heart tightens for a moment. She is young, no older than he on the surface, though perhaps far older than he could imagine. And although the mage is beautiful, her smile has an animalistic quality and she surveys him with predatory interest. She walks barefoot, and despite being dressed in fur and hide, her unprotected feet do not seem to perturb her.

"What happened to your wings?" she asks. She speaks in the old language. The language often favoured by Glacians.

Ryon looks reflexively over his shoulder, and it is only then he notices the way his arms pin to the dirt wall behind him, roots snaking out of the earth and wrapping tightly around his wrists. There are no wings to speak of. They remain vanished. Ryon doubts he could summon them if his life depended on it.

"How—"

"I see them," the strange mage says. "Tucked away beneath your skin." The final word hisses.

Ryon's eyes finally track to his surrounds. They follow the light blaring in from a wide opening. Pine trees loom beyond it in the distance.

A cave, he thinks.

"What happened to them?" the mage asks again, her head tilting to the opposite side. She shuffles as though to see them better, despite their concealment.

"Let me go," Ryon says feebly in the old language, his eyelids closing without his permission. "I have no quarrel with you."

"Ah," she says. "And yet you fought your way through our wards. What other reason could you have to venture so far, night wing?"

Ryon's legs shake unbearably, they struggle to hold him upright to offset the strain on his arms. "I..." he begins, but his train of thought disintegrates. "I..."

"A surprise it was, to have three wings penetrate the wards at once. None so far from death. Was it protection you sought by coming here, where all are forbidden? Did you wish to be healed?"

Ryon shakes his head, feeling it loll onto his chest. "Three?"

"Your company," the mage answers. Suddenly her fingers are at the cusp of Ryon's chin, lifting it upward. "Another night wing. The fire wing."

Tasheem, he thinks. *Rivdan.*

"The last time we found you in our territory, you almost did not make it out alive, Ryon Mesrich," she whispers.

Ryon shudders. Despite the years between, he remembers the encounter well.

"It was only the generosity of our sister that allowed you to leave with your skin intact. You were a boy then." The mage inhales deeply, as though to discern his scent. "Far more spirited."

Ryon groans. His legs shake and his shoulders protest. Every muscle screams.

"Where is our sister?" the mage says now. "Where is Baltisse?"

But Ryon does not answer, he has already turned limp. His mind carries him beneath the surface once more, into that sweet, dulling abyss, where he does not have to think of pain, or Baltisse, or wonder where Dawsyn is, if she is not with him.

Chapter Thirty-One

Yennes spent the night in a squalid back alley behind the tavern.

When she banged the knockers of three separate doors and asked for a bed, the occupants threw the doors back in her face. It may have been the sick that soiled her clothes, or the way she swayed where she stood. In any case, the reception was reminiscent of one she might have received on the Ledge.

On the fourth attempt, an older woman within raked her gaze over Yennes' figure and then shrugged. "Worth a farthing if not a coin pouch," she said, and threw the door wide open. But a man suddenly stumbled over the stoop and nearly bowled Yennes over. His belt buckle dangled precariously about his waist.

Yennes backed away, frowning at the matron with the overflowing bosom.

"A bed's still a bed, miss," she hollered to her, jutting a prominent hip to hold the door open as another man entered. "Don't matter who shares it."

Yennes found her way to a patch of cobblestone unmarred by mud and fell asleep against the wall of a stable instead. She listened to the strange nickers and chuffs of the creatures within until her eyelids drooped and finally closed, forgetting entirely the ring that rested in the bottom of her pocket.

When she awoke, her body took its vengeance.

The sun had risen with an insatiable kind of malice. Yennes was sweating through her clothing from the first. The only solace to be taken was the sure knowledge that waking beneath the sun's menace was far better than the frost's. The people on the Ledge awoke this morn in no better surroundings than they had the day before. Tomorrow, it would be just as bleak. Here in Terrsaw, her biggest qualm was the unforgiving ground, for even the exposure of night had left her unharmed. Mostly.

The steady beat pounding in her forehead was made worse by the chatter of male voices.

"Woah, there," one said, followed by the indignant huff of a horse. "Henry, pass me that rope."

Yennes turned cautiously, noting the flip her stomach took at even this small movement. She could not see within the stable, but the timber wall was thin enough that she could hear every sound of the occupants within.

"Another?" a second voice grumbled. "How many horses we saddlin'?"

"Captain said the whole lot."

There was a low whistle. "Reckon them guards are on some kind of expedition?" the second – seemingly younger – voice asked.

"You ain't heard? Queen Cressida's on her death bed."

"Yeah, I heard."

"Then add it up, yeh dolt. Her Majesty's desperate. She's sending out the battalion to find a cure. Seems she'll do whatever it takes to save her."

Silence. And then, "Reckon she's lookin' for a mage?"

"Ha!" the first voice scoffed roughly. The conversation grew distant, accompanied by the clops of hooves. "Ain't no mages left round here, Henry. Smoked those fuckers out a long time ago."

Not all, Yennes thought.

The boy named Henry chuckled. She heard him move about the stable, whistling and nattering to the horses.

Yennes rose. She dusted off her skirts and straightened her blouse. She tried to remember the spell Baltisse had shown her not several days before. "*Cristique,*" she muttered, holding her palm to her soiled front. She watched the stains disappear.

Yennes followed the wall of the stables, her back to the wood as she crept along, guided by the sounds of the men. At the stables' corner she stopped. The palace rose before her, surrounded by a great stone wall.

Somehow, in last night's haze, she'd managed to find her way to the very edge of the Terrsaw palace and slept at its feet.

Fragments of possibility collected rapidly in her mind.

"*Dangerous thoughts,*" she heard once more, Baltisse's voice intruding.

And yet, there it was. The palace, and inside it an ailing queen. Something that those Queens needed, and something she could grant them.

Inside her skirt pocket, Baltisse's ring seemed to grow warm. A warning. Yennes dug her fingers in until she had the ring in her grasp. She clutched it tightly.

Immediately, she felt a pull, an invisible hand on her shoulder bidding her to turn around and go right back the way she'd come.

Instead, Yennes stayed hidden in the shadows of the alley, ducking behind stacked wooden pales to avoid notice. She stayed clutching that ring until the sun rose higher, until men in polished armour spilled out of an iron gate and claimed their horses. She stayed until Henry and his superior waved them off and ambled away, their work done. She stayed until the clop of horse hooves dissipated and the road emptied.

Then, Yennes followed her dangerous thoughts out of the alley. She let the ring fall back to the bottom of her pocket, and approached that foreboding iron gate.

"Stand back," came a gruff warning from the other side – a faceless helmed guard. "What is your business here?"

Yennes reached within herself for the tenacity that once governed her. She willed it to return now. "I..." she began, though her voice hitched. "I wish to see the Queen."

The guard chuckled and shook his head at the sky as though consulting it. "Go on home, miss. The Queen don't take tea with commoners."

Yennes swallowed. Her hands came before her in a tumble of overriding nerves. But she kept her gaze levelled with the guard's and did not back away from the gate. "And what if the commoner could cure her wife?" she said slowly, deliberately. "Would she see me then?"

Without waiting to hear the guard's dismissal, Yennes muttered the spell that would call fire to her palm, and she watched it reflect in the guard's muddy eyes.

It took less time than Yennes had anticipated to find herself in the palace's throne room, though she had not expected to arrive shackled and flanked by armoured guards.

They stood on intricately tiled floor beneath a vast glass-domed ceiling. The empty wooden thrones on the dais were bathed in morning light, as though awaiting the Mother herself to adorn them. The Terrsaw palace was a world removed from the throne room she had last stood in, whose only light was gleaned from dim sconces and the magnificent reflection of the Pool of Iskra.

Hurried footsteps sounded from the corridor to the left. The guards at her shoulders tightened their grip on her arms and Yennes held her breath. The footsteps gathered momentum and out of the arched entry spilled a woman in the most elaborate dress Yennes could imagine.

Yennes had the immediate impression that she was being picked apart. The Queen, an older, austere woman, scanned her from head to toe. Yennes could not help but notice the shadows that darkened the delicate skin beneath her eyes, or the hair that had come unfastened from the clasps that held it back. Her forehead was heavily lined and gave the appearance of a perpetual frown. Even glittering with jewels and embellishments, Yennes could not help but see the Queen of Terrsaw as little more than a dishevelled woman.

"Bow your head," one of the guards ordered Yennes and she did so hastily, diverting her eyes to the mosaic on the floor.

"Who are you?" the Queen's voice rang out. It filled the entire room, reaching the heights of the domed ceiling. It sent an inexplicable chill down Yennes' spine.

"She says she's come from the other side of the river," one guard offers.

"Not *you*," Alvira snapped. Yennes lifted her face carefully to see that the Queen's gaze was still firmly raking her. "I am speaking to the girl bold enough to claim she can cure my wife."

Yennes' hands rattled in their shackles as they gripped and released. "My name is Yennes," she said, hoping the volume of her voice hid its tremor.

The Queen's voice was dull as she spoke, but there was no mistaking the roll in her jaw, nor the violent glint in her eyes. "I will ask you this question once, Yennes," she said. "And if I find the answer lacking, you'll be thrown into a cell below ground until I forget your name." She paused and the pressure in the room seemed to swell. "Are you a mage?"

Yennes' heart stuttered. "N-no," she said. "I am no mage."

The Queen eyes seemed to blacken. She turned to the guard on Yennes' right and sneered in his direction. "Did you not claim you saw her conjure fire?"

"She did, Your Majesty!" the guard implored. "Saw it with my own eyes."

"Take her to the keep," the Queen said by way of reply, already turning to leave. "You have wasted enough of my time."

The guards were already lifting Yennes off her feet. "Wait!" she shouted, thrashing against their hold. She slammed her eyes shut and reached for the iskra. "Igniss!"

The flame erupted from her palm. It captured the sleeve of one of the guards handling her and set it alight. He jumped away, aghast, stifling the wool against his chest plate with little success.

But the Queen halted her exit. She watched the guard's sleeve with widened eyes, and it wasn't until the singed smell of burning wool faded that she looked to Yennes' once more.

"You lied," she accused, though her lips turned upward. Her eyes gleamed.

"No ma'am–"

"Your Majesty."

"No, Your Majesty," Yennes repeated. "I am not mage-born. I came about this magic by other means."

"What 'other means'?" Alvira demanded, each syllable striking Yennes squarely.

Yennes readied to reveal herself. She sensed this was not a woman who would linger while she hesitated. Her patience seemed gossamer thin. "I took it," Yennes said. "From the Glacians."

All fell still and silent. Even their breaths seemed to falter under the resonance of her confession. It was the Queen who spoke first, of course, but only after she had traded side-long glances with her guards. Only after she had masked her expression with a dry, indiscernible veneer. Only two words were pushed past her lips: "Prove it."

Yennes looked down at her own body, as though she might suddenly find some means to avail herself. "I am Ledge-born," she said, her eyes darting from person to person. "I was taken over the Chasm by the Glacians... thrown into their pool. But I survived it and journeyed here."

But the Queen was already laughing, already swallowing the ends of Yennes' story. "A woeful tale to hide your true heritage, mage," she said. "Though I can understand it. The prejudice some still wage against your kind is regrettable."

"I am not–"

"There are still some who would seek to strap you to a pyre. Certainly something to avoid."

Yennes could not be sure – the Queen's expression was still a mask of careful dispassion – but she thought the words might have been a threat.

"I, too, would wish for privacy, should I possess *unnatural* abilities."

"I–"

"Useful, perhaps," Alvira continued. "But dangerous in the wrong hands. Some believe such things ought to be eradicated all togeth–"

The Queen's words fell short as Yennes raised her palms. The guards rushed to protect their Queen, drawing their short swords and moving to surround her.

But there was no lightning bolt that lashed from Yennes' hands. They simply glowed brightly, a lattice work of ice and frost coating her skin from fingertip to wrist.

Yennes called the iskra to her palms but did not coax it further than that. Whatever threat the Queen perceived her to be, she did not encourage the idea now.

Alvira had clutched her hand to her chest, falling back into the folds of her guards' protection, but now, she straightened. Her piercing gaze fixed to Yennes' hands, mouth agape. "Mother almighty," she intoned. "Iskra."

Yennes held the magic in her palms and nodded cautiously.

Alvira pressed her hands to her gown, wiping them against the fabric. "Leave us," she said suddenly, and it did not seem that she was addressing Yennes.

The guard nearest the Queen faltered. His mouth opened and closed before he uttered, "Your Majesty?"

"*Get out!*" she commanded. "Now."

The guards did not question her. They eyed Yennes with trepidation as they melted down their various corridors, disappearing into the walls of the palace until it was just the Queen and Yennes, alone.

Alvira did not come closer. If she had thoughts, Yennes could not speculate their nature. Everything, from the Queen's stance to the exact degree of her smile seemed precisely controlled. Yennes could not tell if she was about to be killed or welcomed.

But Yennes had seen the weapons toted by the guards. She could guess at the sheer number of men she had at her disposal. And hadn't she just now demonstrated their obedience to her? The power with which she commanded them?

The thought bolstered Yennes, for if there was someone in this kingdom who might bear the means to fight Glacians, surely it was the woman before her.

"Iskra witch," the Queen said.

Yennes balked at the name.

"How very... *interesting* it is to meet you. Why have you come?" her gaze darted back to Yennes' palms.

"I heard your wife had taken ill," she said cautiously. "I came here to offer my magic to heal her."

"Her Majesty," the Queen corrected.

"Her Majesty." Yennes blinked.

Queen Alvira considered her for a moment. The silence stretched. "Well," she ushered impatiently. "And what of the rest?"

"The rest?" Yennes frowned.

"Yes, child. The *rest.* Surely you did not come to my palace gate out of sheer benevolence. You would be the very first in history if that were the case. Now, what is it that you came here for, in exchange for curing my ailing wife."

"So she *is* ailing?" Yennes asked, a remnant of her former self escaping.

Alvira's careful smile dropped slightly, "I am afraid so."

Yennes nodded. Whatever else this woman was, she was quite obviously heart-sore, dread-stricken. "I will not keep you from her bedside," Yennes offered. "As I've said, I come from the Ledge–"

"Ah," Alvira breathed. "And you wish to be its liberator?"

Yennes considered the question. It was not exactly what she wished. Each day since leaving the Chasm, her mind had waged a war against her memories – it clawed at her with remembrances of Glacia and the Ledge that made her shudder. It tore her in half with other wretched invasions – longing, sorrow... regret. People she'd left behind. Faces she would never see again.

Sometimes, she was thrown back into that ocean and she hoped to simply drown this time.

She was no saviour. No liberator. She was the outer layer that remained of a once stronger woman. She was a shade of someone far more familiar than the failing consciousness that inhabited her now. Whoever this person was, she was no heroine.

"I cannot return there," she told the Queen, shaking her head. "I'm... I cannot go back." It was the truth. And to think of those children, those babies, those men and women that remained was to bring tears falling to her cheeks. "But I must do what little I am still capable of," she continued. "I must offer my help. And in return, I ask you for yours."

Alvira tugged on the folds of her dress, hesitating. "And what would you have me do?"

"Take your soldiers to the mountain," Yennes said. "And fight."

The Queen shook her head slowly. "If only it were so simple a remedy."

"There are children up there," Yennes said. Surely it would be enough to persuade anyone.

"And there are children here, too. Children who would be orphaned should their parents die in a pointless battle against superior creatures."

Yennes sighed, frustration brewing hot and fast. How easily this queen disregarded the plight of her own people – a forgone conclusion. "There are those in this valley who told me about your deal with the Glacian King. It was you who condemned my people. My *parents*. Was it not?"

Alvira tilted her head to the side. "Most people in this valley are hapless, mouth-breathing fools. It is why they do not sit where I sit."

Yennes tasted acid. "I had found it difficult to believe that one could be so callous toward her own people. I thought I might find you repentant."

"Oh, I have regrets," Alvira said evenly. "In fact, I have found to be a queen is to be perpetually sorry for miracles I could not weave and to constantly defend those I did."

Yennes' chest rose and fell with barely tempered ire. "So, I am to take it that those people on the Ledge are counted among your miracles? That they should remain there so that *you* may remain?"

"Ah, so we understand each other," Alvira said. "And now we must discuss whether *you* may remain." Her eyes swept over Yennes once more, pausing on her palms before shifting over the rest of her.

Yennes balked. "Whether I may remain?"

"Indeed," the Queen said. "I'm afraid you pose rather a large threat. *Glacian* magic? Well, if the people of Terrsaw thought such a thing existed, they would be moved to stamp it out. Fear runs errant when those beasts are merely mentioned."

Yennes swallowed. "I am no threat. I came here to *help.*"

"And what a help you could be to me," the Queen agreed. "I have been looking in every crevice of this kingdom for the very brand of help you might offer, in fact. And so, you see, there *is* a way I can repay you for your services to the palace." The Queen smiled kindly at her, as though she were offering something charitable. "I can allow you to live peacefully here, in this valley, where you need never think of the mountain again. Where you needn't return. No one need know of your... *abilities*, or hunt you down in our forests. In return, you can rid my wife of that which slowly takes her from me." At the mention of the Queen Consort, Alvira's jaw twitched, her eyes turned distant. When she spoke next, the words did not bear the same barbed edges. Her voice was softer, less controlled. "If you were to save her... I would be forever in your debt."

Yennes thought of the life she was suggesting, one forced into silence, into hiding. One where she could languish in sunshine while the mountain loomed behind her, a constant reminder of that which she had failed to help.

Surely, she had not survived this much, journeyed so far, for it to amount to nothing.

"No," she spat, and the word imbued her, fortified her. This was right. She felt it at her core. "I won't accept such a wanting deal."

"Wanting?" Alvira asked coldly.

"If I cure the Queen, you must act to free the Ledge," Yennes declared.

"And if I make no such promise?" the Queen questioned, her eyebrow rising.

Yennes lifted her chin. "Then you must hope your men return with that mage you sent them to look for, though I hear they are difficult to find."

Alvira's eyebrow rose. "I'm impressed," she said. "You have quite a bit more spine than I'd guessed."

Yennes smiled, despite herself. Perhaps her old impetuousness was returning.

Alvira turned her head. "Guards!"

Yennes' heart stuttered. She heard the clatter of armour returning down the halls and looked pleadingly to the Queen. But there was no change in Alvira's expression, nothing to warn Yennes of any threat.

The contingent of guards returned to the room and Alvira smiled at them. "We have a new guest to the palace," she said to no one in particular. "Ensure she feels our welcome."

Something collided with the back of Yennes' head. She heard the crack as it connected, felt the instant, splitting pain. Then the room tilted sideways.

And she saw nothing more.

CHAPTER THIRTY-TWO

Before the sun rises, Dawsyn wakes the others. They have camped beneath the outcropped boulders of the slope, huddled around a fire, but now she stomps the low flames to ashes.

They had lost light soon after finding Salem and Abertha, and though Dawsyn would have continued on in the dark, the others were slower. Abertha was weak. The winds picked up and became impossible to push against, so she agreed to stop.

But within the hour, the sun would illuminate the ground enough, and somewhere on this mountain, Ryon, Tasheem and Rivdan were waiting... wounded.

"Get your wits about you," she says for the second time, kicking the soles of Esra's feet. Hector and Abertha are already standing. Salem and Esra are slow to rise. They shiver and complain, pulling their furs and cloaks tighter with furrowed brows.

"Have we anything to eat?" Esra grumbles.

"Aye. Go swing that ax, Dawsyn. I can make a meal of anythin' yeh find."

Dawsyn frowns. "We ate last night."

"Aye," Salem says. "And tha' hare din't sit so well with me. 'Fraid it made a hasty return soon after."

"Ugh," Abertha grunts, regarding Salem with pinched brows.

"We don't have time to *eat*," Dawsyn says tersely, letting the heel of the ax thump against the ground to expel her frustration. "Get off your arse and walk."

Esra rubs his eyes. "Mother above, Dawsyn! Such vile lang–"

"Get. *Up!*"

"You worry needlessly," Esra tries to pacify. "If *I've* survived the Chasm and the big bird lady, then surely Ryon did."

"He's wounded," Dawsyn spits. "So are Tasheem and Rivdan."

"At least let a man relieve himself," Esra scowls at her. "Hector, look away. I don't want to leave you with a diminished impression. It is too cold for gloating."

Dawsyn grabs Esra by the scruff and hauls him upright. It is surprisingly easy in her state of building fury. "We're leaving," she says between gritted teeth. "Do not slow me."

They walk the entire day through, and each hour only intensifies her worry. She has no clue where to lead them. There are no tracks to follow. The further they go, the more impossible it seems that she will simply stumble across them. They could have been expelled anywhere on the mountain.

By nightfall, Dawsyn's mind is made. Once they've found a suitable spot to rest for the evening, Dawsyn proclaims, "I'm going to fold," and tries to quash the trepidation she feels. "It is the only chance we have of finding them."

The others look to one another. Hector gives Dawsyn a familiar glare. One of disapproval and resignation. He often scowled just so on the Ledge when she'd rejected his offers of marriage or tried to press supplies into her hands. He knows her well enough to see when her mind is decided. "Do you know *how?*"

Dawsyn nods once. "I cannot go far," she admits. "But I must try."

"That magic is dangerous, lass," Salem says, voice laced with concern. "Even Baltisse..." Here he gulps and turns his eyes downcast, as though the name pains him to say. "Even Baltisse were challenged by it."

"I know," Dawsyn sighs heavily. "But I will not lose him."

Salem shakes his head. "He's alive, lass. Holed up somewhere, biding his time and lettin' his wings heal. This cold don't touch him the way it does us."

"Will you swear it, Salem?" she asks the older man, the first human Ryon ever befriended. "Will you swear to me that he's alive? That he is not fading as we speak?"

Salem doesn't offer any answer; he seals his lips into a flat line. His eyes turn pleading.

"I can feel it," Dawsyn tells him, her hands shaking with the consuming dread of it. "I feel him fading away. I cannot explain it."

Salem eyes the frost that coats her palms, glowing in the night. "You needn't explain it to me," he says. "But tha' boy loves yeh," he sighs. "Bloody well told me enough times. If Ryon heard yeh'd fizzled yerself out tryin' to reach 'im, I don't reckon he'd survive it."

Dawsyn turns away until she can be sure her voice will be even. She swallows whatever desperate sounds her lungs wish to release. Then she admits that which her grandmother always warned her against.

"Do you think I'll fare any better if he dies first, Salem? If he leaves me here?"

"Lass, I–"

"I will not survive him," Dawsyn says, walking away. "I can survive many things… but I won't survive that."

Dawsyn leaves them standing around the fire Hector made and trudges through deep snow into the shadows. Squalls bite at her eyes and face. It finds ways to her skin through her clothing.

She can source the mage light with ease now. It is not hard to imagine warmth, safety, love. No, it is no longer hard to imagine love.

She reaches for the sense of arms encasing her, of kisses caressing her cheek bones, her temple, her throat. It only takes a heartbeat to bring that spark to the forefront of her mind and will it to expand.

The iskra and mage magic coalesce like old friends reuniting. They balance perfectly between warmth and cold, light and dark.

To fold, she must simply imagine the place she wishes to be and let that place expand in her mind. She must imagine it unfolding before her and so it shall be. Therein lies the magic's limitation – she cannot bring to mind a place she has not been.

Dawsyn breathes in deeply, feeling the burn of frost in the back of her throat. "Please," she utters to the air. "Baltisse. Guide me." She closes her eyes.

She pictures a familiar warren – one where Ryon had stashed belongings in his once-regular trips down the slopes. It is one of the only places on the mountain she can remember with any detail.

She feels the magic expand in her and then abruptly retract. The bones of her limbs condense, her chest sinks inward. Time and space fold and she feels an instant of excruciating, unbearable pain. But she manages to hold the image in her mind, and when space expands, abrupt relief rushes in.

The image within her mind becomes her surroundings. She lands on all fours with a graceless thud, her hands and knees sinking into the snow. She gasps against the protestations of her stomach, but at least manages to hold onto its contents.

It worked. The warren is before her, unchanged since their last acquaintance. But he isn't here.

"Fuck," Dawsyn huffs shakily, spitting bile. She stands on unsteady legs.

No footprints mark the snow in any direction she can see. The warren entrance is piled in fresh snow. The mountain breathes fiercely down the slope and beyond her, and she knows there is no one here but her. "RYON!" she shouts anyway, though it hardly travels.

There is no reply.

Dawsyn lets her head fall back on her shoulders, closing her eyes until her breaths ease. She can feel the depletion of power like a tapped well, painstakingly refilling ounce by ounce. It will take all night to replenish. She cannot afford to burn out.

She clambers toward the warren and begins to dig out the snow covering its entrance. Her fingers are gloved and ineffectual, so she takes the axe from her shoulder straps and uses its wide blade.

When the hole is deep enough, she stomps at the edges with her boot, then lowers herself through.

"Igniss," she says, and a weak flame unfolds in her palm. Her breath seizes in her chest at the sight of the place. She remembers those nooks in the tree's underbelly, where Ryon's supplies are still stashed. A knife. Burlap draw-string bags of dried food – likely fouled now. She remembers waking to the crackle of weak flames, to the same smell of fresh earth, and the imposing form of a Glacian, staring at her intently beneath hooded eyes. Wary eyes. *"Relax, girl. You are safe."*

Dawsyn swallows. How little they knew of each other then.

There is a small array of kindling and dried pine needles spread across the ground, likely disturbed by an animal of some kind. She gathers them together now and expertly lights them.

She has no food. The fire will soon consume these meagre twigs. There is little left of her power, and she is tired. But she curls up beside the little flames and gathers her cloak tightly around her. She closes her eyes and sees Ryon, thick brows raised in amusement. He smirks as she taunts and threatens him, his eyes subtly drinking her in.

Dawsyn smiles back. "I'll find you," she murmurs aloud.

* * *

Dawsyn repeats the process for three days. She rests and folds. Rests and folds.

The exhaustion she feels after each journey begins to feel lighter, less consuming. Soon, it begins to feel like stretched muscles. She finds she can grit her teeth and push beyond it. She needs less and less time to rest in between.

She sets traps and eats whatever prey she can catch while she sleeps off the fog of fatigue. She drinks regularly and finds that her strength is not fading. Rather, she is growing stronger.

Yet, there is no triumph in it. Only failure.

She has imagined every scene of the slopes in her memory. The place where the water ran over the cliffside, the cave they sequestered Baltisse in while she recovered. The tree she pinned Ryon against when she learned he was not dead.

She has shouted Ryon's name until her throat felt shredded, and no one has called back.

Now she cannot call to mind any other memories. Every place she knows has been drawn in her thoughts and willed into existence and she feels no closer to finding them.

"Fuck!" Dawsyn shouts and a flock of ravens disperse from their branches, fleeing the echo of her voice as it reaches their midst.

He is not dead. She feels sure of it. Whatever ties saw fit to bond the two of them would surely hurt to cut. She does not feel their severance. Ryon is not dead.

But whatever condition he might be in, it must be dire.

And she cannot find him to fix it.

Dawsyn's jaw aches from clenching it so tightly closed. Her eyes burn from the wind. Her hands throb with chilblains, but she throws her fist into a tree trunk still. She snaps the loose bark with her knuckles and ignores the reverberations that rattle her bones.

Defeated, she slams her eyelids down and imagines the campsite where she had last parted ways with the others. Her body begins to collapse inward.

Dawsyn unfolds with a wrenching gasp into the snow. Her stomach rolls, but she has come to expect it.

Before her is the small opening to a cave against a steep cliffside.

"Dawsyn?"

She turns. Approaching her from the forest is Hector, his arms laden in stripped branches.

"You didn't find them?"

Before she can answer, there is a clamour from within the cave, and Salem appears in its mouth.

"Dawsyn!" he calls, his face stricken. "Yer back! Thank the saints."

Dawsyn nods, bracing for interrogation. *Where are they? Where are the others?* She opens her mouth to stay the questions, the band of sick dread tightening around her ribcage.

But Salem speaks again before Dawsyn can. "Come quick, lass! She's getting worse."

Dawsyn hesitates, her legs locking in shin-deep snow. "What?"

"It's Abertha," Hector tells her, reaching her side. "Her wound has fouled."

"Wound?" Dawsyn repeats, hastening toward the cave opening. "What are you talking about?"

"A cut on her leg," Hector answers, following. "She says she slipped in the Chasm."

Dawsyn groans internally. Abertha hadn't mentioned a wound. "Is she awake?"

"No," Hector says. "Fever took her under two nights ago."

Dawsyn's grandmother had an adage for infection – *three days to set, two days to sleep, one day to steal.* Dawsyn had seen it happen in real time to a neighbour on the Ledge. Infection took three days to make itself known. By the time it did its host was not long for this world. Even the best medicine woman could not delay the death sleep.

Dawsyn crouches inside the cave.

Esra kneels beside the girl's body. He pats her forehead with a swath of wet rags, looking horribly unsure and inept. "Dawsyn!" he says as she crawls toward him. "Where have you *been?*"

Abertha's face resembles a corpse's already, save for the beads of sweat at her hairline and across her upper lip. She shivers intermittently, her limbs twitching. There is, at least, a snowpack tied to her calf. It leaks onto the cave floor and wets the leg of her pants.

"Two days?" Dawsyn confirms with Hector, who hovers over Dawsyn's shoulder.

"Thereabouts," Hector answers. "She's weakening. We didn't know..." his voice trails off, and he sighs. "She did not say she was hurt."

Dawsyn gently unties the snowpack, made from whatever shirt was generously given and torn to pieces. Abertha's lips part as Dawsyn's fingers work, but the sound that escapes is so faint, Dawsyn cannot be sure it is one of pain or the murmurings of sleep. The girl smells of death already.

The fabric of her pants is badly stained in blood and dried puss – so much so, the fabric has melded to the wound. Dawsyn sighs.

"Must you remove it?" Hector asks. "Can you heal her first?"

Dawsyn considers. "I'd rather see the magic working, so I might know the extent of the wound, and know when to stop."

Hector grimaces back, but nods. "Do it quick."

Dawsyn pulls out a knife and carefully makes a cut at the hem. Then, with one swift movement, she tears the fabric, splitting it up Abertha's calf, and separating it from the wound.

Abertha's leg jerks, and she moans pitifully, new sweat beads forming along her brow, but the fever keeps her sedated.

The wound is... ghastly. It makes a wretched mess of her skin, mottling the flesh. The cut has yellowed with a foul-smelling excretion, while the surrounding skin remains bright red. It stretches from the inside of her knee and disappears into her boot.

Abertha's shoes are already unlaced, but it would be madness to leave her without boots, even for a short time. The cold finds its way to the skin without provocation, which is why Dawsyn blanches to find the seam of Abertha's boot broken – the sole peeling away. Such an easy route for the cold.

"Mother mercy."

"What is it?" Esra asks.

As an answer, Dawsyn slowly pulls the ruined boot from Abertha's foot. The insides are well insulated with layers of hide and fur-lining, and if it weren't for the gaping seam at the toe, it would have made a fine boot for long-wear. Dawsyn cringes. How long had she walked through the snow? What havoc has the frost wrecked on her?

"Shit," Dawsyn breathes.

"Holy Mother," Esra gapes.

Hector curses and backs away, as though it is catching.

Frostbite.

Two of Abertha's toes have blackened, as though dipped in ink. The others are ominously white and bubbled in blisters, the flesh slower to die.

"Idiot," Dawsyn mutters, though her throat closes for the girl. "Why would she say nothing?" The wound, the ruined shoe – why travel in silence rather than alert them? "Close your eyes," Dawsyn says roughly, and presses her palms to the burning flesh of Abertha's leg, avoiding the wound. "*Cristique.*"

Light fills the cave, and she urges magic into Abertha. Dawsyn cleans the wound first, clears the blood of infection. Then she mutters the spell to repair it and feels the power ebb. The wound begins to stitch slowly, the flesh resisting the effort to rejoin. Dawsyn can feel it pulling back but coaxes it to continue. *A little longer,* she thinks, feeling the fever dissipate from Abertha's skin.

Release me, Dawsyn hears, and feels the pressure of resistance intensify.

Dawsyn lets it go. She feels the magic sprint back through her veins, thin and feeble. But the wound at Abertha's leg is now a fresh pink scar. It is not completely healed, but Abertha's eyes are open and searching. Her cheeks pinken delicately with the chill in the cave.

Dawsyn feels an intense pounding in her head, and her vision swims.

"Bertie?" Hector says, grasping her shoulders. "Are you well?"

Abertha looks at him, then Dawsyn. "I... Yes. I think so."

But Dawsyn's waning gaze has found Abertha's toes once more, and though the white-tipped smaller toes have returned to their healthy pink, the first two remain black as coal.

"Dawsyn...Thank you," Abertha says, leaning up on her elbows. She bends her leg to view the scar better and winces.

"Do not thank me," Dawsyn says, sighing sadly.

Abertha frowns. "Without you, I would have died."

"You should have told us you were cut." Dawsyn closes her eyes against the thumping in her skull. "Surely you knew better."

Abertha looked suddenly uncomfortable. "I saw what happened to that blonde mage in the Chasm. I didn't want you to use your powers if you were depleted. It was only a cut."

"A cut that can become easily *fouled.* As you ought to know."

"I wasn't *aware* it had fouled," Abertha bites, oddly petulant. It strokes a long-gone memory Dawsyn can't quite reach. Her mind is addled enough.

"And were you *aware* your boot had split at the sole?"

"My boot?"

Dawsyn holds it aloft. The frayed stitching dangles.

The girl looks mystified. "No. I was not aware."

"If tha' fever set in early, she won't've felt a bloody thin' beneath the ankle, Dawsyn," Salem offers from somewhere behind her.

Abertha shakes her head, baffled. "I will mend it before we continue."

"We will not be continuing for a while," Dawsyn utters, scrubbing her face.

"What? Why?"

Dawsyn takes a breath. She grips her knees and flexes her fingers, preparing. "You are frostbitten."

Abertha's eyes widen, then she sits up, staring down at the deadened flesh of what was once her toes.

"Can you heal them?" Hector asks Dawsyn in a hushed voice. "Once you are rested?"

But Dawsyn healed the other toes, and if it were possible to restore dead flesh, she imagines the magic would have made its mark on the ruined ones. She turns to Hector and lets him read the answer in her eyes.

Hector's face falls.

"Perhaps in a day or so," Abertha offers. "Once your magic returns?"

Dawsyn looks back at Abertha and works her face into a smile. "Of course," she says.

Abertha sighs, then chuckles incredulously. "Thank the Mother. I apologise, I am normally more vigilant. But I am grateful to you, Dawsyn, truly."

"As I said," Dawsyn answers, quietly taking a blade from inside her cloak. "Do not thank me."

She waits for Abertha to grin and look away. Then she grits her teeth. "Hold her."

Hector leaps forward, throwing his full weight over the girl's legs.

And Dawsyn takes the knife to Abertha's toes, pressing the blade all the way through flesh and bone until it meets the ground.

CHAPTER THIRTY-THREE

Ryon awakens with a groan.

His shoulders scream, the tendons torn and throbbing with a menace he has never met. But this cave he knows. It all comes crashing back to him.

"Awake again," says the same voice as before – low and melodic. The mage with the braids tips a clay cup to his lips. "Drink, night wing," she says.

Ryon splutters at the liquid forced passed his lips. It burns, leaving his throat scorched. "Ugh," he moans, his head swimming. "Riv?" he mutters. He is not sure if the word fully forms. "Tash?"

"Your fellows are alive, though they have fared worse than you," the mage says in the old language, choking any reply Ryon could give with another wash of the hot, fiery liquid.

Ryon thrashes, turning his head away, but it only tears at his shoulders and another moan escapes him.

"Easy, Glacian," the mage says. "You'll separate those arms from the rest of you."

The substance works its way down his throat and makes his eyes water, but the pain coursing through his body quickly dulls. It makes it easier to think, to concentrate. His feet slip on the rocky floor, but he can focus on the mage, he can peer at the receding light from the entrance. Receding or dawning? He has no concept of time.

"How long have I been here?"

"Days," the mage said. "You are stronger than I predicted."

Ryon tries to steady the shake of his legs. "Please," he says. "Let me go. I want no fight with you."

"Ah," the woman says. "Then you should not have wandered through our wards."

"I was *brought* here. I did not come of my own means."

The mage tilts her head to the side. "And who delivered you? Surely not Baltisse. Unless she is in trouble?"

"No…" Ryon hesitates. "No. Not her."

The mention of her name brings to mind the first time Ryon stumbled upon this clan of mages – of how they intended to kill him. Were it not for Baltisse's arrival, her ability to read minds and find his intention well-meant, they likely would have.

"Where is she? She has not visited in a long while," the mage asks now, her eyes burning fiercely.

Ryon cannot answer. Doing so will surely bring about a swift death. He defers instead. "Yerdos folded me from the Chasm," he says. "She brought us here."

It has the affect he imagined. The mage's eyes widen – bright beacons in this dark cavern. Her hand reaches out toward his neck, as though she might squeeze it, but her fingers retract. "Yerdos?" she repeats, the name hushed. She says it with reverence. "She sent you here?"

Ryon nods once.

"A gift," the mage utters. "An offering."

The muscles in his stomach recoil. Offerings tend to infer food. From what he knows of this ancient clan, it would not seem undue for them to consume Glacians and call it sustenance.

"She showed us mercy," Ryon says, his voice softer. So soft he fears she will not hear. "She returned us to the mountain."

The mage only stares with that lopsided tilt, the flame in her palm dancing haphazardly.

"What is your name?" Ryon winces.

"Samskia," she answers, gaze unbroken.

"Samskia… Yerdos had other plans for me," he grunts, his eyelids drooping. "There is a woman on this mountain. She needs me."

"Women do not have need of men," Samskia rebukes. "It is only men who suffer and destruct when women withdraw their attention."

Ryon closes his eyes, feeling Dawsyn reaching for him through the dark. He thinks of the way her eyes search and search until they find him and thinks that this assertion might have been true once, but it isn't true now.

She needs him, just as he needs her.

"In two nights, the moon will glow red. Perhaps you'll live to see it, night wing, and your lover will come to find you. Far stranger things have happened on a blood moon."

Ryon looks to the cavern entrance, where the light has brightened the snow beyond. "And if she does not?"

"Then we will bleed you dry in Yerdos' name," Samskia says with a sinister smile. Her teeth glisten. "You and the rest of your winged friends."

With that, she thrusts her hand sideways, and the flame that she had held bounces along the cavern walls, lighting torches as it goes. It illuminates the tunnel-like cave foot by foot, until the unfathomably long expanse is thrown into relief.

Tied by vine to the earthy walls are the wilting bodies of not just three Glacians – though Rivdan and Tasheem hang limply beside him – but many.

And their skin is ghostly white.

"I hope you live to see the moon, night wing," Samskia says, gliding toward the cave opening. "You were a fool to leave your woman." With that, the mage disappears, stepping out onto the snow with bare feet.

Ryon turns his head as far as he can manage to his left, straining to see Tasheem and Rivdan. Their forearms and shoulders are encased in the same vine, their heads lolling forward onto their chests. Tasheem's lips are rimmed in blood and drops of it seep from her mouth and fall to the ground. Rivdan trembles in his sleep. His eyes are only half-closed. Ryon can see the whites of them beneath the slits of his eyelids.

"Fuck," Ryon breathes. He cannot strain against the vine. It only seems to wind itself tighter when he tries. In any case, his shoulders are too injured for the movement, stretched beyond their capacity from holding up his weight. "Mother help us."

"Oh, I doubt the Mother will turn her head for the likes of us, Ryon," a weak voice says.

It comes from the wall opposite, where the torch flames are beginning to flicker out and throw the bodies of the other captured Glacians into shadow.

Ryon squints and can just make out the shape of the nose, the lengths of steely hair, the sunken, translucent skin.

Vasteel lifts his chin to meet Ryon's stare.

Ryon's stomach lurches.

"The bastard son of Mesrich," the former king says. "How odd that we should meet again."

Chapter Thirty-Four

Abertha only screams for a few seconds before she slumps back, unconscious.

"Dawsyn!" Esra yells, falling back onto his arse. "What the fuck did you do?"

Hector is already snatching the rags from Esra's hands and passing them to Dawsyn, who presses them firmly to the gushing wounds at the ends of Abertha's foot.

"Why... good god, Dawsyn! Why'd yeh do tha'?" Salem gasps. He watches on in horror, his skin tinged green.

"Better to have it over with," Hector intones, ripping fabric from the bottom of his tunic. He begins tying it around Abertha's foot. "The flesh was dead."

"But... fucking *hell!* To cut off her – her – Could yeh not've tried to heal her, Dawsyn?"

Dawsyn chews on her tongue as she helps Hector wrap the wound. It will need to stay dry and clean – as well as can be kept in their current setting.

"Surely, there was something else you could've done!" Esra protests. He glares at Hector with something like disgust.

The bleeding is already slowing, Dawsyn notes.

"Dawsyn? Are yeh hearin' me? Yeh should've given the girl some warnin', at *least*. She should 'ave some say o'er her own goddamn feet!"

"The flesh was black. Dead. I cannot bring back something perished."

"But to cut them clean off like that? *Mother above*, Daw–"

"Would it have been better to wait?" Dawsyn asks, her voice rising. "To let the frost spread? Let her foster the delusion I could possibly restore

214

what I cannot? As for her *say*, Salem, what say has she? Dead flesh cannot stay. Frost that creeps in and takes hold can only be cut away."

Esra scoffs, scrubbing his face with his hand. "Some warning may have been polite," he says to both Hector and Dawsyn. "To hold her down like that…"

"We saved her the anticipation, Es," Hector says calmly, carefully holding his bloodied hands away from his clothes. "Warning her wouldn't have changed what needed to be done. Better that she didn't have to think on it at all."

"We did her a favour," Dawsyn says, watching Abertha twitch and jerk in her sleep. The throb of the wound will awaken her soon. "The expectance of pain is as bad as the reality. We could at least save her from the former."

"But when she *wakes*," Esra says. "Fucking hell, Dawsyn. Surely she will be–"

"Grateful," Dawsyn interjects, her raised voice making Abertha jerk again. "She will be grateful. She is Ledge-born and she understands the whims of frost as well as Hector and I."

"I don't know," Salem mutters, pushing the hood of his cloak back over his head in agitation. "I don't know about tha'."

"No, you do not," says Hector, not bothering to look back at the old man. Instead, he levels his gaze with Esra's. "You did not live constantly fighting for warmth as we did. You lived beneath the sun, and you have no wisdom to give in matters of the cold." Hector stands, nodding at Dawsyn. "I will see about finding some bollybark," he says, then leaves, taking long strides past Salem and out in the open wind.

There is a tense silence. Esra, whose eyes have not left the place where Hector disappeared, clears his throat. "What is bollybark?"

"A pain suppressor. It tastes like shit. But if you can stand to chew it, it numbs the senses for a little while."

Abertha whimpers in her sleep, and Dawsyn gently rests her bandaged foot on the cavern floor. "She will live," Dawsyn says firmly. "And that is what matters."

Salem shifts uncomfortably from side to side. His lips part as though he wishes to say something more, but then they close again.

"Perhaps I seem callous to you," Dawsyn says quietly. She has never denied as such. "That is quite well, but Abertha will awaken. She will walk again soon. I will heal the wounds once I am restored enough to do so and–"

"We do not think you callous, love," Salem interrupts. His features have turned softer, apologetic.

"It was..." Esra hesitates. "Just quite a shock, is all." And indeed, he appears rattled to the core.

Dawsyn sighs. She feels suddenly uneasy in her own skin. The knife at her side glints accusingly at her.

"Dawsyn," Salem begins, finally meeting her eye. "I – I'm sorry. It ain't my place to cast judgments. I'm older, but I don't reckon I've seen half the life yeh had up there on that ice shelf. This mountain," Salem looks out to the slopes. "Well, I can't imagine how anyone survives it long."

Dawsyn nods and stands. She spies Esra shaking his head, as though he can't rid the butchery from his mind. "I may seem cold to you," she tells him. "But you should not tarnish Hector with the same opinion. He is far kinder than I, and had you been made to live as he lived, you might appreciate the oddity he is." Dawsyn's heart tightens, remembering the skinny boy on the Ledge. "Hector merely understands what needs to be done. Rest assured he will berate himself. He will not need your assistance."

Dawsyn makes to follow Hector out into the wind. "I'll go help him."

"No," Esra calls, gathering his feet beneath him. "Let me." He crouches as he makes his way toward her, his head in danger of glancing off the rocky ceiling. As he passes Dawsyn, he takes her hand, squeezes it. "I do not think either of you unkind. Just far stronger than anyone ought to be." He smiles in his lopsided way, then departs, pulling his furs tightly around his torso as the squalls lash at him.

Another whimper sounds and Dawsyn turns to see Abertha's eyes open. Tears well in the corners and her lips shake. She utters small noises that she clearly tries to absorb. She breathes heavily through her nose.

Dawsyn ducks by her head, crouching on her haunches. "I'm sorry, Bertie," she says quietly, her voice oddly choked. She finds she can barely look at the girl. Instead, she looks at her own hands, clasped together and stained red.

"Th-thank you," Abertha whispers, the words hitching. One hand reaches up and clasps tightly around Dawsyn's wrist. "Thank you f-for doing it swiftly."

"I will heal you come morning," Dawsyn vows, clasping her own hand atop Abertha's. "At first light."

"Promise?"

Dawsyn sees her watery eyes, the wildness of her hair, and thinks of another girl she once made promises to, who looked up at her with that same shrewd insight.

"I promise," Dawsyn says.

And though she is not one to offer comfort, she seeks her own. An inexplicable starvation urges her to lie in the place beside Abertha, feeling the girl's arm aligned against hers. Their shoulders press together, side-by-side. Dawsyn closes her eyes, and she is in her den of girls, the wind beating its mighty gale beyond their walls. But she is not afraid. She is not alone.

They survive a fretful night.

The mountain blizzards with impressive intensity and the fire struggles to endure. Hector and Esra find enough bollybark to subdue Abertha's pain for a couple of hours, but she spends the remainder of the night restless, unable to find relief from the throbbing in her foot. Dawsyn tends to the fire before Hector takes over, bidding her to find her sleep so that she can be of use come morning. He ensures Abertha's feet stay close to the flames – her exposed toes are still in danger of frostbite if they cannot not bring warmth to them.

By morning, Hector's face is drawn and weary, but not defeated. He smiles wanly as Dawsyn sits upright, giving up on the pretence of rest. The sky outside has finally begun to lighten, and the wind has breathed its last. The mountain is now a sleeping beast – eerily silent and still after having rampaged and wreaked havoc in the dark.

Esra and Salem are curled in on themselves on the other side of the fire and they likely found no more sleep than she. Their eyes move behind their eyelids with the chaos of the restless.

But Abertha is wide awake. Sweat dampens her hair. "Is it morning?" she breathes toward Dawsyn, eyes pleading.

Dawsyn nods. Without further preamble, she pulls her gloves away from her hands and gently lifts the leg of Abertha's pants. Dawsyn places her hand on the part of her foot that is not wrapped in bandages, then closes her eyes.

The iskra is sluggish, but responsive. It moves to coalesce with the dim light of her mind. Together they flow from her palms and into Abertha.

It only takes a moment. It is all she can expend before the magic retreats again. But Abertha breathes a sigh of deep relief. She lets her head fall back and closes her eyes, the tension lines in her forehead and around her mouth now gone. "Thank you," she mouths.

Dawsyn unwraps the bandaging gently. It is heavy with congealed blood, but the flesh beneath bears no wound. Only the fresh, angry pink of new skin in the absence of two toes.

She sighs, relieved, and wrings her hands together to loosen their tension. "You will repair your boots today."

Abertha stares at her balefully. "I'll consider the advice."

"And check them every day."

"Obviously."

"And wrap your remaining toes, lest they blacken and break off mid-journey."

Abertha rolls her eyes. "You need not mother me. I am capable of–"

"Of almost succumbing to infection? Of walking miles with snow in your boot?"

Abertha frowns, then looks at Hector. "Is she always so insufferable?"

Hector grins.

"If you act like an infant, I'll treat you as such," Dawsyn says, but Abertha is grinning at her, the amusement clear on her face.

"I cannot imagine anyone less suited to raising infants."

"And yet, here I am, chaperoning three of them across a mountain," Dawsyn mutters, rising to her feet. "Now, get ready. Let us see if you can walk without falling on your face."

Dawsyn waits while Abertha mends her boot and wraps her feet. When each are done, they slowly venture from the gap in the boulders that served as their shelter.

Abertha walks unsteadily.

"It may take some getting used to," Dawsyn says, leading her out into open air. "My grandmother cut away more than two before she died. She always said the adjustment was difficult."

Abertha breathes deeply, her nose turned upward. "It is good to be standing at all."

The forest before them has been reshaped, renewed. That is the beauty that follows the brutality of snowstorms – the landscape afterward is reborn. The blemishes of yesterday are buried.

"So clear," Abertha says, staring at her surroundings. Dawsyn knows what she means. On the Ledge, a permanent mist remains. They lived among oppressive cloud. It clung to the mountain top and only ever afforded them a world of grey. Here, where the cloud does not always reach, the forest is pristine. Without the wind to shift the powder, everything is thrown into sharp relief.

"I remember your grandmother," Abertha says now, walking cautiously forward through the snow. "She was a force to be reckoned with. Scarier even than my own mother."

Dawsyn grins slightly. "A fitting description."

"But she was sympathetic. I spied on her through the trees as a child. I watched her say a prayer over the Garisson brothers. They were dead in the grove. Do you remember them?"

Dawsyn remembered. Burly men with a penchant for muscling the trees from others where they saw fit.

"They were bastards and yet your grandmother still spared their souls a prayer," Abertha says. "I never forgot that."

Dawsyn laughs grimly, kicking snow off the toe of her boot.

"What?"

"My grandmother killed the Garrison brothers," Dawsyn admits, shrugging her shoulders. "Whether she prayed over their everlasting souls or not seems forfeit."

"Oh," Abertha says, seeming to consider that for a moment. "Well, I watched my father kill a man once, and I don't recall him imparting any words of salvation, save for a kick in the side before he stepped over the body."

"I no longer believe in the power of prayer," Dawsyn says, following Abertha around a copse of bushels. "If prayer had any sway, we would all be standing on newfound land on the other side of this fucking mountain. Instead, I led us to fire and brimstone."

Abertha studies her for a moment. "Do you still believe the Queen is corralling the others into a trap?"

Dawsyn looks her in the eye. "I know she is."

"Then we are most fortunate indeed."

"Forgive me, but I cannot bring myself to celebrate." At that, Dawsyn's heart thuds heavily. Any capacity for optimism she once had has long since been laid to waste.

She has failed to find safe settlement.

Failed to find Ryon.

"You will see him again," Abertha says, as though she had read her mind. She looks around as though Ryon were likely to appear from behind a tree. "Mother knows, you won't stop until you do."

Dawsyn says nothing. In truth, she has not considered the alternative. She knows she will search for Ryon for as long as it takes to find him. But should she find him already dead...

"You'll find him, Dawsyn," Abertha says again. "You are too stubborn for the fates to thwart you."

If only it were so simple. "Will you tell me something, Abertha?"

"Bertie," she says. "It is what my friends call me."

"Bertie. When I found you in the Chasm, fighting off Wes–"

Abertha shudders delicately. Her shoulders tense.

"Why did you absolve him?" It had gnawed at Dawsyn all this time, that Abertha would not allow Dawsyn or Ryon to simply cut the boy down where he stood. Mother knew, they were more than willing.

Abertha sighs. "You must think less of me."

"No," Dawsyn says firmly. "I only wonder at your reasoning."

Abertha ambles onward, placing one foot before the other carefully, and does not answer immediately. Dawsyn thinks she may not answer at all, before she hears the girl utter a sound of annoyance. "I stole his sisters' clothes after they died. Not *all* of them," she iterates. "But a cloak, a pair of gloves, boots. Wes caught me with them in the Chasm." She holds up her hands now to display the hide gloves. They are crudely made, but thick. "I thought he'd kill me."

Dawsyn waits. "But he didn't."

"No," she says. "He was furious, but he had always had affection for me – even asked me to marry him last season."

Dawsyn shakes her head. "That wasn't affection."

"No. And perhaps he deserved a swift death for forcing himself on me. But... when we were all scrambling for our belongings on the Ledge, I saw Wes and his father bending over the bodies of his sisters and kissing their foreheads, and my first thought was to loot their cabin while their heads were turned. So, perhaps I deserved a swift death, too." Dawsyn watches Abertha lift her face to the sunlight filtering in through the thick brush of pine needles, contemplating them. "I suppose I'd thought us no better than each other."

Dawsyn presses her lips together, considering her words. She has never been well-versed in words of comfort, but it seems suddenly imperative that she ease whatever burden Abertha carries. "My sister was the best thief I knew," she says, and it turns Abertha's attention away from the sky and whatever thoughts afflict her. "She somehow managed to fit herself within the tightest holes, through the narrowest of gaps. She was deathly quiet, too. I cannot count the times I turned to find her standing behind me, holding a blade she'd filched from my belt or my boot. Truly, she was a reckoning. It drove our mother wild."

"Briar," Abertha frowns, remembering. "Yes?"

"Yes," Dawsyn affirms. "And my sister was Maya. She almost got herself bludgeoned more times than I can count."

"But people were afraid of you," Abertha adds. "Your grandmother, too."

"Maya wasn't afraid of us. Of anyone, actually. She would never have apologised for the things she thieved."

Abertha chuckles.

"You remind me of her," Dawsyn admits. "You are the age Maya would be now, had she lived."

Abertha pauses before answering. "I wish I'd known her better."

"If you had, you might have taught her some forgiveness or compassion. They are difficult to come by in our kind. Someone of such character does not deserve a swift death. They deserve freedom. Safety." Dawsyn looks out at the endlessly undulating slopes and shakes her head bitterly. "I am sorry I could not lead you to it."

Abertha reaches out to place her hand on Dawsyn's shoulder. "You led me here," she says. "And even if I should perish tomorrow, at least I stepped foot on land that was not tilted to the Chasm."

Dawsyn feels her lips upturn despite herself. As Maya once had, Abertha has a way of forcing her to good humour.

"Now, tell me," Abertha bids, continuing through the drifts. "How does one come to find themselves intertwined with a Glacian?"

Dawsyn huffs a sad laugh. "Do you have any understanding of what it is to fall in love?"

Abertha blinks at her.

"No, I didn't either," Dawsyn says. "But rest assured, it was not something I could prevent."

"But why him?" Abertha's curiosity seems genuine, and it betrays her youth.

Dawsyn thinks carefully, then shakes her head. "It was not something within my control. When we were first acquainted, I thought him no different than the pure-blooded Glacians. I might have walked away then wholly intact. Now… it feels like parts of me have been carved out."

"What changed?"

Dawsyn thinks of the slopes and how her heart leapt with each quip, each cutting word and its counter. She thinks of how it thrilled her to challenge him. How, after seven years in solitude on the Ledge, she found herself leaning into the companionship, rather than away.

She thinks of the inexplicable magnetism between them and how difficult it was to ignore. She thinks of how he watched her, wherever she went, and how difficult it was not to stare at him. The sly touch of his fingers along hers, the secret pass of a hand on her hip. She thinks of the way the warmth of him made her shiver with newness. How the circle of his arms feels impenetrable. How she breathes for the next moment she finds herself in their embrace.

"I learned we were not so different," Dawsyn says, smiling unknowingly. "He is a difficult man to ignore."

"I will not deny you that. He is quite… magnificent. In bed sport too, I'd imagine?"

"If your thoughts keep wandering to Ryon and bed sport, I may have to cut off the rest of your toes."

Abertha smirks. "Love to see you try."

Dawsyn does not say anything more. Her eyes instead are fixed on a spot downhill, where the pine trees grow closer together along the slope. They look almost purposefully placed. It reminds Dawsyn of the pine grove on the Ledge, where the saplings were planted in rows.

"Dawsyn?" Abertha says, stopping alongside her. She skirts their surrounds, looking for any imminent threat.

"Do you see that?" Dawsyn asks, nodding downhill.

"The cedar trees?"

Dawsyn's gaze is not concentrated on the trees themselves, but rather the haze that seems to hang in their midst. Where the rest of the mountain is clear and virginal, the copse of cedars in the distance seems… distorted.

Abertha, however, seems perturbed not by the strange fog, but by Dawsyn. "I suppose they *do* seem to have grown closely."

"Not that. The *mist*. Do you not see it?"

Again, Abertha only squints, then gives Dawsyn a perplexed look.

Dawsyn grits her teeth. "It is right *there*."

"I don't see any mist, Dawsyn."

"Go back to the others," she says stiffly. "I will return soon."

But Abertha follows her down the slope, her footfalls slightly uneven. "Where are you going?"

"There is mist among those trees. And yet the rest of the slope is clear of it."

"I see no mist, Dawsyn. Slow down!"

But Dawsyn feels seized by something she cannot name. She trudges through the drifts without minding the snow that slips into her boots, her stare fixed upon that odd cluster of cedar, so uniformly placed in their unnatural line, almost as though they were grown deliberately.

A division.

A gate.

The light in Dawsyn's mind grows inexplicably warmer as she hastens. It seems to urge her onward.

"Dawsyn! Mother above, these boots are newly stitched!"

But Dawsyn barely registers her voice. The cedars tower above her as she grows closer, and her eyes track their height. They disappear into the sky, taller than that of any other tree around them. And between their vast trunks, clinging to the bark, is that barricade.

Not mist, Dawsyn realises, but something other. A filmy haze.

It hums with magic. She can feel it in her blood.

"Ouch," Abertha complains, coming to a halt at her side. "I would remind you of my very recent dismemberment, but as you were the butcher, it seems pointless."

Dawsyn holds up a hand to stay the girl's complaints. "Do you hear that?"

The humming grows louder. It is the swelling of a storm, the amalgamating power before the burn of lightning.

"*No*," Abertha emphasises. "Dawsyn, what—"

"And the mist?" Dawsyn queries, studying the barrier before her made of trees and haze. "You still do not see it before you?"

Abertha appears truly incredulous now, looking left to right as though the blanket of grey does not distort her view in every direction. "I do not see it," she says, her voice quieter. "I swear it."

Dawsyn frowns warily at the film, the magic. Her hand reaches forward.

"What are you doing?"

She hears nothing but that alluring hum. The mage light within courses down her arm and she does not give thought to the fingertip that stretches before her, gently glancing off the haze...

A shout leaves her as she is thrust into the air. Dawsyn is flung backward, her feet leaving the ground for one long second before her back collides with it again, the snow softening the fall, but a strike of pain sizzles up her arm, quickly dissipating.

"Mother above!"

Dawsyn sees only the tips of cedar and blue sky, before the view is impeded by Abertha's face. "Fucking hell! Are you all right?" Her eyes are wide with alarm. "What was *that?*"

But Dawsyn only groans softly, the fall having pushed all air from her lungs.

A voice travels to them from uphill. "Is that Dawsyn I see on the ground?" Esra's hovering face joins Abertha's. "Having a kip, are you?"

Dawsyn gives him a lethal glare, still struggling to suck in a breath.

"What're yeh doin' down there?" Salem adds, his face appearing among the others. "Weren't yeh the one tellin' us all to keep our arses off the snow?"

"Yes, Dawsyn. If you must swoon, do as I do and ensure there is a strapping lad whose arms will catch you," Esra says.

"Shut up, Es," Salem mutters. "Ain't nary a man strong enough to catch tha' thick skull."

"On the contrary, I have delicate features, but a huge phallus. So, I suppose, the ratios balance in the end. Dawsyn? Are you having some sort of episode?"

Abertha answers for her. "She was thrown backward."

"Dawsyn?" Hector's voice hails from the distance. "Why is she lying in the snow?"

"She is having an episode!" Esra shouts back.

Dawsyn groans once more and sits up. She feels snow drip down the back of her neck. "There was an entire pit of molten lava waiting inside that Chasm," she says on a shallow breath. "If I was wiser, I would have pitched myself into it."

"Has she maddened?" Esra asks.

"Fuck me, but these people are annoying," Abertha says with a sigh. She proffers a hand, and Dawsyn accepts it, getting her feet beneath her. Then Abertha's gaze returns to the place between the cedars where Dawsyn had been standing moments before. "What *was* that?"

Dawsyn's mind hums insistently, the bright spark pulsing behind her eyes. "Something to keep one out," she says. She does not know where the knowledge comes from, but it is there, throbbing behind the beating drum of her own mage blood.

"Yeh said she were thrown?" Salem asks, his eyes assessing Abertha. "What'd yeh mean, thrown?"

"I mean one moment, she was standing amongst that tree line," – she gestures toward the cedars – "and the next she was on her back."

"Well," Esra says, pulling the waist of his pants higher. "Let us see what foe lies beyond!"

"I wouldn't, Esra," Dawsyn warns, but the man has already passed, striding determinedly toward the opaque wall of grey that he so obviously cannot see. "You'll be sorry."

"Come out, you cowardly f–" His sentence is cut short by the high-pitched shriek he emits as he sails through the air, landing a foot before them and spraying them with snow.

"Mother's tits!" Salem shouts, backing away, his eyes darting around the forest. "What the fuck was that?"

"A *barrier*," Dawsyn answers, staring with fresh awe at the strange magic. "A ward."

"Glacians?" Hector asks, pulling forth a long dagger from his sleeve. He looks to the skies, as though white wings might suddenly appear above the treetops.

But Dawsyn's eyes remain on the magic. "No," she says. "Mages."

Chapter Thirty-Five

Yennes awoke with Baltisse's voice echoing in the chambers of her mind. She told her what a fool she'd been. How heedless she was. How she knew nothing of this kingdom and how it worked.

Her head rolled back and connected with something unforgiving – a wall. She was surrounded by them.

What little light there was revealed stone, an iron grid, and little else. Her hands were shackled to the wall. She could not use them to push hair from her face. Something viscous ran down the back of her neck, a rivulet of blood from where she'd been struck.

Bright spots clouded her vision when she blinked, but she had enough wit left in her to summon the iskra. It wound its way willingly to her palms, as though it had been waiting for her to finally wake.

"*Bruvex,*" she whispered and the iron links around her wrists broke. Her numb arms dropped to the ground, and she winced as the blood rushed back to them. Next, she tried the iron gate, but the same enchantment made no mark whatsoever. Some invisible protection, perhaps. A magicked lock.

"Baltisse," she whispered weakly. "Where are you?"

But Baltisse was back in her cove, doing as Yennes should have done, keeping her distance.

The only tell-tale sign of passing time was the candle that sat inside the sconce beyond the gate. She watched it burn down and guessed at the hours that passed. With each one, the slippery voices of the Chasm returned, louder than before. The torment she could not rid herself of. They whispered that they were a part of her now. Sewn into her skin. Married to the flesh.

And Yennes whimpered. She cried and prayed and pleaded with the Mother. Whatever strength she'd harboured in reserve was gone now. This world had taken every last piece. If humans were born to withstand a measure of trial, then she'd had the portion of three.

She let herself crumble and did not care for the sounds she emitted.

"My, my," a voice said, jolting Yennes from near sleep. She looked to the gate, the candlelight now eclipsed by a figure. Alvira. "How pitiful you are. This place has a way of smothering the fire within a person, but I thought it might take a while longer to stamp out *yours*."

Yennes did not bother to lift her head, she simply closed her eyes, aware that whimpers still escaped her lips, but not much caring. She hoped the Queen was here to finally kill her, do what the Ledge and Glacia and the Chasm had failed to.

"Have you had enough now, iskra witch?"

Yennes nodded. *Yes,* she thought. *I've had more than my share.*

"Then I'll offer again what you were too stupid to accept before. You will cure my wife, and I will let you live. Surely, it is not such a terrible trade?"

Yennes moaned. She did not wish to live.

"Oh, come now. I think you'll find Terrsaw a grand place to start a new life. Think of it, witch. You could find a home. Lure a husband. Have a child—"

Yennes' eyes snapped open.

"—you could leave the past where it ought to remain and start anew. Is that not why you escaped that hellish place? Surely it was not to die here on my floor."

Yennes pulled her knees in tighter, until she resembled an infant. She let the Queen's words circle inside her mind, caught in an endless loop. They became louder and louder, until she had to squeeze her eyes shut again.

"I'll return this evening," Alvira told her. "Once you've had time to think it over."

"No!" Yennes called, her voice choked and cracked. She could not remember when she had last had anything to drink. "No. I… I need to get out…"

"Yes, it is rather a despairing place," Alvira agreed, looking about the keep as though they were discussing the décor. "Smells terrible."

"Let me out," Yennes begged, voice rising. "Please."

"And the Queen Consort?" Alvira asked, her hands suddenly gripping the rungs, knuckles white. "Let me be blunt, witch. If she dies, *you* die. Do we understand each other?"

Cressida was asleep when Yennes entered the bed chamber on shaking legs.

Grey-skinned and cheeks sunken, she seemed not long for this world. Her short, shallow breaths rattled on inhale, as though it could not quite reach her lungs. It was a sound Yennes was acquainted with. The sound of drowning. On the Ledge, most died young, but if the cold could not pry one from this realm quickly, then it would settle for stealth. Lung sickness took those who survived every other test of the Ledge, and the rattle of their last breaths always sounded the same.

Servants hovered around the Queen Consort's bed, useless in their frivolous ministrations. No amount of cold compress or treacle could cure what had already set it. Alvira knew it. She looked upon her wife with glazed eyes, the lines around her mouth deepening with the effort it took to conceal emotion – but the anguish was clear. It was emanating from her in waves. "Get out," she ordered the lady's maids and they hastened to scramble away.

Yennes waited for the doors to close before speaking and as soon as the room was empty of any other, she took a trembling breath. "Do I have your word that I will be released, should I save her?"

Alvira answered hastily, impatiently, as though Yennes' life was of little consequence. "You have it," she said. "Hurry. Please."

Cressida coughed and her body jolted with the force of it. Dark specks dotted her lips and chin and Yennes quailed. The Terrsaw Queen was right to worry.

Doubt quickly interceded as Yennes lowered the bed covers from Cressida's chest. What if she was unable to do what had already been promised? Did she have strength enough to heal a person so close to death?

She pressed her unsteady hands to the woman's chest, feeling the rapid movements as her body fought its last. Yennes closed her eyes and, in silent prayer, beckoned to the iskra.

Mercifully, it unravelled within her.

"Ishveet."

She had practiced this spell with Baltisse, with her own cuts and abrasions, with the mending of tools and fabric. It was not difficult for the magic to find what was damaged. The iskra flowed through her palms easily. It seeped into the Queen Consort and entangled with her blood.

When Yennes opened her eyes, Cressida's cheeks were less hollow, her eyelids less veined. Her cracked lips became fuller, pinker, and her breaths eased into a steady rhythm.

The Queen's wife awakened, healed.

Yennes was pushed to the side as Alvira rushed forward, kneeling beside the bed and grasping Cressida's hand in her own. "My darling," she whispered, bringing the hand to her lips. "Mother, bless us."

Cressida's eyes roam the room, pausing on Yennes first, and then finding her wife. "Alvira," she said. "What did you do?"

But Alvira stood and pressed her mouth to Cressida's, thwarting the woman's confusion.

Yennes smiled. Not at the Queens. Not them. But at her hands.

Cressida blushed slightly at the open display before company, then looked to the company in question. "Am I to assume you managed to smoke out that mage you threatened me with?" she asks wryly.

"Something of the sort," Alvira answered. "Do you feel any pain?"

"None."

Indeed, the more the seconds passed, the more colour returned to her complexion. She sat upright, groaning as she cricked her neck. "Saints, that feels divine."

"I'm glad for your improvement, ma'am."

"Your Majesty," Cressida corrected.

"Your Majesty. Lung sickness took my mother up on the Ledge. It is a cruel way to die."

Cressida's eyes widened. "The Ledge," she muttered, to herself perhaps, and then to Alvira. "Surely not?"

"It would seem our friend Yennes has somehow stumbled across Glacian magic," Alvira confirmed. "Though I am yet to hear the full tale."

"Yennes?" Cressida repeated, a note of recognition in her voice. "Survivor?"

Yennes nodded tiredly. "It is what they called me."

"They?" Both monarchs seemed to lean closer.

"The Glacians," Yennes murmured. "I... I lived with them for a time."

The Queens gave her an incredulous look. "Lived?" Alvira asked. "What could you mean?"

"What is your real name, if not 'Yennes'?" Cressida interceded, her eyes sweeping across Yennes entirely.

Yennes' fingers curled inward to her palms. She had not uttered it aloud since she found herself within that Chasm. It felt false on her tongue, a version of herself long since left to rot.

"Farra," she finally said, as though uttering someone else's name.

"Well, Farra," Alvira seated herself on the mattress beside her wife. "You ought to tell us the rest. You will not leave from here until you do."

Chapter Thirty-Six

Farra was taken from the Ledge and brought before the King of Glacia in the same cruel fashion as each Ledge-dweller before her. She was blindfolded and stripped and chained before being thrown into the dungeon to wait the night. When the morning came, she and the other captives were herded up a narrow winding staircase and thrust through enormous oak doors, where the Pool of Iskra awaited, where Vasteel awaited.

Yet it was not Vasteel that caught her attention first, nor that fucking pool with its strange whispers. The room pounded a frenetic beat as the Glacians roared and jeered and thumped their empty chalices against the tabletops, but it could do nothing to distract from the Glacian that stood at the King's side. The very Glacian whose talons had sunk into her shoulders and snatched her from her home.

He bore the marks of her fight. There was a cut along his cheekbone. A split in his lip. Her very own fingers had gouged those lines across his chest. She could see clearly where the scratches disappeared beneath his tunic. He had not put up much of a fight when they landed, releasing her as soon as they were close enough to ground. She had turned with ruined arms and drawn her knife, ignoring the screaming of her shoulders as she sliced and scratched. The Glacian had hit the knife away and taken her wrists in one of his hands, pinning her against his front within moments. Farra got the impression he could have done so sooner.

"I am sorry," she thought he had said. But the wind was howling. Other captives screamed and shouted around them as they were held in mid-air, their tendons straining. The more Farra thought of it, the more ludicrous it seemed that she had heard the Glacian say anything at all.

He stared back at her, across the expanse of the hall, and a slow smile stretched across his face. And what a face it was. Pale and chiselled, as though cut from stone. His hair was short and a dark smoky grey. It perfectly imitated the colour of his eyes, the colour of his wings. Those wings hung perfectly still, folded inward behind the vast expanse of his shoulders. He was, in every possible way, dangerous. Terrifying. Beautiful.

And he watched her as though he might consume her.

Vasteel preached and Farra heard nothing of what was said. She focussed on keeping her sights set on her captor. She would die this night – she had already deduced as much and was shocked it had not already come to pass – and so, as her neighbours stepped to the edge of the pool, one by one, she speared the Glacian with every ounce of spite and malice she was capable of. She would die cursing him, and if the Holy Mother was merciful, she would ensure this beast never knew peace again.

"Move, girl," a gruff voice demanded, and she was shoved forward. She stepped toward the pool with her head high, her lips pressed tightly shut, and she looked her last at the Glacian by Vasteel's side, praying he felt her hatred.

But the Glacian had stepped forward. "Wait!" he called to her, to the room at large. "Halt!" his hand reached out and for a moment Farra thought she recognised panic. But then the Glacian's eyes fell to his master and they became coolly indifferent. Mirthful, perhaps. "Your Grace," he said. "Pardon the interruption. But it has been so *long* since I had a servant to… *tend* to me."

The confusion that had narrowed Vasteel's eyes turned to amusement. The King's head tilted back and he laughed.

Soon, all the Glacians around the hall were laughing. Laughing at her.

Farra turned to cut them with her stare too.

"She *is* spirited," Vasteel guffawed, as though she were little more than a wild animal fighting against the hold of his trap. "But we have many a human walking these halls, Mesrich. Take who you please to your chambers."

The Glacian named Mesrich grinned. "I want this one," he said, and there was an edge to his voice, a slip in his otherwise oily countenance. "I relish a challenge."

Vasteel laughed again and slapped Mesrich on the back. "I see you've returned to yourself, my friend. Consider the girl a gift from me to you. No noble shall hunger tonight!"

The Glacians roared their approval, tankards clashed, but Farra turned her gaze to the pool before her. It glowed invitingly, swirling with some matter she could not name, and though it were inexplicable, she could *hear it*. It urged her closer, promised a gentle embrace.

At thirty-one, Farra had fought off her share of men who believed she was little more than a means of satisfaction. She would not fight off another. With one last loathsome glance toward the Glacian named Mesrich – the one who had dragged her across the Chasm – she held her breath, then hurled herself into the pool.

There was no sensation of falling. No collision. She fell into the depths of the pool, and it ensconced her immediately, cradling her in its warmth. She felt utterly weightless, thoughtless. The pool sung to her and she smiled. She closed her eyes obediently. What blissful relief to rest within its depths. The pool delivered her gently down its current, and she went willingly.

A tug in the opposite direction was the only source of discomfort, but even that was easily ignored. She curled herself away from it. *Yes*, the pool said. *Stay. Sleep.*

There was nothing she wanted more, but something strong had her. It wrenched her away.

Her head broke the surface to the return of wild laughter, the sting of the cold. She was mercilessly dragged over the lip of the pool and dropped onto the stone – its sharp edges prodding her uncomfortably. Farra tried to lift her heavy eyelids. How harsh this world was. Better to return to the pool. Perhaps she could roll herself over the edge.

"No," a voice said. It reached her above the harsh echo of mirth and merriment. Cold fingers clasped her wrist. "Please. Stop."

Farra blinked again and Mesrich's face came into view, hovering close to hers. Grim concern marred his otherwise flawless features.

"Well," Vasteel's voice called, reverberating from the stone walls. "I've never seen you look so starved, Mesrich. What say you all? Should we deprive our friend his fill of flesh?"

There was a roar of dissent in reply.

"Or should we take what the Mother has offered us?"

A rumble of enthusiastic approval followed.

Mesrich did not join the chorus. His stare was saved for Farra.

"Ha! Very well. Then take what is yours, feral beasts! Let us drink!"

A resounding roar followed, but Farra barely noticed. She was being lifted from the cold floor, into even colder arms.

"Let go of me," she mumbled weakly, her words blending into one another.

The Glacian did not reply. She watched the underside of his jaw strain, watched his eyes darken as they left the noise behind them, and before her eyes closed again, she thought she heard him whisper to her that he would keep her safe.

Once more, she slipped beneath the surface.

She awoke upon a bed, one wider than any she'd known to exist. She was warm. Soft blankets were laid carefully atop her. Her limbs felt oddly heavy, as though the muscle had dissolved and left nothing behind but useless weights that kept her anchored down. But she had to get her bearings, had to find a weapon, had to get out.

She wrenched herself upright, vision swimming.

"Easy," a voice said, and then a hand was against her chest, urging her onto her back again.

She found the face – the very same face that had haunted her in restless sleep – and she spat into it.

He had her wrists wrapped up in a heartbeat. She had hardly raised them to rake down his face, to tear out his eyes. "LET ME GO!" she screamed as loudly as her lungs would allow.

But he only watched her with morbid finality. "I cannot."

Whatever the pool's magic, it had sapped her strength. Quickly, she found her efforts waning, she was sinking back to the bed, gasping for breath. Tears escaped the corners of her eyes. They coursed down the sides of her face and got lost in her hair. "What do you want from me?" she asked, her lips trembling. If he ripped the clothes from her body now and forced himself upon her, she could hardly stop him.

His eyelids drooped with something like disdain. His jaw ticked. "I want nothing from you."

"Then let me go. Or throw me into the pool."

"You will never see the inside of that pool again." His voice became a growl. "You will rest here. Heal." He motioned toward her shoulders, which Farra only now noticed were bandaged. "When you are well, I will help you find your escape."

Her heart stuttered. She tried to find the trickery in the words, but the Glacian's eyes did not err from hers, his lips did not falter from the way they pressed firmly together.

"Escape?"

He merely nodded. There was nothing sardonic about the way he perused her shoulders. The concern seemed somehow genuine. "I stitched the wounds again," he said flatly. "They had opened."

"Am I supposed to thank you?"

Mesrich cursed in the old language. "Of course not. But you should rest until they heal. Stay upon the bed."

"And if I do not wish to stay?" Farra pushed. "Have you forgotten to tie me to it? Or do you intend to guard me day and night?"

The Glacian smirked in his small way, scrubbing his face tiredly. "You won't venture far in this place, should you make your bid for escape without my help."

"And why would you help me," she said impatiently, her voice unsteady. "You brought me here, did you not?"

Mesrich stared at her and in his eyes, she thought she detected anguish, indecision. Some turmoil that couldn't be voiced. He nodded. "I did," he said. "But it was not by choice."

Farra contemplated his words but could find no meaning in them. Instead, she simply watched him, unwilling to take her eyes from his while he remained so close.

He grinned again, despite himself, his eyes locked to hers. "Your eyes," he said. "I've never felt quite so eviscerated as when you set them upon me in that hall." He shook his head. "You have no fear, do you?"

Farra jutted her chin, preparing to lie. "No."

"You should," he said, finally wrenching his gaze from hers. "You will not survive here."

"I should think you care little for my survival, Glacian."

"Thaddius," he said. "My name is Thaddius."

"I do not care to know the name of my captor," Farra spat.

"I saved you from the pool," he reminded her, though even he did not sound convinced. "That surely grants me your name."

"Fuck you."

"Fearless," he chuckled darkly, looking skyward. "Mother help me."

"The Mother will spit on your sorry soul should you ever find yourself at Her gate."

Thaddius Mesrich turned to her once more. "I've come to believe the same." He stood then, and for the first time, Farra noticed the absence of his wings. Without them, he looked oddly... human. Large and hauntingly pale, but human. "The bath is drawn," he said, gesturing toward a brass tub in the corner. "You should wash before the water turns cold."

And then the Glacian left the room, closing a heavy wooden door behind him.

Farra waited a beat, then another, and then flung the covers from her body. She lurched unsteadily toward the door, but when she pulled on the handle, she found it locked. The hinges clattered but did not give and she hit it with her fist, letting loose a shriek of frustration.

She turned and let her back rest against the frame, panting from the exertion. She tried to find reason, sense. She needed to think.

She looked around the sparse room. The ceiling was adorned with an intricate candelabra she'd never seen the likes of. There was an armoire she did not recognise, and a bathtub, steam rising invitingly from its depths.

There was no escaping, it seemed. She could not break her way out of this room without causing considerable noise. Even if she could, she did not know the way, and this palace was crawling with Glacians. Thaddius was right, she would not venture far.

She shuddered at the thought of his name. She hung her head to her chest and let more tears fall. It did not seem the Glacian would kill her himself. At least, not yet. Every cryptic reply led her to believe that he was remorseful, despite the improbability of it. Whatever threat lay ahead, it no longer appeared to be imminent. She had time. With time, came opportunity.

She shuffled toward the ridiculous tub, too big for anything but a castle. The water *did* look inviting. Her feet ached with the cold of the stone floor.

Ridding herself of the ragged garb she'd been vested in upon her arrival to Glacia, she let the rough, thin fabric fall to the ground, and stepped carefully into the water. A hiss escaped her teeth as she lowered her body beneath the surface. The heat stung, so at odds with her icy skin, but moments later, she was groaning with deep satisfaction. Never had she felt the luxury of being fully submerged.

That is, of course, except for the magical pool she had thrown herself into.

Farra kept her ruined shoulders propped up out of the water but found they did not ache quite as badly as before, wrapped tightly in their clean bandaging. The Glacian had obviously taken measures to ensure the job was done properly. Farra looked down at her breasts and wondered if Thaddius had disrobed her in the process. She blanched.

Was it merely her body, he wanted? He had told his King as much, hadn't he? *It has been an age since I had a servant to tend to me.* Is that what he intended to do with her? Keep her locked away in this room and fuck her when it pleased him?

And if she refused? What would he do with her then?

Farra thought of the pool and the inhabitants that were fished out. All except her had been docile, empty. Was that the alternative, should Thaddius Mesrich find no use for her?

Farra snarled and sank lower into the tub. There was an escape somewhere. There had to be. A way out, all she needed was time to find it.

In that moment, beneath the water, there was no part of Farra that believed Thaddius Mesrich would help her escape, that he would make good on his word and release her. She would have to make her own way out.

Thaddius would need to be stalled. She thought of the sharp lines of his face, his shoulders, and swallowed. To be a woman of the Ledge was to endure. She could surely endure this too.

She could fell a grown man with a pick, a hammer, a knife. She could go days and days without a morsel to eat. She could sear her own wounds closed. She could knock a rotting tooth from her mouth. She could bear the brunt of a blizzard as it tried resolutely to pull her toward the Chasm.

She could borrow time. She could seduce a Glacian.

Farra waited alone for two days.

Food appeared at her bedside as she slept. It unsettled her to think she had not awoken to the sound of someone entering. And yet, she remained unharmed.

She paced and gnawed on her own thoughts, waiting for the moment Thaddius Mesrich would re-enter the room, but the Glacian remained resolutely and inexplicably on the other side of the great wooden door.

She could hear him. When she pressed her ear to the woodgrain, she could discern the heavy breaths of someone standing sentry. In the night, those breaths drew longer as they slept. Farra was sure it was him.

But still, he did not enter the room.

She ought to count her blessings, she thought. She was safe in this room after all. Instead, after two days, she was wearing a path into the stone as she circled the room. She pulled on her hair and cursed with increasing frequency. Despite all the things she was capable of enduring, she thought this – this tedious anticipation – might be the thing to thwart her.

Eventually, she stalked to the door and hammered her fists against it. "Are you going to leave me in here forever, Glacian?" she shouted.

There was a rough mumbling from the other side and then suddenly the handle rattled. The door pushed inward. It caught her off guard, made her stumble backward.

Thaddius Mesrich stepped into his chambers, swiftly closing the door behind him and locking it.

"You think I'll try to run?" Farra asked, half hysterical.

The strange Glacian did not meet her eye. "I cannot allow you to. The others–"

"Will drink my soul if I try?"

She thought the Glacian might make some snide aside. Instead, he just said, "Or worse."

Farra wondered if it was a threat. "Surely you can't mean to keep me in here forever."

Thaddius frowned. "It has only been two days."

"Two days as a trapped animal!"

The ringing pitch of her voice made the Glacian grin slightly. His eyes perused the room. "Quite the cage," he muttered. "I assure you that sleeping on the floor in the corridor was far less appealing than my own bed."

Farra's stomach curled at the mention of his bed.

"Your wounds need time to heal," he sighed, already turning back toward the door.

"Wait!" she said, her hand reaching out to stop him.

Thaddius paused but did not look back at her. Instead, he looked warily at her fingers against the inside of his wrist, as though they were something to fear.

Her mind was sprinting. She had not given much forethought to this encounter or what she would do when she saw the Glacian again. She only knew that she needed to find a way to make him drop his guard. The Glacian was vigilant, cautious. That much was clear. If she was to outsmart him, outrun him, she would need to make him pliant, malleable. He would need to believe she was of no concern.

"I am sorry," she said, softly this time, if a little breathless. "I am not used to... to being so alone."

The Glacian's eyes were hard – impenetrably so.

"Please," she said, though the words sounded false, even to her. "Stay with me. It is surely better than guarding my door."

Something in his expression faltered. His gaze swivelled back to the door in question.

"No," she said, diverting his attention again. This time she dropped his wrist. She walked backward toward the bed. "Sit by me," she said. The way his eyes darkened, she knew her voice was soft enough, tempting enough. "Distract me."

"From what?"

"Fear," she said, and she made her voice even smaller. "Loneliness."

Thaddius' expression immediately solidified. He grinned once more in that icy, dangerous way she now recognised as derision. "You do not make a convincing mouse," he said, staking her where she stood. "Fear doesn't seem to concern you. Though, it should."

Then he left, closing and locking the door behind him. Farra was left alone for another night. Alone, but alive.

The following days were a series of failed attempts on Farra's behalf.

Each time Thaddius entered the room to deliver her food and water, she tried to engage him in conversation, in anything that would see him linger for more than a few seconds. Sometimes, he sent humans in – slaves with their tongues cut out. People she recognised from the Ledge. They came to collect her bed pans and redress Thaddius' bed. They looked at her with mournful eyes and departed, unable to answer her questions. Would she wind up like them? Muted and enslaved?

Thaddius remained steadfast in his supposed dispassion for her, though she did not believe it. He had brought her here for a reason – *her* specifically. At times, he betrayed a flicker of interest, of attraction. But whatever emotion came to pass over him was then quickly thwarted by a stony veneer.

Farra took to sleeping as much as she could to pass the time. It was odd, how very lax she had become in such a short period. How complacent. She no longer woke to the sounds that echoed through the castle walls. She knew Thaddius remained outside and it somehow comforted her. She slept with her back to the door and did not fear she would be ripped from her bed in the night.

She was plagued by terrible dreams, mostly of falling. Each time she closed her eyes, she was tipped over the edge of some great height, and the sensation of plummeting turned her stomach over; it seized her.

One such dream was filled with nothing but that unending fall. No surrounds, no sound at all, just an interminable, sightless drop. She could not see the ground rushing up to meet her from below, could not wake herself before the collision came. This time, she collided with ground, and she felt herself burst on impact.

She awoke to the sound of screaming, to large, cool hands on her cheeks, and it took a second longer to realise the screams came from her.

"Shhh," a voice whispered in the dark. "You are well."

She blinked, gulping a lungful of air. The bed covers were twisted around her body from where she had likely thrashed. She wore nothing beneath them, but the Glacian did not look at the slithers of skin that were revealed. Instead, his eyes trapped hers. "It was a dream," he said now, his voice so achingly gentle it was difficult not to melt into the hands that stroked her jaw. It was difficult not to take comfort from them.

She swallowed past the pain in her throat, raw from her shrieks, and simply stared back at the creature poised above her, over her, wiping the tears from her face.

"Normally, you do not wake," he said in that same voice, low and melodic.

Farra frowned. "I've screamed before?"

He sighed quietly. "Every night."

Her stomach fluttered. She wondered if he'd comforted her before exactly like this, without her knowing.

"What do you dream of?" he asked suddenly, uncharacteristically. In all their interactions, he had never once lingered. Now, it seemed as though he could not stop himself. He searched her face with need, with some sort of deep-seated curiosity.

Farra found herself wanting to tell him. "I dream of falling."

"Falling?"

She nodded.

He considered her answer for a moment, then smiled inadvertently. "My greatest fear as a child was falling. I dreamt of it often."

"One with wings still fears falling?"

"One must learn to use the wings first." He grimaced. "It requires repeated failure."

Farra tried to conjure an image she had not considered before – a Glacian offspring. "I cannot think of you as a child."

"We all were once. However long ago it may have been."

"Exactly how old are you, Glacian?"

"Far older than any creature ought to be."

Farra had awaited a moment like this. A moment where she could make him vulnerable, make him talk to her, trust her, but instead of calculating her next remark, she found herself speaking freely. Some spark of curiosity within her had been set alight.

"When I was a girl, my biggest fear was falling into the Chasm," she said. "I soon learned there were worse ways to die."

"Glacians?"

"The people of the Ledge believe the Glacians devour them."

Thaddius raised his eyebrows. "Is the truth better, or worse?"

Farra considered before answering, then sighed. "It is both better and worse. The end may be less gruesome, but you harvest humans not for hunger, but to prolong life. We die for greed alone."

Thaddius grimaced. "Not one of them considers the cost," he admitted.

"But you do?"

The Glacian became still. "Remorse has its own costs," he said simply, and Farra could not guess at his meaning.

She sat upright. The sconces had long since flickered and died, and she moved to see his face clearly. She found herself much closer than she had intended. The Glacian did not veer away. He remained seated at her side, body facing her, his cool breaths glancing off her lips.

"Did you save me?" she asked, and sincerity leaked into her voice, made it quiet and feeble. She needed to know if this was a game and if he were the villain.

"Yes," he breathed. He seemed unable to remove his eyes from hers. Farra fared no better.

"Why?"

"Do you not want to be saved, girl?"

"Farra," she corrected. "And I wanted to be left on the Ledge. You were not so merciful when you saw me from the sky on Selection Day."

He closed his eyes for a moment. "I did not want to."

"Then why–"

"Because I am as trapped here as you were on the Ledge," he said. "And this place does not care for my remorse." He made to turn away, to stand.

For the second time, Farra reached out and grasped his wrist. Her fingers barely encircled it. "Wait," she said.

No other words came. She had no good reason to stop the Glacian from leaving the room. She could not voice this unquenchable need to speak with him, to make meaning of his cryptic remarks. She did not want to hear his even breaths through the doorframe and wonder what he was thinking, what his intentions might be. She wanted to hear it from his lips. She wanted to see his eyes when he spoke. She...wanted. And it had little to do with plans for escape. "Tell me..." she fumbled, unsure of how to articulate it. "Tell me the truth."

He sighed and his shoulders looked too heavy. She wondered if it was tiring to carry his wings – if even while sequestered they still weighed him down. "What do you want to know?" he asked. His hand turned over slowly in hers, until their palms were lightly touching, his fingertips glancing off the inside of her own wrist, making her pulse thrum.

"Everything," she said on an exhale. "Tell me everything."

CHAPTER THIRTY-SEVEN

There were several nights similar, where they would meet stiffly, warily, and by the end of the hour, both would be seated in the middle of the bed, hands touching. Thaddius told Farra everything. He told her of how the pure-bloods do not breed, and of the colony to the west of the kingdom, filled with Glacians of mixed parentage. He explained the days he had spent there – learning who the mixed bloods were, befriending them, and how he had come to slowly despise Vasteel and his nobles. How it had taken years and years to undo the prejudice, the notions of his superiority, and begin to feel the burn of regret, of blame.

"There was a young mixed boy in the Colony," Thaddius told her. "He was the first I was acquainted with. He was winged, but his skin was like yours," he said, running a hand over Farra's forearm with something like reverence. "He was tasked with bringing repaired clothing to the palace from his mother and father, who tailor our clothes. All measures of labour are outsourced to the Colony," he explained. "There is very little that a pure-blood does but drink and hunt for sport.

"I collected the clothes from him at the palace gates for a time. But he always approached on foot. At some point, I asked him why he did not fly, and he told me a brute had sliced through the membrane on one side. It was the first time I heard them call us that. *'Brutes'.*" Thaddius gave a small smile. "The child was bold to say it in front of me. I think he expected me to punish him. But instead, I asked him his name. It was Ryon. I offered to teach him to fly."

"With a torn wing?" Farra asked, captivated by the strange story. "Is that possible?"

"If it is stitched correctly, yes. Wing injuries are rife in our world. We've found the ways to mend them. I took him home to the Colony. His mother nearly keeled over when I entered her shelter." He smiled. "I helped her repair Ryon's wings and then I taught him to fly again. It took weeks, but he was a determined sort – far more than any other Glacian I'd met." Thaddius' smile faded and his gaze turned distant. "But he was reckless. One evening, he crossed the boundaries and flew into the forest. He was quickly found. A group of hunting Glacians cut his wings to ribbons as punishment. They flew him back to the Colony and dumped him at its centre for all to witness. He was likely already dead. When I arrived the next day to visit, I found his mother and father weeping over his body. It was the first time I'd truly hated what I was. *Who* I was."

Farra turned her eyes to their fingers. His were turned up and limp. She slid hers among them. "We cannot change what we are," she said quietly. She had never met someone quite so filled with self-loathing.

"But we can change what we do," Thaddius said resolutely, the sharp angles of his face softening some when he looked upon her. "Despite the rules that bind us."

"You could leave this place," Farra suggested. "Find some other ice palace to live in."

He smirked. "Tempting. But I cannot. Vasteel would search for me, and I will not live out my remaining days in hiding."

"Your remaining days?" Farra repeated slowly. "You make it sound as though they are numbered."

Thaddius' fingers tensed around hers. "All our days are numbered," was his reply. "If I were honourable, I would shorten my stack."

"Glacians do not age," Farra argued, frowning. "Your days are innumerable."

"I've come to believe that nothing should last forever, malishka. While the outside remains pristine, the inside rots and decays."

"Malishka?" she repeated, taking the word and turning it over.

Thaddius only shook his head. "An old language word," he said simply.

A gamut of emotion ghosted the Glacian's features as they sat there in the waning torchlight. Farra had never seen one so haunted by their own existence. It pained her to watch it – the way he sliced himself open to get out the ugliness.

She leaned forward, bracing herself on the bed. Her shoulders gave a shallow twinge of pain, but it was easily ignored. With one hand she grasped his chin – how she had longed to feel her way along it – and turned his face back to hers. She viewed the planes of his face and marvelled. "You said nothing should last forever," she accused, her voice sharper than her stare. "As though you *intend* to shorten the stack."

He seemed too captivated to answer. His lips parted, erringly close to hers, but no words escaped.

"But you are not rotten within, Thaddius," she told him. "You do not scare me."

Thaddius swallowed. "I have done terrible things," he said hoarsely, his voice hardly more than a whisper. "You should be scared."

Farra's hand moved unbidden to the Glacian's throat, feeling the rapid pulse beneath her fingers.

He sighed, as though resigning himself. "Keep your distance from me, malishka."

"My days are numbered too," she replied, her lips glancing off his.

"Not yet they aren't."

She continued as though he hadn't spoken. "I might use the precious few I have any way I choose."

He cursed. "Last chance."

But Farra had never met a challenge she could not face. She counted the beat of blood beneath her fingers. *One... two...*

There was a low growl that made her insides ripple and then his mouth was on hers.

He was softer than she anticipated, not made of the stone she had imagined him cut from, but he was as cold. A shiver thrilled through her as his hand pressed into the small of her back. She was filled with something heady and exasperating. She was rid of all thought as his lips explored hers; there was only feeling. He seemed hungry for her. His tongue slid along hers and she sighed. Her hands wound around his neck and pulled him closer and it stirred a feral noise from him, rising from somewhere deep in his chest. His hands wrapped around her back, and he pulled her into his lap.

She wore very little. She had precious few garments and had taken to sparing them upon returning to bed each evening. Her scrap of tunic fell low, past her hips, and she wore nothing beneath. Her bare legs wrapped around the Glacian's waist, his fingertips skirting up her thighs slowly.

"God," he murmured into her neck, so quietly she barely discerned the words. "Have mercy on me."

Farra spared no thought for the Mother at all. She had not come to her aid on the Ledge, nor here in Glacia. She had not stepped in to save those who had sunk to the bottom of the pool. This bed, this moment, was not the design of a god, and Farra preferred it. This bed was wicked, unnatural, and she would delight in it to spite the Mother and all Her idleness.

She lifted the ragged hem of the tunic slowly, revealing inch after inch of skin, until the fabric rose over her face. She discarded it to the side.

And Thaddius' eyes turned wild.

He revered her naked form, hands skating over her flesh, heavy exhales escaping his lips and hitting her skin. Another shiver thrilled her, and he felt it.

"Do you fear me now, malishka?" he asked her, in a voice that should be feared, in a way that should quell her.

Instead, she only felt want. Greed. Lust. And the dark glint of his eyes trapped in her stare revealed he was no better, no more controlled. "I don't fear you," she said. With her own hands, she cupped the weight of her breasts, kneading them without looking away. "Do you fear me?"

Thaddius did not respond. His eyes had left her face to watch her hands and his fingers on her hips began to bite into her flesh. He bared his teeth slightly. Whatever control he'd retained slipped away and he became a creature made of nothing but thirst, desire.

She found herself on her back, his face suddenly pressed between the valley of her breasts, and then lower, and she had to close her eyes at the exquisite feel of his cool tongue on her flesh, tasting her, suckling her. He reared up only to pull the clothes from his body – first his tunic, then the ties of his breeches – and Farra laid her eyes on the expanse of him and was awed.

The muscles entrenched in his torso heaved with each breath, and she was only spared a few aching moments before he returned his mouth to her, to her stomach, her neck, while she writhed. The pleasure elicited whines from the back of her throat and her sex clenched.

Thaddius' face suddenly hovered over hers and he blocked out her surroundings, her senses, and any other sign that she might be a captive of the Glacian Kingdom. His forehead pressed gently to hers, his restraint clearly waning. "Will you let me have you, Farra?" he asked.

Her hands tracked down his stomach as he spoke, finally finding and gripping his cock.

He groaned, pressing his lips together in an expression that bordered on pain. "*Fuck.*"

"I'm yours," she vowed, hardly aware of the weight in the words, the fate she was sealing.

He took her bottom lip between his teeth, only releasing it to say, "Are you sure, malishka?" He gasped as she stroked him. "Because once I take you, I'll want to keep you."

She pressed her lips to the cool skin beneath his ear and felt him shiver in return. "Then keep me," she whispered darkly, heeding no sense. Only desire.

Fingers suddenly pressed against her entrance, and she gasped.

"So wet... warm," he murmured, moving his finger upward to that collection of nerves, pulsing with anticipation. He caressed her until she was trembling, begging for him, her body undulating, and every roll of her hips seemed to tip him closer and closer to madness. Finally, with a hissed curse, he reared up and pressed his length inside her.

Farra's walls clenched around the size of him, the heaviness. For a moment, she wondered if she could withstand him. But he moved with grace, with measured strokes, and soon she was meeting each thrust, welcoming all of him, until he was seated to the hilt, and he buried his face in her neck.

"Farra," he murmured, his pace quickening. The slide of their bodies against each other only fuelled her. Her limbs were wrapped around him, as though they might be merged, might coalesce and combust. The combined sensations overwhelmed her – the feel of him sliding within her, the frenetic pace of his torso along hers, the gentle worship of his lips. She moaned a plea, and the Glacian heeded it. Without slowing, his fingers came between them, and he stroked her once, twice, three times.

The sensation built to an unbearable point, and there she was suspended, weightless. And then she fell.

He swallowed her cries, eclipsing her mouth with his own, and she gripped his neck as he claimed his own release, his entire form shuddering with the strength of it. Both of them falling, falling, but never crashing.

In the moments that followed, they simply lay staring at each other, their foreheads touching, and they passed revere between them like a silent language.

The next evening, when Thaddius stepped inside his own chambers, Farra was waiting for him, and it took them only seconds to collide and come completely undone.

Farra's shoulders had long since healed enough that she could be moved and yet she said nothing to Thaddius, nor he to her, when they joined together after nightfall. She found herself delaying the moment, day by day, when they would need to confront reality.

While alone, she berated herself. She made herself promises that she would not continue what she had started. She thought of ways out of the Glacian Kingdom and wondered where she would go if it were not back to the Ledge.

She had heard the stories of a green valley, of course. Her mother, before she died, would let slip tales of the village she was born to. Farra thought she would ask Thaddius to take her there. But then she would think of the moment they would part ways, for she belonged in the glow of the sun, and he on his mountaintop, and she would delay the request another day. Just one more day.

When the door opened earlier than she had expected, before the light had dimmed in the singular narrow window, she turned smiling, expecting Thaddius.

Another Glacian stood upon the threshold and Thaddius was nowhere in sight.

All the fear she had stowed away and forgotten returned to her. She backed away.

But the Glacian merely rolled his eyes and scoffed at the ceiling. "Good god," he said acidly. "What feeble trade."

Farra inferred that he spoke of her, though she could not grasp his meaning. "Who are you?" she asked with far more valour than she felt.

He pinned her with a derisive stare. "Phineas," he spat. "And you are the human who has possessed my oldest friend."

Farra allowed her eyes to sweep over the Glacian once, taking in his considerable height, his long, unkempt hair. She watched for any sign of attack. "What do you want? Thaddius will return any moment."

"No, he won't. Unfortunately for both of us, he has tasked me with standing sentry by the door while he eats and sleeps. If I didn't, there is little doubt he would have starved himself to keep you safe, by now."

Farra narrowed her eyes. "You've guarded my door?"

"*Your* door?" Phineas repeats. "As though you've already laid claim to what is his. Was his sanity not enough?"

"I do not know—"

"Come now," Phineas interrupted, making a gesture of impatience. He paced the width of the room and back, his agitation apparent. "You are not the first human to be bedded by a Glacian. Question is, for how long does he intend to fuck you?"

Farra's jaw ticked. She felt hot, vicious anger swell in her chest. "Why?" she asked. "Have I taken your place?"

His laugh was mirthless – lip upturned to reveal his teeth. "It is a clever ruse, seducing him at a time of... weakness."

Farra thought of all Thaddius Mesrich had confessed to her. The hairs along her neck stood on end. "Weakness? You refer to his morality, I presume?"

"I refer to his stupidity. His morality has long been his worst enemy, admirable as it is. You are merely the newest poison."

Farra's eyes did not swerve from the Glacian before her. "And so you've come in his defence?" she goaded. "Are my wiles so effective that even a weaponless human becomes a threat?"

Phineas' fists clenched and he gave a withering smirk. "I see what he means. You are indeed dauntless."

Farra spoke clearly, hiding a rising tremor. "This is no ruse," she said. "I... I care for him." She realised it was true as she said it. Somehow, the ploy and reality had tangled.

"And he for you," Phineas said immediately. "And you have no clue of the danger he places himself in by doing so. The King will have his head if he learns the extent of his devotion. Already, he walks a thin line between deception and treachery."

"Because I am human?"

"Because he is a *noble*, one of the King's preferred, and you are serving to unravel *everything*."

Farra hesitated, Phineas' proclamation rocking her.

"Should the King know his most prized has turned to the affections of a human, he will be killed. Do you understand that?" He pierced her with an accusatory stare, one that told her he did not understand the appeal. "Of all the prospects in Glacia, he had to go and fall in love with a human from the Ledge." He shook his head, tired, exasperated.

"Will you reveal him to your King?"

"I will not need to," Phineas said, turning back for the door. "You will be the death of him, not I. If you care for him… you will not allow this to go any further."

"And then what should I do? Offer myself to the pool, or to the Chasm?" she called, a desperation taking hold of her.

Phineas looked at her one last time, raking her with his derisive judgement. "He will not allow either. Go to the Colony, and *stay* there," he said. "When he comes to you, send him away."

"And if I ask you to take me elsewhere?" Farra questioned, stopping him before he could close the door. "Somewhere beyond Glacia? Allow me to be where I belong?"

"I would deny you," he said cuttingly. "Unlike him, I would not risk my life to save yours."

He closed the door firmly behind him.

Farra pushed Thaddius until he relented. She made him admit that everything Phineas had said was true, and though the thought of leaving her in the Colony sent his fist flying into his armoire, he assented with heavy eyes. She could not deny either of them one last evening together, but before dawn broke, they untangled their bodies reluctantly.

The Colony seemed a place of colour, where the palace was made of greys. The lean-tos and huts and makeshift tents made a kaleidoscope of chaotic rows. The mixed were even more variant, their skin no different to those on the Ledge. The differences between these Glacians and herself were more subtle. They were larger than her, their shoulders broader. Their facial structure more angular, still giving the impression of having been once cut from stone, even if their skin was of conflicting hue.

Farra was taken aback by the sheer volume of them. There must be twice as many as those on the Ledge, perhaps even three times as many.

"Do not trust all of them," Thaddius murmured frantically. He guided her through the Colony with a hand clutched around her upper arm, his eyes skirting their surrounds ceaselessly. "They may have no interest in your soul the way the pure-bloods do, but they may very well alert your presence to the palace if they believe they can leverage it."

But contrary to his words, every pair of eyes they encountered saw Thaddius and quickly diverted. She noticed how quickly the pathways emptied as they progressed down them.

"They fear you," she stated quietly, watching a cluster of children break apart and scatter as they neared. "I do not think they will dare defy you, knowing you brought me here yourself."

"Pray you are right," he grunted. "Because I will balance on a knife's edge every day, fearing it will tip."

"You will tell them you sent me to the slave quarters if they ask. Tell them you've made better use of me... whatever you need to."

His jaw went taut, flexing menacingly beneath the skin, and he said nothing. His pace quickened, and she struggled to keep up.

They arrived at the entrance to a hut made of varying-sized timbers and pine thatching, and he led her beneath the cloth that covered the door without bothering to announce himself.

"Thaddius? Wha–" A female stood from her pallet on the ground.

"Annika," Thaddius greeted her. "I– I am sorry, but..."

"This is her then," Annika said in the absence of any explanation for entering her home unannounced. She was older. Her hair had streaks of silver that in no way resembled Thaddius'. Her face was delicately lined by the hand of time, her stature still impeding in the space. She stood tall and frowned at Farra, shaking her head slightly. "Please, do not ask it of me, Thaddius."

The Glacian looked contrite. "I must."

Annika scoffed harshly. "Take her where she belongs, you fool! You brought her to that fucking palace; *you* help her find safety."

"I will," Thaddius vowed. "But not yet. There are dozens of brutes swarming the slopes as we speak, hunting. There will be dozens more tomorrow. I cannot simply whisk her away without being seen. I need time to plan. I need to be careful."

"You need a knee to the crotch," Annika added, rubbing her forehead. "What trouble you've brought upon yourself, Thaddius, and now me."

"I only need you to keep her safe for a week. Perhaps two. We were not seen leaving the palace."

"Thaddius, I–"

"*Please*!" he implored, his neck tensing with the force of his urgency. "Please," he said again, only this time his tone was tempered. He seemed to be making a great effort to calm himself. "You're the only one I trust with her."

Annika stared at him for a moment. "You went and fell in love, didn't you?"

Farra flinched, but turned in time to see Thaddius nod. He swallowed and did not meet her eye.

"Stupid of you," Annika quipped, but her expression was one of pity, rather than admonishment. "Of all the females–"

"I assure you," Thaddius interrupted. "I tried not to."

Annika cursed, then turned her back on them both. "The next time you're sent over that godforsaken Chasm, try snatching up a man." She disappeared behind another door made of hanging cloth.

"It's not quite so easy to discern the difference from the sky. They wrap themselves in heavy fur," Thaddius called to her, rolling his eyes. Farra elbowed him.

"Speaking of which," Annika returned, a bundle of fur in her arms. "Wrap yourself up, human. You're turning blue."

Indeed, Farra had walked the distance to the Colony in nothing but the prisoner garb she'd been forced into weeks before. Thaddius suddenly regarded her with an appalled expression. "Fuck," he gritted out, closing his eyes. "I am sorry, malishka."

Farra touched his arm. "I am fine."

"No, you're not," Annika argued. "You keep telling him that and death will find you quicker than we can hide you." She threw the bundle at Farra, who caught it and unravelled a heavy hide-backed blanket.

"It will also be your bed," Annika told her, shrugging. "Try not to wet it in the snow."

Farra wrapped it around her shoulders. "Thank you."

"I will repay you, Annika," Thaddius said. "And I will return tomorrow with food."

Annika made a tsking noise. "No, Thaddius. You'll stay away from here. Do you understand me?"

"I..." he hesitated, his fingers intertwining with Farra's. "I cannot–"

"You can and you shall. If you truly care for her, you will leave her be." Annika's eyes bore into his. "Return when you are ready to whisk her down those slopes."

"I am grateful for your aid," he said roughly. "But I will not abandon her here and keep my distance."

"Yes," Farra insisted. "You will."

Thaddius turned his back on Annika, his eyes boring into Farra's. "You needn't fear, malishka. I will not reveal you."

"It is not *myself* I fear for," she said, turning her hand over so that their wrists were pressed together, their pulses beating in tandem. "If you are caught, your King will kill you, will he not?"

"I will not be caught."

"Stay away, Thaddius," Farra told him firmly, her eyes wetting. "Please."

He pulled her against him then, lowering his mouth to hers and catching her in an urgent kiss. A kiss that was an apology, a promise, and a salvation all at once. "I'm afraid it's too late for that," he said against her lips. He kissed her once more, then moved away on a deep sigh.

"Tell no one," he said to Annika.

"Ha!" the female barked. "Half the Colony will know by now, Thaddius. Nothing is secret here."

"Then tell them I will stomp down their houses and breathe fire if they open their mouths."

Annika only rolled her eyes.

Thaddius looked back at Farra once more before departing, regret and panic breaking his façade for a moment. And then he was gone.

Farra turned back to her newest keeper. "Thank you for the fur," she said, uncertainty making her fidget.

Annika glared at her. It rather reminded Farra of her own mother's reproach when Farra would spill or break or burn something. "It was my son's," she said. "Ryon's."

Farra turned her eyes downcast and nodded a little. "Thaddius told me of him."

"Did he?" Annika said bluntly. It was apparent the female did not want her here in her home, wearing her son's bed pallet, endangering her safety. "Did he bed you afterward?"

Farra's throat constricted. She stilled.

And Annika nodded dolefully. "When is your next cycle, girl?"

"My…" Farra reeled, her mind racing. "I… uh…"

"Mother above," Annika murmured. "Do you humans have no sense of preservation?"

The barb stung more than it should. Farra swallowed, determined to regain composure. "Any day now."

"Well," Annika said sharply, turning for the flap of cloth concealing the other half of her home. "We will soon see just how much trouble you are in."

She disappeared behind the divider and Farra let loose a shuddering exhale. Her mind whirred, eclipsing all thought of escape plans. She looked to her abdomen, and closed her eyes as a curse escaped her lips. "Have mercy," she uttered, shaking hands coming over her stomach. Then she sank to the floor, and for the first time since she was a child, she prayed.

Chapter Thirty-Eight

Thaddius stayed his distance for seven days.

In truth, Farra had expected him sooner. He entered Annika's home with apology eking from every pore of his being. "I am sorry, malishka," he said, lowering himself to her pallet beside her. "I was sent to hunt."

"You aren't supposed to return at all," she reminded him, though she could not completely disguise the hurt in her voice. She never thought it would be quite so easy for him to leave her alone.

"Are you well?" he asked, eyes scanning her for any hint of abuse or injury.

"I have not bled," she blurted, forcing the words past her lips. She had thought on what to say to him when he came, but painful news was better delivered quickly.

It took the Glacian longer than she had expected to understand her meaning. A line appeared between his eyebrows first, but then his face became blank, stark, before his eyes dipped to her stomach.

"It is still too soon to tell," she said, though it was in complete contradiction to the sickness that had begun to keep her awake at night, the listlessness she felt.

Still, the Glacian said nothing.

"I should have thought of it sooner," Farra said, her sight blurring, as it had often done these past days. "We shouldn't... shouldn't have–"

Thaddius stood abruptly. His gaze had turned watery, and he looked at her as though she had thrust a sword through his chest.

Annika appeared through the draped divider and she gave Thaddius a wary glare. "Easy, Thaddius."

"A child?" he asked, the word cracking as it released.

Annika levelled him with a cutting sniff. "Have you just thought of its probability *now*, mighty noble? It didn't occur to you when you were on top of her?"

"Stop," he breathed, closing his eyes. Then, to Farra's astonishment, he fell to his knees, as though they could hold him upright no longer and buried his face in his hands. "Mother above."

"Doubt your prayers will help you now," Annika said. "Though, I suppose there is little else to be done."

"There must be something," he argued, lifting his face, eyes pleading. He did not address Farra at all. Did not look her way. "You must know of some... tonic? Some method?"

"None known for their effectiveness, nor safety."

Thaddius groaned, as though that sword in his chest had twisted, entrenched deeper.

Farra watched the scene unfold as though she were a mere observer and not the source of its anguish. Frowning, she rose to her feet. "It is not for either of you to decide the course ahead," she said firmly, ignoring the wave of nausea that rolled through her. "Take me to the valley," she said to Thaddius. "Now. Before anyone should see the pregnancy for themselves, and I will have the child there."

But neither Thaddius nor Annika readily agreed. Neither would hold her gaze.

"I cannot stay," she told them. "Surely, you both know that. If it is known Thaddius sired a child with me, they will kill me. They may very well kill *you*," she said to him.

"Our deaths are already upon us, malishka," he said, a tear escaping the corner of his eye. "No human can survive the birth of a Glacian child." Finally, he deigned to look her way. "And I will not remain and watch you die."

The child inside Farra grew, as did the gaps between visits from Thaddius. It seemed to pain him to see her, slowly swelling from her middle. He would blanch, his eyes dipping to her stomach, and then turn away. He did not dare touch her.

It had been many weeks since he last came to her, and she had begun to ache in the most unexpected places. The small of her back, the inner tendons of her thighs, the bottom of her ribcage. Her chest burned when she ate, or drank, or moved. It was as though this baby was punishing her for forcing its existence. She could not blame it. What a world she would bring it into, before swiftly departing it herself.

That admission had struck her like lightning at first – seared through her core and staked her in place. The baby would kill her. She could not survive it.

Annika gently described the way the baby would grow too large to be birthed, but that she would birth it anyway, and the trauma it would cause would take her life.

"If anyone should survive it, I'd rather think it would be you, Yennes," she had said, clutching Farra's hand.

"Yennes?" she murmured coarsely.

"A survivor," Annika told her. "One who endures all."

Farra hardly thought the moniker would save her now, yet she warmed to the name. The idea of being someone else was, at times, what she yearned for.

She became oddly at peace with her impending death. There was only so much time one could borrow, after all. Had her death not been secured the moment Thaddius' talons pierced her skin? Every day she lived was a mockery to fate's whims. Time would catch up with her – it was an enemy she could not fight.

She blamed herself. She had been a fool. It had been easy to forget the world, a reality outside of the room she'd been confined to in the Glacian palace. She had lost track of time in there, lost track of reason, lost herself.

For a while, however long time had stretched within those walls, she had begun to think the Glacian *loved* her. That perhaps, she loved him.

But the Glacian's absence stretched. And when he did come, she seemed to make him shrivel.

"There is good within him, Yennes," Annika told her, more than once. "More so than any other brute you'll find in that palace. But he was born in a world designed exactly for him and he grew believing the space he occupied was more significant than another's. I fear that, for all the good in him, there is simply too much to unlearn. You must know he regrets his actions. He blames himself, even if he does not have enough sense to say it."

"I am not without fault," Farra said, not wishing to speak on the subject any longer than she had to. "What's done is done."

She tried to find consolation in the days that remained. The hut kept
her out of the wind. She was kept fed and warm and safe. Others came
to visit Annika, who mended their clothes and fashioned new ones in
constant rotation, and soon, the visitors began to know her too. They
called her Yennes and asked for tales of the Ledge.

She told them all she could recall – what reason had she not to? She
spoke of the Selection Days, the pine grove, the tilt of the shelf down to
the Chasm. She told them what it was like to fossick the Drop, the never-
ending violence of the desperate. She told them of her parents, and her
only friend, Harlow Sabar.

When there was no audience, Annika prodded her with questions until
she thought of another story to tell – Harlow climbing a pine only to get
stuck in it, the games they would play as children, the boys they would
fend off as teenagers. She wondered where Harlow was now on the Ledge
and how she was passing the days, without Farra to call on her.

"She was family to you," Annika said when Farra fell silent, lost in
thought. "This Harlow Sabar?"

Farra nodded.

"You speak of her often," she remarked.

Farra ran her hands over her distended belly. "There are no others to
speak of."

Annika pushed her thread through the hide she stitched and frowned
in thought. "It seems your Ledge and this Colony have much in common.
Both trapped by brutes, living by their mercy alone. Though your kind
seem to have a penchant for killing one another." Her nose wrinkled. "It
is odd you have not found unity together."

"It is difficult to be unified when one can die for the simple impudence
of stepping outside."

Annika dropped her gaze then, her lips pressed tightly shut. Farra knew
the female kept her speaking for distraction. She did not allow Farra to
wallow. Yet now silence stretched between them, as she pulled on her
thread and chewed on her tongue.

Farra thought she seemed regretful.

Finally, Annika said, "Humans do not belong on this mountain." She
lifted her eyes and let them travel over Farra's limbs, pressed in tightly
beneath her bundles of furs. Still, Farra trembled with the cold. A blizzard
blew outside and it found easy entrance to them both through the many
cracks and crevices of this hut. It did not seem to bother Annika at all.

"We mixed do not live easily here," Annika continued. "We eat what we can trap and what the brutes deign to feed us. We are restricted to the borders they created, kept tightly beneath their reign. They take our children, our iskra when it suits them, if not as often as they take yours. But this mountain – the cold – it is still our home," she said. "And we do not fight its touch each day that we dare to live." She returned to her work once again, uncharacteristically leaving Farra to her thoughts.

"You had a child. Ryon," Farra said slowly, cautiously. "Thaddius told me a little about him."

Annika's hands stilled, but her eyes stayed averted. She sighed before continuing. "Yes," she said, her voice sadder than before. "He was beautiful, but too spirited for this place." She shook her head, smiling. "I imagine him flying somewhere out of reach now. A boy like that was never going to remain confined for long."

"And... his father?" Farra pressed.

"He was killed soon after," she said, her voice cracking slightly. "He was heartbroken. Filled with rage. It overcame him, as hatred often does." She shook her head. "It was only a matter of time before he did something stupid."

"What did he do?"

"He tried to kill a brute," Annika said, sniffing derisively. "As though killing just one would do any good." She reshuffled the piles of garments she was working on and stood, clothing in hand. "The difficulties you face are... unthinkable." Her voice was far softer, meeker, than Farra had ever heard it. "But if there had been a way to trade my life for Ryon's, I would have gladly taken it. It would be a relief, not having to endure without him. Mothers are supposed to pass before their children, Yennes. You suffer now, but you will not suffer long. There is some solace to be found there, I think."

She shuffled away then, disappearing beyond the drape, and Farra traced small circles around the top of her stomach, feeling the life of the child within.

Another month passed without Thaddius' presence and Farra felt it with every twitch and kick of the baby in her womb.

When the threadbare drape of the shelter's entrance was finally pushed aside by a stark hand, it was not Thaddius who ducked his head through the opening, but Phineas, and his biting glare found Farra immediately.

Annika backed away, fear widening her eyes. "Wait—"

"Hush," Phineas said, stepping inside. "I have not come to tie you to the stocks. Though I *should*."

"Phineas," Farra said stiffly.

"So, it is true." His eyes had lowered to the swell of her abdomen. His expression changed into one of disgust. "Holy Mother," he muttered. "What trouble you've brought upon yourself."

"What do you want?" Farra said abrasively. The revulsion in his stare made her skin crawl.

"Only to see with my own eyes what Thaddius has told me." He scrubbed his face with his hand. "The thing that has swallowed him whole and spat him out."

"And what concern is it of yours?"

"*He* is my concern," Phineas growled. "He does not eat. Does not drink. Does not follow orders. And it is *you* who drives his madness!"

"And do you suppose I asked to be taken from the Ledge? To be wrenched out of the pool? Has it not occurred to you, Glacian, that perhaps I would rather have let that pool take my soul, than be before you as I am now?" She huffed with exertion, unable to catch sufficient breath.

"He loves you. Do you understand that, human?" Phineas growled. "He is… killing himself. Slowly. You must convince him not to."

Farra laughed shallowly, darkly, though there was a twinge of pain that could not be ignored. An involuntary response to the thought of Thaddius dying. "I have not seen him in many weeks, Phineas," she said. "And I have little time remaining. His child will make its presence any day."

Phineas cursed loudly. His presence was too big for the shelter, too imposing. His very width threatened to knock the walls of Annika's home to the ground. "And if there was a way to save you…" he growled, the tension apparent in his neck, in the quake of his wings. "Would you accept its course?"

"What?" Farra blurted, brow furrowed.

"If there was a *way* to… to *mend* you afterward," Phineas bit out, his eyes filled with malice. "Would you be *willing*?" This last seemed to pain him, as though he were reticent to heed the will of a human.

Farra fell silent. She stared at the Glacian with nothing short of blatant suspicion. "And why would you go to any lengths to help me?"

"It is not *you* I wish to help." There could be no arguing the callousness with which he said it. "Thaddius is my brother. I will not see his life squandered by some human he professes to love. If he insists on this insanity –" Phineas paused, readying his words. "Then I will do what is necessary to save him. Even if it means saving *you*." He said it as though the entire idea was absurd – that a Glacian could love a human, or that a human could be worth saving.

"By what means?" Annika said, still stricken in her place. She watched Phineas as though he might tear her to pieces at any moment, a complete contrast to the way she regarded Thaddius.

"When will the child come?" he asked.

"Such things aren't certain," Annika answered. "I expect by next moon."

"You will send word when it begins," Phineas told her. "Send someone you trust. I will be waiting by the East gate."

"And then what?" Farra demanded, clutching her stomach with her hands.

"Then Mother help you," he said giving her one last look of exasperation before leaving. Farra was left with her heart in her throat and a rapidly intensifying sense of foreboding.

Chapter Thirty-Nine

Annika had prepared her as best she could. With failing delicacy she'd described the tight cramps that would come in her lower stomach and intensify with the passing of time. She'd described the waves of pain, building until she would be blinded by them, until she would become nonsensical, and then she described the blood, the broken bones, the last moments of Farra's life, spent in agony.

"Will you care for the baby after I'm gone?" Farra whispered to her one evening, back when the swell of her stomach still seemed innocuous. "They will belong here, after all. Among your kind."

Annika had sighed and patted Farra's hand. "Of course, Yennes," she said, but her expression clearly told Farra what she already knew – the female was advanced in years. She would not survive to see this baby grow to maturity. Annika shook herself from her reverie and laid her hand reassuringly along Farra's cheek. "He will be raised in our village and this village protects its own. If there's one thing I'm sure of, it is that there will be many a hand to help guide this young one. Just as I was raised. Just as my Ryon was raised."

"Tell me what he was like," Farra asked suddenly. Annika gladly told her tale after tale of a boy running through the Colony with his wings following, making mischief from nothing, his heart too free to heed the dangers that surrounded him.

"He was fiercely brave," she told Farra, a sad smile appearing. "Too brave for one such as us. Too confined for his wild spirit."

The shelter filled with Annika's palpable grief. Farra could almost see the boy running through the drapes, launching himself out into the open air. She felt the heaviness of his absence, and clutched Annika's hands.

The female's tears had begun to slip down her face. How must it feel to have the ghosts of your family living within you? The sounds of their laughter, their chatter. The smell of their skin and the feel of their hands, their expressions and tenor, and the exact sound their footsteps made when they came home. How heavy the weight of their memory must be.

"I pray this child grows to be just as fierce," Farra told her. "And his spirit as strong."

Hours later, in the dead of night, Farra awakened to a telling clench at the bottom of her stomach, and she prayed for the same once more.

She waited until dawn broke to wake Annika. By then, the tightening of her stomach had begun to force beads of sweat to coat her forehead and chest. Her back ached terribly, and she found she could not lie down.

"Mercy be with us," Annika murmured, going still and pale. Then she disappeared out into the morning air.

There was a blizzard coming – of that Farra was sure. She could smell it. The stillness of the wind outside, the biting smell of frost, the charge in the atmosphere. As though the mountain knew something of consequence was imminent, that fate would bring this day a being of great magnitude – an existence immense enough to move it.

Farra curled over her stomach and howled.

Annika stayed with her through each shuddering wave. It was not long before they began to eclipse her – blocking sight and sound and sense so she was nothing but agony. When the iron-like clenching of her belly released and the pain ebbed, she heard the words Annika tried desperately to fill her with. Reassurances, encouragement, prayer. Farra could only nod, her breaths ragged and hitched. The wind outside whistled through the cracks of the shelter, finding the exposed parts of her skin, but she found the cold could not touch her. She was aflame. She was combusting.

"Malishka?"

A face appeared above hers. She blinked away the sting of sweat to bring it into focus. It had been months since she had seen it last. "Thaddius," she breathed, feeling his fingers wiping the hair from her face. His own crumpled. She saw his eyes well, his lips shudder. He whispered, "This is my doing. My selfishness."

Farra could not tell if he spoke to her or to himself.

For a moment, while sense was suspended, she could only feel relief that he was there, running his fingers over her cheek, leaning to press his

lips to her forehead. She forgot to summon the anger she had carefully
harboured these past weeks. Farra clasped his wrist and relished the feel
of his forehead pressed to hers.

"You will be well," he told her, as though it were a command. "I'm
going to make sure of it."

"Fucking hell," came Phineas' voice, though Farra could not see him.
"Of course it comes the night of a blizzard."

"Say nothing, brother," Thaddius rasped. "Or wait outside if you cannot
restrain yourself."

There was a snort of derision. "*Now* you speak of restraint?"

"Go!" Thaddius roared, and it aligned with Farra's own as another
wave overcame her, burying her. When she surfaced again, there was
only Thaddius, and he looked at her as though the sight of her pain might
split him in two.

"Forgive me," he said brokenly. "Forgive me." He said it over and over
as the day wore on, as her body revolted, threatening to break her apart.

"I should have come," he said aloud. "I should have come sooner."

"No," Annika answered. "You shouldn't have."

"I could have been with her. Comforted her–"

"Comforted *yourself,* you mean," Annika quipped. "The damage was
done, Thaddius. Returning to this shelter only risked exposing her.
Exposing yourself."

"I could have–"

"There is nothing you could have done, Glacian. Stop pitying yourself.
There is little time remaining. What exactly do you and the moron have
planned for her?"

Farra lifted her eyelids long enough to see Thaddius become taut with
worry, with dread. "We will take her to the pool," he said. "And she will
drink from it."

Farra's strength was waning, but her repulsion was fierce enough to lift
her shoulders from her pallet. "No," she bit out, and was then seized by
the grip of pain. She grit her teeth, her vision blurring until it subsided.
He wrapped his arms around her, and she gasped into his chest. "No," she
repeated into the fabric of his tunic. "No. I'd sooner... sooner die." She
crumpled again, the pressure strengthening around her middle. She was
sure she would snap soon. Her bones would break and there would be no
need to speak of her drinking from the pool in some absurd attempt to
keep her alive. She would already be at the Mother's Gate.

Thaddius begged her, pleaded with her, but she heeded none of it. Eventually Annika pushed his hands aside, and Farra heard no one, nothing. She was being sliced from within. A fire scorched through her, starting from her middle. She tilted her head back and screamed.

Then all became black.

Was this death?

Farra dearly hoped so. Death was quiet. It was sightless. Voiceless. There was no sensation. Just the tender suspension of thought, her mind ambling to make meaning of this oblivion, fighting backward to remember. Remember what? How had she found this place? How to escape from it?

But what could possibly compel her to flee its embrace?

"Yennes!"

How out of place it was, the sound of panic amid the peace.

"YENNES!"

Yennes. It meant survivor. Annika had given her the name.

"Yennes! The baby!"

The baby.

The baby. Her baby. The one made of Glacian and Ledge blood, both.

She found her heavy limbs, her heavy eyelids, and forced them open. It took the strength of a titan. The strength of a mountain, but she opened her eyes. The darkness fled and pain gripped her anew.

A terrible roar left her, but it was cut short when her throat closed, her lungs empty of breath.

"Yennes, you must push. Now!"

And this was all that was left. This last thing she would have to endure. She would accept the pain and gift the world this life that never should have been, and then she could rest forever. She need only suffer a while longer.

She was well-versed in suffering. In surviving. She was Ledge-born.

The squalls outside blew in pursuit of her. The frost crept in and tried to take hold, and she pushed it away. She fought it back. She reared up and bore down, feeling each snap within her, and though the pain was beyond description she pushed still, until there was no feeling at all. Just the absence of pressure, of fear, and the first brays of a baby, freshly born into a world not its choosing.

"Farra," Thaddius murmured reverently, as though she were the Holy Mother Herself. His lips pressed to hers gently, for a moment. "You did it."

"Take him, Yennes," Annika's voice bid her. But she could not feel her limbs. Could not command their movements.

Farra opened her eyes as Annika placed the form of a baby to her chest, then picked up Farra's arms and wrapped them over its warm, slippery flesh.

"A boy," Annika said, her eyes wet. "Your boy."

Farra blinked slowly at the shape cradled to her chest and for a moment, her vision focussed. She looked long enough to see the warm hue of his skin, perfectly matched to hers, the exquisite dimples of his knuckles, the delicate slope of his small nose. He opened his eyes long enough for her to see that they resembled hers and that of her own Mother's, and she smiled.

"Ryon," she said, though she could not be sure her voice would carry. "Call him Ryon."

She felt his heart, beating resolutely against her weakening one, and sighed contentedly. This child must be a design of fate, for how could something so perfect, so improbable not be?

She looked her last at her son, smiling weakly, and then the darkness reached up. It clawed her back down into its embrace. Farra was too weak. Too tired.

But she did not want to go. She wished suddenly, fiercely, to stay.

Death ambled, slow to collect her.

Life came in flashes of anguish. There was a glimpse of the night sky and the excruciating jostle of movement. She felt a moment of wind, lancing her cheeks, before the dark pulled her back. Over and over reality returned, and she clawed to stay each time. She heard the swoop of wings. Felt the shudder ripple through her as something collided. She heard a voice, *his* voice, giving desperate commands.

"Phineas, she is *fading!*"

"Hurry," came the answer, then more jostling. More pain.

Doors closed, footsteps glanced off stone, and then a glow burned beyond her eyelids.

"Lay her down," came Phineas' hushed voice. "God, the blood. Quickly! We only have a moment."

"Drink, malishka," Thaddius told her, and she felt the press of metal against her closed lips, felt the strange matter press against her mouth, neither wet nor solid. "Please," he said again more urgently, and she felt fingers pulling her chin down.

But suddenly, her ears were filled with swoops and clatters, a cacophony of activity. And she heard Thaddius moan in despair as his hands left her.

Her head hit the stone.

"Let go of me!" he shouted, his voice quaking the ground around her.

There were other shouts. Voices that made little sense, curses and braying anger. Only one other voice seemed able to usurp the discord and Farra recognised it.

Mother help them all, she knew that voice.

"Mesrich," Vasteel said. His voice trembled with something deeper than mere rage. It was betrayal. It was pain. "You fool."

There was a scrambling from behind, then a shout of pain.

"The time for struggle has passed, deshun," Vasteel said. "Though I ought to tie you up and let you throw yourself against the chains for an eternity. I might, if I could bear the sight of you. And *you*, Phineas. What am I to do with you?"

Farra wrenched her eyes open. She found Thaddius, lurching against the Glacians that tried to restrain him. Their thick hands wound around his biceps and wrists, struggling to subdue him. Phineas stood alongside, ceding to his own detainers. "Thaddius," he said, desperately. "Stop, brother. It's over."

"NO!" Thaddius roared, and he slipped the hold of his captors, lunging to Farra, his body caging hers where she lay on the floor. "I'm *sorry*," he gasped to her, his voice breaking, crumbling.

Then he was gone. She heard his screams as he was hauled away.

"Take him to the Chasm," Vasteel said. "Phineas, too."

"Not him!" Thaddius shouted. "He played no part!"

"Your loyalty warms me," Vasteel said, no hint of mirth remaining. The words were festered around their edges. "Ill-placed as it is. Have I not given you everything, Mesrich? Have I not offered you the place at my side and shown you eternity?" The words shook. They rose in volume with each passing second. "Was *I* not also owed your loyalty?"

"Let them both go," Thaddius begged, though there was little conviction left in his voice. "Please. Kill *me*."

"No pure Glacian muddies their blood and lives, Mesrich. Your death is not for bargaining."

"My death..." Thaddius grunted, panting heavily. "Will be a welcome reprieve. So long as it departs me from your tyranny. Your greed." A heavy silence followed. "You speak of eternity, but your fear is plain to me. Soon, your pure-bloods will dwindle, until this world is finally free of us, and the Mother will rejoice."

A slow laugh began, and it was full of the fear Thaddius spoke of. "My," Vasteel rumbled. "How far into madness you have fallen. Much further than even *I* thought. Though you did try to warn me, did you not, Phineas? Was it not you that suggested I send him to the Ledge for Selection? That it would shake him from his reverie? Return his spirit?"

Phineas closed his eyes and lowered his head.

"It returned quite a bit more than we bargained for," Vasteel said icily. The King's anger seemed barely contained. "Though fear not, Mesrich. It was not Phineas who revealed your treachery to me. I have my own *acquaintances* in the Colony who bore witness to a pregnant human, visited by Glacians this night. Though the girl does not seem to be with child any longer," he remarks, his tone dropping to a deadly timbre. "Where is it, Mesrich?"

"Kill me," was his only answer, and then the crunch of his knees hitting the floor. "Kill me and let it be over."

"Very well," Vasteel said, his heavy footfalls finding Farra's ears. He passed close by her, his talons glancing off the stone, and came to stand before Thaddius. "It pains me to know this is the last time you will kneel before me, Mesrich," he muttered coldly, taking a sword from a nearby Glacian's scabbard. "My only consolation is knowing that your offspring is out there still and that they will continue to pay for your stupidity."

There was ringing sound as the sword passed through the air and then the hall was torn by the sound of pure anguish. Thaddius' wings lay broken and bloody.

Farra faded, unable to hold onto her consciousness any longer. Her thighs were slick with blood that continued to flow from her, and it promised a kinder demise. She whispered Thaddius' name, her heart splintering to pieces, and begged death to come.

"Take him to the Chasm!" Vasteel roared. "And push him in." A frenzied cheering followed.

"As for you, Phineas, I am loathe to spill more pure blood–"

"Please!" Phineas begged. "Please, Your Grace. I'll do anything. It was a mistake!"

"You will learn to heed your King again, Phineas. Or find yourself devested of your wings."

"Yes, Your Grace."

"You sink to the bottom of our ranks. Do you understand me?"

"Yes. Thank you."

"Now," Vasteel said, though his voice had become muted. Farra wasn't sure she truly heard it at all. Was not sure if she were still there, in that realm of hell with mountain beasts. "Let us see what spark resides in this one."

Farra was kicked onto her side.

And she fell.

Pain was absent.

But it was not death that relieved her. Of that, she was certain. She had touched death, seen its insides, and they were hollow. Death was dark and voiceless. It did not sing to her as she was serenaded now – lulled to sleep by choirs.

They sung of escaped sorrows.

They sealed her eyes shut.

They coaxed her to follow the current of this river to its end, where death would embrace her.

But this was not death. Death was bloody. Death was a freefalling abyss. Death did not lure its prey into its clutches, it wrenched the living from their perches and shut out the light. One had to fight to reach the surface again.

She felt the pressure against her lips, her eyes, warm tendrils of an indescribable substance holding them shut. But she could not breathe, could not find the will to try.

That matter was inside her now. Warming the inside of her nose and sliding down her throat. Searching... searching.

For what, she could not fathom. All that she had been made of had been left for ruin. Stripped from her.

Her home, her lover, her baby...

Ryon.

She could bring to mind his name but not his face. Not the exact shade of his skin and eyes and hair. Not the feel of his weight on her chest. She had to find it. Had to find that memory.

No, she thought. *Wait.*

Sleep, the whispers told her gently, hushing her. Her eyelids were shuttered so tightly she could not move them.

But she could find the seam of her lips, could prise them open. She gulped, expecting to choke on whatever substance trapped her, but found it as gentle, as fortifying as air.

She breathed again.

Suddenly, she was pulled, not along the current, but out of it, in the opposite direction.

Her face felt the sting of the cold and she was abruptly hauled onto stone.

She blinked and the Glacian palace took shape once more. She lay on her side, immediately noticing the absence of injury, of pain.

Beside her, the Pool of Iskra swirled, glowing impetuously, as though it had been cheated.

"Your first task in your repentance is upon you, Phineas," Vasteel's voice rang out, reverberating in her ears. "Send her into the Chasm. I have a new set of wings to hang on my walls."

She watched the distant shapes of Vasteel and his nobles depart and a cold hand reached beneath her upper arm.

"Stand," said a hollow, broken voice.

She turned her head and looked up. Phineas stared back at her, the tresses of his long hair falling into his face, but not concealing the alarm that struck him.

And despite the fresh panic blossoming inside her, she levelled her stare, her bottom lip trembling. "Try to throw me into the Chasm," she whispered. "And I will drag you in with me."

Phineas' breath left him. His eyes widened in awe. "Farra?"

In response, Farra merely glared.

"Don't speak!" Phineas rasped suddenly, eyes darting around the throne room. "Do as I say. And *do not* try to run." It was spoken in a rush, his lips barely moving as he uttered the demand.

It was only then that Farra remembered how the pool had made the other humans lame, had sucked the will from their bodies.

"They're *watching*," Phineas murmured to her, so low she had to focus on his lips to understand him. "Stand."

There was little choice in the matter. There was only this, the friend of a Glacian who had sired her child, and the hope of his lingering loyalty.

She stood.

"Walk," he said, a little louder now, as though it were not for her benefit.

She walked, wondering if the tremor she felt was showing on the outside, whether the walls of her chest could withstand the pounding of her heart, whether her throat would collapse amidst the pressure that gripped it. She wanted to cry. Wanted to scream or run.

"Don't," Phineas whispered, gripping her arm tighter. "Trust me."

An impossible ask.

He led her out of the throne room and down a wide hall, down a stairwell, until it opened to a tunnel. A tunnel that led them to the ice plane before the Chasm.

"What will you do with me?" she whispered to Phineas.

He only gave her a look of warning and swallowed hard.

His strange magic opened the portcullis at the end of the tunnel and the force of the blizzard squalls almost sent her tumbling backward. But Phineas took hold and pulled her forward.

The wind sliced at her cheeks, her neck. The sleet forced her eyes closed and she could not see where she was being led, she only knew that somewhere before them was the Chasm and beyond that the Ledge.

Perhaps Phineas would take her back where she belonged. She could return home.

It suddenly did not seem so bleak a place.

Phineas stopped on the ice, stabilizing her when she pitched forward. She could hear his panicked breaths, even over the howl of the wind.

Farra turned her head inside the shelter of her cloak hood to look at him. But his eyes were elsewhere, locked on something before them. Farra followed his gaze.

The Chasm was a mere foot away. They stood before the lip, achingly close to the void. She did not dare move, lest she slip.

"Please," she rasped, turning her head toward him. Desperation overcame her. It roiled in her core, streaked down her arms and burned her palms with its cold fear. She looked at them and found them coated in frost.

"I owed my life to him," Phineas said, holding her still as she wrestled with the wind. "Many times over."

"Please," she said again. "D-do not throw me to the Chasm. *Please!*"

"Yennes," he said, shaking his head in wonder. "It is a fitting name."

Farra said nothing, shielding her face instead from the onslaught of ice and snow that lanced her skin.

"My last favour to you, my brother," Farra heard, and then her feet left the ground.

She was plummeting into that dark abyss, identical to the belly of death she had clawed her way out of. Only this time, the fall was accompanied by the swoop of wings, the strong encompassing of pale arms, and the sensation of her spirit leaving her body as she dropped and dropped and dropped.

Chapter Forty

Within the Terrsaw palace, the Queens sat aghast, astonished by the woman at the end of the bed.

A woman with frost covered hands and wary eyes.

A woman who spoke as though her own voice frightened her.

"You… you journeyed through the Chasm?" Alvira uttered, though it was clear to her that the tale was true. How else to explain the Glacian magic she held in her palms?

"I did."

"And you bore a child. With one of *them*?"

Yennes blanched at the accusation in her tone. "Yes. Which brings me to the favour you promised," she said, attempting to stand taller, to broaden her shoulders. "I have cured her," she said, gaze flicking to Cressida. "Let me leave from here."

"And where will you go?"

Yennes did not answer immediately. There was calculation in her eyes. "If you can offer me no hope to retrieve my son, then I… I will make my peace with it. Start anew." The lie burned her throat on its way out. She recalled with perfect clarity the Glacian King's taunts to punish Thaddius' son as he'd cut the wings from his back. There was no peace to be found now. None.

"Ah," Alvira answered. "Yes. Well, such a request comes with a few conditions of course."

Colour leached from Yennes' face. The smell of the dungeons below returned to her. Her hands twisted together.

"An iskra witch walking amongst good folk? It would be rather rash of me to let you leave from here and do as you will."

"I only mean to return to my lodgings," Yennes said.

"I shall need to know where you will stay," Alvira continued. "And should I call on you, you will obey the summons."

"Call on me?" Yennes asked, her eyes narrowing. "What–"

"So that you may continue to serve the palace, of course." Alvira smiled. "It is quite a prize, Yennes. Have you any idea what my people would do to you should they learn the truth? That you fucked a Glacian? That you bore its child? I ought to send you to the pyre now." Alvira watched with an air of satisfaction as Yennes reared away. "I assure you, it is quite an allowance to let you live at all."

Yennes' eyes welled. The last of her resolve drawn away from its husk.

"So," Alvira said. "Where will you go from here, iskra witch?"

Yennes stood on the bank of the river, holding a ring in her hand with a black stone at its centre. The tighter she held it, the more she felt the tug of her limbs, the one that led her through the Mecca, through the fields and forests and to the water's edge. Without Baltisse's ring, she would have wandered haplessly through the kingdom, unaware of how far she'd travelled.

She wondered if Alvira had snuck into the keep and bowled out her insides as she'd slept. It would explain the emptiness she felt now.

"Yennes?" a voice called, and she looked up to see someone familiar on the other side of the river. A woman with long, golden hair and beautiful clothes. There one moment, gone the next.

She reappeared beside Yennes, a small chain necklace woven tightly around her fingers. Yennes' ring grew hot in her hand.

"Yennes," Baltisse breathed, looking her over shrewdly, and then into her eyes, delving into her mind.

Yennes could only imagine what she saw.

The mage sighed heavily, sadly. But she did not insult Yennes with pity. It was understanding she exuded now. Tiredness. Anger. "Fucking crowns," she muttered, taking Yennes' hand.

"You tried to warn me."

But the mage shook her head. "I cannot curb your course," she said simply, though Yennes did not know what she meant. "It is not for me to decide what you will do."

"You must teach me to fold," she pronounced, tears dripping from her chin. When had she begun to cry?

"So that you can go to Glacia and find your boy? What did you say his name was?"

"Ryon," Yennes whispered, swaying to one side.

Baltisse held her upright. "I meant what I said before, Yennes. You do not need to cling to what was left up there. Unburden yourself."

"I cannot simply–"

"You *can*," Baltisse pressed. "Because that boy? He belongs amongst his kind."

"Vasteel… he said he would hurt him."

"And how will you stop him, Yennes? What power could you wield that would thwart him? Thwart them all? And even if you could, what will you do with your son, when the Queen comes to call on you and learns that you brought him here? She is just as dangerous as them, Yennes. I suspect you know that now."

Yennes teetered until she found her forehead pressed to the mage's shoulder. Her body shuddered with the force of the past and present colliding.

"What is done, is done," Baltisse told her, though her voice leaked with regret. Sorrow. "There is little we can change. We just live, Farra. That is how we defy our enemies, how we honour those we love. We live."

Chapter Forty-One

In the den of a mage clan, the former King of Glacia barely resembles that which fled his own palace months before. He is diminished. Sunken. The mage light casts shadows on his limbs where the bones all but protrude from his skin. His once lustrous hair and beard now hang sparsely. It is the first time Ryon has seen him without wings – he doubts his frame could support them.

Vasteel lifts his head, and the movement is not without immense effort. Indeed, he trembles with the weight of it. Ryon wonders if the iskra he consumed is eking out by degrees, slowly aging him. How long has it been since he last drank from the pool?

Despite the pain, the corners of Ryon's mouth lift a little. "Mortality does not become you, Vasteel," he murmurs, ignoring the sting of sweat trickling into his eyes. His breaths are short, but he can summon enough for this.

"No," Vasteel says on a ragged exhale. His own breaths threaten to cave him in. "One of the many reasons I've avoided it."

Ryon laughs darkly, though it sends spikes of pain through his chest. "I've always imagined what awaits the wicked in the underworld. Those in the Colony speak of many tortures there. Water that turns to acid in one's throat, food that turns to dust. The ground made of spikes and sky of fire. They say there is a special circle saved for the most ruined of souls. A place where the skin is cut from the body until it lies unsheathed. One is healed instantly, only to be peeled again, over and over." Ryon watches Vasteel closely. "We both know that you are promised to that circle, Vasteel. I think you avoid mortality for its reckoning, not for your vanity."

Vasteel says nothing. Indeed, he may have slipped back to

unconsciousness, the way his head hangs limply on his thin neck. But a quiet murmur still reaches Ryon across the cavern. "Alas, if only I could reach death sooner," he says, a hint of dry mirth in the words. "I would face that reckoning humbly, deshun. But the iskra… it keeps me here, decaying whilst I still breathe, and it is torture enough."

Ryon hopes not. He hopes the afterlife makes him suffer for an eternity. He hopes every soul he consumed awaits him, ready to cast their stone and take their share of his flesh.

"I know what you think of me," Vasteel whispers now, his head lolling to peer at Ryon through clumps of filthy hair. "You think me a villain. Your father thought the same."

Ryon does not quail at the mention of Thaddius Mesrich. He has long since grown immune to the brutes spitting his name through their teeth. Using it as though it were something to cut him with. It has been many years since he felt its sting. But Vasteel's tongue does not curl at its citing now. Instead, he sounds sorrowful.

"Thaddius tried to curb my tastes once," he continues, his breaths becoming even more shallow. "Tried to… to reason with me. To negotiate. Ha! He wondered if we hadn't taken our fill of life, taken too many of the living to defy our own deaths. And I… I should have killed him then. Should have prevented the events that would unfold. I should have denied fate its tangled designs to kill me, but I couldn't see it. I couldn't see how maddened he had become.

"But worse than that, I did not see what *you* had become, Ryon," Vasteel rasps. "And so, I was twice a fool – once for believing in Thaddius and again when I believed in his bastard. But I swear to you. I cared a great deal for your father. And I could not help but care a great deal for you too." He looks at Ryon with watery, ancient eyes, and shakes his head slowly. "I should have staked you both."

Ryon meets that gaze, ice curling up his spine. He musters a smirk. "You would never have killed me, *Your Grace*," he says coldly. "I was too good at charming your affections and you were too stupid to notice."

A jostle sounds from Ryon's side – Tasheem awakening. A breath of relief loosens from Ryon's chest to see her eyelids rise and fall. Her feet slip on the wet rock beneath her, slick with her blood.

"Tash," he says, trying to make his voice reach. "Tash, go easy."

She groans soundly, looking about the cavern with eyes that threaten to shutter. Her mouth hangs open, her breaths too short. "Ry…?"

"I'm here," he tells her, watching the vine tighten around her wrists. "Be still, Tasheem." But her eyes have fallen to the Glacian on the wall adjacent and they widen in panic. Reality seems to return to her then. She finds Rivdan tied to the wall beside her, then Ryon, the other Glacians. "What—"

"Ah, a party," a voice simpers, floating through the cave.

Samskia strides toward them, her fingers trailing along the low ceiling, moss and vine appearing where she touches. "So many awake to see the blood on the moon."

Ryon's throat closes. "Samskia."

"You've survived, night wing." She nods to him, her irises glowing. "I hoped you would."

Tasheem stares at her balefully. "Who—?"

"She's a mage," Ryon groans, looking to the cave opening, where the light is dimming.

"Let us go," Tasheem spits. Blood dribbles down her chin, her eyes roll.

Samskia tilts her head over and watches the blood fall in droplets, adding to the stain at her feet. Then she smiles brilliantly. "Very well," she says and waves a hand through the air once.

Ryon feels the immediate release of the vine wrapped around his wrists and arms, and they drop like stones to his side. His legs have no strength with which to hold him, and he crumbles. There is a chorus of flesh colliding with stone as they all fall, only the ones still alive utter a cry. Ryon's shoulders are ablaze, he curses wildly into the stone.

Samskia bends to him, tracing a line across his brow. "I'm afraid there is no time left for your woman, night wing," she says. "I had hoped we'd see the blessings of the blood moon bring her to you."

Ryon tries to brush her fingers away from him, but the fire in his arms burns on.

"Do not try to move, Glacian," she tsks. "Your limbs will be of no use to you now."

Indeed, he cannot summon movement from his legs, his arms making him bite down on his own tongue to keep from screaming.

"Baltisse saw something in you that I do not see," she says, peering into his eyes intensely, turning her head on its side like a curious animal. "She insisted you live. But Yerdos… she wishes otherwise."

"No," Ryon urges.

But Samskia's eyes widen before she turns her face away, beckons to something he cannot see. She stands abruptly, dropping his head to the stone. "The wards," she utters, and then the air leaves the cave. The mage inhales as though she could hold the entire atmosphere in her chest.

For a moment, Ryon is breathless, suspended. Then Samskia exhales in a gust and air returns to his lungs.

She turns to face him once more, a wide smile alighting her features. "Your woman has made it after all, Glacian," she says.

CHAPTER FORTY-TWO

Dawsyn brings mage fire to her palm and approaches the barrier once more.

"Dawsyn!" Salem hollers. "Are you daft?"

But Dawsyn can still feel the hum of that magic, can still see that strange haze, and something within propels her forward.

Above her, the moon is glowing in spite of the sun, a pink hue tinging its face.

She comes to the barrier's edge. The flame in her hand seems to lean toward it, as though wishing to touch it.

Bracing to be hurled through the air once more, she shuts her eyes, and reaches forward.

Nothing happens. When she opens her eyes again, she finds her arm extended through the barrier, the mage light still dancing in her palm.

"Dawsyn?" Hector calls to her.

"I'm all right," she says incredulously, a bubble of laughter catching in her throat. She goes to step forward.

"Don't!" Hector calls again.

But Dawsyn is already through. Already standing on the other side, and no force tries to expel her.

She looks back at the others, standing on the slope. But their gazes are darting in every direction and they call out her name.

"I am well!" she tells them, but they do not seem to hear her.

"Dawsyn!" Salem bellows, his hands cupped around his mouth. His face is stricken, panicked.

"He cannot see you," comes a voice.

Dawsyn whips around, pulling her ax from its sheath. Where before there had been no-one, now stands a group amongst the trees. Men and women, with animal skin draped over their shoulders and fire in their eyes.

Mages.

"Who are you, ax-wielder?" the closest of them says. A woman with black hair, thin lips.

Dawsyn's heart beats rapidly in her chest, but she does not dare back away. "Dawsyn Sabar," she says, wondering if they can hear the awe in her voice, wondering if they can feel the warmth she suddenly feels. Her mind is flooded with it.

"Sabar?" the woman asks, her eyebrow rising. "A descendant of Melares?"

Dawsyn recalls the name. Baltisse used it not so long ago.

"Yes," she says.

"A foolish girl," the woman says ruefully, "to marry a king of Terrsaw. Monarchs only take and never give." Her eyes hold Dawsyn in their grip, the colour within them swirling viciously. "Is that why you have come, princess?" she asks. "Have you come to take?"

Dawsyn sees their stance subtly change, becoming defensive. Ready.

"No," she says.

"Then why have you come?"

She grips the ax handle tightly. "I… I saw the haze. The barrier. I could feel it."

"This is not your mountain, child. Go back to your castle."

"I have no castle," Dawsyn says, her voice rising. "And I am no royal."

"Have they cast you out, child?" the mage asks, her head tilting to the side. "Did they too learn of your blood?"

"No. I am not from Terrsaw."

"You are a Sabar–"

"Born on the Ledge," Dawsyn finishes. "And I did not ask to be on this mountain."

Silence follows. The woman's companions share glances. Confusion.

The dark-haired mage turns to them, speaking a language Dawsyn does not understand. But their eyes roil as she speaks. Their lips lift. They seem… entertained.

"A Glacian prisoner!" the mage says, smiling brilliantly back at Dawsyn. "So, it was the *blood moon* that brought you to us this day. It always finds those in need of retribution. You are in luck, Dawsyn Sabar, mage of the

Ledge. For tonight, we will bleed the Glacians who claim our mountain as their own, and you will have your vengeance on your captors."

Dawsyn hesitates, pulling back toward the calls of her friends, pacing frantically just feet away. But that same hum she believed had come from the barrier seems to resonate, instead, within these mages. There is a flux of energy passing among them, between them, and out to her. It courses through Dawsyn – a gentle current. It is curiosity that moves her feet forward, rather than away.

"Who are you?" she asks of them. But only one answers.

"I am Roznier," the black-haired mage says, taking Dawsyn's hand. She feels a thrill run the path of her spine at her touch. "This is our clan."

It seems to Dawsyn the mage clan has carved a piece of the mountain for themselves. Roznier leads her past huts made of tree root, as though they had risen from the ground simply to form shelter. Signs of mage magic are all around her, from the pines that curve inward, protecting the clearing, to the paths cleared of deep snow. Sunlight filters down into the circular space, making patterns on the snow, and Dawsyn feels warmed by its touch.

There's no wind, no bite to the air. Indeed, Dawsyn feels she could do away with her furs here, so mild is the weather.

"What are you?" Roznier asks suddenly. She had been leading Dawsyn down a winding path miraculously clear of snow. They pass huts on either side, but Roznier pays little attention to the surrounds. Her discerning gaze is on Dawsyn.

Dawsyn frowns, she is unsure which answer is fitting. Mage? Human? Vagrant?

"I cannot distinguish what I sense," Roznier continues. "What I smell."

"You can likely smell a great many things." Dawsyn scowls. "It has been an age since I bathed."

"Ah yes! What a journey you've had. How did you come to find yourself off the Ledge, young one?"

"A long story," Dawsyn defers, pausing to see a deer standing unafraid only several feet from them, its eyes closing as it tips its head toward the sun.

"Who taught you to use magic?" Roznier asks next, her curiosity obvious. Her companions have left the path, venturing in different directions. Roznier and Dawsyn walk on alone.

Dawsyn sighs. "A friend of mine. A mage named Baltisse," she says, though her throat thickens to mention it.

Roznier smiles widely, then lets out a crow of laughter. "Baltisse!" she says, affection winding through each syllable. "Yes, she holds much admiration for you Sabars. Tell me, how does she fare? She has not paid us a visit in many moons." Roznier looks expectantly at Dawsyn, searching her with new understanding. "I assume she was the one to rescue you from the Ledge?"

Dawsyn smiles sadly. She recalls again, as she often does, the sensation of freefall as she slides down the ice and over the lip of the Chasm, the second of suspended time before she and Ryon fell, and the hand that clasped her wrist and pulled them between realms. "Something of the sort."

"You are most fortunate indeed, young one. She is a powerful being. And she has always lamented those on the Ledge. In many ways, she believes *we* are to blame."

"We?" Dawsyn asks. "Mages?"

But Roznier sighs, her sight far-reaching and glassy with memory, and Dawsyn is suddenly struck by a thought. "Roznier," she whispers, and the mage turns back to her. But Dawsyn is merely turning the name over in her mouth, a niggling sensation gnawing at her. Had Baltisse used that name when she spoke of King Vasteel and his reign in Terrsaw?

"He welcomed us into his fold of advisors and treated us like nobility. Me, two others by the names of Roznier and Grigori, and my mother, Indriss."

Dawsyn lifts her eyes to the woman beside her and stops in her tracks. "Roznier," she repeats. "Creator of the Pool of Iskra."

Roznier's lips flatten into an even thinner line, but she does not deny it. "One of four," she says. "I cannot take all credit."

Dawsyn does not answer. Instead, she takes the mage's measure anew. Roznier seems to sag under the weight of the moniker, the same way Baltisse had. A similar sorrow that once darkened Baltisse's features now darkens Roznier's.

"Whatever hatred you feel now, Dawsyn Sabar. I assure you, it will not amount to the centuries I've spent in this skin, loathing every inch of it. I've learned to put my mind to what can be controlled and make peace with what I can't."

Dawsyn shakes her head. "There is no hatred." She helped Baltisse to protect Terrsaw after all. She pulled boulders from the earth to form the Boulder Gate. There are too many to hate for Dawsyn to add another.

"Where is Baltisse now?" Roznier asks, looking past Dawsyn's shoulder, as though she might appear there. "It is not like her to stay away on a blood moon."

Dawsyn's shoulders fall, but she makes herself say what Roznier has still not grasped. "She is gone," she says tightly, lips reluctant to relinquish the words.

Roznier's gaze becomes blank. Taller than Dawsyn, she looks over her head, staring resolutely away. "She cannot be."

"I am sorry." It is all Dawsyn can say, for that familiar wave of sorrow is upon her, and she cannot allow it to bury her now.

Roznier's lips part and a broken breath leaves her. She squeezes her eyes shut and Dawsyn watches in wonder as Roznier lifts her palms to the sun, her face too, and murmurs something Dawsyn does not understand, in a voice that rings through Dawsyn's blood, raises the hairs on her neck.

She cannot explain it, but for an achingly short moment Dawsyn feels her. She feels Baltisse's palms on her shoulders, her long fingers pressing into the flesh. She feels the touch of Baltisse's forehead against her own, feels their breaths combine. She sees her molten eyes, burning brightly in her mind – and that hum that existed inside of Dawsyn is suddenly released. It is all around. It finds the sparks of life in everything nearby. And Dawsyn's own spark – the one that exists in her mind – expands and widens and fills every inch of her, every corner.

A mere moment, then it is all gone.

And Dawsyn wants it back. She needs it back.

Tears fall thickly. They are swallowed beneath the neck of her cloak. She cannot seem to stop them.

"Not gone," Roznier says, placing a hand where Baltisse's had lain. "She exists still."

Dawsyn shakes her head, blindly denying. "I saw her die," she mumbles. "I left her there. Left her body behind as though she meant nothing to me," the words come on waves of shudders she cannot control.

"We have no use for our bodies in the other realm," Roznier tells her. "She is not gone, Dawsyn. She surrounds you. She is... everywhere." The woman places a hand to Dawsyn's chest. And the hum grows louder, vibrating within. "What we cannot see, we can feel. She still exists. Not in this place, but the next." Roznier smiles gently, though her own sadness is plain. "You will be joined again one day."

Dawsyn does not know what it means. She does not understand the realms and the paths between. But she knows that, for a moment, the two were bridged. She wonders who else lingers on the other side. She wonders if they are all just across the way.

She breathes and this time her chest feels lighter, filled with warmth.

"Come," Roznier says, taking Dawsyn's hand in her own. "We will celebrate tonight and there is much to prepare."

CHAPTER FORTY-THREE

Ruby alights from her horse and curses.

It has been an age since horseback has rendered her quite as limp. Her thighs tremble as she walks, passing the reins to the stable hands with breathless thanks.

"Captain," comes a voice from the shadows.

Curse the Mother. She should have returned hours before, as dawn broke. But those that had survived the journey through the Chasm were in no shape to swim through the ocean's current at its end. They were forced to wait until the tide receded enough that they could wade through, and even that had threatened to thwart a few of the weakest.

Now, night has fallen, and the voice that beckons her is unlikely to allow her to find a bed, as much as her body requires it.

Ruby follows the voice to the back of the stables – stables that smell strongly of shit but serve to provide some privacy.

"Cressida," Ruby says grimly. "This can likely wait till morning."

"No, Ruby," the Queen Consort snaps. "It cannot."

It is a quite a sight to see the woman here at all, much less cloaked in dark grey. Gone are the brilliance and opulence of her finer clothes.

"Are they safe?" Cressida asks first, a hint of stress in her voice. "The Ledge people?"

Ruby grimaces, her throat stricken. "Of the ones that remain, I expect many will recover, yes."

"Of the ones that *remain*?"

"They were near death when we caught up to them," Ruby says. "Taken by a strange illness. Some did not make it much further."

Cressida curses in a way that seems unnatural. Ruby is sure she has never heard Her Majesty curse. "The Glacians are coming."

Ruby blanches. She reels back a step. *"Now?"*

"Tomorrow, or the next day, perhaps," Cressida spits. "I can hold them off no longer. They are impatient."

"Fuck," Ruby mutters, running her hands through her filthy hair. "*Fuck.*"

"So, no, we cannot wait," Cressida answers. "The Queen's Jubilee will be held tomorrow morning. I will make the announcement then."

Ruby stares at her, dumbfounded. "At the *Jubilee?*"

"Was it not your idea to 'lead them into the dragon's den' so to speak? What better way to corner Alvira than by announcing the return of our lost ones while all are gathered beneath her balcony?"

"You'll be executed," Ruby breathes. "This is not the plan."

"The plan has been escalated," Cressida says evenly. "You will ready yourself for it. Even if we are lucky and the Glacians await the celebrations to be over, Alvira will have very little time to change her tune and align it with ours. Even if she cedes to the call of her people, time will be needed to rally. *You* will need to ready the battalions."

"I am no longer their captain."

"You will be so again," Cressida says forcefully. "And when the Glacians come, you will be ready to fight them off."

Ruby feels a splinter of panic within, cracking her resolve. "It won't be enough," she breathes, remembering her time in Glacia, the sheer *number* of them.

Cressida's eyes darken. "It is too late to bow out now, Ruby," she says icily. "You gave me your word."

Ruby only shakes her head. "We will need to evacuate the Mecca. The Glacians will come for them if they cannot reach the Ledge-dwellers."

"There will not be time. Are the survivors waiting in the Fallen Village?"

"Yes. Like sheep for slaughter."

"How many guard them?"

"Twenty."

Cressida huffs. "I will send more to them tonight. As many as I can allow without Alvira becoming wise to it. We must hope the Glacians do not arrive sooner."

Ruby almost laughs, the circumstances are so dire. "We must hope their number does not decimate us entirely. Or this plan will only lead to the slaughter of all."

A rustle sounds from behind them.

Ruby turns, reaching for her sword. "Who's there?"

"There are others who can be called upon," a quiet voice says. From out of the shadows, steps Yennes. "Those who will be willing to fight."

"The iskra witch," Cressida hisses, then turns to Ruby. "Are you not able to tell when you are being *followed*?"

"How much did you hear?" Ruby asks, holding her sword in line with the woman's chest.

Yennes hesitates, her hands moving skittishly. "All of it."

It will be difficult to kill and dispose of her, Ruby knows, but there seems to be little other choice. The woman is a puppet, and Alvira has always grasped the strings.

"That's unfortunate," Ruby mutters.

"I only wish to help." Yennes watches the sword tip warily. "Please. I swear it."

"What do you mean, there are *others*?" Cressida asks abruptly. "Speak plainly, witch."

Yennes bites her lip. "The mixed-blooded Glacians," she says.

"The mixed-blooded have seized control of Glacia, imbecile," Cressida snaps. "It is *them* we must now fight."

"No," Yennes says shaking her head. "No, I know them."

"You *knew* them," Cressida corrects. "Many years have passed since, Yennes."

"The ones I saw in the palace didn't lament those left on the Ledge," Ruby confirms. "Why would they turn on Adrik, and help to save them now?"

"Because they are not our enemy," Yennes says forcefully, more forcefully then either Cressida or Ruby have ever heard her speak. "And if someone else has taken rule of Glacia and that fucking pool, there will be those who wish against it. Those who will do anything to be rid of it for good."

"Be rid of it?" Cressida asks. "It cannot be done."

Yennes sighs, hesitates. And Ruby senses something banking up in the silence. A mounting swell. A shudder in the constellations. Yennes finally releases a gust of breath. "There is a way," she says, "And I can trade the knowledge for the Colony's allegiance in this fight."

Ruby only stares, stunned, her sword tip hitting the ground.

Yennes continues, as though she hadn't just split the sky above them, poured its secrets to the earth. "They will agree. I am sure of it."

Cressida's breaths are hushed. "Do you speak truthfully?" she utters. "Do you truly know how to destroy the Pool of Iskra?"

Yennes seems to shrink as she answers. "I do."

"How could you possibly?" Ruby exhales.

"I knew its maker," Yennes says simply. "And she showed me the way. We only need the one with means to see it through."

CHAPTER FORTY-FOUR

The blood moon rises quickly and Dawsyn watches on as the clan prepares their celebration.

There are dozens of them. The mages greet each other with nods and small touches of palms but rarely speak. They work and weave amongst one another like a current, harmonious and synchronised. Dawsyn wonders how many centuries in each other's company it took to achieve such peace.

There are children too. They play in the snow and disappear into the trees, leaves dancing at their heels. The other mages pay them little mind, at ease with the sight of them disappearing into the woods. Their wards will protect their young, after all.

Roznier seems something of a leader to Dawsyn. The others confer with her quietly on occasion, approaching with a light touch of a palm and then speaking with deference. Whatever she says in return, it is spoken in the old language; Dawsyn does not understand a word.

The mages stare curiously at Dawsyn, and it makes her wary, but none approach. None seem to question Roznier bringing her here and so Dawsyn only watches this community, hewn from the mountain like her, living so conversely from that of the Ledge people.

"How easy you make it seem," she says to Roznier late in the afternoon, as the light begins to ebb. "To live amongst one another, with the cold." They are seated on a log bench before a large campfire. It burns brighter and hotter than any Dawsyn has seen. She almost forgets she is on the mountain, that the cold exists at all.

Roznier accepts a plate of food from a passing mage and offers it to Dawsyn. "It is easy to be peaceful when one is abundant," she says simply. "I imagine it was not so on the Ledge where those Glacians caged you."

"No," Dawsyn replies flatly.

"I've had many years to think on the matters of peace and abundance," Roznier says conversationally. "Greed is what impedes peace, invokes war. Greed is what led Baltisse and I to create the Pool of Iskra. Greed is what led Vasteel to drink from it. The Glacians were born from greed. They are made of it," she says. "In that, we can take some solace. They will never know peace."

Dawsyn agrees. But it is not Vasteel or even Adrik she thinks of. It is those in the Colony of Glacia. It is Rivdan, Tasheem... Ryon. They may never know peace either. All for the greed of another. "Not all of them deserve it," Dawsyn says in reply. "Not all of them drink from the pool."

"Ah. You sound just like Baltisse," Roznier says. "She often tried to convince me of the same. But whether they drink from the pool or not, they remain unnatural beings."

Dawsyn cannot agree this time. She thinks that nothing seems more natural than Ryon in flight. How can something so beautiful be an abomination? Heat prickles beneath her skin.

Roznier chuckles darkly. "Even the mutts among them have the pool running through their veins, Dawsyn, if not by their own choice."

"Then surely you are to blame, Roznier," Dawsyn says. "Were it not for you creating the magic that transformed Vasteel, no Glacian would walk these slopes."

"Indeed," Roznier agrees easily. "Though as I've said, I have had much time to consider my actions, and whilst there are parts of my past I cannot forgive, I at least know I did not act with ill intent. None of us did. Not in the beginning, anyway." Her stare becomes far-reaching. Dawsyn wonders what she sees. "If I had the foresight to know what would become of the pool, I would have thwarted its creation. I would destroy it now, if I could."

Dawsyn becomes still. "Destroy it?" she says slowly, watching the mage's narrow eyes for any hint of jest. "Can such a thing be done?"

"Everything made can be unmade."

"I grow tired of poetry," Dawsyn says evenly, though her mind runs rampant. "Speak plainly, mage. Can the Pool of Iskra truly be destroyed?"

Roznier eyes her warily. "How odd you are, Dawsyn Sabar. A woman of the Ledge who sympathises with Glacians. I see the blood-thirst in your eyes. You champion the Glacians and yet still want their life source destroyed?"

"I champion those who do not live freely," Dawsyn says. "And I wish their oppressors a merciless death."

"Hm. Just like Baltisse," Roznier mutters to herself shaking her head. "Well, Dawsyn Sabar. I am sorry to say that the Pool of Iskra will remain until there is someone willing to draw all of its magic into their being and play host to it."

Dawsyn recalls Baltisse speaking of similar acts, as though magic could simply be carried from place to place. *"We carried it inside us and brought it to a place of Vasteel's choosing; high up on the mountain where no one would dare go."*

"And *you* are not willing?" Dawsyn asks.

"Ah, but there is no mage alone who can play host to magic so dark and so large. Not for long, anyway. Mage magic and iskra were not meant to combine. Absorbing so much magic would only bring destruction. The detonation would be… cataclysmic, I believe."

Dawsyn well knows how combustible mage magic and iskra are when they compete. "What of a human, then? Or a Glacian? Someone without the hindrance of mage blood."

"But what human has the power to say the incantation? To invoke the energy needed to complete the task? It is a complicated spell, Dawsyn. That is the great trap of the magic we created. Magic that can only be undone by itself, but *destroys* itself. If self-sacrifice were the only price, I'd have paid it long ago. But absorbing that magic turns us into a weapon only the Mother should wield. The cost outweighs the reward, I'm afraid."

Dawsyn shakes her head. "There must be an answer."

"Not without risking the annihilation of all," Roznier says.

But has Dawsyn not lived with both dark and light inside her and learned to combine the two? Has there ever been another in existence who has held both in balance?

Dawsyn very much doubts there will ever be another like herself.

Roznier suddenly looks up to the sky. "Ah," she says. "The blood moon is here."

Dawsyn follows her gaze, looking to the pink hue of the moon's surface. "What happens on a blood moon?" she asks. She has watched the mages prepare the fire and cook food enough for all, but there has been no mention of what comes next.

The mages converge around the flames – flames that grow inexplicably higher as daylight recedes.

Roznier chuckles. "We vanquish the unnatural, Dawsyn Sabar. Are you feeling vengeful?"

Dawsyn raises her eyebrows. "I am rarely not."

"Then the blood moon brought you to us by design. Samskia!" Roznier calls, and a woman with wide eyes and bare feet emerges from the back of the circle. "Ve verdina oi Glacians," Roznier tells her, and the woman named Samskia smiles wickedly. Her eyes dart to Dawsyn's, and they turn molten, churning with anticipation. She quickly disappears. There one moment and gone in the next.

"Where did she go?" Dawsyn asks, frowning at the place where the mage had been.

"To fetch our offerings," Roznier answers. "We've collected many this past season. Much more than is ordinary."

Dawsyn's feels a sudden thrill of fear. It begins at her scalp and travels down her neck, leaving gooseflesh in its wake. "Offerings?"

But Roznier does not answer. She stands suddenly and the mages surrounding fall quiet.

The hum in Dawsyn's blood suddenly rings loudly and she shivers. It fills her completely as it had before, and she feels all powerful. Every inch of her suddenly strengthened, made new. She smiles at the warmth of it, the sureness of it. She sees that intangible light in every pair of eyes she encounters. They are all made of the same.

The mages begin to sing.

Their voices build and build, reaching ratcheting heights that give Dawsyn the sensation that the noise might burst within her, split her apart. She closes her eyes as it grows, letting it imbue her. It is heady, this music. It quickens her blood. It reaches into her chest and grips her heart, forcing it to beat in time with its tempo. And by the time their song finally dissolves, she opens her eyes to a setting she barely recognises, to a body she does not know. Her own skin feels blissfully unfamiliar.

But there is movement beyond the flames of the campfire, and she blinks to bring them to focus.

A line of bound bodies kneels. Bodies that had not been there before. Bodies tangled in roots that break skin. Bodies so broken that the heads sag upon necks, some slumping to the snow.

But there are three she recognises, three bodies her eyes stick to. Her heart defies her chest and becomes lodged in her throat, trying to escape her body altogether.

Her knees almost buckle. "Ryon," she says, and it is only a breath. It barely passes her lips.

But he hears it.

He is a shadow. His bare chest and arms hold bruises that make her stomach turn over. Every breath seems laborious. He trembles with each pull, moments from collapse.

Tasheem and Rivdan are worse. Rivdan lies sideways in the snow, and Dawsyn is not certain he is alive at all. Tasheem sways, blood dripping from her mouth.

The ecstasy that had filled Dawsyn is gone instantly. In its place, she is filled only with cold certainty.

She tears her eyes from Ryon and looks at Roznier beside her, who smiles radiantly down at her clan and has the righteousness to speak of peace. Dawsyn's ax is within her hand in a moment. It is at Roznier's throat in the next.

Silence falls. Quickly and terribly.

There is only one who breaks it, and it comes in the form of gentle melodic laughter. The mage named Samskia runs her finger down Ryon's cheek and watches Dawsyn with glee.

Roznier turns slowly toward Dawsyn. Her eyes flit down to the ax blade, as though it were a curiosity and not the thing piercing the skin of her throat. "Interesting," she murmurs, then looks at Dawsyn anew, her eyes filled with flames. "Though, not intelligent."

Pain grips Dawsyn then, curling her insides upon themselves and reducing her to a squirming, screeching ball on the ground. The ax falls beside her head.

"Do not pick it up, Dawsyn Sabar," Roznier says from above. "Baltisse may have taught you tricks, but she has not taught you enough for this."

Dawsyn pants, struggling to raise herself from the ground. "Let him go," she grunts, then again, louder. "Let him *go*!"

Roznier looks at the Glacians, ten of them at least, in various states of decline before the fire. She raises her eyebrows, clearly at a loss in understanding her pleads.

"*Dawsyn*," Ryon says, his voice reed thin. She can barely hear it. But she gets to her feet and staggers toward him. There is no thought connected to the action. She simply knows she must go to him. Fix him. Now. She stumbles, crawls, falls.

She rounds the fire in moments and crashes to her knees in front of him, shuddering at the extent of his injuries and the deep, dark circles around his eyes. She presses her hands to his face; ignores the way they shake.

He leans into her touch, closing his eyes.

"I've been looking for you," she tells him, the words breaking as she releases them.

He smiles weakly. "I've been waiting."

Dawsyn presses her forehead to his and closes her eyes. She finds the light is already there waiting. Already joined by the iskra that will seep out of her and into him, repairing everything that threatens to tear him away from her.

"Ishveet," Dawsyn says, and the magic gives way. It floods into him, as though it knows how interlaced their existences are. As though his healed parts are hers as well. The magic pours and somewhere outside of herself she can feel white light encasing them. Blocking out all else.

When it fades, Dawsyn opens her eyes, and they find his – bottomless and familiar. Saturated in adoration. "Hello, malishka," he whispers.

CHAPTER FORTY-FIVE

Ryon hears the word whispered around the clearing, rising to the strange moon above them "Malishka?" They say, passing it between them. A question.

But Samskia cackles again in her deep timbre, watching Ryon and Dawsyn exultantly. "Did I not tell you, night wing?" she says to Ryon. "I told you your woman would find you this night!"

"What is this?" another mage demands. Ryon recognises her. She was here the last time he had become ensnared within the mountain clan's traps. A tall woman with black hair.

"A fated pairing, Roznier!" Samskia says and she makes to approach Dawsyn. Ryon tries to move his hands to come between them, but his wrists remain bound. His strength may have returned, but the tangles of roots still rise from the earth and bite into his flesh, holding him there.

Dawsyn pulls a blade from her side and holds it in line with one of Samskia's eyes. The mage merely turns cross-eyed, completely unperturbed. "Unbind him," Dawsyn says, promising death in every syllable.

"She is foul-tempered, night wing," Samskia says in the old language. "I relish the foul-tempered ones."

Dawsyn does not drop her blade nor her sights. "What is she saying?"

"That you are… spirited."

The mage called Roznier tsks. "Lower the blade, Sabar. There is no need to fight."

"Cut him free," Dawsyn repeats, "and I shall do whatever you wish."

"Ah," Roznier mutters. "A promise no mage should ever make. But fear not. If Samskia says this Glacian is yours I shall not take him from you, child. Be at ease." Roznier eyes Ryon balefully, then curls the fingers of her left hand inward. At the movement, the root that binds his arms and legs fall away.

"The half-breed," Roznier says as Ryon comes to his feet. "I hadn't known you'd returned. Very unwise of you."

But Ryon is reaching for Dawsyn. He takes her arm and pulls her back into his chest. "I'd agree," he says. "But I did not come by choice."

Roznier dismisses him with a wave of her hand. "Very well, Dawsyn. You have what the blood moon intended for you this night. You can be away if you wish, though I do question the fates' designs if they have brought a Glacian and a mage together."

Dawsyn turns rigid, the lines of her body tensing against his. "I'll be taking these as well," she says firmly, gesturing down to where Tasheem and Rivdan still await their deaths. Both now unconscious.

Roznier tsks. "You cannot spare them all, Dawsyn. However much you might sympathise with them. The moon calls for blood tonight and we will heed it!"

"Not these," Dawsyn says again, and she moves to stand in front of them.

Ryon bares his teeth at Roznier. He summons his wings.

"You disappoint me," Roznier says now. "I would not expect a descendant of Melares to defy her own kind in favour of the bats of Glacia."

Ryon's fists clench, but he knows better than to start brawls among mages.

"You disappoint me too," Dawsyn counters. "You hide behind your wards, ensnaring roaming Glacians you can sacrifice, rather than take back the mountain they took from you. You hide in corners and refuse to fix what you ruined."

Roznier smiles icily, but it does nothing to conceal the touched nerves. "You know very little of this mountain, child."

"I know little else *but* this mountain," Dawsyn says. "And I know what it is to be confined to one small piece of it, and *you*–" Dawsyn looks to the clan collectively, "–you are as trapped as I once was. Seeking your small vengeance. Afraid to do more than that."

At the bite of her words, the mages surrounding them become eerily still. For reasons Ryon cannot explain the air becomes thick. Metallic. He tastes rust on his tongue. Ryon knows well the smell of violence that precedes a battle. It smells like this, like blood.

He wishes there were swords on his back. He comes closer to Dawsyn, eyes tracking those mages closest.

Roznier laughs without parting her lips, but the sound is not mollifying. It elicits fear. Ryon is suddenly sure the women could smite them where they stand. "And what more would you do, Dawsyn?" she asks slowly, her voice slick and deadly. "Tell us."

Tasheem groans suddenly, then coughs, spluttering blood to the snow. Ryon bends to lift her upright. He looks at Dawsyn desperately.

"Your friends are close to death," Roznier says redundantly, for blood spills down Tasheem's front and Rivdan has still not opened his eyes.

"*Dawsyn,*" Ryon utters. "Help them."

"She cannot," Roznier answers instead. Ryon's eyes dart to the mage's, then Dawsyn's. Dawsyn is looking down at Tasheem determinedly, her lips pressed tightly together.

"She spent all she had on you, half-breed," Roznier remarks, eyes alight. "And now she must make a deal with me to heal them for her. So, make your ask, Dawsyn. Go ahead and tell us whatever it is you can do, that we apparently cannot. Make it worth my while, child. I have no desire to let three Glacians walk free from our midst this night."

Dawsyn's eyes find Ryon's and in them is a storm. They waver once, then quickly solidify. She turns back to Roznier, her chin lifted, blade lowered.

And Ryon feels inexplicable dread flood through him.

"Heal them and cut them loose," she says. "And I will destroy the Pool of Iskra myself."

Chapter Forty-Six

The leader of the clan sneers at Dawsyn, any warmth there may have been now gone.

The other mages watch on. Some with morbid curiosity, as though she were a strange insect among them, speaking her strange language. But others have wide eyes that swivel back and forth between the two black-haired women, and their lips part at the mention of the pool.

"Oh?" Roznier says, her eyebrow quirking. "And you think yourself able?" A laugh bubbles past her lips. "I can see why Baltisse took a liking to you, Dawsyn Sabar. You have fire."

"You said no mage could withstand the iskra for long." Dawsyn ensures her voice reaches them all. The air before her fogs with each word. "And yet here I am. Alive."

Roznier hesitates. She looks Dawsyn over warily. "What do you mean?"

"Dawsyn," Ryon says, and she feels his hand curl over her wrist, an edge of panic in his voice. "What are you doing?"

"I have both mage and iskra magic within me," she continues, ignoring the tightening grip of Ryon's hand. "Iskra that I absorbed from the pool."

Some of the mages back away. They speak rapidly to one another beneath their breath. It does not escape Dawsyn that any one of them could debilitate her in an instant.

Ryon stands beside her now, his wings extending to their full scale. Even weaponless, the sight is menacing. "Don't," he says to a mage who raises their hand and his voice curdles blood. It ignites flames down her spine.

"Yes. Let us hear the whole of it," Roznier says, her predatory stare widening. "I thought I smelt something strange about you," she says. "Iskra, you say?"

Dawsyn does not dare look away. "It coincides with the mage magic. Baltisse taught me to hold them both."

"Prove it," Roznier says.

Dawsyn does not lower her eyes as she calls the iskra to her fingertips and lets it coat her skin. It was already there, waiting, begging to be released. It mists over her hands and burns her knuckles, and she sees its glow reflected in Roznier's eyes. She can only hold onto it for a moment before it recedes, too weakened to do any more than that.

Roznier lets loose a breath. "So, it is true," she says on a whisper, and then she turns away. After a pause, she says, "You stole it from them? The Glacians?"

"I did."

"And the mage magic did not reject it? Try to oust it?"

"It was a challenge to begin with," Dawsyn admits, remembering the times she was struck down. "Now it is natural. I can use them both."

More permeating silence. The only sound comes from Samskia, who hops from foot to foot, giggling quietly.

"Tell me, Roznier, creator of the pool–"

"One of *four.*"

"–has there ever been another like me?"

Ryon bristles. Dawsyn can feel his reproach pouring from him. He scolds her without speaking, wary of this pact she's making. What will he say, once he knows it all?

"You believe you can hold the pool's power?" Roznier asks, but this time it is without snide. Without derision. Her face is softer, unsure.

"I do not know," Dawsyn says. "But if there is someone who might…"

"And you would willingly take the risk, knowing what failure could bring?"

Dawsyn's eyes dart to Ryon's once and then away. She braces. "I do not need to hold it for long."

"The release of that much power will obliterate all within its circumference, Dawsyn, and you do not know how far the ripple travels."

"There is a place it can be contained," Dawsyn says, though the flatness of her voice has alerted Ryon once more and he comes closer.

"Dawsyn, wait–"

"If I cannot keep my grip on it, then I will fold myself into the Chasm. Into Yerdos' pit."

Dawsyn wishes the resulting shockwave did not ring so mightily, maybe then she wouldn't feel the finality of it sink into her bones. But the mages gasp and grip each other's shoulders. Yerdos' name is whispered amongst them, and Roznier looks moments from ripping free of her skin. She swells where she stands, her hope too big for her body. "But how could you fold to a place you have not been?"

Hysterical laughter suddenly resounds through the forests, shaking the snow from the surrounding treetops. The mage called Samskia spins in a circle, her eyes gleeful. "Sur menska oi vesh! Yerdos ve nay dieski!"

Dawsyn looks to Ryon. "What did she say?"

"'But they have been to the pit,'" Ryon translates. "'And Yerdos set them free.'"

Roznier does not question Samskia further. She stares at the strange, dancing mage, and seems to take her words as they are. Then, she clasps her hands and the roots that hold Rivdan and Tasheem fall away, slithering back into the earth from whence they came. Neither move, too weak to react.

Roznier looks, for the first time, afraid. She closes her eyes and wrings her hands together, her face drawn. When she opens them, they pierce Dawsyn anew. "Very well," she says. "Then it is a deal."

"I will need time to prepare," Dawsyn utters, already backing toward Rivdan and Tasheem. "I cannot go to Glacia this night."

"I will not come to drag you back, Dawsyn Sabar," Roznier shakes her head. "Nor you," she adds to Ryon. "Though I must bid you to stay just a while a longer. I told you before, this is a night for vengeance."

"They cannot wait," Dawsyn spits, gesturing to Tasheem and Rivdan. "Heal them."

Roznier sighs, then nods to no one in particular.

Two mages step forward, one man and one woman, both adorned in layers of necklaces that rattle as they approach. They touch their hands to the foreheads of Rivdan and Tasheem, and Dawsyn squeezes her eyes shut as the blinding light erupts from their fingertips.

When it dissipates, Ryon bends to take Riv's shoulders in his hands and shakes them. Gone are the patterns of blue and purple that had blossomed beneath the male's skin. His jaw no longer hangs like a corpse. The male blinks his familiar blue eyes and finds Ryon's. "Mesrich?"

"Can you stand?" Ryon asks, but Rivdan's eyes are darting around the clan of mages and the pyre before him, and his hand goes to his shoulder, to reach a sword no longer there.

"*No,*" Ryon tells him sharply. "Go easy. You're safe."

"What the fuck is happening?" comes Tasheem's voice.

Dawsyn tries to put herself in the female's line of sight. "A mage clan," Dawsyn mutters. "No sudden movements."

Tasheem's eyes widen, and she begins to check over her body, now whole and well.

"Stand, Glacians!" Roznier calls to them. A frenetic drumbeat has begun, though Dawsyn cannot tell where it comes from. The fire licks at the night sky, reaching impossible heights once more, and the mages surrounding it begin to sing disjointed verses, not together, but not apart from each other either. Choruses interweave and break free, and Dawsyn and Ryon tear their eyes away from the sight to look to one another. Ryon's fingers find her wrist again and he pulls her slowly away.

"You cannot walk through the wards or *fly* out of them," Roznier says, her voice reaching them despite the crescendo of noise. "Stay. Watch what the blood moon brings, Glacians. Watch what happens to those who wander too far from their nest."

Dawsyn watches as Samskia skips to where a Glacian lays crumpled beside Rivdan. The roots that bind him fall away, and Samskia whispers something in the male's ear.

When he fails to move, Samskia buries her long nails into the clothes on his back, and he wails pitifully. She pulls him across the ground, closer to the raging fire, and is joined by other mages, who shriek and claw like animals.

They lift his considerable mass from the snow as one and haul him into the flames. The sounds of the Glacian's cries are quickly vanquished.

Dawsyn, Ryon, Rivdan and Tasheem watch on, frozen, as the Glacian within blackens, all to the sound of exultant cheering.

Over and over, the mages repeat the ritual, dragging hapless Glacians in various forms of enervation to the pyre, and throwing them in. Some never open their eyes or utter a noise, making Dawsyn think them already dead. Some scream so long, that even Dawsyn grimaces. But she finds she cannot bring herself to pity them. She cannot claim there is no satisfaction to be gained from watching their unnatural skin bubble and meld into their flesh. It brings her some measure of despicable pleasure to see the white wings that stalked her childhood skies burnt to ash.

"And the finest of our offerings," Roznier suddenly calls, her voice enacting a hush over the raucous celebrations. "The very first Glacian himself!"

Dawsyn's head snaps up. She looks at Ryon, but his expression is steely, set determinedly ahead on the orange flames.

Surely, not…

Samskia brings him forward, and he walks on two feet. His knees buckle some as he staggers; his wings are torn, his hair hangs in ropes. His face is skeletal, all traces of superiority now erased.

But it is him. Vasteel. And despite herself, Dawsyn's breaths come sharper. She clenches her fists. "Mother above," she mutters.

Vasteel, held prisoner this entire time. By a mage clan, no less.

He turns his head toward them as he reaches the edges of the pyre, his burning nobles heaped in its middle. He sees Dawsyn, and then Ryon, and he smiles serenely. "I will see you in that circle, Mesrich," he says. "The one saved for us."

Ryon takes three measured steps toward him, and Dawsyn watches the muscles of his shoulders ripple as he shoves Vasteel, lifting him off his feet. He falls atop the pyre, and his cries last longer than any other before him. Dawsyn watches his face within the blaze contorting into something unrecognisable, something that does not resemble any creature that Dawsyn has encountered. He screams until his voice chokes off, unable to draw breath, his body blackening.

It is many minutes before Dawsyn looks away. She needs to ensure that only cinders remain. Only ash, quickly swallowed by the passing breeze. She ignores the shaking in her hands and keeps her eyes trained on the form that was once the King of Glacia, and thinks, *one less to find. One less to kill.*

Eventually, some of the mages begin singing and dancing again. They eat and drink and circle the fire. The hum in Dawsyn's blood rings soundly.

Roznier approaches Dawsyn and her friends, standing stunned in the snow. Despite the festivities, Roznier's expression is grave. She touches Dawsyn's hand with her own and presses her ax into her palm. "Go now. And blessings, Dawsyn," Roznier says, squeezing her fingers. "You will surely need them."

"And if I should fail?" Dawsyn queries.

"Then it shan't be the greatest failure at the hands of a mage," she says, her lips quirking sadly. "And when you meet Baltisse across that bridge, please tell her that I… I am sorry," she says pleadingly. "And tell her thank you."

"Thank you for what?"

"For finding you," Roznier says. "And seeing what you were."

Before Dawsyn can take apart the words, she feels a warm touch upon her forehead. The last thing she sees is Samskia's benign smile over her shoulder.

And then everything folds inward.

CHAPTER FORTY-SEVEN

Dawsyn unfolds onto the very incline she had been on that morning.

She gasps as her lungs expand again. Samskia smiles back at her, teeth unnaturally white in the dark. Above them, the moon casts its strange-tinged glow.

Seconds later, Ryon appears. And then Tasheem and Rivdan, all escorted unfolding by the hand of a mage, who quickly disappears once they have delivered their burden onto the slope. Dawsyn can see the hazy barrier of their magical wards ahead.

But Samskia remains. She tilts her head and peers at Dawsyn. "Vey ty sosud yerd iskra," she whispers.

Dawsyn does not understand it. Cannot begin to fathom the translation, but she feels a lick of heat along her spine at the utterance and it ignites the spark in her mind. She blinks, her mind repeating the tangle of sounds back to her, like an echo.

"What does it mean?"

Samskia only gives her a conspiratorial grin. She turns to where Ryon kneels in the snow, bending to kiss his cheek.

Then she is gone.

Tasheem stands, shaking snow from her woven hair. Rivdan curses and vomits onto the incline.

"What the fuck was that?" Tasheem spits, bending to rest her hands on her knees.

Dawsyn barely hears her words. Her attention is saved for Ryon, who is here, alive.

She goes to him, and he catches her, there on the ground in a clumsy embrace. She holds him tightly, feeling the slide of his stubble against her cheek, the warmth of his breath on her neck. She feels his heart thump between their layers and sighs.

She remembers the last time she set eyes on him, in the Chasm. Both desperate and half-crazed with exhaustion. "I've been looking for you," Dawsyn murmurs once more, so that only he can hear.

His broad shoulders heave with the weight of his own relief and he wraps her up tighter, pressing his lips to the skin beneath her ear. "What took you so long?"

Dawsyn closes her eyes and escapes to the peace of it all, that he is here. That no danger surrounds them.

But Ryon sighs. "The promise that you made–"

"Not yet," Dawsyn tells him, unwilling to think past this moment. There will be a time to speak of it, to plan and devise and fight about what is to come. But it will keep.

She pulls back and peers at him properly, losing herself in his warm eyes, in the long lashes that frame them, in the lines and shadows of his face. "If you nearly die again, I'll not forgive you."

His lips quirk. He presses his forehead to hers. "Yes, you will."

"Ryon?" comes a voice from higher up the slope. Esra's. Dawsyn would recognise it amid a blizzard. "SALEM! They're HERE!"

"Fuck me," Tash says beneath her breath. "SHUT UP, ESRA! YOU'LL CAUSE AN AVALANCHE!"

Ryon groans and helps Dawsyn stand. "Perhaps we should have left her with the clan."

Dawsyn smirks.

"Is that what they were?" Tash huffs, looking thoroughly rattled. "Looked like a family of savages setting Glacians on fire."

"Vasteel," Rivdan says suddenly. It seems his body has ceased its retching. "They... they had Vasteel. All this time?"

"I'd wondered where he'd fled to," Ryon comments casually, though his jaw ticks at the mention of his name. "Seems he hardly fled at all. Managed to find himself ensnared in mage traps instead."

The conversation is interrupted by the chaotic approach of Esra, Salem, Hector and Abertha, who send snow spraying in every direction as they run downhill.

"Dawsyn?" Hector says, reaching them first. He grabs her shoulders and peruses her, then looks to Tasheem and Rivdan. "What happened to you?" he demands.

Abertha joins them next. But Salem has fallen halfway down the decline and Esra tries unsuccessfully to drag him out of the drift by his foot. "Get *up*, old man!"

Ryon curses beneath his breath and goes to their aid.

"You found them," Abertha says incredulously. "How?"

"It's a long story," Dawsyn sighs happily. "It's telling can wait."

"Wait for what?"

"Until we've eaten. I fear Tash might entertain cannibalism soon."

Tasheem grunts. "There's no 'might' about it."

Abertha takes a careful step away.

Dawsyn and Ryon are the only ones that remain awake.

The others lie asleep around the fire, in the same cave where Dawsyn and Hector cut Abertha's toes away.

It isn't a coincidence that neither have fallen asleep. It is as though Ryon's presence has awakened that same ringing thrum she had felt within the mage wards. She feels unsettled in her own skin. Sitting across from him as they ate was almost intolerable. And she sensed it was no better for him. He stared at her unerringly, his expression not always content. There was too much heat in his gaze to feel comfortable. Her heart was beating too quickly to relax. When had they last stood beside one another without the barrier of impending doom firmly between them? There had been so few hours like these, where no guillotine hung from above.

She did not want to sleep.

As soon as Esra's eyes close, half-way through one of his many tales, Ryon rises.

He is before Dawsyn in the next moment, taking her hand and pulling her to her feet. Then, they are back in the moonlight, finally escaping to the surrounding forest. Before Dawsyn can lead ahead, Ryon wraps her in his arms and leaps into the air, his wings unfurling in the same moment. Suddenly, they are skyborne.

He flies her into the treetops, and they glide a short way down the slope until craggy rockface appears below. Ryon descends upon it immediately, setting them both down at the base of a slow-trickling waterfall. Here, the slope flattens and water cuts through the snow in a staggered line before falling over the next cliff edge. The black rock face is smoother here, made even by the near constant persuasion of water.

But tonight, the water runs thin, and the rockface is merely a shield to the icy wind.

Dawsyn barely feels the cold. She is made of fire.

If Ryon boils too, he does not act upon it. After setting her down, he steps back from her, lets his hands fall from her waist and turns away. He runs his hands over his head and looks out over the sheer drop before them. "Dawsyn," he says, and the word is riddled with accusation.

No, Dawsyn thinks. *Not yet.*

"Did you mean what you said to Roznier?" he asks. He knows that answer already, surely. He knows her.

Dawsyn doesn't respond immediately. She watches the muscle along the back of his neck contract. She wishes he would come closer.

"*Dawsyn,*" he says, firmer this time. "Answer me. Did you mean it?"

"Mean what?"

"That you would *martyr* yourself?" Ryon snarls, turning to face her, and Dawsyn finally sees the heat in his eyes for what it is. Not lust. But anger. Betrayal.

Dawsyn swallows. She knows he won't let the conversation be avoided. He will not allow her this one night to pretend.

She considers refusal. Distraction. Denial. Anything to trace the edges of the truth and not touch it. The dawn will see their next reckoning. For tonight, she wants only reward.

But Ryon grits his teeth, widens his stance. His wings retract and vanish from view. And he appears like the mountain around him – immoveable.

"I meant what I said," Dawsyn allows. "I believe that I can absorb the pool's iskra. I believe I can contain it."

Ryon shakes his head in disbelief. "You cannot possibly. Malishka, *please.*" He comes toward her. "Listen to me. It cannot be done."

She cannot bring herself to become indignant or arrogant. Because she knows. She knows all of this already. And she owes him a thousand lives but can only give him this one. And perhaps they won't survive each other, and the thought is unendurable. And yet…

"Ryon," she says, "I have to *try.*"

He groans, eyes shuttering. Ryon turns away from her and even with his face hidden, his strain is apparent. Dawsyn hears him muttering to himself and she steps toward him, her fingers drawn to the places where his shoulders bunch and flex. But he suddenly rounds on her.

"The incantation!" The words surge from him, his eyes widening with some shallow sense of hope. "Roznier mentioned an incantation would be needed. An incantation we *don't* have."

Pain lances her to see him clutch so desperately at anything that might dissuade her. She wishes it were possible.

She repeats the words that Samskia muttered to her. Words in a tongue she knows little of. "Vey ty sosud yerd iskra," she recites. It is committed to memory. The old vocabulary may elude Dawsyn, but there are some terms she is intimately knowledgeable in. The phrase feels etched into her skull and Dawsyn suspects Samskia's hand carved it there.

The utterance knocks the air from Ryon's lungs, and he exhales in a gust. It deflates him. She can see the tenuous hope spilling from him, leaving him slack and empty.

"That's the incantation. Isn't it?" Dawsyn says, though she need not hear his answer. His reaction is confirmation enough. "Samskia whispered it to me, and I've heard it over and over since. I… I *feel* it," she closes her eyes, and there it is. Waiting in the background. An ever-persistent pulse.

Ryon closes his eyes again. "It won't work, Dawsyn," he says, though his voice lacks conviction. "And you will die in the attempt."

"You cannot know that." She tries for gentle.

"The pool was created by *four* powerful mages. Each of them cutting away a piece of their power to procure it. *Dark* magic. It cannot be contained by just one person!"

Dawsyn has already come to the same conclusion. She has already admitted to herself that her hopes of survival are slim.

But she does not need to confess her doubts to Ryon. "Baltisse once told me that I would decide what I was born for," she says now. "I believe this was it."

"You're a liar," Ryon growls. "You know it won't work, and you will willingly throw yourself in hellfire. You'll take yourself away from me."

"I'll destroy the Pool of Iskra."

"YOU WILL TAKE YOURSELF AWAY FROM ME!" His voice rebounds off the rockface. It echoes across the mountain. He pants, his chest heaving, and the air before him fogs.

There is a crack in Dawsyn's chest that spreads and spreads. She shakes her head. "Not willingly," she says weakly. "I will do everything I can to keep that from happening."

"Tell me this one thing, Dawsyn. Please," he says, coming toward her, close enough to touch. "When we first met... when we walked these slopes together... did you feel what I felt?"

She swallows, her skin prickling. "What did you feel?"

His eyes trap hers. "I felt something cut its way into my chest and bind around my heart, and you've lived within me ever since. Wherever I go, it remains, and it seeks you out. Nothing feels right unless I can see you, hear your voice." He looks down at her, and when Dawsyn tries to avert her eyes, he takes her chin and lifts it, so that she can see nothing but his glare. A glare that strips her, always. Turns her inside out. *Look at me* and tell me that you were not carved apart and remade with a piece of me."

She feels her throat tighten, her eyes sting. "I was."

"And do you feel it still, that thing that does not allow you to sleep without me? The thing that demands satisfaction?"

Dawsyn swallows again, shivering to the current that comes to life beneath her skin. She nods.

"That's me," he tells her, slowing his words so that they puncture her skin, stealing pieces of her. "That ache that you feel in your chest... that's me too. Don't you crave me, Dawsyn?"

She nods, absently reaching up toward his mouth, rising to the tips of her toes.

"And have we not sacrificed enough of each other? Of ourselves?"

Dawsyn's lips are a hairsbreadth from his, but he holds her chin away, and stares down on her, denying her this last inch. "Yes."

"But you would *throw* yourself into that pit and take my heart with you."

She closes her eyes, shakes her head.

"Yes," Ryon says roughly. "That is your plan. Is it not? To leave me here. Alone."

"No," she murmurs quietly.

"I don't believe you."

"*No*," she urges. And there is pain in the word. Pain and love and resolve, and she opens her eyes to his, finding the flecks of black around his irises. "No. I *love* you."

He drops his hand from her jaw, removing that one barrier between them. "*Prove* it," he growls.

Her mouth collides with his in the same moment and it takes the breath from her lungs. Her hands scratch at his neck, trying to find purchase on him to leverage herself closer, despite all the ways they press together. It is not enough. Not close enough. Not hard enough. The ache he spoke of begs relief and she seeks it in every piece of exposed skin she can reach. She groans when he lifts her higher, where she can angle her lips with his, dig her fingers into him. "Please," she breathes.

"Please, what?"

"Let me have you."

"I told you," he says, his voice more controlled than hers. "You already do." He takes her to the rockface then, pressing her back to its smooth surface. As it always does, his strength baffles her. His size overwhelms her, eclipses her. She reaches for his shirt at his waist and pulls it over the hard planes of his stomach, then higher. She lets him pull it over his head while she marvels at the sculpting of his body. Then she pulls at her own clothes slowly, relishing the heat in his gaze as they reveal more and more of her skin. The furs fall to the ground. Then her leathers. Her blouse is tugged free. The control he so recently held slips a little as she pulls the last laces of her stays and lets them stretch over her breasts, lets the straps fall slack over her shoulders and hang loosely, until she is barely covered at all.

"Pull it away, Dawsyn," Ryon says, and the deep timbre resonates within her. "Don't play with me."

She wants to play with him, if only to prolong the moment. She wants to watch him crack and come undone. But the heat of his glare is too much. His hands on her waist are too much, and she finds she can do little more than obey him. Heed to him. She slides down his body until her feet touch the ground and undresses before him fully, sighing with each pass his hand takes over her body.

"Perfect," he says evenly, tracing a line from her throat, between her breasts, and down the middle of her stomach. Not stopping until he reaches her sex. He cups it, watching carefully as she arches into him.

Perhaps she'd feel the cold if she weren't ablaze. Perhaps she would notice the sting of the air if it weren't for his body so close to hers, emanating waves of heat. When she pulls at the ties of his trousers, he makes no move to stop her, or help her, so she frantically wills her shaking fingers to untie them, reaching within to grip him.

He hisses at the feel of her hand wrapped around his cock, then again when she pulls, sliding her hand up its length.

Dawsyn feels his fingers move against her slickness, sinking into her, and she struggles to keep focus. Her eyes roll into the back of her head as he slowly chases the rapid tempo of her breath, invoking each moan, each beckoning of his name. But her hand manages to maintain its clasp, and it lavishes him with her own need. He grows hotter in her palm, harder. And soon, he is thrusting back into her hand, his need as large and urgent as hers.

She lines the head of his cock against her sex and lets it slide against her. His lips crash into hers, nipping and tasting and stealing her sense, and she pulls away only to tell him, "I ache for you. Always."

His pupils dilate, then he is lifting her off her feet once more, pressing her back into the stone, and sliding inside her.

Her gasp is swallowed by his shoulder. She has yearned to feel this way again, so full with him, so heady. She moves her hips against his without a mind to do so, and he moans. "Not this night, malishka," he tells her, stilling her hips with his hands. "Tonight, we take what we need."

His thrusts are slow and languid, and they make the blood in Dawsyn's veins pound with impatience. Every absence of him feels torturous, each filling is bliss. "Did you think of this, Dawsyn? Those nights we spent apart?"

She barely sees, barely thinks, but nods, murmurs yes, over and over.

"I think of little else. You consume me. Do you understand?"

She takes his mouth and licks into it, trying to convey her acknowledgment where words elude her. He rewards her by increasing his rhythm and she holds on tighter. She meets him thrust for thrust and feels the first quickening deep in her belly. "Ryon," she pants.

He releases her, putting her feet on the ground and turning her to face the stone. But though she cannot see his face, she feels the wall of his chest against her back, his arms wrapped around her like a vice. She arches her back, her hands finding purchase on the rockface.

He tells her other things that make her blood sing, and all the while she hurtles toward a pinnacle of ecstasy, her mind falling into a trance. He pushes into her harder, faster, until she is unaware of where he ends and she begins, until their shared pieces are indiscernible from the others, and she detonates. She calls his name, and he responds, pounding against her until the tension snaps.

They come apart together.

And are remade with pieces of each other.

They sink to the snow, Dawsyn cradled away from its touch, and in the lingering bliss is only his heartbeat, the most significant sound in the world.

"Stay with me," he whispers to her. "Vow it."

This promise, in part, she can swear to. "You took my heart long ago, Ryon," she says. "It stays with you."

CHAPTER FORTY-EIGHT

This iskra witch has always been something of a curiosity to Cressida.

Timid, but not careful. Quiet, but opinionated. Hardened as glass and just as breakable. The splinters are plain to see. One could easily find the fractures and tap a finger to watch them spread. What a fascination she has been.

Now, she inspires nothing but fear.

Cressida watches Yennes as she departs, taking a horse marked with Terrsaw emblems through the back alleys of the Mecca, quickly swallowed by night.

"This plan is folly," Cressida hisses to Ruby.

The former captain looks as doubtful as Cressida does. "What other choice have we?"

A million choices cross the Queen Consort's mind. This is not the first juncture in their haphazard plot that has made her consider abandonment. How easy it would be to walk away and return to the palace? To lay next to her wife and be awash in the same sin. She has certainly done it well these past fifty years.

If only she could sleep, she might just do it.

But she is profoundly aware of what will happen when she lays her head down. She will see those faceless visitors. She'll hear wings and shouts and the cries of children. Slowly, her toes will curl and her throat will clench. She'll be gradually pulverised by some invisible weight that cannot be lifted. She'll lie awake, bound to her bed, slowly corroding.

So long has Cressida wrestled with the cost of her complicity. She is too old, too tired to keep the guilt at bay.

No, they are too far down the path already. There are no other choices.

"Get some sleep while you can, Ruby," Cressida murmurs. "Leave for the Fallen Village before the sun rises."

"And you?" Ruby asks, her young face turned up to Cressida's. The older woman remembers looking in a mirror to see a face just as unlined as this, blessed by youth. How insidious the years are, leaching the body so gradually you barely notice life draining away.

Ruby awaits an answer, watching Cressida carefully. When no reply comes, she asks again; "What will you do, *Your Majesty*, when Alvira learns of your deception?"

Cressida smiles bleakly, ignoring the hammering of her heart. It would hardly do for it to give out now. "I suspect the knife in my chest will make it difficult to do much of anything, Ruby," she says, nodding to her one last time. "Good luck to you."

She leaves the woman in the shadows of the stables, walking swiftly back from whence she came, and the palace beckons her. The gates open before she can touch them, the guards nod their heads and make no mention of her being out of her chambers in the middle of the night. It is not their place to question someone of her station. It is not their place to comment on the welling of her eyes. They avert their gazes and allow her passage through the outer tunnels and up the servant stairwell, down the orange-bathed corridors, and through to the quarters where Alvira waits.

She pushes the doors to the bed chamber softly, then lets them click behind her.

Her wife's familiar form is outlined – despite the utter darkness of the room – huddled there beneath the blankets, smaller in sleep. Less substantial without the weight of that fucking crown.

Here, in this bed, she is just a woman. A woman she has loved well these decades past. A woman who once read aloud her journals of how she would purify the corrupt, right all wrongs, defend the vulnerable, cure the ailed. A woman who once held her face in her hands and declared Cressida the greatest gift on Terrsaw land. A woman who carried her, bruised and bleeding through the streets of the Mecca, promising her a future free of persecution for two women like them. Free of judgement. A world they would rule together.

Cressida lays herself upon the pillow beside her wife for the last time and does not close her eyes. She watches her through the night, brushing the silver hairs away from her face and wondering how she sleeps so soundly while their bed is surrounded by ghosts.

The carriage sways precariously as they trundle through the Mecca.

Alvira and Cressida sit on opposing benches, watching beyond the small windows. The town square is filled with undulating crowds that press forward as the carriage draws near. They throw their rice paper confetti and holler their anthems. The musicians bleat relentlessly, strumming their lutes and banging their drums. But inside the coach, the noise is muted. The faces are blurry. Cressida cannot help but stare at Alvira's careful joviality, the gentle crinkle in the outer corners of her eyes. She waves graciously, no citizen too lowly for her attentions.

Performers, Cressida thinks. *The both of us.*

"Did I not ask for that *shrine* to be cleaned up?" Alvira asks. Her smile does not falter, but her eyes have found the steps that lead to the *Fallen Woman.* It remains cluttered by hundreds of unlit candles. Despite the crowd's size, no one dares tread upon the dais.

"The advisors decided against it," Cressida tells her. "With all the attention on the Sabar girl, they thought it might rouse the rebels." Indeed, their chants can still be heard through the more peaceful celebrations.

Alvira allows a slight frown to ruin her otherwise perfect portrayal. "Why haven't they been detained? I remembered the advisors agreeing to that much, at least."

But any orders to have the protestors removed had been undone by Cressida just that morning. "There are so many of them now, dear," Cressida says placatingly. "It is not possible to gag them all."

"I should have the archers pick them off from the parapet," Alvira says icily, waving to a child on the shoulders of his father. "Be done with this... *obsession.*"

The carriage trundles on toward the palace gates, passing through the thickest cluster of spectators. As soon as the wrought iron clangs shut behind them, the crowd moves in, pressing against it to claim their position. Soon, their Queen will address them from her balcony.

They had passed through the Mecca on their traditional route without incident. The skies were clear of Glacians and the crowd, though split in their affections, were docile enough.

Cressida breathes a sigh of relief.

"Let's get this over with," Alvira grumbles. "Adrik will be at the Boulder Gate by nightfall, and we should be too." The carriage door swings outward and a hand is proffered to help the Queen alight.

The courtyard is behind palace walls, free from the townsfolk's view. Only two guards await them here and Alvira notices immediately. She searches the courtyard, her brow furrowed. "Where is the rest of our escort?" she demands of the guards present, as though they are to blame for the miserly security.

"They've been sent to the Fallen Village, dear," Cressida says lazily, flattening the lines in her skirts. "The last thing we need is for the Ledge escapees to run off now."

Alvira looks as though she might argue. After all, it was not an order she had sanctioned. But her eyes dart to the sky and she shudders delicately. "Very well," she says, holding her hand out to Cressida. "Come, dearest. Let us remind our people of what we've given them."

Cressida ensures her lips press into a thin smile. She makes her fingers intertwine with Alvira's and she tries to still their quaking.

"Are you cold?" Alvira asks, then turns to a footman waiting at the stairwell. "Fetch Her Majesty's pelisse!"

"No," Cressida says amiably, squeezing Alvira's hand. "Do not fret, Veer. Let us have this business over with."

Alvira stops her before they can begin to ascend the stairs that will take them to the balcony. The guards at their backs halt in turn, their armour clattering at the sudden movement. The Queen holds Cressida in her stare, cradles her there, as she always has. And Cressida knows what words will come next. Words of placation, of reassurance. A reminder that everything in Cressida's life will be well. Alvira will make it so.

No matter the cost.

"This day will pass soon enough and tomorrow everything will be returned to the way it should be."

Cressida denies herself the cowardice of turning her eyes to her feet. She forces herself to look at her wife and to hide the feeling of her chest caving in. "Of course."

Like the courtyard, the balcony is empty of waiting guards, but this time, Alvira does not comment. The archers on the parapet above are enough to console her fears of a revolt and though the crowd swirls menacingly beneath them, they hardly seem a threat from this height. They are insects funnelling through the Mecca's winding streets, easily squashed.

That is how Cressida has always thought of them. It is far easier to do so, than to think of the faces and minds and families they are made of.

It is why they loathe me, she thinks. *They notice the way I look at them, desperately trying not to see.*

That is where Alvira and her differ. Alvira looks wilfully at them now, eyes darting from face to face, scrutinising carefully. She sees the patched clothing of the children, the wayward hobble of an amputee. She sees the elderly jostled by the well-dressed, the women with black eyes and bruised jaws. She sees those of high station, seated within the palace gates below, and those that must remain behind, separated by the luck of their birth. She sees them all and it does nothing to her.

When Cressida looks, bile collects in her mouth. It has always been better not to see.

"Good people of Terrsaw!" Alvira calls, her voice projected onward by the town criers who repeat her words like an echo down the streets. "I humbly thank you for these illustrious celebrations!"

There is a cheer from the crowd, though its effect is watered-down some by the corresponding heckles. *All hail the Queen!* is interlaced with the ever persistent *Bring Sabar home!* The maelstrom below builds.

"On this day, my Jubilee, we commemorate those who fell so that we could remain, and we celebrate fifty years of freedom!"

Another resounding compilation of applause and jeering. Cressida spots members of crowd being dragged to its edges by the Queen's guard.

"We will eat the food of our lands, reap the rewards of our labour, and sleep peacefully in Terrsaw's bosom without fear! Tomorrow, we will begin another decade free of threat. Another era on the land the Holy Mother granted us. Each day takes us further from those years spent in darkness. Our children will continue to grow, looking to the sky unflinchingly, and we, as a people, will continue to prosper!"

Cressida's breath quickens. In the distance, she can see that great mountain looming, and she knows she must do it now.

"So, bow your heads with me now, good people. Let us acknowledge those brave souls who shield us from horror and pain. Thank them for their sacrifice. For without them, we would be returned to those dark days."

"YOU SACRIFICED THEM!" comes a shout, though Cressida cannot find the speaker among the crowd. The words are met by a rumble of assent. The crowd roils.

"Bow your heads!" Alvira shouts, her voice amplifying. Only Cressida can see the blue veins stretched taut down the column of her throat. *"And be thankful for this era of peace and safety.* Let us pray our blessings will continue!"

But silence and prayers do not reign. The quiet is broken by the growing cries of the rebels interspersed among those too fearful or too selfish to follow suit. It starts small. The call of "Bring them home," hardly reaches the queens up on that balcony at first. But soon it is ten who take up the chant, then double that. By the third call, it is a hundred or more – too many for the guards to silence and Alvira's cheeks pinken. Her eyes flash with violence.

And the time is now.

The time is now.

Cressida steps forward.

She leaves the shadow Alvira casts, aligning herself with the Queen. And oh, how she loathes it.

The crowd does not quiet upon her approach to the balustrade, but Alvira does. She looks sideways at Cressida as though she had threatened to throw herself over the edge. A sight, Cressida is sure, many people in Terrsaw would be happy to see.

Cressida fills her lungs, lifts her chin, and quietens the voice within begging her to stop. To step away. "An addition to our celebrations today!"

The upper classes and first waves of the crowd fall quieter, likely taken aback to have her address them. It takes a while longer for the message to ripple back through the town criers. By then, Alvira's confusion is plain.

But it is only mere confusion she pins Cressida with. Not betrayal. Not yet.

"Terrsaw, we come to you today with news of good fortune! News you've long awaited hearing!"

The crowd jostles in anticipation, but it does not break. It waits, breath baited.

"Cressida," Alvira says quietly, the last sounds floating from her lips as her breath catches. "What–?"

Cressida continues before courage escapes her. "The Ledge-dwellers have been liberated!" she calls to them, the words clear.

They rebound. She sees it as comprehension dawns. As it spreads.

She hears Alvira's intake of breath, the first prickles of duplicity reaching out to clutch her heart.

"The people of the Ledge have been returned to our lands!" Cressida continues. She feels that window of time narrowing. Will Alvira set her guards on her now and call her insane? Or will she follow where Cressida leads her. Is she capable of doing so? "They wait and rest in the Fallen Village. Reuniting with the home they were taken from!"

Bafflement seems to ring out, suspending time. It heightens as the crowd stares at her, at each other, and then it begins to break. Mutters turn to cheers, wails. They grasp one another, frenzied and jubilant. Parents hoist children into the air. Grandmothers weep. Lovers kiss.

"Never shall we allow our people to be forsaken to the Glacians!" Cressida shouts now and it sounds like a battle-cry. "Never shall we repeat the mistakes of our history! We will welcome our fallen ones back into our kingdom and we will stand together against any who wish to haul us back up that mountain. We are of Terrsaw!"

"WE ARE OF TERRSAW!" the crowd calls back, greater than any chant before it. "BRING THEM HOME! BRING THEM HOME! BRING THEM HOME!" On and on it goes, the crowd dancing to its chorus, exultant.

But Cressida takes little notice. She studies Alvira instead and waits for the ax to fall.

Alvira does not call for the guards. She does not pretend to smile at the crowd with good grace. She merely stares at Cressida, shock and treason colliding.

The Queen does not act, and it unnerves her.

"Alvir–"

But Alvira turns and walks away, her heels glancing off the balcony tiles in quick succession and she disappears behind the curtains that shield the corridor within.

The guards do not come for Cressida. They will remain still until they are given their orders. Cressida follows her wife, abandoning the raucous mob behind her and pushes the curtain aside.

She feels the sting of Alvira's hand before it leaves her face. Cressida does not reel. She closes her eyes until the ringing in her ear dissipates, but stands stoic, unmoving. When she opens her eyes to Alvira, it is to find tears falling thickly, her wife's lips trembling, cheeks mottled in high colour.

"You..." she says, stammering. "You... *betrayed* me?" she barely voices the words. They seem trapped inside her, unable to convey the depth of her pain. Her face crumples and she raises her hand again, surely to lash it against Cressida's cheek once more but she cannot seem to bring herself to. It sags back by her side again, her arm limp. Alvira turns away from her.

Cressida's voice trembles, her throat shrieks in pain. She wants to take Alvira's shoulders in her hands. She wants to kneel before her and apologise, repent.

But she cannot. They are too old for that, anyway.

"Time to face it, my love," Cressida says shakily, another piece of her heart breaking free. "Time to undo it."

But Alvira does not turn to face her. She hangs her head and Cressida hears the beginnings of a sob.

They were girls when last she heard Alvira sob. Girls caught kissing in a cobblestoned alleyway. Girls spat on and mocked by bigoted louts with stale breath. *One day, we'll make the rules.* Alvira had told her, wiping away her own tears.

Cressida goes to Alvira now. Hesitantly, she touches the nape of her neck with her fingertips. "Veer," she says. "It isn't too late. Even the greatest queens must right what is wrong."

Alvira's back tenses. Her chin rises. She turns to meet Cressida's eyes. "I do not recognise you," she says coldly, and her voice is so filled with ire, Cressida takes a step back. How many times has she seen this fire in her wife's eyes? Now she burns in it.

"There is a choice to be made, Alvira." Her voice is beginning to fail her. Fear returns. "There will be a battle. You will need to pick a side."

"And you ask me to side with those who cannot win?" she seethes. "You ask me to throw Terrsaw to the mercy of the Glacians?"

"The guards will fight with us," Cressida rushes. "The Ledge people will not be taken peaceably. And the mixed-blooded... Yennes believes they will join us, Alvira. The fight will be even!"

Alvira only stares without blinking, shadows clouding her irises. "I rid the world of Dawsyn Sabar, only to have my *wife* betray me."

Cressida swallows. "Please..."

"The fight will not be even," she says icily. "The guards will follow my orders alone when I place myself on that battlefield and you will stand beside me."

"Alvira, I cannot–"

"YOU ARE MY *WIFE!*" she shouts, spit flying from her lips and speckling Cressida's eyelids. "And you will not leave me to stand alone in the mess you have made!"

Cressida shudders, the weight she has carried on her shoulders sinking to her feet. Grounding her. She meets the eyes of the woman she loves. "I've stood by you in every failing, every triumph, every transgression," she tells her, her own tears finally breaking free. "And I can stand by no longer."

Cressida watches her wife's eyes shutter with each word. Alvira swallows thickly. She leans forward, until the sides of their noses come together, their foreheads touching. Alvira's fingers gently slide through Cressida's hair behind her ear, tender and familiar. And Cressida sighs. They loved each other well, didn't they? They stood the test of time. Surely, enough love remains that some compromise can be found, some–

"Then you have betrayed me a second time," Alvira says.

Cressida feels the shunt of the blade as it buries between her ribs, but the pain is slower, more subdued. She has already sunk to the floor by the time it begins to bloom, blood climbing up the walls of her throat and filling her mouth, dribbling over her lips.

And the ghosts arrive. Only now, they do not care to stay. They nod to Cressida and leave, one by one.

Alvira's face is the last thing Cressida sees. It hovers over her, wretched and anguished. Her love. Her wife. Hands stroke her face lovingly. Whispers beg Cressida for forgiveness, but she cannot give it. She is already slipping away.

The Queen Consort closes her eyes and listens to the last remnants of Alvira's voice, and she does not fear.

Finally, she sleeps.

CHAPTER FORTY-NINE

Dawsyn knows she is being watched.

Ryon hovers persistently, as though she might fold away to Glacia at any moment and drink the pool dry. He remains at her heel as their party prepares to leave the mountainside camp, not allowing her out of his sight.

They will soon fly to the outskirts of the Colony and make their plans to infiltrate it. *It is the best way to reach the palace undetected,* Rivdan had said. *After that, Mother help us.*

"Where are you going?" Ryon's low voice reaches her. She halts in the process of turning away from the cave, where the others are gathering their belongings.

Dawsyn sighs quietly. "Would it pacify you to come with me?"

He grumbles something but crouches his way out of the cave behind her, straightening to his full height in the morning sun. He rolls his shoulders with a groan and for a moment the tips of his wings appear, then quickly vanish before they can extend.

Mother above, but he is an impressive creature.

"Come," Dawsyn says, taking one of his hands in hers.

"Where are we going?"

"I only wished to walk a while," she tells him. "And it seems I'm not trusted to do so alone."

Ryon narrows his eyes. "It is not a matter of trust."

Dawsyn sighs but pulls him to stride beside her. "Oh?" she says ambling along in the snow, for once not hurrying in any particular direction. It feels foreign to dawdle. "You don't fear I'll run off to Glacia without you?"

"Won't you?" he fires back, fingers unintentionally biting into her palm.

She smiles weakly. "So you do not trust me."

"I trust that your mind is turning over the same thoughts as mine," he says. "I trust that you'll act exactly as I expect you to."

Dawsyn grits her teeth; the barb begs her to pull at it. "And what is it that you expect of me?"

"Bravery," he says, pulling her to a stop so he can watch her face. "Recklessness."

"I am not *reckless*."

Ryon's expression is flat. "You stormed the Terrsaw palace. Twice. You tried to kill Alvira on a whim, and Adrik, and–"

"Those were calculations," Dawsyn says, smirking. "I knew you were standing behind me."

"So, it is only my strength you admire me for?"

"No. I admire your wings, too. Walking is tiresome."

His smile is not lasting. "Baltisse once warned me to stay away from you, you know? She told me I'd met my match. In more ways than one."

Dawsyn tsks. "Are you regretting your choices, my love?"

"Choices?" he asks. "There was no *choice*, malishka."

Dawsyn walks ahead, ignoring the ache in her chest. "I felt her... Baltisse. In that mage clan. She seemed peaceful."

Ryon stares, eyes widening.

"Inside the wards, Roznier said something to you," Dawsyn continues. "Something about you having returned to the clan? Had you been there before?"

"Ah, that's a long story. It was where I first met Baltisse."

Dawsyn's mouth falls open. "You jest."

But Ryon is laughing in earnest now, shaking his head. "It was during one of my first expeditions down the mountain in the night. One moment I was a travelling down the slope, next, I was wrapped in vine, trapped. I found myself gagged and dragged back behind their wards, tied to a tree. They left me there and went about their business, talking about their plans to cook me when the sun set. I was shouting and braying like a fool when Baltisse walked by. She dressed differently from the others. Spoke differently. She inspected me like I was an insect, sniffed the air around me, and said, 'What is your name?' I spat it out, and she sighed, as though she'd known the answer already. As though she was hoping I'd say otherwise. Then, she said, 'Well, I suppose I cannot leave you here.'

"She spoke to Roznier, told her I was 'an important piece in the game.'

I had no idea what she spoke of. All I knew was that I was freed and then folded outside the wards. Baltisse asked me what I was doing so far from Glacia and of course she could read the answer in my mind. She knew of all my grand plans within the moment and she smiled. She described to me an inn not far past the Fallen Village in the valley. She said it was owned by a drunk named Salem, who would offer me lodgings far away from the Mecca, should I need it. She told me I could find her there. And then she disappeared."

Ryon smiled. "I met Salem on my very next venture. Esra soon after. They became my home away from home quicker than I could imagine. Baltisse healed me. Counselled me when I needed it, and when you finally came along, Dawsyn, she told me that if I could not stay away from you, then I should stand by you. Protect you." Ryon halts and his hand pulls Dawsyn to a stop alongside him. "But I won't stand by you this time, Dawsyn." All traces of humour evaporate. "If you sacrifice yourself to that pool, I won't stand behind your decision. I won't forgive you. Do you understand me?"

Dawsyn sighs. She reaches up to touch his chest, laying her hand on his heart. "I made a promise to you," she says. "I do not intend to break it."

He looks over her head. "Whether you intend it or not, I fear it matters very little. The moment before the sword drops, if the chance avails itself... you'll change your mind."

She does not meet his eye. She has never been a good liar, never needed to resort to coercion to achieve any end. It pains her to do so now.

"You don't need to fear," she says, bringing her body up against his, wrapping her arms around his waist. She lays her head against his breastbone, where he cannot see her eyes, and she breathes him in.

How cruel life is, to ration the time between lovers. Each time she finds herself here, in the circle of his arms, she feels sure she is home.

Has she ever told him that? That he is the place she thinks of when warmth evades her? Has she told him how the spark in her mind grows brighter when they touch?

"We go to Glacia to kill Adrik," Ryon says to her. "And we will find some other way to be rid of that fucking pool. We'll fill it with stone, bury it in the rubble of the palace."

Dawsyn clutches his collar and brings his lips down to meet hers. She willingly loses herself in the press of his mouth, in the clutch of his wide hands at the dips of her waist. She feels his deep exhale when her tongue slides past his teeth and pulls him tighter, anything to smooth the lines in his furrow. She tucks away the truth, the great unavoidable certainties she feels.

The first is that there is no other way to destroy the pool.

The second is the surety that there will always be someone willing to use it, as long as it still exists.

The third is that her own life is not such a great sacrifice.

And the final certainty is that Ryon will never allow her to make it.

They fly to Glacia knowing the task ahead won't be clean or even quick. It may take weeks to find a way into the palace, maybe more. Rivdan and Tasheem shake their heads doubtfully. "It will be a hive, Dawsyn," Tash says. "Every member of the Izgoi will be within its walls."

"It's the only path left," Dawsyn tells the others, not meeting their eyes. "Killing Adrik is the only chance we have left."

"And if we fail?" Hector asks, his hand gripping Esra's. Dawsyn wonders if she shouldn't have left them all behind. Kept them from the relentless pursuit of danger.

But she looks around at them, her friends: Rivdan and Tasheem, who abandoned their home to help her; Hector, who was dragged into their circle of bandits; Abertha, who she cannot look at without seeing Maya; Esra and Salem, who have suffered much and offered her more comfort and affection than she ever deserved... and then Ryon, who chose to tether himself to someone such as her, knowing she would drag him over precipices.

She cannot abandon them now. She is past the point of pretending she'd rather court loneliness.

No. She'd rather this. Or rather, she needs them. A terrifying proposition.

"If we fail," Dawsyn says, swallowing. "Then we'll know... we'll know we took every measure. We turned every stone."

"And you would be satisfied with that?" Hector pushes, eyes narrowing. "With letting fate decide what happens to people like us?"

Dawsyn's eyes flicker to Ryon's before she can bid them not to. He is staring at her intently, awaiting an answer she cannot possibly deliver with any measure of honesty. No matter how her tongue tries to shape the words, they will never sound true. Not to her. Certainly not to him.

But it is not time to break her promise. Not yet.

"No," she finally says, opting for a modicum of honesty. "I won't be satisfied. But there are worse things to live with. I will learn to live with this. Perhaps the future will bring us another opportunity, another path."

"A path you needn't walk," Rivdan says now. "It is not your burden, Dawsyn. You only think it so."

Dawsyn grimaces, for how many have said the same? How many have told her to set down the weight she carries? How to tell them that she'll feel it still, despite the distance?

If not me, then who? She wants to shout it, bellow it.

Instead, she gives a thin smile. "Wherever I go, I won't be walking," she says. "A hybrid once made me a promise and I intend to make sure he keeps it." She turns to Ryon and finds him looking straight through her.

"I'll take you there now, malishka," he says, voice hollow. "Just ask me."

It is so ardent that she looks away again. She sheaths her ax. "Not yet," she says, unable to bear the feeling of being turned inside out. How remarkable and dangerous it is, to be seen all the way through.

"I, for one, will be opening my own tavern, if anyone was wondering," Esra says, slinging his arm over Hector's shoulder. "Called, *Well Hung.*"

"No one was wonderin', Es."

"I'll be getting the fuck off this mountain if I can," Tasheem shudders. "If I ever come back, it will be too fucking soon."

"What will you do, Bertie?" Hector asks, nudging the girl with his elbow. "Once all this is over?"

Abertha considers for a moment. "I want to see the valley," she says, looking surreptitiously at Dawsyn. "I want to see where we came from."

Dawsyn wonders if it will be possible for someone like her to make a life in the valley and leave their origins behind. She hopes so. She prays for it.

She listens to each of them, making their plans to carry on. They sound to Dawsyn as fantastical as walking through the Chasm, as unlikely as a pool of dark magic. She wishes she could feel the draw of contentedness that they feel, the nearness of peace.

To her, peace feels idealistic. Naïve. How nice it must be, to feel its proximity.

"Come," she says to them, though her boots are heavy. Already, she wishes to turn back. "We can celebrate in Esra's godforsaken tavern after the task is done."

The rest give a cheer, renewed with purpose. All but Ryon, whose eyes grow darker with shadows each passing second.

Ryon flies with Dawsyn in his arms. He does not wait for Rivdan or Tasheem. He simply lifts her without warning from behind and leaps from the slope into the sky.

They stay low beneath the treetops, dodging the pine and using the mist to stay hidden. Ryon does not speak to her, but his hands grip her tightly, his blood pounds beneath the skin, and she feels his unease. His suspicion.

But he doesn't voice it.

And neither does she.

She supposes he will settle for keeping her within his sights when they reach Glacia. And she will settle for that moment when the sword falls… when the chance avails itself.

It takes very little time for Glacia to appear before them, rising into the cloud-clogged atmosphere, bleakly grey and threatening. The palace spires pierce the sky, while the Colony stretches beneath it. From a distance, the slum appears nothing more than a mass of craggy, colourless rock.

Ryon, Tasheem and Rivdan land in the forest down the slope, not daring to come closer. It is difficult to know if sentries will be watching the skies, as the Glacians once did under Vasteel's command.

"I doubt Adrik would bother with such things," Rivdan says as they trudge the rest of the way up the slope. "He seemed quite averse to imposing any order among the Izgoi once the palace was theirs."

"No. Just drinking and fucking and ensuring there were still those doing his labour. Arrogant bastard," Tash intones. "Always thought himself superior."

"*We* encouraged him," Ryon says. "Fed his ego."

"He manipulated us all, Ryon. We thought he'd lead us to freedom," Tash sniffs. "We were young, and he fed us visions of glory."

"But we are not so young anymore. And still, we didn't see it."

"Perhaps it was never his intention to take Glacia for himself, to drink from the pool," Dawsyn says suddenly, the words falling from her lips in a tangle of thought. She barely pauses to dissect them before allowing them passage. "The pool speaks. It lures those near enough to heed its commands. Perhaps Adrik is merely a victim to its call."

"A *victim?*" Tash says now, her voice rising. Rivdan lays a heavy hand on her shoulder, placating her.

"It is possible, is it not?" Dawsyn shrugs. "So long as the pool resides in Glacia, it is a threat. Its magic will keep reaching out to touch those who come too close. The temptation will be too great."

Silence follows, save the press of their boots in the snow. Ryon is grinding his teeth. Rivdan's head tilts to the side, considering her words.

But Tasheem scoffs, her ire plain. "Temptation only threatens those who already lack a heart."

In that, Dawsyn agrees. She cannot imagine any amount of temptation that would lead her to consume another's soul.

The first glimpses of the Colony appear ahead. Oblong shapes that become struts and flags and lean-tos as they slink closer.

"Stay behind me," Ryon murmurs to them. "And be quiet."

The border of the Colony is not guarded by sentries. In fact, they continue to escape notice as Ryon guides them slowly behind the first of the crooked shelters. They had planned to enter slowly, finding those who Ryon, Tasheem and Rivdan considered friends to hide them. Perhaps find those who have already pitted themselves against Adrik and his self-appointed reign and lean on their assistance as they move to storm the palace.

But the wind that whistles through the Colony is devoid of accompanying sound. There is no conversation, no clatter or clamour of an entire race living shoulder to shoulder. They stalk slowly down the narrow lanes between shelters and find no one in their path. Curtains of fabric flap wildly in the frigid breeze, revealing empty interiors. Snow builds at the edges of the lean-tos, spilling within. The lanes, once slick with slurry and ice from incessant traffic, are now blanketed in virgin snow.

Ryon looks over his shoulder at Dawsyn and she sees her thoughts matched in his expression.

There is no one here.

The Colony is empty.

"Where are they all?" Salem asks, his gruff voice cutting through the silence much the same way a horn would. Esra hits him in the stomach.

"Ugh. Esra! Yeh–"

"Shut up," Ryon says lowly, dangerously, dissolving whatever slander Salem had been ready to bestow. "Or I'll have Dawsyn shut you up."

Esra frowns. "She doesn't have that spell."

"She has an ax," Ryon says clearly. "And my blessing to use it."

Dawsyn's lip quirks.

They continue onward without encountering traces of anyone that still resides in the Colony. It feels and sounds devoid of all but them. It raises the hairs on her neck, unsettles her. For if the mixed are not here in the Colony, then where?

They turn a corner, coming to a large opening Dawsyn recognises. Stocks adorn its middle, laden in snow. The small dais is now a small white mound, the mountain taking back what has been left unguarded.

Dawsyn can still envision Ryon sitting on that dais, shoulders slumped in defeat, her body curled around him in a moment of forfeit.

The vision is impeded, however, when a figure appears across its space, stepping into the open, skin as white as the snow around him.

He holds a crudely made knife and the skin of an animal – a hare, it seems. It dangles from his grasp.

The Glacian halts immediately and raises his knife, head turning to view their party, counting the number. His wings do not appear. In fact, his feet shuffle backward, as though he means to flee.

The moment he appears, his name rises to Dawsyn's lips.

"Phineas," Ryon says, the name escaping on a breath. His eyes widen at the sight of the male, teetering in place on the other side of the clearing. No longer does he stand tall and righteous. He stoops. He quails. The hand around the small knife clenches it tightly. Long straggly hair hangs over his forehead.

It reminds Dawsyn of the Glacians they had found with the mage clan. They too were diminished. Defeated.

"Stay back!" Phineas calls, retreating back the way he came – a gap between shelters. His voice is strangled with panic.

Ryon reaches over his shoulder and slowly pulls forth a sword. "Phineas?" he says again, louder this time.

Dawsyn spins the ax in her grasp, feeling the woodgrain slide along her palm. It seems to sing through the air as it moves.

Phineas – the man who betrayed Ryon to Vasteel.

Phineas – the iskra-drinking Glacian noble.

"What are you doing out of your cage, Phineas?" Ryon asks now, his shoulders stiffening. He moves forward toward the dais but makes a motion for the rest to stay back. The message is clear – the brute is his.

Phineas suddenly stills once more. His feet cease sliding backward through the snow. "Ryon," he says in recognition, his knife dropping an inch. Though the Glacian's stance slackens some, the fear in his voice only intensifies. He drops the animal skin and holds his bloodied hand up placatingly. Dawsyn marks how it quivers. "Ryon," he says again, shaking his head. "What are you doing here?"

"Me?" Ryon asks, stalking closer. His slow footfalls round the dais – a hunter cornering prey. "No, not I. This is my home. What are *you* doing here, Phineas?" Ryon's sword flashes menacingly as he adjusts his grip and Phineas does not miss it.

He speaks carefully, as though warding off a rogue animal. "They sent me here," he says. "King Adrik released us all and sent us here."

A noise escapes Tasheem somewhere behind Dawsyn. It sounds like derision.

"All?"

"The remaining pure-blooded," Phineas elaborates.

"He freed you. Gave you the Colony," Ryon says. It is not a question. "How charitable."

"It did not come without a cost," Phineas replies and then he lowers his knife to his side. Wings extend from his back, or rather, what is left of them.

Splintered bones unfold and jut out over his shoulders. There is nothing else, just the broken remnants of what was once an impressive span of translucent membrane. A flash of malevolence crosses Phineas' expression, and then his broken wings vanish from view.

"Consider yourself fortunate," Ryon intones. "I would have bled you dry." He advances.

"Wait, deshun!"

"Call me that again," Ryon says, continuing to stride towards him. "And I'll cut your tongue out."

"Ryon! Please," Phineas holds his hands before him. "I... I can help you!"

"Yes, you can," Ryon says, and he brings the hilt of his sword crashing into Phineas' temple. The Glacian crumples immediately, his eyes rolling into unconsciousness.

Ryon sheaths his sword again. "Hurry," he says over his shoulder.

Dawsyn's heart pounds. She rushes forward, beaten by Tasheem and Rivdan, who help Ryon to lift Phineas' limp body.

"We need to hide," Ryon utters. "We've made too much noise."

"Where?" Tasheem asks. "We don't know where the rest of the Izgoi are."

"Come," Ryon says, leading hurriedly back into the maze of the Colony.

* * *

Stuffed inside the limited space of a frozen timber hut, Ryon slaps Phineas' cheek. It takes him several moments to come to, his eyes finally tightening with fear when they focus on Ryon.

The Glacian breathes heavily, his shoulders rising and falling. He pulls at the restraints that tether his wrists together behind his back. "Ryon, please," he says. "I only ever protected you."

Ryon's jaw ticks. "Be useful," he says, "and you stay alive."

Phineas' eyes dart between all those crowded into the small shelter. His cracked lips, veined eyes, sallow skin appear more human than they ever have before. Dawsyn wonders if the deprivation of iskra is killing him or keeping him here.

Phineas licks his lips nervously. "What is it you need?"

"Knowledge," Rivdan says simply. "Where are the others?"

"In the noble's village," Phineas answers immediately. "The new king's orders. Vasteel's pure-blooded are to remain in the Colony, without the privilege of flight."

"He always nursed a complex where wings were concerned," Tash quips.

"The mixed who did not fight are housed in the noble village," Phineas continues. "The Izgoi have free reign of the castle."

Ryon turns to Dawsyn. "There are hundreds of Izgoi," he tells her. "Too many to fight."

"Not anymore," Phineas interrupts and Ryon's head whips back to him. "There were many who stood against Adrik, once they knew that... well, once they could see–"

"That he was consuming iskra," Ryon says plainly.

Phineas nods. "Any of those who spoke against him were turned out of the palace. He called it sedition. Most remain in the village, from what I can tell."

"How many remain?"

"Of the Izgoi? Perhaps fifty. Maybe more."

Fifty, Dawsyn thinks. *Still too many.*

"But you won't find them in the palace," Phineas suddenly adds.

All in the shelter fall still, silent. Ryon is the first to break it. "You just said–"

"They left." Phineas speaks cautiously, watching Ryon's reactions for any sudden movements. His eyes flit to his weapons often. "I do not know where they were going."

Dawsyn's heart gallops. "When?" she asks forcefully.

Phineas does not turn his head toward her. "Midday," he says. "The entire flock."

He could be lying, Dawsyn thinks, but every wisp of instinct she possesses tells her otherwise. "They've gone to Terrsaw," she says aloud, for surely it was always Alvira's plan.

"The Ledge people," Ryon says. "They've reached the valley?"

They must have. For what other reason would Adrik abandon his pool? His throne?

"The Queen will hand 'em right over," Salem utters, jaw hanging open. "Mother above. Yeh gotta get back there!"

Ryon stands upright, leaving Phineas on the ground. "We cannot go alone," Ryon says, his voice hurried. He is already making to leave. "Not if we hope to win."

Abertha sniffs. "If you think those people will be recaptured peaceably, you underestimate them. This is no Selection Day. They'll fight with us."

"It won't be enough," Dawsyn says. She clasps Ryon's arm as he tries to pass her. "It won't be enough," she tells him again, lower this time.

He halts, meeting her eyes. He reads what she tries to convey. His head begins to shake. Slowly at first and then vigorously. "No," he tells her.

"Ryon–"

"*No*," he growls once more, piercing her with his glare. "You promised me. Did you not?"

Dawsyn glares back. How are they to defend so many in Terrsaw against fifty trained Izgoi, filled to the brim with iskra, as well as whatever battalion the Queen brings to the fray?

It is an impossible feat. They cannot win. Not unless–

"Do you hear that?" Hector says suddenly, breaking her reverie. He rounds Ryon to peek through the gap in the flimsy drape.

Dawsyn falls still with the rest. Together, they let the sounds of shouting reach them. A distant rumble of voices finds its way to their hut on the wind. Ryon's eyes darken.

"Mesrich, wait!" Rivdan calls, but Ryon does not heed him. He slips outside, his eyes turned to the sky. Dawsyn watches the fleeting shadows come over him and disappear, and he mutters something awed.

Dawsyn follows him, tilting her head back.

The sky is filled. Wings disrupt the normally impermeable blanket of cloud. Glacians in varying hue circle above, dipping and disappearing into the fog. They make whorls of the mist, allowing dappled light to pierce through.

The others in the hut follow them outside, and they too stare up at the sky in awe. Tasheem murmurs something in the old language, eyes glassy. Dawsyn wonders if she has ever seen so many of her kind flying freely above.

"Ah... should we be running?" Esra asks nervously, backing into the tent. "Ryon? Is the swarm likely to kill us?"

Ryon does not turn his eyes away. "No," he says, his voice contemplative. "They are the mixed-blooded."

"Yes," Esra continues. "But why exactly are they in the sky?"

No one answers, but they continue to watch together as more mixed-Glacians rise from somewhere east of the Colony – the noble village.

Tasheem suddenly laughs, breaking the tension immediately. She steps forward, cupping her hands around her mouth, and a wordless high-pitched call rips from her throat. She beckons to those in the sky, as though she were calling to old friends. After a moment, they cry back, their exultant calls echoing down around them.

CHAPTER FIFTY

The old noble village is a hive of activity.

Males and females alike gather weapons, sheath their swords. Some seem to bear nothing but expressions of determination. Eagerness. Some cry. Embrace each other. Others slam doors shut and remain inside.

Many stare as Ryon and Dawsyn pass, leading their party through the alleyways, dragging Phineas along with them. Tasheem clasps his upper arm solidly in her grasp. Some come forward to clap Ryon on the back.

"Mesrich!" one says, sheathing a blade as he approaches. Ryon and the male clasp hands. He does the same with Tasheem and then Rivdan. He offers the rest a cursory nod. The male is bearded, with familiar scars cutting a line through his lips. Ryon recalls the day Brennick earned them from a brute who'd hauled him to the Kyph. He had spat at a passing pure-blood at the witless age of seven. Those scars gained him no small amount of admiration amongst the children of the Colony. "We thought Adrik threw you into the Chasm!" he says now, smiling widely.

Ryon sneers. "Adrik? When did he ever lift a finger of his own?"

Brennick guffaws, tapping the hilt of his sword. "He'll find himself amongst the fray soon enough."

Ryon's eyebrows rise. "You're going to Terrsaw? All of you?"

Brennick shrugs, his enthusiasm plain. "Adrik tried to win our favour by giving us the noble village, but I don't relish spending the rest of my life on this fucking rock." He turns to look at those moving with haste around them. "It seemed the sentiment was shared. We already rid ourselves of one dickless king. No one here is much interested in the rise of another." Brennick winks at Dawsyn. "So. War it is."

Ryon barely dares to hope. He turns his sights to the sky once more, watching the joyous flight of so many, wheeling wildly, laughing freely. He shakes his head incredulously. "Why now?"

"Well, for one thing, the hapless idiots have flown to the valley, and it's a battlefield that works in our favour. They won't fare so well in the heat. For another, the human woman was hard to ignore. Very convincing, she was. Had a whole speech prepared." Brennick affects a high-pitched voice. "'If Adrik is to be stopped, the time is nye.'" He chuckles. "She'll have us believe some of the Terrsaw guards will be waiting to side with us too."

"Human woman?" Dawsyn cuts in. She steps forward. "What human woman?"

Brennick reads the tension that suddenly becomes Ryon, as well as the vicious curl of Dawsyn's tongue as she says the name. His eyes dart between them. "Some sort of magic woman," he says. "She appeared out of nowhere right in the middle of the village. Yennes, she called herself."

Ryon's belly rolls. He pictures once more the way Yennes had averted her eyes as she'd left them in the middle of the Chasm, answering the beckons of Alvira. His hand flexes. He resists the urge to reach for a sword.

Dawsyn, however, does not bother flirting with resistance. Her ax is already in her hand – a hand coated in frost.

"Where is she?" Ryon asks evenly, though he cannot supress the edge of malice that escapes.

Brennick frowns at him. "Do you know her?" he asks, all traces of eagerness quickly dissipating. "Who is she?"

"A traitor," Ryon says, eyes already scouring the lane ahead. "One that is likely leading you all into a trap."

Brennick runs agitated hands through his hair. "*Fuck*," he spits.

"Get everyone on the ground," Ryon tells him, marching past him down the lane. "No one leaves Glacia, Bren, do you hear me?"

"I hear you," he says, following hurriedly, stride for stride. "What about this Yennes? There were a few who seemed to know her. Trust her."

Ryon barely hears him. "Where is she?" he repeats.

"Headed toward the palace. Said she needed time to recover some. She was dead on her feet when she turned up."

"She folded a long way," Dawsyn murmurs. She walks swiftly on Ryon's other side, her sights set on the spires ahead. "She will be weak."

"We'll find her. Get everyone out of the skies," Ryon tells Brennick again. "Tell them to wait."

"What are you going to do?"

Ryon feels his blood cool in his veins. He feels the violence come over him. "I'm going to pry the truth from her."

It takes them little time to reach the castle and they do not bother to hesitate at its gates. They enter the tunnels, Dawsyn unlocking the portcullises they meet.

"Keep up," Ryon calls over his shoulder to the others. They do not have time for Esra and Salem to gawk at their surroundings.

The palace feels colder than usual when they finally set foot within its walls. It is eerily quiet despite the unending stone that quickly reverberates each tiny movement. They move swiftly along its corridors and Ryon cannot shake this feeling of unease, of apprehension.

How he detests these walls. These ceilings. He longs to see it burn.

"What is she doing here?" Dawsyn asks aloud. It is the question on every mind.

Ryon's jaw is set hard. "The better question is, what has Alvira sent her here to do?"

"It doesn't make sense," Dawsyn continues. "What ploy would include luring the mixed to the valley if they resist Adrik? Surely if he wants them dead, he would use them for the pool?"

Ryon cannot think on her words around his own rage. Had he not had his reservations towards Yennes on first sight? He should have listened to his instincts. There was always something about her that was shrouded, difficult to discern.

They hear nothing as they walk the vast hallways, coming closer and closer to the throne room. He cannot imagine finding her anywhere else. Where else would an iskra witch be but beside the pool that made her?

And there she is.

Yennes is draped in layers of shawl and delicate fabrics designed to keep her hidden. It is in keeping with his experience of her. She only ever showed glimpses of herself: in the nervousness of her hands, the twitch of her lips, the shirking glances that bolted if ever one tried to hold her gaze.

The woman stands before the pool, her back turned to them. She does not come close to its edge, but still, she seems taken by it. It illuminates her, already absorbing whatever vibrancy she is made of, turning her to shadow.

She turns slowly at their approach, for they have not come quietly. They come with revenge in mind, her betrayal still fresh, and she seems to know it, to expect it. She holds her hands at her sides rather than clasped together, clumsily folding and unfolding. She stands tall and ready. Unflinching.

For the first time since their meeting, Ryon finally recognises her as not a woman diminished of spirit, but a woman unafraid.

A woman born of the Ledge.

Ryon reaches for his sword.

"Farra?" a voice impedes.

The name, so out of place, echoes through the chamber of Ryon's chest. A name rarely spoken, and yet it is said aloud now, of all places. Of all times.

It is Phineas who speaks. With his wrists bound, he stumbles forward into Ryon's periphery. His sights are set on Yennes, his expression aghast, awed. "Farra," he speaks again.

Yennes' lips press into a thin line. "Phineas," she replies, as if the two were familiar with one another. As if they were acquaintances of old, meeting unexpectantly.

Ryon's chest is amid slow collapse. His mind does not find sense immediately. It does not connect the pieces the rest of him already has. He hears his mother's name and cannot fathom it.

Yennes is watching him, and him alone. It is a familiar stare. Curious and intense. Pained and uneasy. She had watched him often before they all became wise to her deceit.

No, Ryon thinks simply. He says nothing. He does not advance. Indeed, he could not will his body to move if he begged it. He is vaguely aware of his hand grasping his sword and the way it shakes. Somewhere outside of himself, he feels the warm touch of Dawsyn's fingers, holding his forearm.

"You're alive," Phineas says, the words steeped in his own disbelief. And then he seems to remember himself, remember his company, and his eyes dart to Ryon.

Ryon only sees the woman before him. A woman who fled Glacia decades ago. A woman with skin like his own.

"Ryon," she says now, her voice soft and breaking. He hears it still. Her hand lifts, reaches for him.

"Farra," Dawsyn says. It is not a call, but an expulsion, as though she tests the name, and upon hearing it again, the woman before Ryon turns toward it despite herself. "*You* are Farra?" Dawsyn asks quietly.

Yennes, the survivor, keeps her liquid stare on Ryon as she nods.

His mother.

She pulls in a deep breath, her attention on Ryon unwavering. "I am sorry," she tells him, tears spilling over her cheeks, but she keeps her shoulders back, her chin up, and her hands do not furl together.

It is anger that strikes Ryon first. He can feel it burning in the centre of his stomach, slowly rising. "Humans cannot survive the bearing of a Glacian child," he says. It is all he can think of to say, anything to deny what is standing before him. A dead mother is preferable to a traitorous one.

As though she can read his thoughts, his quiet seething, Yennes' lips tremble, but she stares still. "I should have died," she nods, agreeing with him. "Many times, I've feared it would have been wiser."

Silence followed. Cold and wrenching. Ryon merely waited. He waited for something sensical to rise from the quiet.

Yennes sighed. "You took a long time to come," she begins, voice uneven. "I laboured for hours. All through the night, and then when you finally came... I did not mind at all that I would die, because I had seen your face. I had held you against me and felt your warmth, your strong heart and I'd never felt so sure of something." She almost smiles. Almost. "Dying didn't seem such a great price to pay for you to live. I should have died." She seems to say it to herself. Her voice recedes to a mutter. Her eyes turn distant.

"Your father saved her, deshun," Phineas says now, his drawn face pleading with Ryon's. "He carried her into the palace and he meant for her to drink from the pool, but..."

"But the brutes found us," Yennes – Farra – says. The term 'brute' snags on his mind again, a word Yennes had used in his presence. A word only those familiar with the Colony would use. "They threw me into the pool instead and something within me still had enough strength to fight. The thought that my soul would linger here inside them... I could not allow it."

The sick ire in his stomach only burns hotter. "And my father?" he asks, and perhaps she can hear the pain he feels, because she flinches.

"They took his wings," she says, closing her eyes. "He went into the Chasm, and then–"

"Phineas saved you," Ryon finishes for her, looking to the Glacian in question. The male nods, looking as ancient as he should.

"Your father loved her," he murmurs sadly. "However foolishly."

"Foolish indeed," Ryon says icily. "I wonder if he'd have guessed we would one day find each other again, only for you to lie to me. Deceive me."

"That is not–"

"Tell me, Farra," Ryon continues, cutting her voice in two. "Why not tell me you bore me? I may have warmed to you, relied on you. Surely every worthwhile fraud knows the best manipulation is to make someone care for you?"

Farra sighs deeply, her shoulders slipping from their careful composure for the first time. "It was never my intention to manipulate or deceive. Baltisse asked me to help a girl made of iskra and mage light, and I came to help her."

"She could have died by your hand!" Ryon roars, the anger finally peaking. "If Dawsyn – if *any* of us had died when you led Alvira to meet us in the Chasm, it would have been by your hand. Do not lie to me once more. You did not come to *help;* you came to ruin us!"

"I had no choice," Farra says, desperation beginning to creep into her tone. "The Queen... I've long since stopped fighting the hold she has on me. But that ends *today,* Ryon. Today, Queen Alvira falls, and the Ledge people will finally be free. There is a plan–"

"Are we to trust a plan outlaid by you?" Dawsyn says suddenly, stepping forward. Ryon sees the ice solidifying over her fingers. "A woman who folds into Glacia for the first time in thirty years, now that her son has outgrown the need for her rescue? Tell me, *Yennes.* Did you ever think of the boy you left in the Colony? Or were you too busy appeasing the Queens you serve?"

The tears that streak down the woman's tired face are answer enough. "I wanted to come back," she says looking back at Ryon. "But the Queens were watching. Baltisse convinced me not to."

"Baltisse?" Ryon hears the name whispered from one of their group.

"I wanted to come for you, Ryon," Farra says and Ryon sees the truth of it in every line of her face. "So many times... I almost did."

"And here you are now," Ryon utters, swaying where he stands. "For what did you finally find the courage?"

Farra nods, as though ceding the loss of his forgiveness perhaps. "There is a plan, one that we stand a chance of completing if we act quickly. I only ask that you listen, *please.* There is no time to squander."

Ryon does not offer her a nod. He lets his eyes bore into hers, and he waits.

She swallows before continuing. "Queen Cressida has turned against her wife."

There is a small intake of breath from Dawsyn. "You lie."

Farra sighs. "She has orchestrated an uprising, a revolt. She and the captain of the guard, Ruby."

The information is jarring. It stuns their party into silence. No one reacts. No one speaks. They listen warily, unsure if what they hear is sinister or of substance.

"By now, the Queen's Jubilee will be over, and the citizens of Terrsaw will know that the Ledge is empty of people and its survivors have arrived in the valley. With a rebellion already growing, Cressida's announcement will place Alvira in a very tight corner. Her only viable choice will be to stand with Ruby and the battalion of soldiers she has waiting in the Fallen Village, ready to defend the Ledge people, rather than sacrifice them to the Glacians."

Ryon's breath catches in his throat. "And yet you are here, staying out of the fray."

"I am here because even with half the Terrsaw guard, it won't be enough," Farra says. "I came to rally any remaining Glacian I could. I came to know a few in my time here. I hoped I would find them, appeal to them."

"And in that, you have succeeded," Ryon says. "The sky is filled."

"It's a trap," Dawsyn says at once. "It must be."

Farra looks at Dawsyn for a moment, eyes soft and rounded in awe. "You are far braver than I, so you may never understand my weakness. Where you would have spat in the face of a queen who watched your every move, I obeyed."

"No," Dawsyn corrects. "You kneeled."

"There was never another end to the Chasm, Dawsyn," she says gently now. "I knew it in my core. In my blood. The voices within... they bid us to run in the opposite direction for a reason. I did what I thought was necessary to save those within it."

"You were a coward," Dawsyn says. "And we've no reason to believe a change in character now."

Farra looks over her shoulder at the glistening pool and for a moment Ryon wonders if she has forgotten where she is or why she is here. But then she speaks. "Whether I am to be believed or not matters little. At dusk, the Glacians will meet the Ledge people in the Fallen Village, and a battle will ensue, with or without your help. But if our people lose, they will be herded back up those slopes, Dawsyn. Back onto the Ledge." Her eyes aren't pleading, nor determined. They are merely weary. They are weighted in regret. In shame. In the violence of her years.

"I prayed each day that you would grow and live well, Ryon," she tells him softly. For a moment, Ryon can glimpse what life might have been like, carved by her hand. A life of soft glances and mild touches and quiet reassurance. A life removed from the one he lived. "You were meant to be born, just as you were, so that you might do great things, as all improbable souls seem to."

She clasps her hands together and they intertwine with one another. "Some of us were meant to die. I've learned the cost of outstaying one's welcome. I've wronged you. Hurt you," she says. "But I will make it right again, I swear to you. I only ask that you give me the chance to do so."

Every fibre of Ryon's being is at war, parrying with indecision. He should kill Farra… his mother. He should *kill* her. Not for revenge, but for the sheer likelihood that she is still a slave to Queen Alvira.

But something aches deep within him, and it begs him to leave her be. He finds he cannot lift the sword in his hand. He turns to Dawsyn, to the others. "Please, give me a moment," he asks of them, and they do not hesitate to comply. All bear the same stunned expressions he likely mirrors, and they nod, backing away. Tasheem pulls Phineas away.

"Leave him," Ryon tells her, looking at his father's friend, his mentor. Tasheem grimaces. "Go, Tasheem, please." And Rivdan leads Tasheem away, nodding once to Ryon.

Brown eyes appear before him, hands on his face. Dawsyn speaks, but he only watches her full lips and hears nothing. "Stay," he says, interrupting her. He does not mean to say it, does not remember giving thought to it, but there it is. He wants her with him in moments like these.

Her hands leave his face, only to intertwine his fingers with hers. "Always," she promises.

Chapter Fifty-One

"You look like your mother," Farra tells Dawsyn, but it doesn't steal her attention from Ryon, who breaks slowly from the inside out.

Dawsyn can see it behind his facade of coolness. It is horribly reminiscent of the way he stood in this very room months ago, crumbling at the thought he had killed his own mother, simply by existing.

Now, here the woman stands.

Dawsyn's own mother had died before she could know her. The cold had taken Harlow Sabar just as it had taken them all, one by one. If she resembled her mother, there was no one left who could confirm it but Farra.

"She was just as strong-willed as you too." Farra smiles sadly. "So unlikely, that the two of you should meet and fall in love. Harlow's daughter. My son. Impossible. Destiny, perhaps. Do you believe in such things, Dawsyn?"

Dawsyn shakes her head. "Only fools trust the fates. Destinies are forged, not written."

Farra almost laughs. "You have no idea how odd it is to hear Harlow's voice from your lips." Farra's eyes had grown distant. "She would mock me my imaginings when we were children. She never dreamt. Never mused on what could be. I, however, have always thought the Mother places us on a map she drew herself. She takes us off when our time comes to leave. It has plagued me these many years to think I clung to the parchment when I ought to have let go." She speaks to Dawsyn, but looks at Ryon, her eyes never wandering far. "Perhaps I clung on only to see you as you are now. As a man." She seems to marvel, finally granted permission to look her fill. Then she deflates. "I would not have been a good mother to you, Ryon. Know that."

Ryon laughs without mirth, running a weary hand over his face. "You have no right to speak to me of what might have been."

Farra flinches and looks away.

"Tell me all of it," Ryon says now, and when he speaks, it is not only to his mother, but to Phineas too. "Now. I am owed this much."

Dawsyn does not drop her hand from Ryon's as the tale is told. She needs to feel his skin, trace his pulse, mark the moments when his hand twitches and tightens around hers. She grips back just as fiercely.

They listen as Farra describes her arrival in Glacia, the bid for her life. They watch Farra's eyes glisten as she speaks of Thaddius, and his promises to keep her safe, to help her escape. Her eyes shutter when she speaks of her months in the Colony, alone and waiting. Her belly slowly growing. She speaks of a woman named Annika, who nursed and housed her in those months. And eventually, she tells them of Ryon's birth, and the chaotic moments that followed.

She turns to Phineas at the end of her account and the male is looking at Ryon with pity in his eyes. "Vasteel ordered me to throw her into the Chasm, but your father..." Phineas shakes his head sadly. "He had been willing to *die* to save her. All those months, I'd watched him deteriorate before my eyes. I'd thought him insane, then. How could one human, one *woman*, make a Glacian so wretched? I will never understand why he wasted himself the way he did, but there was something I understood in all of it, deshun." He sighs. "Your father loved her, and so I could not be the one to kill her."

Dawsyn wonders about that baby in the Colony, opening his eyes for the very first time as his father was killed and his mother taken into the Chasm.

"It was Baltisse who found me at the Chasm's end," Farra continues. Her voice breaking at the mention of her name. "She pulled me from the ocean, brought me to shore."

"Baltisse?" Ryon says, his first murmur since the story began.

Farra nods. "She taught me to channel the iskra, offered me her home in the bay. She warned me not to go to the Queens. She tried to prevent me. But..."

"But you went," Dawsyn finishes for her, for she knows that madness well. Had she not stormed the palace herself, certain those within would want to help the people of the Ledge?

"I wanted my *son*," Farra says now, her voice more forceful than

Dawsyn has ever heard it. The words spit from her lips, saturated in anger, in despair. "But I was too cowardly to return here myself. Too weak. So I sought their help."

Dawsyn can only imagine how easy it must have been. Alvira must have salivated to have a magical being arrive on her stoop, already so vulnerable, so malleable. "She threatened you," Dawsyn states. She does not need to ask.

"She threw me into her dungeons," Farra corrects. "And I didn't have it within me to die then either." Tears fall in earnest.

Ryon is silent beside Dawsyn in the moments that follow, but then his hand leaves hers and he walks toward Farra slowly.

The woman holds her gaze steady, as though ready to accept whatever justice he might impart. But Ryon stops a foot away. He holds out a hand.

Dawsyn watches as Farra places her palm in his, their skin matched in hue. "I'm sorry," she tells him softly, her lips trembling, tears dripping from her jaw. "More sorry than you will ever know."

Ryon lifts his free hand to her cheek, wiping tears aside with the backs of his fingers. He does not embrace her, does not afford himself to utter his forgiveness, but in this small way, he gives her solace. "There is not a corner of this continent that has treated you kindly," he says to his mother. "You deserved more."

Farra sobs then, as though every ounce of her existence presses against her chest and forces the breath from her. Her head falls forward and is braced by Ryon's chest, and he lets her rest there. He lets her catch her breath.

When she raises her head again, it is with clear eyes. A steady tongue. "Go now, son," she says, trapping his hand in both of hers. "There are people in the valley who need your help. Ledge blood resides within you, after all." She smiles wanly.

Ryon sighs, his expression marred with determination now, his decision made. He pulls his hand from his mother's and turns to face Phineas.

"I will allow you to live," he tells him. "Because I know somewhere within you exists a creature of some decency. But know this," he says, pointing a threatening finger at the Glacian. "You did not *save* my mother. You put her in the belly of a mountain and washed your hands of responsibility."

"Can I prove myself to you, deshun?" Phineas says now. "I will fight with you. I–"

"If I see you on the battlefield, I will count you as my enemy." Ryon's voice resonates, deflecting off the stone walls around them. "Go from here."

Phineas does not resist. He nods once, giving Farra and Ryon both one long remorseful look, and turns to leave.

"You ought to be on your way too, Ryon," Farra says. "Rally the mixed. There is little time."

Ryon nods. "I will come to find you after," he says. "If... if you want to be found."

Dawsyn sees the light in Farra's eyes at Ryon's words, the satisfaction it brings her. Farra smiles in her small way.

Ryon turns his back, reaching his hand for Dawsyn's. But she hesitates to take it. The pool before her swirls in its lazy patterns, not quite liquid and not quite air. The words impregnated on her mind only need be said once and the entire well will dry.

So long as the pool exists...

"Go," Farra says, this time to Dawsyn. She watches her with a knowing grimace. "You do not belong up here, Dawsyn. Our kind never has." It makes Dawsyn think of the Ledge people cloistered in the valley. Farra nods encouragingly at her. "Be in the valley. And take my son with you. Please."

Dawsyn tears her eyes away from the glare of the pool. She looks at Ryon, proffering his hand, waiting for her, begging her not to break her vow, praying she doesn't choose the pool, the Chasm, Yerdos' pit, rather than him.

It is in that moment, pulled in opposite directions, that Baltisse's voice once again returns to her. *You were not born for destruction,* she reminds her, as she once had, *or for the Ledge. You were born for Terrsaw.*

Perhaps she should listen.

Perhaps destruction is not all she was made for.

Dawsyn places her hand in Ryon's, and it fills her with a light that is neither mage nor Glacian, but the rightness of two souls such as theirs, and the assuredness that they should collide.

Chapter Fifty-Two

Under Farra's instruction, the small army they had gathered flies toward the Boulder Gate. They clog the sky with their multi-hued wings, brimming with freedom, and Ryon's chest swells to see it, to join them.

Long has he fought for those in the Colony to experience exactly this, the feel of the frigid wind beneath them, the thrill of the descent. The endless expanse of sky all around, too big for any one Glacian to claim. They tumble and wheel over treetops, nudging one another out of the way as they soar, laughing loudly, and Ryon thinks that even if they should forfeit some to this battle against Adrik, at least they have tasted the air and seen the world as Gods do.

He clutches Dawsyn tightly now against his chest, but she does not seem bothered by the altitude nor speed. Somewhere between holding a knife to his throat and saving his life, she has built a tolerance for flight.

"Why are you smiling?" she asks suddenly. Without taking her arms from his neck, she brushes his bottom lip with her thumb.

"I was thinking of the first time I took you from the ground."

Dawsyn huffs. "You tried to take my ax and I almost cut your hand off."

"That wasn't the first time."

Ryon cannot see her face properly, but he imagines her frown. He knows it well. "Then, what was the first?"

"You held a knife to my throat, and I flew you into the trees to hide."

"Ah," Dawsyn nods against him. "That was uncomfortable."

"Not for me," Ryon smirks. "I was fond of that dress you wore." He can still picture the way it had hugged her frame, how delicate it had made her seem, even after she'd drawn blood from his neck.

"You were fonder of me removing it," Dawsyn says then and Ryon feels all the blood in his body rush south.

"That was foul play," Ryon scowls. "Trying to weaken my resolve like that. By then, it was tenuous enough."

"Men are easily weakened."

"Near you?" Ryon asks. "They stand little chance. I stood little chance. That entire journey down those slopes with you was torture." Dawsyn's fingernails scrape the back of his neck, as he speaks, and he shivers. "Yet, I want to return to those days with you. If I were able, I would." It is the truth. There have been so few days that have belonged to him and Dawsyn alone. Their beginning seems like a luxury now, time wasted.

Dawsyn shifts, pushing her face out of his periphery and into view. "I want to tell you something," she says. "But I – I lack the ways to say it."

"You lack nothing," Ryon says and means it.

They are coming to land. The Boulder Gate awaits them below. The treetops have thinned. There isn't a hope that their descent has been left unseen. There are too many of them.

It is with urgency that Dawsyn speaks. The moment Ryon's feet touch the ground, the words come, and he does not put her down.

"When Baltisse taught me to use the mage magic, she described a light that existed in my mind, something that was shrouded, dim. I'd never noticed it before. Baltisse told me that to find it, I must think of something that brought me happiness, but no memory was strong enough. Nothing of my childhood on the Ledge came close. The only thing that worked… was when I thought of you." As with anything Dawsyn says, the words are weighted. Sincere. They ring with significance. Ryon does not dare interrupt. He prays she'll say more.

"It is only you that I think of when I need to find it," Dawsyn continues. "There is nothing else strong enough, no other feeling that casts the same light. The magic grows warmer, brighter in your presence. If you depart this world before me, I will never find that light again, because the love I feel for you… it is the ruining kind. I won't survive it twice."

Ryon wonders if she has any clue the gift she has given him. They are words enough to eclipse any suffering that might find him next, words enough to win wars.

Ryon tries to speak around the emotion banking up in his throat. "Will you make a deal with me?" he asks her. "It won't be for your ax this time, I swear it."

She grins. "Yes."

"Let's live through this last fight," he says, "so that I can fly you away and make you my wife."

He'd never dared to dream it until just then, in that second, but suddenly he wants it with every fibre of his being. He wants it more than he wants Adrik dead, more than he wants Alvira thwarted.

He wants only Dawsyn Sabar to be his. And he wants to be hers.

Still in his arms, Dawsyn winds hers tighter around his neck. "What makes you think I'm looking for a husband?"

"You just declared your undying love for me."

"Love and marriage are not the same." Dawsyn smiles. "What if I tell you no?"

"Then I will ask it each day until you finally give in."

Dawsyn laughs, the sound of it never failing to make his heart race. She deserves a life of laughter, of love.

"Very well," she says. "But no rings."

"No rings," Ryon agrees. Mother knows they have brought them enough grief. He presses his forehead to hers, savouring the warmth of her eyes. "Do not die," he says to her once more and vows silently that it will be the last.

Her eyes fall to his mouth. "I never do." She presses her lips to his, clinging to him with that same fervour he felt the first time she kissed him.

When they part, her feet are set on the ground and all around them the other mixed-Glacians land in the valley for the very first time.

"Stay close to me," Ryon tells Dawsyn, and it is more for his own comfort than for hers. "Please."

"Always."

CHAPTER FIFTY-THREE

The sun barely glances the shoulders of the mixed before it begins its descent, shrouding the valley in shadow. They prowl quietly, slowly through the thick brush of forest that precedes the Fallen Village, but even from this distance the clamour of armour and voices and wings can be heard.

Dawsyn looks behind her, to where Esra, Salem and Hector follow, resolutely ignoring her bids for them to remain behind, near the safety of the Boulder Gate. They all stalk through the darkening forest now, crude weapons in their hands, bodies alert and ready.

"Salem and Esra cannot join this fight," Dawsyn whispers. She does not know whether the words are intended for Ryon, or for herself.

Ryon merely takes her fingers for a moment, cradles them tenderly in his palm, then lets them go. His silent way of telling her that it is not her choice. Not her life. "I have my eye on them," he says. "Rivdan and Tasheem will be near."

Dawsyn is accustomed to the slow approach of death. It has stalked her many times before this one, following her into the fray. She has always traipsed forward with her ax before her, breaths steady, even. No threat seemed greater than the one before. The probability of losing did not sway her path. It did not weight her feet, as it does now.

This night, she drags herself unwillingly to the last battlefield. Death is a burden perched on her shoulders. The ax in her palm feels like an unwelcome visitor. For the first time, she does not want to fight, for she fears they might lose.

The difference does not lie in the enemy, for the enemy has rarely varied. No. The difference lies in the company she marches with, for while forfeiting her own life has never worried her, the thought of losing theirs is a price too high.

She is suddenly sure she is unwilling to pay it.

Not Abertha, who has only just arrived.

Not Esra, who is too alive to die.

Not Salem, who loves too deeply to bleed.

Not Hector, who has already bled enough.

Not Rivdan and Tasheem, who have given too much, too willingly.

Not Ryon, who has pulled her from the deepest trenches of herself and loved her still.

Not even herself, who has only just begun to feel thawed. Renewed. Not now that she has found this family.

But the shouts ahead continue and they call her forward.

Just this one last fight.

She calls to mind every morning she woke to dig the snow from her doorway on the Ledge, every tree that she felled, every song her grandmother sang. She thinks of Maya, of Briar, of all the days stolen from them.

She hears the shouts ahead and there is little else that matters more.

The price is high, but it is not her who will pay it alone.

Light suddenly begins to impede the darkness. The thinning of trees ahead allows the Fallen Village to come into view and reveals the beginnings of ruins. Of crumbled homes choked in vine and weed. Beyond them, a structure looms. Large wooden beams stand fast in freshly dug trenches. An entire perimeter of high fencing. Through the narrow gaps, Dawsyn can see those inside teeming.

Like animals confined to a cage, the Ledge people batter its walls, ramming their bodies against its supports until they tilt.

And above, hovering like vultures, several Glacians circle. They glide over their prisoners as they have always done, taking time to select their prey.

The line of the mixed-blooded halt in the woods, not venturing further yet. Ryon holds his hand raised and steady, alerting them to be still, silent.

"Where are the Terrsaw guards?" Dawsyn whispers. She stands behind a wide oak trunk and surveys the clearing before her. But the fence that imprisons the Ledge people is tall and impedes her view.

"Taking their fucking time," Ryon mutters.

The sound of steel on wood rings out and Dawsyn's eyes fly back to the enclosure. She catches a glimpse of silver armour, a flash of steel, and hears again the telling thwack of metal meeting timber. There is a roar of outrage from the bearer within as the effort renders nothing.

"The guards have been captured," Ryon whispers and he curses quietly, lowering to his haunches.

Dawsyn sees more of them, squinting through the dimness. She sees the swords protrude through the gaps in the fence, hears the clinking of their armour. Someone shunts their body into a tilting beam and it cracks a little. The gap allows Dawsyn a better view and she recognises the thin, straight nose, the glossy hair, the rich brown skin. She watches the guard shove her shoulder relentlessly against the teetering beam and hears her shouts of exertion.

Ruby.

Ryon and Dawsyn turn to each other with a shared understanding. Ryon frowns already, shaking his head. "We need to re-strategize," he says.

"There's no time," is her answer, already formulated.

"Anyone want to share?" Tasheem quips, shuffling forward on her own haunches, keeping low to the ground. "What's happening?"

Ryon holds his hand high to the line of mixed, signalling them to hold their position. He nods to Rivdan, to Brennick, and they creep inward, forming a tight circle on the forest floor.

Hector, Abertha, Esra and Salem, their bodies crouched, lean toward Ryon, straining to hear.

"They've fenced the Ledge-dwellers in," Ryon whispers. "Some of the Terrsaw guards too."

There is a brief silence. "What does it mean?" Tash asks.

"One of two things," Dawsyn answers. "Either a battle ensues as we speak between Adrik and Alvira, and the guards are losing."

"If there were a battle nearby, we'd hear it," Rivdan says. "This empty land echoes."

"Which makes the second possibility the most likely," Dawsyn says. "It seems Alvira did not cede to our side, and the dissenting guards have been overpowered."

As she says it, they hear the swoop overhead as more Glacians take flight, circling high, awaiting an order. They glide leisurely, wasting away the remaining daylight.

"So, we fight the Glacians... *and* the Queen's loyal guard?" Brennick frowns, his voice thick with disbelief. "Fucking hell."

Ryon speaks to Dawsyn now, though his gaze doesn't meet hers, as though he'd prefer not to hear her answer. "Can you break through the fence?"

Dawsyn narrows her eyes, the ax in her hand answer enough.

"It's a game of distraction then," Ryon says, eyeing the gathering wings above them. "I'm fairly certain that once we round the fence, we'll find Adrik and that fucking queen on the other side, shaking hands."

"So, we attack," Rivdan says plainly, his sword turning over in his grip. Even in the dark, the act is menacing. "By wing or on foot?"

"Both," Ryon replies, his sight stuck on those above, his jaw strained. "We split in two and send half to the sky."

"And me?" Hector asks, his shoulder bumping into Ryon's.

"Make yourself useful, Ledge boy," Ryon grins at him. "Go get your people."

"Make it quick," Tasheem adds, shaking her head as she draws a sword from her back sheath. "We no longer have numbers on our side."

"There are a hundred people in that pen," Dawsyn says, looking skyward once more. "And they've been waiting fifty years for an opportunity to tear Glacians to shreds."

"Dawsyn, take Hector. Salem, Abertha and Esra can help. Get them out as quickly as you can. There won't be much time."

"I'll take ten to the sky," Brennick says now. "You'll need more on the ground."

"Wait for my call," Ryon tells him. "I'll distract Adrik for as long as I can."

The sun falls further, urging them onward, and firelight illuminates in the distance. Ryon glances once more to Dawsyn, conveying what he needn't tell her, that their chances are now likely futile, the risk great. "Ready?"

She nods to him. She turns without saying the words that choke her.

They have said what they need to already.

Crouching, she and the others near the border of the clearing, leaving the Glacians behind.

She feels the relentless thrum of her pulse, grips her ax, and waits. "Will you do something for me, Hector?" she murmurs, making her voice so quiet, Salem, Esra and Abertha do not hear.

He raises his brows, ice-blue eyes piercing hers through the dark. "Anything, Dawsyn."

"When it starts, take the Ledge children into the trees," her voice is thick with urgency. "Salem and Esra cannot fight. Abertha is too young. Take them with you and run. Do not look back."

Hector closes his eyes for moment, turning his head away. When he looks back at her, unshed tears shine in his eyes. But his jaw is set. "And after?" he whispers. "Where will I find you when it is done?"

Dawsyn brushes his cheek, catches the first droplet on the tip of her thumb as it falls. She thinks about how his face has hardly changed since they were children. "I won't be far," she tells him, though even to her, it sounds flimsy. An unlikely contingence. "I'll never be far," she promises.

And this, at least, she means.

Chapter Fifty-Four

Ryon tears his eyes from Dawsyn's back.

It seems he is always made to let her go in the moments he wants to fly her away. She waits by the treeline, out of sight from the Glacians circling above. Ryon turns to face his friends, his allies, one last time before he leaves them, too. "Take to the skies and retreat if the tide turns," Ryon tells Rivdan, Tasheem and Brennick. The former two nod gravely, shuffling quietly away to spread the word amongst the rest. But Rivdan stays. He looks steadfastly back at Ryon, his stare determined.

"I'll be following you, Mesrich," he says evenly, as though the matter isn't to be argued.

Ryon sighs. "Riv–"

"I'll be following you," he says again.

Ryon presses his forehead to his clasped hands. If Alvira's army awaits beyond them, there is little to be done. The human army will outnumber the mixed. Adrik's men will defend any aerial attack. The fight will be long, and it will eventually be lost, and he cannot imagine one such as Rivdan withdrawing his honour. He will fight to the end too, whether it is at Ryon's side or not.

If this is Ryon's last stand among enemies, he can at least face it in the company of a friend.

Ryon lifts his head. "If I fall," he murmurs to Rivdan, "find Dawsyn. Take her with you. Please."

Rivdan nods once, the weight of his promise heavy in his eyes.

"Thank you," Ryon says, laying a hand on his shoulder. "For everything."

"If there are two in this valley worthy of following, they are not out there,"

Rivdan says, looking to the Fallen Village. "They are here in this wood. I will follow you again, *Gervalti*. We will be victors today. Fortune from misfortune," he says, a small grin appearing. "If you will it, it will be so."

Ryon thinks of the Colony and all the times Rivdan and Tasheem appeared at his shoulder, by his side. He wonders if he will be granted the chance to thank them after, for a lifetime of loyalty. "Fortune from misfortune," Ryon repeats, shaking his head incredulously. "Let us hope the name holds this night."

With a contingent of mixed waiting in the shadows, Ryon and Rivdan step into the clearing, their wings visible but tucked, their weapons drawn, but not raised.

The Glacians in the sky see them immediately. They begin to descend, as Ryon suspected. They will likely retreat to Adrik. Warn him. Receive his next orders.

Ryon and Rivdan stalk past the pen of humans, some old, some so young it sends cold-blooded rage to every extremity.

"Ryon!" someone calls from within. Ruby's face appears in the space between wooden beams, she presses her cheeks firmly to the timber. "Ryon, Alvira—"

"Get everyone toward the north corner," Ryon tells her quietly. He hopes she hears it over the din of moving bodies, of panicked cries. "Look for Dawsyn."

Ruby's eyes sharpen, she nods and disappears, quickly calling to those closest within their holding.

Ryon however, has his eyes ahead, where the opposing corner of the human enclosure nears. Rounding it will reveal the expanse of the army that lies in wait. It will tell him the outcome before the fight begins.

But round it he must.

He looks over his shoulder and nods one time.

Dawsyn runs for the fence.

And Ryon steps out into the open, where the rolling hills of Terrsaw unfold for as far as the eye can see.

The sun is a sliver of orange sinking into the knolls. It glints off a thousand pieces of armour, a thousand different helms. It burns pink through the filmy skin of Glacian wings. Row upon row upon row of Terrsaw guards, fronted by mountain creatures.

Closer to him and on horseback at the foot of the hill is the Queen of Terrsaw and Adrik, King of Glacians.

They are swarmed by several white-winged Glacians, gliding low toward Adrik while Alvira's horse paces and shrinks away, clearly afraid. They fly next over the hills of armed soldiers, both man and not, calling their warnings, readying them to fight.

"Mesrich," Adrik calls loudly to him and the sound bounces from the landscape, echoing across the planes. It fills the valley with the promise of violence. Of destruction.

Ryon cannot help the quickening of his blood at the sound of his voice, the sight of him standing there, so assured by the many men that wait beyond him.

If they all die this day, it will not be before Adrik. Ryon must make sure of it.

They halt well before Alvira and Adrik both, so that whatever they might say will be called into the wind and heard for miles around. "Archers sit on the hills," Rivdan murmurs to Ryon, his sights in the distance, scrutinising the scene. "To the east and west as well."

"When the time comes," Ryon says. "Pick them off first."

Adrik stretches his lips into an unconvincing smile. His eyes widen in something like disbelief. "You live, deshun," he calls loudly, and his teeth seem unwilling to part. "Tell me, how is it that you always manage to crawl your way out of death's clutch?"

Black hatred climbs Ryon's throat. "It is no hardship. I simply give him your name and promise to bring you in my stead."

Adrik's gaze darkens considerably. A flash of wing appears over his shoulder, but it disappears just as quickly. "I should have kept you in the Colony, deshun," he says now, voice cold. Gone is the careless tone. The only thing left is annoyance, a gnawing sense of irritation at being unable to foil this one recurring foe. "I've given you the misconception that you were worth more than your bastard breeding suggests."

The comment does not rankle Ryon as it once did. After all, he is the son of a Ledge woman. If there is anything righteous in his blood, it was bred of her. "It was not I who put on a stolen crown and called myself royalty. That is a trespass only the two of *you* share," Ryon looks to Alvira as he says it, spotting the crown on her head, dull and tarnished in the dusk.

"Where is she?" Alvira asks now. Her watery eyes have lost their hardened edge. She seems almost untethered. Skittish. Her sights dart to every corner of the Fallen Village, to the forest beyond. They search frenetically and find nothing. "Where is the girl?"

Ryon smirks despite the gravity of the affair, despite the whisper of death swirling around their ankles. "Which girl?"

"*Sabar,*" the Queen spits. She alights from her horse clumsily. She paces to gain a better vantage of the land over Ryon's shoulder. She barely takes heed of the Glacian beside her, the ones before her, the army behind. Every facet of her seems intent on finding Dawsyn. "I know she is here. *Where is she?*"

"Is she dead, Mesrich?" Adrik says, grinning hopefully, as though this one factor might cheer him.

"Of course she isn't *dead,* you fucking imbecile," the Queen rants, her breaths coming heavier, faster. "Of *course* she isn't! DAWSYN!" the Queen screeches. "FACE ME NOW! DO NOT HIDE IN THE SHADOWS LIKE A COWARD!"

Ryon tilts his head to the side. He gives a huff of laughter to see the Queen's cheeks ruddy, her eyes bulging with the force of her cry. "She will wait in the shadows until she is ready to greet you, Alvira," Ryon allows, and he watches the flash of panic grip her momentarily. "I dare say she watches you now."

The Queen's mask is gone. Only a mad woman remains, her collar and bodice speckled with blood so dark, it could be ink. She blanches again and turns her back to Ryon. "READY THE ARCHERS!" she cries and Ryon hears the order passed on down the line, reaching into the hills.

His stomach jolts. "Where is your wife?" he asks, the attempt to distract made successful when Alvira's shoulders bunch, when her feet halt in place. And Ryon needs no further information than that. He need only see the way the Queen's chin drops toward the spattered fabric on her chest. "We expected to find Cressida in these hills," Ryon continues, hoping fiercely that Dawsyn has found a way through the fence, that she is leading its prisoners into the trees.

Alvira turns to him, her eyes alight with hatred, with bitterness. "I am sure you did," she says, her voice shaking with the force of her rage. Tears slip over her cheek, though she pays them no mind. Ryon is unsure if the Queen notices how she teeters where she stands, if she feels the shaking of her frame. "Did you and the Sabar girl laugh together, knowing my own wife was plotting to overthrow me?"

Ryon says nothing, he merely waits as the Queen unravels, ribbons of her unspooling at her feet.

She nods, as if to herself. "Yes. You must have. How you must have celebrated to learn of it! You must have thought yourself victorious before the battle had even begun. *She made a fool of me,*" she growls, spittle collecting at the corners of her mouth. "You made a fool of me," she says, not to Ryon, but to the wind. She runs clawed fingers through her hair. "You abandoned me." Alvira's face collapses in pain for a moment. She breathes against the waves of whatever emotion tries to overthrow her, but they do not win. Soon, the lines on her face vanish, her eyes become dangerously large and unblinking. "I ran a knife through my wife's heart," she tells them all, detached and hollow. "I'm afraid she will not be here this night."

Ryon wonders what colour her blood will be when they cut her, or whether she has bargained it all away to make her wretched deals. He wonders if it will be as black and cold as the heart that homes it.

Thunder rumbles.

It is the type of thunder that moves slowly, grows discreetly, until it eclipses all other sound. Until it shakes the ground beneath your feet.

Ryon raises his sword, fearing the battalion of men on the hills have begun advancing, but a thousand heads are turning to the direction of the sound. They look toward the south, where the first torches become visible. A handful of orange specks, that soon become a sea, spilling over the unoccupied hills.

Alvira and Adrik call for the men to halt, shouting incessant orders as the people come. As the sea nears, faces become discernible beneath torchlight. Men, women and children of Terrsaw, in their labourers' clothing or noble attire. By cart or wagon or horseback or on foot. Hundreds and hundreds of them are added to the hills before the Fallen Village, some with knifes at their belt, but most without a weapon at all. They are not dressed for battle. They arrive in no formation, and as they spot the winged creatures in the failing light, they halt. Some scream and back away, unaware of the battlefield they have invited themselves upon.

Ryon sees Alvira dither, sees her try to retreat into the folds of her guards, and he means to call to her, but he is saved the trouble.

"Alvira!" comes Dawsyn's voice from his back. And he looks to see her approaching him, her ax resting upon her shoulder. "Do not go so soon."

CHAPTER FIFTY-FIVE

Two swings of her ax. Three. Four. Hold and breathe.

Swing again.

The pattern returns to her like a loyal friend, moving familiar muscles in familiar ways. She swings the ax into the unstripped timber posts, buried hastily into the ground. The fence is no match for those born on the Ledge.

Two posts are felled quickly, and it is all they need. They split with a weak-sounding crack. Hector catches them before they can clatter to the earth.

Within, Ruby waits, a crowd of her guards on either side of her, whispering fiercely among the crowd.

Dawsyn slides her arm through the gap and gestures for Ruby to hurry, *hurry.*

The children are passed through first, whether by Ruby's order or not, Dawsyn cannot be sure. She grabs their arms and pulls them through one by one, handing them off to Hector, who hurries them back into the tree line.

He looks back at Dawsyn from there in the underbrush, his eyes wide and anguished. She gives him a strained smile, nods once, and he disappears from sight, taking with him Abertha's youth, Esra's irreplaceable light, Salem's warmth, and the hope of children who will grow away from the fucking mountain that looms beyond.

"Dawsyn," Ruby calls to her, familiar brown eyes beseeching her from within the enclosure.

"Hello, captain," Dawsyn says, stepping through the breach and into the holding.

Ruby smiles. "I expected an ax to the throat."

Dawsyn shakes her head. "I found it difficult to accept that you'd turned on us." She grasps Ruby's plated shoulder. "I'm happy to find that you are on our side."

Ruby pierces Dawsyn with an intense stare. "I never left it."

Dawsyn looks out to the flock of people, filthy and bleeding. Some remain on the ground, too injured or sick to rise. But there are many so filled with rage that they stand tall, facing Dawsyn with bunched fists. She addresses them now.

"This night gives you your last chance of freedom," she tells them, her voice low and careful. "The Queen of this land says we must go back to where we came. Back to the Ledge. But that is not the land we were made for. Our lungs were made for valley air. Our skin sewn for its sun. The hands of our parents and grandparents toiled this land, and our hands were meant to feel how it yields." The last time Dawsyn spoke to her people in such a way, it was in the snow, on the precipice of their descent into the Chasm. She asked them to wager their lives on a chance for freedom then, and it was met with wariness, with fear.

But there is no Chasm here in the valley, nothing that threatens to tip them off the side of a cliff. The frost does not creep in, cracking their lips and burning their fingers. The cold is not a threat here, where the warmth of the sun sticks to the earth even after it sets. When Dawsyn looks to her people now, she sees not wariness, but eagerness. Not fear, but the kind of courage bred in those who have survived many storms and are yet to be thwarted.

"We are outnumbered," she continues. "But we have the mixed-blooded Glacians on our side and fifty years of vengeance. And we will have to let it be enough."

"Then it will be enough," comes a familiar voice.

Nevrak steps forward, his eyes illuminated by nothing more than a deep, deep hunger. And Dawsyn wonders if he might be right. What match are those in Terrsaw, against those who fought the cold and won?

"Our allies wait in the trees," Dawsyn says. "They will lend you weapons. Move quickly and stay hidden. Wait for my call to reveal yourselves."

Ruby smiles viciously. "Do not keep us waiting long," she says and leads the way through the fence.

* * *

Dawsyn walks alone out into the open now and it is not to the opponent she has long since come to expect. It is to a woman who cowers back into the ranks of her guard. It is to a Glacian King who breathes heavily beneath the oppressive heat of the fertile season.

Despite the overwhelming number of Terrsaw guards who choke the hills of the valley, Dawsyn approaches unafraid. She swings her ax to her shoulder and rests it there. She watches civilians of Terrsaw stutter in their attempt to welcome the Ledge survivors with welcome arms, only to find the Fallen Village primed for battle. She can feel their confusion, their fear.

She wonders how Queen Alvira can possibly continue to rule them, after this night bleeds to morning.

She wonders if maybe this battle can be won before it begins.

"Alvira!" she calls, letting her voice ring out. She sees the heads of the Terrsaw men and women turn to the sound of it. She sees them jostle one another, point toward her in the bowl of the hills, sauntering out of the Fallen Village. "Do not go so soon."

Alvira whips around, eyes bulging at the sight of her. "Sabar," she mouths.

"Do not delay on my account," Dawsyn continues, gaining ground. "The Glacians are naturally weakened by the heat and your numbers far outweigh theirs. Command your soldiers to kill the Glacians."

There is a silence and in it she sees Ryon stare at her in wonder, she sees Rivdan smile. She hears Adrik curse her and take out his sword and she raises her ax in response.

But Alvira does nothing.

And all of Terrsaw watches on.

"You've an entire army at your back, Your Majesty!" Dawsyn shouts. "Do you mean to have them kill the Glacians or your own people?"

She hears the hushed murmurs, the first rumblings of dissent. The same dissent that has been simmering since she first found herself in a Terrsaw dungeon. She remembers their chants, there was suspicion arising even then.

Surely the Queen will not wage this war before them.

But there is no calculation in Alvira's eyes. No careful manipulation shaping her lips. From the way she breathes through her teeth, Dawsyn suspects that sense and logic no longer drive her.

"I am the Queen of this kingdom," she heaves. "I have served it, devoted my *life* to it, and it will serve me in return for what I have given, what I have sacrificed! I will not allow a *child* to take it from me."

The Terrsaw guards nearest to her break from their steadfast positions. They look amongst one another, their understanding of this battle now changed. Who are they fighting for? For what cause?

"It is over," Dawsyn says loudly. "And we need not heed to the whims of this pathetic King and his contingent."

"Ah," Adrik calls to her. "But you are wrong there, girl. We Glacians must drink after all. I insist on it. We may retreat today if the need arises. But know that we will return in larger numbers every week, *every day* if we must, and we will take any human in reach." Adrik turns to the people of Terrsaw, his voice ripping across the distance. "WE TAKE THE LEDGE PEOPLE NOW," he roars. "OR WE RETURN TO TAKE YOU ALL!"

Rivdan laughs, a low rumble that does not fail to reach Adrik's ears. "You were always far-reaching, Adrik," he says. "I used to think it optimism. Now I know it is only stupidity. How exactly do you propose to take them all?"

"I am the *King* of Glacia," Adrik says righteously, his chin lifted. "And the mixed-blooded that I liberated from the Colony will do whatever I ask of them!"

Rivdan grins then. It is only just visible beneath his unruly beard. He raises his fingers to his lips and whistles once. It is loud and piercing, and at its sounding the reverberations of wings rent the air.

The sky fills with them, hundreds, rising from the trees, and flying toward them. They circle the sky above and Dawsyn watches with her heart in her throat as the archers on the hills change the trajectory of their arrows, tracking the mixed-blooded in flight.

"They do obey their liberator, Adrik," Ryon says, his expression blank and indifferent. "Though it was never you. Was it?"

Adrik's mouth gapes as he watches the mixed come to land behind Dawsyn, stretching in a line on either side of her, unsheathing their weapons threateningly, their steel flashing.

And the first lines of Terrsaw guards begin to back away, unsure now, unwilling.

Alvira stumbles forward, madness seemingly having claimed her. "The Ledge-dwellers are beasts!" she screeches, and she hardly resembles the regal Queen her people recognise. "They belong on the mountain, with the rest of the Mother's base creatures! I will not allow them on this land! I will not allow an ax-wielding *savage* to take the throne!"

Dawsyn only smiles. She takes the ax from her shoulder and turns it over in her hand. She does not miss the way it makes Alvira recoil. "If I wanted your crown, I'd have passed this ax through your neck and relieved you of it upon our first meeting," Dawsyn says. "It is what we savages do."

She raises her ax over her head then, holding it there, and she does not turn to watch as the survivors of the Ledge, the ancestors of the Fallen, move from the trees to join her. But she feels them. She sees it in the eyes of the army before her, in the eyes of Alvira and Adrik. She hears it in the cheers of the Terrsaw civilians. They cry and chant at the approach of the Ledge-dwellers, battered and bruised but returned to the valley. Returned to their own kind.

"I *will* relieve you of your head now, Your Majesty," Dawsyn says loudly, cutting through the cheers renting the air. "Unless you surrender."

"Enough of this!" Adrik calls, summoning his wings. "Give the order!" he commands Alvira.

And Alvira, with lips that shudder with the force of her rage, bares her teeth, then shouts. "ARCHERS! FIRE!"

And the arrows rain down.

They are impossible to see against the night sky. There is only the repeated sound of strings released, and then the pending silence before they land.

"Take cover!" Ryon shouts, but there is nowhere to hide, nowhere to take shelter out here in the open. And though the guards nearest to them have become reluctant, frightened even, the archers atop those hills have not heard the declarations of a maddened Queen. They fire upon her order.

Dawsyn does not duck as the arrows fall. She does not turn her back and run, nor lift her hands to shield her face. Instead, she feels all the blistering heat in her mind combine with the burning cold of her core, and she lets it all out. She allows it to obliterate.

She sends her power into the air, picturing every one of those arrows splintering down to their shafts, and she roars as it escapes her. She wills her body not to splinter with them.

The smell of burning wood fills the air as the arrows explode. All at once, they shatter mid-flight, dropping shards of wood and metal arrowheads harmlessly down to the ground.

Silence follows.

Alvira gapes at the sky, then looks at Dawsyn, shock marring the hatred she is made of.

Dawsyn feels her limbs become lead and her lungs struggle for breath, acutely aware of how empty she is of any remaining power.

Ryon, too. He moves backwards toward her, his swords raised. "You have one last chance to end this now, Alvira," Ryon says only to her. "You cannot win this fight."

"That is where you misunderstand me, half-breed," Alvira says, her maddened eyes set on Dawsyn. "I do not intend to survive another day, if I must surrender this crown."

And Dawsyn sees it then, that there will be nothing said or done that could dissuade her, nothing could ever satiate the need for power.

"KILL THEM!" she roars to her army, her voice echoing along the hills.

But the army does not heed the call. It rustles with confusion, the men on the frontline unwilling to move forward.

"We need not heed the commands of a mad woman!" comes Ruby's voice instead. She steps forward among the mixed, her armour marking her as one of the army's own.

"KILL THEM!" Alvira shouts again. "CHARGE. NOW!"

Again, the army barely stirs. The witnesses continue their chanting and cheering, and the mixed Glacians stand behind a human, unwilling to attack until she summons them to.

But Adrik waits no longer.

With a curse, he lifts his sword. "ENOUGH! If there is to be a fight, then let it begin." And he charges forward, meeting Rivdan halfway and bringing his sword down upon the male's own, the two coming together with a thunderous clash.

Now the other white-winged Glacians rush forward, their weapons drawn, and Dawsyn and Ryon are already swinging, already leading their battalion forward into this inevitable fray.

Dawsyn's ax meets the sword of a Glacian, and she parries it, drawing a blade in her free hand. She ducks low as he swings again, sinking the knife into his side and pulling it free. She fells another before he can truly reach her, throwing her ax into his chest as he runs, sword raised. She retrieves it before he falls and moves onward.

It is Alvira she seeks. Alvira pushing her men into the battle, ordering them to join the fight. Some dive into the ravel, but most refuse, ignoring her commands.

Dawsyn approaches and Alvira stills, her face going slack with fear.

Dawsyn does not fear. She stands before the Queen of Terrsaw, the maelstrom of battle continuing behind her, and lets her ax fall to the ground.

"This will be your last chance to kill me," Dawsyn says, hands out and empty. "Be sure you do it properly."

Alvira turns and grabs the collar chest plate of the nearest soldier, thrusting him forward. "Execute her!" she demands, vessels popping in her eyes. "NOW! Execute her!" But the soldier refuses. He takes off his helm and throws it to the ground along with his sword.

Dawsyn tilts her head at Alvira. "The time for delegating murder is over. It will need to be you, Alvira."

Roaring her ire to the sky, Alvira stumbles forward. She takes the discarded sword from the dirt and, without skill, raises it with two hands above her head. She hurtles to where Dawsyn stands, bellowing to the stars.

And Dawsyn smiles. That old, inherited wrath that was bred into her from her mother, her grandmother, awaits this moment, and it is enough to replenish whatever strength had been sapped.

She knocks the sword aside easily as Alvira brings it down. She lets the momentum of the woman's clumsy footing guide her body toward Dawsyn's waiting arms. She hears the clatter as the sword falls to the ground and pushes her forearm tightly against Alvira's throat.

The Queen struggles, her back to Dawsyn's front, each movement finding her windpipe constricted beneath the hold of Dawsyn's arm.

There is nowhere for her to go, not against a Sabar. Not against a girl from the Ledge.

Dawsyn's other hand rests against the back of Alvira's head.

Her lips move beside Alvira's ear.

"For Valmanere Austrina Sabar," Dawsyn tells her, "And every soul lost to the cold, to the Ledge."

Dawsyn pulls her hand to the right and listens for the sharp snap of the Queen's neck.

The sound elicits not a single ounce of remorse.

CHAPTER FIFTY-SIX

The woman once named Farra stands alone in the middle of the Glacian palace, thirty years after she last escaped it. She feels every one of those years like weights chained to her feet. She has dragged them along behind her long enough.

When she closes her eyes, she sees her child in the only phases of life that she had known him and the gaps she cannot fill feel like a curse, a punishment.

Next, she thinks of Thaddius, but not for longer than the time it takes to reconcile that whatever love they had exchanged had created a warrior.

Last, she thinks of the Ledge.

She thinks of how it must look now, empty of its prisoners, as it should be. It brings a smile to her face.

Farra hugs her arms to her body and relishes the gooseflesh rising along her neck. The cold *is* alive. It is a faceless enemy easily thwarted and its grip cannot hold her.

She opens her eyes to the pool's enduring glow, and it speaks to her. It whispers promises of peace in death. It sings to her of rivers that will deliver her to soft endings. It lies and schemes and lures her toward it.

But she has long since stopped listening to bodiless voices.

The iskra within her stirs restlessly and she finally allows it passage through her extremities, into her palms. It waits obediently for her direction. It waits to serve its last.

Farra shuts out the world she should have left long ago and has rarely felt as still, as restful.

"Vey ty sosud yerd iskra!" she calls, and the walls ring with the strength of her voice.

The substance in the pool spills over its edges, seeping into creases of stone. Its silvery glow trails over the floor of the Glacian palace in small streams, diverting and then intersecting at the soles of Farra's feet.

She feels it as it seeps inside her, filling her quickly. Like the ocean, it is a current she cannot fight against. It gathers on all sides and thrusts her one way and then the other, until the pool runs dry, and she contains every inch of magic within.

Farra screams.

Every inch of her is stretching, splitting. She is nothing but dark matter in a vessel too small to contain it, but she cannot break apart.

Not here.

She turns toward the great oak doors, but topples. Her body does not obey her. It belongs to the iskra now. And she cannot make it to the tunnels, she cannot make it to the lip of the Chasm. The iskra tears her at the seams from within and there is little she can do but roar in agony, beg for mercy.

She sees Phineas kneel before her, though her sight is darkening, the iskra clouding it. He says nothing as he lifts her from the floor, despite the way she thrashes. Despite the ear-splitting cries she emits.

"I've got you," he tells her, over and over. "I have you, Farra. Hold on."

He carries her out of the palace, onto the ice. He stumbles beneath her weight as they near the lip of the Chasm, and just as Farra's sight blackens altogether, she sees the Ledge.

She sees the tops of the pine trees, ordered in their lines. She sees the gleaming face in the distance, black as night.

And then she sees nothing at all.

"I've got you," Phineas says, one last time.

And then they are weightless. They are falling.

Phineas' arms remain wrapped around her as Farra splits apart.

CHAPTER FIFTY-SEVEN

The valley quakes.

It splinters in places, disrupting the ruins of the Fallen Village. But the tremors are nothing compared to the blast.

Dawsyn lets Alvira's limp body fall to ground as the quaking begins. She steps over her and collects her ax, looking around for Ryon, Tasheem, Rivdan and Ruby, the ground concussing.

But the air suddenly turns scolding and in the next moment a force knocks her from her feet.

She is thrown through the air and as she lands, her head collides with rock. She slumps down the side of a crumbling stone wall, her ax flying from her hand.

Her ears ring. She feels the warm trickle of blood spilling down her neck, slipping over her shoulder. And her vision blurs, turning to distorted shapes she cannot quite discern.

Ryon, she thinks. *Where is Ryon?*

But it is Rivdan that crawls to her side, shaking the ring of the blast from his own head.

Dawsyn can only think of one thing immense enough, one thing that could shake the earth like that...

Rivdan's blue eyes widen as his hand goes to the back of Dawsyn's head and comes away brilliant red. He reaches for her and though she cannot hear him, she sees his mouth moving.

She wants to ask him where the others are, ask him if they are alive. But the dark edges of her mind are collapsing, gently folding inward.

Dawsyn feels him grasping her arms to pull her upright, but she sways and so he doesn't let go. She feels her legs knocked from beneath her as Rivdan bundles her body to his chest, and she opens her eyes.

All around them, chaos ensues. Bodies rise from the earth and continue the fight. Steel against steel in the dark.

How fitting, Dawsyn thinks, that they should wage this last war in the dark.

Amid the fray, Ryon can be seen, taller than the rest, narrowly missing the descent of a fired arrow. Their eyes meet, and though she cannot understand why, he nods. Shouts something.

Rivdan's wings unfurl. They stretch over either shoulder, lifting.

Suddenly, Dawsyn's head clears. She turns to see the determined set of the male's jaw. She sees his returned nod.

"Put me down," she says, though she cannot hear her own voice. "PUT ME DOWN!"

But Rivdan is already airborne, already pulling away from the ground with her in his arms. She thinks the words he mouths over and over are *Sorry, Prishmyr. I'm sorry.*

The ground falls away, the tangles of Glacian and human becoming smaller and smaller. And Dawsyn is too weak to struggle against him, and not stupid enough to try, so she merely shouts and begs him not to take her away. Not without him.

Dawsyn's shouts do not persist for long, for they are not alone in the sky. Soon, from the darkness comes ghostly shapes of several Glacians, tailing them.

Rivdan dips beneath them, wheels over them in tight circles, and Dawsyn's stomach twists with every movement. She can barely make sense of the direction in which they fly, but she hears the outraged shriek of a Glacian when Rivdan tears into the membrane of a wing with his talons. She feels the strain of every muscle in his chest as he outflies them, carrying her to safety.

And there is nothing she can do but hold on.

Below, Dawsyn can just make out the winding serpent of the river, glistening in the distance beneath the moonlight and spilling all the way out to sea, and she means to tell Rivdan to follow its path.

Suddenly, the air is filled with a keen whistling. Arrows fly past them, puncturing the wings of nearby Glacians.

At first, Dawsyn does not realise they are falling.

Rivdan's eyes, so close to hers, go wide. He rolls, his wings sticking to his sides, and she finds herself looking up at the moon, and then further, to the cloud-shrouded mountain top. A shudder ripples through him. She hears a harsh grunt of pain and then nothing more.

The moon falls away, or perhaps Dawsyn and Rivdan do. The wind howling past her gives weight to it. The plummeting sensation in her stomach makes her brace for impact, but Rivdan's arms remain wrapped tightly around her and she is not afraid.

When they collide with the ground, darkness, familiar and heavy, is there to greet her.

CHAPTER FIFTY-EIGHT

Blood runs down the back of her neck. It makes his stomach lurch. He nods to Rivdan.

Ryon ducks beneath a flying arrow and watches Rivdan leap into the air, Dawsyn cradled against his breastbone. He swallows the bile and exhales in a gust.

She'll live, he placates himself. *She'll live. They both will.*

The ground has stopped quaking but remains charged with some invisible energy and he can think of only one thing that could make the world shake like that. When he looks up to the mountain, he can see snow cascading furiously down its slope, barrelling over trees. The sound is immense.

But none of it is enough to keep the Glacians on the ground for long. Many are already in flight. The others already have their weapons back in hand. The fight continues as though it had never stopped.

"The bastard son of Mesrich," comes a voice. Adrik staggers toward him, one leg badly slashed. His face is creased with fury, but still the sword in his grasp is steady.

Ryon faces him. He can feel that same bloodlust coat his tongue.

He remembers every backslap of his childhood. Every cleverly crafted word that came from Adrik's lips. "Do you remember what you would tell me, Adrik? When that moniker was thrown my way?"

Adrik spits blood to the ground.

"You told me that one day I would shove my sword down their throat, force them to swallow their words."

Adrik smiles without humour, without even an ounce of sanity. "You were so easy to use, Ryon," he says. "You believed everything, anything I said. You *idolised* me."

"I did," Ryon agrees, clenching a sword handle in either hand. "But you can make good on at least one of your promises."

Ryon lunges forward, and his sword clashes with Adrik. The reverberations scream through his limbs, but he doesn't allow the male a moment to find his footing. Adrik stumbles backward as he parries, grunting with exertion, eyes wild with something like fear. The male has spent most of his years scheming, strategizing. He is no real swordsman. He had relied on Ryon, leader of the Izgoi, to fight his battles.

It only takes a single bluff to fell him. Ryon pitches one sword at Adrik's head and the male throws himself backward to avoid it. But Ryon is ready. He rushes Adrik onto his back, hearing the breath expel from his lungs on impact. Ryon kicks the sword from Adrik's hand and presses a knee to the male's chest.

"The Pool of Iskra is gone," Ryon tells him. "Did you feel that blast? The destruction of all that magic?"

Adrik laughs weakly, brokenly. "Impossible." But the laughter cuts off when Ryon's second sword hovers over Adrik's mouth. "Wait," he utters, desperate. "Please."

"You traded your honour for that pool," Ryon tells him, feeding the sword through the parting of Adrik's lips. "And now you'll die knowing it was for nothing."

He watches the male's eyes go wide, watches his hands mindlessly grasp the sword, panicking. Ryon shunts the sword into the back of Adrik's throat.

It takes several moments for this final King of Glacia to drown. Ryon uses every passing second to recall a different memory of the king, and then lets it die with Adrik.

Ryon pulls his sword free and does not spare the male another glance.

As though the King of Glacia's death had sounded a warning, the tide of battle turns.

All around, white-winged Glacians take to the sky. One after the other they retreat, weakened by the warmth of the valley, unsupported by the Terrsaw guard. They leap for the skies and turn back to the mountain.

And Ryon's chest loosens. They've won. They've finally won. And they are still alive.

Dawsyn, he thinks victoriously. *Where are you?*

Ryon cranes his neck to find a pair of wings he recognises. He searches the sky for Rivdan and the woman he loves.

But high on the hills behind Ryon, where the archers stand, a fervent call rings out: "ARCHERS!" it commands. "FIRE!"

Time seems to slow. Ryon's blood turns cold.

It is the humans on that hill, wearing Terrsaw emblems, that finish the war. They follow no Queen's command. They see the Glacians retreating, and it seems that they cannot simply let them escape. They let their arrows fly.

And Ryon's heart sinks. *Dawsyn!* Dawsyn is in the sky. She and Rivdan.

The arrows shred holes through wings and chests. The soldiers on the ground cheer to see Glacians rain from the sky, landing with sickening thuds atop crumbling houses, broken chimneys and dry, cracked earth.

All around Ryon, they crash to the earth.

A flash of red hair catches his eye, high above.

He watches the arrows as they bury in Rivdan's back.

He watches the male falter and try to fly on.

And then they fall.

They fall.

CHAPTER FIFTY-NINE

Her den of girls is warm for such a blizzard-worn night. The fire crackles, her shoulders are donned by threadbare blankets, and Dawsyn marvels at the absence of cold. Her toes do not curl up inside her leather boots. Her bones do not ache.

In the crook of her arm, her sister Maya huddles, peacefully asleep against her side, mouth agape. Her wild tangle of black hair tickles Dawsyn's neck.

Briar stokes the fire. Her long-braided hair dangles over her shoulder and she flicks it back with a curse.

Valma sits on a cot. She is sewing something together and frowns at Dawsyn when she looks up. "What are you doing here, Dawsyn?" she asks, her fingers continuing to weave thread.

Dawsyn smiles to hear her voice again. It is unbroken, uninterrupted by wet, lung-deep coughs. It is coarse and abrupt, and it rings long after the last word leaves her mouth. "Am I not welcome in my own cabin?"

Her grandmother smirks, raising her eyebrow. "*Your* cabin, aye?"

"Leave her be," Briar grins, eyes sparkling as they regard Dawsyn. Those dark eyes seem filled again. Filled with love and warmth and peace. It has been so long since Dawsyn last saw them this way. "Let her stay."

"Here?" her grandmother argues. "In this den? No," she laughs. "She was never meant for this speck on the map, Briar."

Dawsyn looks to her sister's young face, untouchable in sleep; then to Briar's, alive and teeming; then to her grandmother's, lined with a lifetime of love and labour. Dawsyn had forgotten how her lips pinched together just so, and how her right hand always rose to scratch a spot beneath her ear, and how her left foot incessantly tapped an off-beat rhythm that matched the wind howling outside.

"I wish to stay," Dawsyn says. And it feels strange that sadness should grip her now, where comfort and warmth is easy to come by. But she feels it. She feels every day spent huddled before a weaker fire, shivering beside them. She feels every moment spent stoking it alone, banishing thoughts of this den when it was filled with women. She learned how to tuck those memories aside, lest this same sadness steal her over the edge of the Chasm. But she lets it sink her now. Lets it fill her up and drown her.

Her grandmother rises and bends to touch her cheek. "No," she tells her simply. "Not yet."

"When?" Dawsyn asks desperately, her throat burning.

But Valma Sabar does not answer. She only smiles gently, brushing Dawsyn's lips with her thumb. "All things find their way back home."

Chapter Sixty

Dawsyn wakes to the sound of a thousand voices, but hears only one.

It is the sound of her own name, repeated over and over.

It is the press of a forehead she feels. It lies against her chest. Wide hands pressed against her forearms.

Howls of pain – the kind that comes from the core of a person.

The thunder of feet.

The stillness in the air.

Lips against her cheek, the bridge of her nose.

The light in her mind, awakening at that familiar touch. It sparks feebly.

"Dawsyn," she hears again. And the sound is so broken, it stirs the iskra in her belly, however weakly.

"Come on," she hears. His voice. Ryon's. He presses his head to her chest, where her heart tries to beat. "*Come on!*" he pleads with it.

Dawsyn opens her eyes and finds the sky empty of anything but stars. The moon.

She raises her weighted arms slowly and presses her hands to Ryon's head. She intertwines her fingers in his hair.

And he jolts. "Dawsyn?" he says, lifting himself to look at her.

She finds his eyes, the universe expanding within them, and is home. "Ryon," she murmurs. She does not know if he hears it.

His lips part with laughter. Still smiling, his mouth presses to hers and he holds them there, drinking her in, and she him.

Tears slip over the sides of her face, over the shells of her ears. She lets them fall freely. She wonders if anything has ever felt as good.

"It's over, malishka," Ryon whispers into her throat, his voice shaking. "It's over now."

But there is an edge to his voice, and it is not one of victory, of glory. The relief is diluted. It is tenuous.

Dawsyn's chest tightens. "Will you help me stand?" she asks.

"You fell," Ryon tells her, making no attempt to move away from her. "You fell a long way Dawsyn... You're hurt."

But Dawsyn can already feel the iskra and mage light moving slowly within her, sluggishly stitching that which was torn. "I'm well enough for this."

Ryon obliges, as he always does. He stands first, lifting her gently. She sees the cuts that mar his arms. A deep gash bleeds insistently at his side. "It's not deep," he tells her quickly. "I'm fine."

"Rivdan," Dawsyn says, her lungs screaming with the effort. "Where is he?" But Ryon need not answer.

All around them lies the toll of war. The broken and bloody are everywhere. Some unseeing, others screaming, some taking their last breaths.

Dawsyn sees the Terrsaw civilians surrounding the injured humans and mixed alike, aiding them where it is possible or else offering comfort in their last moments.

And beside Ryon and Dawsyn, crouched low, is Tasheem. She bows her head over the form of Rivdan.

He is as peaceful in death as he was in life, his eyes hooded, lips parted. And if not for the arrowheads that protrude through the wall of his chest, Dawsyn might believe he is merely lying upon the earth, gazing at the stars and telling them stories of Glacian legend.

Too much has transpired for Dawsyn to cage the savagery of pain. She makes no attempt to hide it now. For a moment, she hates that he died in her place before she remembers that he was nothing if not noble, honourable, kind and generous.

She sinks to her knees and lets the violence of grief find its outlet. She takes Tash's hand and Ryon's, and for long moments they simply sit side by side by the body of their friend, and they say nothing aloud that won't be heard in death anyway.

Dawsyn's pain is surely nothing to that of Ryon's, or Tasheem's, for this friend they grew up with in the Colony. She steps back and leaves them with their storyteller. She watches as Ryon grips his hand, then lays his own on Rivdan's heart. Tasheem does the same. Dawsyn can hardly stand to see the devastation in her eyes.

She turns on shaky legs and it is to find many faces looking back at her; a strange collection – men and women, armour-clad soldiers and mixed-blooded Glacians. They watch her expectantly, but she cannot move her feet forward.

Ruby strides before her and Dawsyn is glad to see her alive, uninjured. In her hand is a familiar crown. The one Dawsyn has seen adorning an imposter's head. Ruby's sword is bloody, and she drives it into the ground before Dawsyn and kneels.

"Your Majesty," she says, bowing her head.

She proffers the crown into the space between them.

Others lower to the ground. A few dozen at first, and then more, until Dawsyn looks over a sea of bowed heads. They kneel, eyes averted, awaiting her word, her command. Though there is a sense of victory here on this battlefield, it is not strong enough to outweigh Dawsyn's weariness.

She is tired.

She walks forward slowly, gingerly, wincing at the pain that lances from every limb. She bends to take Ruby's hand and urges the woman back onto her feet.

With all of Terrsaw watching, Dawsyn takes the crown. She looks at it for a moment, notes the silver and jewels that adorn it. She thinks of the Sabars that wore it in eras past, her ancestors. She thinks that perhaps their bloodline has served enough, suffered enough, and that whatever days remain should be spent idle. It need not be her enemy any longer.

Dawsyn lifts the crown and places it carefully on Ruby's head. When the woman's eyes widen, and her head shakes, Dawsyn places her hands on her cheeks and holds her still.

"You were destined for glory, Ruby. Take it."

"I cannot."

Dawsyn musters all the conviction she is left with. "You can," she says, then turns the captain around to face her kingdom and kneels at her side. Slowly, one by one and then altogether, the crowd follows suit.

Ruby seems baffled, awe-struck. "What is the third lesson?" Ruby blurts, her chest heaving. "You never told me."

Dawsyn only shakes her head as she stands again. "Nothing you need learn." She has never been more certain of anything.

Dawsyn turns away, turns back to the only thing she will only ever seek in her remaining years. Ryon is waiting for her, warring with uncertainty.

"Are you sure?" he asks, and she closes her arms around him. "You would make a fine queen."

Dawsyn smiles into the wall of his chest. "You made me a promise," she tells him. "I intend to make sure you keep it."

By dawn, the Fallen Village is empty of all but the dead and their mourners, Dawsyn among them.

They sit by Rivdan's side all night and no one speaks. They simply spend these last moments with their friend, with their brother. They do not think of what comes next.

When first light arrives, they stand wordlessly. They wipe the blood and dirt from their hands and wait for the first person to break the quiet.

"I want to bury him here," Tasheem says. "On *this* side of the fucking Boulder Gate."

So they do.

They take the shovels offered to them by other mourners and they find a place by the tree line where Rivdan can sleep in the shade. They dig and dig without relenting, letting blisters form on their fingers. They do not stop until Rivdan lies in its base, until Ryon's knees crumble beside his grave. The only pause comes from the sounds of his apology, as he tries and fails to explain a lifetime's worth of gratitude.

But words have never been enough to slake that particular need. Dawsyn knows this much. She kneels beside Ryon and takes his head in her lap. She cradles him until the breaking slows.

Around them, the same scene repeats, again and again. The dead are laid to rest by those that loved them, or they rot alone. Dawsyn supposes all one can hope for in this realm is that they can collect enough mourners before they pass on.

There is no glory in war. There is only this, the pieces that remain.

At some point, Esra, Salem, Hector and Abertha find their way back to them, there in the battlefield.

Hector takes her hand, Esra takes Tasheem's. Salem sits beside Ryon and puts a hand to his back.

"What now?" Abertha asks. It is unclear of who she asks.

But Dawsyn answers.

"Now, we live," she says. It comes on a whisper, travelling on the wind, all the way throughout the valley.

Epilogue

They carved a statue of Dawsyn Sabar.

She was placed beside her grandmother, the crown princess of Terrsaw, though Dawsyn, like Valma, never did sit on the throne.

In fact, Dawsyn never even saw how perfectly her likeness was captured in that marble. She never stood at its base and marvelled at the way the sunlight glanced off the stone ax. There is very little left in the histories to suggest what transpired after the destruction of the Pool of Iskra and so Dawsyn Sabar's disappearance remains a great mystery to the people of Terrsaw, even centuries after the Ledge people returned.

According to Queen Ruby's journals, Sabar attended the new monarch's coronation, which gave way to a new era. It is the very last known proof that Dawsyn Sabar ever stepped foot on Terrsaw land again.

Some believe she returned to the Ledge, where she had been born.

Some believe the great Glacian warrior, Ryon Mesrich, finally took her to the other side of that mountain, where she found the paradise that alluded her.

Some believe she died. She had suffered through too much.

But if the chaotic writings of Esra, the infamous Solstice Braggard, are to be counted, the remainder of Dawsyn Sabar's life was spent somewhere else.

It is said that an inn was built in the forgotten parts of the Terrsaw forest, beyond the river, where nary a single traveller would wander. The musings describe a band of mixed-blooded Glacians and humans alike, cutting trees to resurrect an establishment that was never recorded in Terrsaw's enterprise accounts. A place Esra and his husband, Hector, called "Salem's Inn."

The scribblings mention other names otherwise unknown: Tasheem, Abertha, Brennick. And then more names of presumed children that were dated later: Tizz, River, Gerrot, Briar and Farra. It is unclear to whom these children were born.

If Esra is to be believed (and other evidence suggests he clearly shouldn't be), then Dawsyn Sabar lived with her husband, Mesrich, the very being who succeeded in bringing the downfall of the last Glacian King.

They lived their remaining days in presumed peace, for the borders between Glacia and Terrsaw were abolished by Queen Ruby, and all were allowed passage beyond the Boulder Gate.

Within a couple of centuries, there were no children born with wings or talons.

Esra's entries detail the last remaining days of Dawsyn Sabar, who lived until the effects of age wore on her, as it does to all who are fortunate.

According to his writings, Dawsyn's last words to those who lived in Salem's Inn were, "I am not cold now. They are waiting for me."

Ryon Mesrich, possessed of wings, flew Dawsyn Sabar over the ocean and disappeared into the horizon. Neither ever returned.

Esra's last journal entry was dated soon after this account, and it read:

Mother, take us all now, if you wish.

We have lived.

Acknowledgements

The other day, my nine year-old daughter told one of her school friends that her mum had written three *entire* (*big arm gestures*) books, then proceeded to ask that poor kid how many books *her* mum had written.

In that light, first thanks must go to Zoe, for making me feel infinitely cool. Also, sorry to that mum, for the completely unwarranted and rude comparison. You didn't deserve that.

As always, I must address my online community of readers, most of whom I've promised a kiss on the lips. I'm well aware of the outstanding indenture and if you'll make a queue, I'll gladly pay up. Thank you for your passion, your words of encouragement, your tears and laughter. I am so incredibly lucky that you took a chance on me.

Speaking of chances, I must give my whole-hearted thanks and love to my brilliant agent, Amy A. Collins of Talcott Notch Literary, who has an excellent rack and an even better work ethic. In 2021, you sent me an email that changed the trajectory of my career, and I'm forever grateful that you did. Thank you for always going above and beyond (and for getting up at three in the morning to attend meetings).

To a phenomenal team of editors and publicists: Gemma Creffield, Caroline Lambe, Amy Portsmouth, Desola Coker and Dan Hanks. Angry Robot Books was the best home for this trilogy, where it was treated with such care. Thank you for your collaboration and general brilliance. I adore working with each of you.

Thank you to Penguin Books Australia, and in particular Lily Croznier, who has held my hand through many a terrifying promotional event. Thank you for the opportunities you've sent my way. I'm forever grateful.

To the McCallums – Mum, Dad, Alycia and Teagan. How lucky I am to be born into a family like ours. Thank you for turning up for me, again and again. My first readers and my first champions.

To each and every friend who has galvanised me along the way, hand-sold my book, demanded early copies and generally made this experience all the brighter – know that I treasure you.

To my found family – Hannah, Amber, Samantha, Kaven and Maggie. How sweet it is to share every success and failing with you.

To my husband, Michael, and my children, Dean and the aforementioned Zoe – thank you for being my home. Anyone who has ever pursued a dream will know that it requires sacrifice, not just from you, but from those you love best. It isn't always easy to share your mum, your wife, with the pursuit. Thank you for coming along for the ride and bearing it with such grace. It is because of your love for me that I can love what I do. I hope I make you proud.

To you, dearest reader. I wrote Dawsyn to personify the rage that would otherwise send me to jail. If there lives inside you a small, tired ax-wielder who was taught to smile politely and bear the brunt of unkindness, know that Dawsyn slays so that we don't have to.

Finally, to this trilogy, that has quite drastically changed my life.
We did it.